The Last App

Tom Alan

For Jill – the chance of a lifetime.

Prologue

Sometime in the very near future, certainly much less than a lifetime away...

Mick Strong: village GP of long standing, father, widower, grandfather, and great-grandfather. He stands and spreads his arms, Christ-the-Redeemer style. Usually he'd simply bellow: *Will you all please shut the duck up!* then bask in the sighs and raised eyebrows from those of his brood who deem his humour to be deficient in political, social or any other fashionable type of 'correctness'. Today, however, he wants to keep the tone serious. Deadly serious, appropriately enough.

He's planning to tell them when he's going to die.

Part One

<u>The Beginning</u>

'Lord, let me know mine end and the number of my days,
that I may be certified how long I have to live.'
—Psalm 39

Chapter One

'Half a glass of red wine a day can add five years to your life,
according to new research...'
—*The Daily Telegraph*, Health News, 30 April 2009

'H*appy birthday to you, happy birthday to you, happy
birthday, Great-Granddad, happy birthday to you!'*

Mick scans the room, nodding with proprietorial satisfaction
as it quietens. They've gathered in his honour (and at his behest)
at the poshest hotel for miles. It might not be Downton Abbey,
he might not be Lord Grantham, but with its silver service and
uniformed waiting staff it's pretty damned impressive.

He tugs his cuffs out of his jacket sleeves. *You can tell a man
by his cufflinks*, he often says. You can also tell that he can afford
to buy shirts without buttons on the sleeves. He adjusts his red
satin dicky bow, to show a bit of class. Some'll grumble it doesn't
go with his three-piece tweed suit and brown brogues, but he'll
dress himself, thanks. A touch of eccentricity is best achieved by
not worrying about what other people think. He arches his back
as if he's recently woken from a refreshing sleep.

'Thank you, thank you,' he drawls, in his mind sounding remarkably like a winner at the Oscars. 'Thank you for coming, thank you for *sharing*.' He catches the eye of his daughter, Michaela: local schoolteacher, elective single mum twice over, 'women's libber', vegetarian eco-warrior. She treats him to a wry smile in acknowledgement of his well-known, and often voiced, disdain for what he calls her 'sharing fetish'. He also hates being ordered to 'enjoy' by waiters, and the hideous modern tic of writing *thanx* and *gr8*. What *does* she have on her silly head? It's his birthday, not a bloody wedding.

'I will just mention my Celia at this point, to say she's in our thoughts on this happy occasion. Gone much too soon, dearest. Please raise your glasses.'

There's a murmur of assent, and Mick stares at Michaela. He has never told her that he and Celia had argued over her name. It was their only serious row. Mick's father and grandfather had both been called Michael, and although Celia had some ideas from her own family tree, Mick had put both feet down. Anyway, Celia's not here to tell, and Mick certainly isn't about to 'share' that.

'So, seventy-five years, eh? There's not many make it this far.' Mick pulls his top-of-the-range Tissot pocket watch from his waistcoat by its twenty-four-carat gold chain. He flips it open and nods, as if it's confirmed his unparalleled judgement. 'I know some of you are going to ask me the same old question: am I finally going to announce my retirement? And you know my usual answer: you tell me when I'm going to *die*...'

'And I'll tell you when I'm going to *retire*,' they answer in weary unison, all except great-grandson Will (William *Michael*, if you were wondering) who's only eleven, and is too busy picking chunks of icing off the back of the cake, safe that Great-Granddad (GG to him, and him alone) will protect him from any parental tut-tutting.

'Well, I might have some news for you on *that* front!' Mick announces rather theatrically, now with his hands flat on the table and his head jutting out defiantly – silverback, and he knows he is.

There is a gasp at the far end of the table. It's Paula, Michaela's daughter, christened Michaela Paula but always Paula to avoid confusion.

'Oh, at last, at *last!*' she squeals in genuine delight, squeezing husband Adam's arm with surprising force. She's been on at Mick to retire for years.

'Oh, well, hold on there, Paula, sweet. I did say *might.*' Mick glances at her and nods conspiratorially. There is no one in this room who Mick is more devoted to than Paula. It won't be long before she reaches the age Celia was when she had her heart attack, and it's Celia's face he sees now. Paula has her hair down today. Mick likes it that way, not that he's ever told her why, and there aren't many pictures of Granny Celia in circulation, so she couldn't know. Mick muses for a moment, a tear threatens to intrude, but he swats it away before it gets anywhere near his stiff upper lip.

'So, when *am* I going to retire? It'll be a big moment, no doubt. I've been the village GP for longer than any of you can remember, and I think I am, or have been, doctor to everyone in this room, with the notable exception of Adam...' All eyes turn to Adam, they know the script, '...but then, he is an *Am-er-i-can!*' The laughter is polite, dutiful – no one would say 'compulsory', but only because no one would dare.

Adam takes it on the chin – he has no choice. He smiles gamely, but it's that nervous smile, usually reserved for the dentist's chair when the phrase, *this won't hurt at all,* is administered with a knowing look. But Adam has good reason to be nervous today.

'So, when will it be? When will it be?' Mick teases, stroking his silver goatee. 'I might have the answer in *here!*'

Mick lifts a white, paperback-sized package above his head. There are official-looking stickers and stamps, and a QR code suggesting it's very important and has arrived by secure delivery. A large holographic *LT* logo is emblazoned across the back. Paula's elder brother, Steve (Steven *Michael*), leans over to her.

'Christ! Is that what I *think* it is?' he grumbles, like Mick's flashing a loaded pistol. 'Isn't that the logo from Adam's company?'

Paula frowns, nudges Adam, and applies her *WTF* glare. Steve joins the quest to catch Adam's eye, but Adam appears to be suddenly fascinated by the remains of the icing off his bit of birthday cake. He studies the chalky pieces like they could be part of a yet-to-be-identified dinosaur awaiting reassembly.

'Stupid old *git!*' Steve snarls, loud enough to turn a few heads.

'I have to thank our American friend for this. Adam, you are a visionary!' At this moment, Adam sinks as far back into his padded chair as he can without breaking it. 'As most of you know, Adam works for the LifeTime Corporation, and as some of you will be aware, if you read the *quality* newspapers, they are at this moment bringing their revolutionary new app to the UK.'

'Oh no, Dad!' Michaela gasps in an almost whisper, her hand snapping up to her mouth, a belated attempt to stop the words from escaping, maybe. Her fears are confirmed by Steve's fixed stare and tight grimace. She and Steve have shared a comment or two about a *Guardian* report on the LifeTime Corporation's pending export to the UK. But, as with most five-minute internet sensations, they hadn't expected to hear much more about it, certainly not at Mick's birthday celebration.

Paula is now digging her nails into Adam's wrist; he looks

like he's pondering whether he has the remains of an Archaeopteryx on his plate. Or maybe it's a baby Tyrannosaurus?

'Have *you* done this?' she hisses in his ear. Adam's eyes remain locked on his plate.

'He's done this himself. He swore me to secrecy. You know what he's like.' Paula stares hard at him, willing him to look at her, but Adam continues his after-dinner palaeontology.

Mick sails serenely on, the *Titanic* out of Southampton dock.

'Now I believe I am *the* first person in the United Kingdom to have purchased membership of this remarkable new service.' He glances towards Adam, who is busy rearranging scraps of coloured icing on his plate. 'That right, Adam?'

'Yep, that's right,' Adam drawls, without lifting his head.

'Is there anyone here who *doesn't* know what this is?' Mick challenges. Those who know keep their eyes well occupied: Adam concentrates on his jigsaw; Steve inspects the faux chandelier with uncharacteristic interest; Michaela busies herself trying to fold her napkin back into its original fan shape. Cathy's shoulders tentatively confess uncertainty. She is Steve's wife and rarely swaps her Jane Austen or PD James for his *Guardian*. 'Then I'll explain,' Mick continues with a satisfied nod. '*This* is my deathday,' he announces gravely.

'No, GG, *birth*day!' Will contradicts, the only person in the room who would.

'Yes, I know today is my birthday, but *this*,' he waves his package again, 'is my *death*day.'

Paula scowls at Adam. Her expression suggests that he might be sleeping on the sofa later that night, but Adam isn't looking.

'Thanks to Adam and his amazing team at LifeTime, I have here the most accurate prediction of the day I'll die that it's possible to obtain. And here's the really important bit: I can now plan the rest of my *life* accordingly.' He smiles proudly but finds it difficult to locate a pair of eyes sharing his pleasure. Most heads are down, although Paula and Adam are now in a tight little discussion that doesn't look like the planning of a second honeymoon. Mick's knocked off his stride for a moment. This deathly quiet, appropriate though it might be, is not what he's been expecting. He has no notes (why would he?) so he's temporarily unsure how to continue. But only temporarily.

'So, let's have a peep, shall we?' He slides a knife under the flap and starts to slice through it. The silence has the air of cheap theatrics mixed with genuine menace. Nobody is sure whether amusing quips are appropriate: is this still a birthday, or has it morphed into an impromptu rehearsal for a wake? Mick stops, a teasing glint in his eye. 'Imagine it says here I'm going to die in five years? In that case, I can tell you now, I'll retire pretty much immediately, liquidate a few assets, then I'm off to see the world...' He smiles again, but still can't lock eyes with anyone except Will, who's lost interest in the cake, his concentration rarely lasting longer than a party popper, and is now looking a little confused, worried even.

'But maybe I'll find I've got ten years to go. If that's what it says, I might work a bit longer, maybe part-time, start a little bit of travelling, but you can see the options this gives. It cuts out the uncertainty.'

Mick continues to slice through the flap and the silence deepens – birthday celebration transformed into public execution at the flick of a steak knife. He peers inside the package and fishes out what looks like a DVD case and a golden envelope.

'Golden ticket!' Will shouts, inveterate Roald Dahl fan. Steve envelops his son in a tight hug and whispers something silent and silencing into his ear.

'I imagine the news is in here?' Mick asks, holding up his envelope and looking down the table towards Adam again. Adam takes a cautious glance back and nods the sort of nod Roman Emperors probably used when it was time for someone to die. Mick wonders if Adam might be about to wiggle his thumb in a half thumbs up, half thumbs down pantomime, as he prepares to reveal the sentence. But Adam shows no inclination to upstage Mick's show.

Adam has warned Mick repeatedly that this sort of public 'surprise opening' isn't a particularly good idea, especially at his age. *Fucking ridiculous* had been his exact phrase, his language emboldened by fear of what Paula might say once news of his role in this caper was revealed. Whatever it says inside, he's explained pleadingly to Mick, his projection will appear short compared to the seventy-five years he's already lived, unless it's an unlikely twenty-odd extra years. But, more probably, Adam has cautioned, given Mick's age, given his history of moderate smoking and immoderate whiskey consumption, the projection will certainly be considerably shorter. Mightn't that put a bit of a dampener on his party? At least open it privately, he advised, so that Mick would know what was coming, and he could have an appropriate comment ready. Or multipacks of Kleenex in case the date is much, *much* sooner than even Mick might think possible.

Mick had bridled at all this, accusing Adam of knowing there was bad news inside. Adam (truthfully) denied this. He simply knew from experience in the States, the sort of reaction that often came from close family when a projection was revealed by an elderly relative. It rarely heralded a celebration – well, not a public one. Would Mick listen? You'd have had as much luck expecting him to buy a ticket for Glastonbury.

Adam isn't even a salesman, but once Mick had heard that LifeTime was going to launch in the UK, he started pestering him to get him the first British membership. Adam's picked up some odd stories from the sales team in the United States, but none of them had ever heard of a customer who put their money on the table so quickly, while asking so few questions.

Mick breaks the seal on the golden envelope. His throat is dry, so he reaches to take a sip of wine. He scans the table, trying to generate a feeling of expectation rather than the sense of dread that seems to flow from each averted gaze. Distracted, he knocks his wine glass over. There's a tinkling and a little crash. Red wine pools then sinks into the heavy damask tablecloth. A white-gloved waiter fusses around Mick like a penguin attempting to mate. It's not a good look, and an even worse idea.

'Leave it!' Mick snaps, almost slapping the waiter's hand away. 'Bring me another.'

The waiter waddles away at speed. Mick wipes a bead of sweat from his craggy forehead, runs his fingers through his silver hair, scratches behind one of his Yorkshire-puddingy ears. The waiter returns, cautiously.

'Thank you,' Mick says with perfect courtesy; he sips and settles. 'So, the prediction...'

'Pro-*jection*,' Adam hisses to himself. '*How* many times?'

The golden envelope folds open so that only Mick can see what's written inside. He licks his bottom lip, narrows his eyes as if he's having trouble reading it. Then he folds it closed again and lays it down on the table.

Now all the eyes have him, but he's staring at the golden card on the table. For what seems like the first time, possibly in all his seventy-five years, he looks uncomfortable being the centre of attention. Even more uncomfortable than Adam.

'Well,' he says, after too long a pause. His lack of notes, lack of forewarning, all now leaving him to process the information and present it off the cufflinked cuff. He's used to delivering this sort of news to patients, it doesn't happen often as a GP, but there'll always be a family member asking, 'how long' a very sick or very elderly relative 'has left'. Mick thinks himself good in these situations. Always honest, *it's difficult to put a figure on it*, he'll say. But then, he'll always manage to hazard a guess.

'Two hundred and seventy days,' he finally says, having failed to find a better way to 'announce' the news. He holds up the golden envelope, Trump-signing-law style, and shows the contents to the room, as if the shiny numerals might add a touch of razzamatazz to the deepening gloom. The silence creeps from deadly to funereal.

'That's nearly a year!' Will chirps excitedly, before Steve can stop him.

Chapter Two

'Eating chocolate at least once a week can reduce your risk of a
heart attack, study finds.'
—*Daily Mirror*, 23 July 2020

'Retiring' to the lounge for coffee, Steve is grabbed by
Michaela on the way, and hauled into a dark, narrow
passage. Sacklow Hall, on the North Norfolk coast, is riddled
with such passages, most of them inhabited by dusty suits of
armour standing ready to ambush clumsy or tipsy guests with an
embarrassing clatter. Cathy follows swiftly and silently, like
backup for a tag-team mugging.

'What on *earth* is he up to? Has he gone *mad?*' Michaela
snaps, ripping off her fascinator and crushing it like it's at least
partly to blame. Had it been a bird, even a medium-sized one,
like a duck or a goose, death would have been instant.

Steve shrugs, relieved that Mick has wandered on ahead.
'He's been mad for a long time.'

'I'm *serious*, Steve. This is a crazy idea. Absolutely stupid.

How could he? How could he put us through this? Bloody old fool!'

'It'll blow over,' Steve counters hopefully, but without much conviction. Steve's spent half his thirty-two years hoping Mick won't do whatever crackpot thing he looks hellbent on doing, and the other half praying he'll do what everyone knows he won't.

'He's telling us he's got a year to live! Is that *true*? I mean, should we write it in our diaries? Arrange a party?'

'Or a funeral?' Steve quips again, unable to resist.

'Steve! Michaela's right. This is serious.' Cathy tugs angrily at his sleeve. 'What do we say after coffee? Enjoy your last two hundred and seventy days?'

Steve shakes his head and sighs deeply. If there's one thing worse than old-man Mick muck-spreading all over an afternoon out, it's Michaela and Cathy ganging up on *him* and suggesting that *he's* got to clean it up.

'This can't be accurate, can it?' Cathy goes on. 'He's not going to drop dead in two hundred and seventy days, is he? That's ridiculous.'

Steve shakes his head. 'There's going to be huge margins of error hidden in the detail; you know what the American legal system's like. Otherwise, you'd have people suing because Uncle Jacob hasn't died, and they haven't inherited his shack in Kansas. Or maybe Great-Aunt Nancy dies a week before predicted and everyone sues for compo cos they weren't ready.'

'Steve, is this *real*? Will Dad be dead in a little under a year?' Michaela sighs.

'Of course not! It'll be surrounded by a Bible-load of legal jargon saying two hundred and seventy days could be anything between a week and ten years. Ask Adam. He's the head statistician at LifeTime, isn't he? He's the one who's sold him the bloody thing.'

While Michaela powders her nose and manages to resist smashing the sinks in the toilet, Steve and Cathy collar Paula and Adam on a pair of sagging double sofas at the back of the lounge. The leaded windows beside them open onto a manicured lawn, and a bleary sun is setting through the branches of a row of old oaks down beyond a lake. It throws a weak light onto Adam who's the centre of Steve's interrogation.

'How accurate is this meant to be?' Steve starts, making it clear he thinks, and hopes, that the answer's *not very*.

Adam takes a deep breath. He's an 'outdoors type', so his (formerly) crisp white shirt, blue silk tie and charcoal grey suit look like a straitjacket that he's been trying, and failing, to escape from all afternoon. His large, hairy hands poke out from his cuffs like clown's gloves. He stifles a sigh. *Positivity...*

'Look, there's an element of this which is entertainment, right? A bit of fun, don't take it too seriously. Buy it for a mate on their twenty-first birthday. But, like it or not, the science and math of calculating how long we're each going to live is improving fast. Medical data, DNA sequencing, longer and more detailed family medical histories, the effects of different foods, medicines, exercise, all that kinda stuff. You know, life expectancy has doubled over the last hundred years, we're simply understanding the causes and measuring them better.'

'But you can't predict a death date from that sort of information.' Steve's no scientist, but this doesn't sound like a question.

'Predict, no. Which is why we don't predict. We never use that word. A *projection* is different. It's based on all the data we have now, and if the data changes, the projection changes too. If Mick stops smoking, for example, his LifeTime projection will increase instantly. At the moment, each cigarette smoked is calculated to take up to fifteen minutes off a life. Stop smoking and you'll see your projected LifeTime rise. No scientist or doctor would doubt that. Being seventy-five, that's not going to add *years* to the projection for Mick, but it'll be measurable; days, maybe a few weeks. The math side of this is about as important as the medical history side. There's so much data on how our life expectancy is affected by so many different things that the accuracy of our projections is getting better week by week. But – and this is the important bit – it's a *projection*, based on all *available* evidence, and we never, *ever* claim we have *all* the evidence. It's only based on what we've got.'

'So, Mick changes his diet and his LifeTime predict–'

'Projection.'

'Oh, who gives a shit! His projection will change?'

'Sure. Start at the beginning: eat nothing and you'll be dead in forty days, give or take, as long as you keep drinking, right?'

Steve shrugs. Right, the bleeding obvious.

'Start eating, and your projected life expectancy will rise. Eat more and eat better and it'll rise further. As a newborn male in the West, assuming that you're going to eat well and exercise moderately and blah blah, you're gonna live nearly eighty years. It used to be more before certain governments here in the UK and at home in the States decided their donors and supporters would no longer foot the bill for poorer folk to enjoy the full spoils of post-war progress. This ain't rocket science, everybody accepts this. It's large-scale math, metadata, hundreds of thousands of studies being refined day by day as more data is added. But the likelihood of extending a projection, of course, is restricted by age; anything Mick changes *now* will have less impact than if a seventeen-year-old does it.

'Smokers, on average, die ten years younger than nonsmokers. Fact. Convince a seventeen-year-old to stop a thirty-a-day habit, and you're gifting them ten *extra* years of life.

Fact. I'm not talking about a projection going up here; I'm talking about hard medical data of hundreds of thousands of cases. Our projections are based on that data. Facts. Convince Mick to quit and he won't see such an increase, simply because he's older. But it's not just smoking, we have a raft of activities that we know, to a fairly high degree of accuracy, will shorten someone's life. Being obese, heavy alcohol consumption, eating red meat, sedentary lifestyle, there are a host more, they'll all shorten your life by amounts that can be measured with increasing precision as more data is gathered. On the other hand, upping your fruit and veg intake, moderating your coffee drinking, being female, *not* living in the Third World and dah-de-dah will all *add* time to your projection. So much of it is obvious common sense; we've simply tried to refine the calculations by crunching as much data as people can give us. Every new, successful cancer treatment goes into the algorithms and adjusts all the projections accordingly, as long as that treatment is available in the country you live in, and you'll have access to it. Developing cancer X in the future might no longer be a death sentence, you might get parole. So, Mick's projection could change if significant medical advances are confirmed, and if it does, he'll be notified.'

'So, back to my question, how accurate is two hundred and seventy days?'

'It's complicated.' Adam steamrollers over Steve's heavy sigh, clearly delighting in having a captive audience chatting statistics at a social event. 'Obviously, the younger you are,' he continues, 'the more unknowns there are regarding the lifestyle you're going to adopt. Are you going to sit in front of the TV chomping red meat and smoking reefers for the rest of your life? Or are you going to be out playing tennis, running marathons, eating bananas and broccoli? So, the margin of error for younger people is going to be pretty big. For older people, the margin of error is obviously smaller. Being older, they are probably much nearer to death than a younger person, so we aren't going to be as far out as we might be with younger folk. Especially as those younger folk have more time ahead of them to break all the healthy promises they've made to themselves – and to us. Alternatively, if they were already on the road to doom, they might have a Damascene conversion in their mid-twenties and suddenly go all tofu and yoga.'

'How far out?' Steve thinks, *blood and stone*, but manages not to sigh this time.

'Again, that depends on how full and how accurate the reporting from the member is. We obviously get their genome sequence from the national database, but how many generations of medical history do we get from the member? How accurate is it? How honest has the member been when reporting their current and past lifestyle habits? Do they really run a marathon every week and only drink wine at Christmas? Every little fib undermines the data and, as we know, people are great fibbers.'

'Is there an answer to my question?'

'Seventy-five-year-old male, no private health insurance, living in the UK – life expectancy is greater in Western Europe than it is in Africa, remember – in general, any projection for that profile would come with about a ten to fifteen per cent margin of error, give or take. Half of that is lack of ancestral medical data, the rest is pure lies – *no, I've never smoked, or drank a lot*. I've heard reports of people with nicotine-stained fingers, teeth and hair swearing they've never smoked. Also note, older people's knowledge of their parents' and grandparents' medical histories will probably be more incomplete than somebody younger, who might be able to get the Holy statistical Grail – digital medical records. The details of Mick's margin of error will be on the data drive that comes with the projection, and it'll be based on the data Mick gave when he enrolled. It's a massive application process, all done online. Ask him for the data drive and I'll be able to dig out his margin of error. Then ask yourself how likely Mick might be to bend the truth of his past lifestyle habits, his current exercise regime, et cetera, when filling in our forms...?'

Steve raises two eyebrows in response to Adam's one, as they both mull Mick's well-known habit of 'embellishing' any anecdote he tells about his past. 'So, fifteen per cent – best-case scenario – of two hundred and seventy days being, what?' He glances quickly at Cathy, who knows his ability to calculate mentally would be shamed by an average ten-year-old.

'Forty days, give or take,' she replies in an instant, saving his blushes, 'meaning his projection is anywhere between what, 230 and 310 days?'

'Assuming we've got full and accurate data.' Adam nods.

'So, he'll definitely be dead some time less than a year from now?' Paula is pale, clearly shocked, she came for a birthday celebration for her granddad. She'd probably have thought twice about putting on make-up and a new dress if she'd known it was going to be his last.

'No,' says Adam, trying hard to remember that not everyone has a master's in stats from Yale. 'We're *not* predicting. There are no guarantees to this. It's all about likelihood, assuming accurate data' – a double eyebrow-bounce from Adam – 'we're *not* saying he is going to die on this date or between these dates, just that it's more likely than not, given the data we've got *now* and trusting its accuracy. Given a thousand seventy-five-year-old males providing *exactly the same data set as Mick*, don't quote me on the figures here, this is simply to illustrate, but maybe eight hundred of them will die within that range. Maybe two or three of them will die on day 270.'

'And some of them will live another ten years?' Paula whispers, hope seeping into her voice.

'Maybe dozens of them, I don't have a computer here to work it out, but yes, we're not *predicting* a death here. We're doing a statistical *projection* of the probability of a death, margins of error and, what do you Brits call them, porkies, included. Some of them might drop dead tomorrow, some will live to a hundred. He could get hit by a bus.'

'We're back to entertainment.' Steve groans, not looking remotely entertained.

Adam shrugs. 'It can shock a few people into changing their lifestyle choices; if we catch them young enough, that seventeen-year-old, thirty-a-day smoker? Statistically, we're adding ten years to his life if we convince him to change his behaviour now.'

'But with someone Mick's age, what do you call that? Enterstistics? Statainment?'

'I don't expect you to believe me, but I tried really hard to talk Mick out of this, particularly because of his age. You ever managed to get Mick to change his mind?'

Steve takes a breath, lets it out slowly. Paula stares at her shoes.

Chapter Three

'How to Live Longer: Swap Animal Protein for Plant Protein to Extend Lifespan, says study.'
—*Daily Express*, 19 February 2021

Mick has taken possession of a winged chair next to the fireplace, poured his coffee, and allowed Will to put another log on the fire. He's also got one of the waitresses to sneak him a sly single-malt Bushmills that he's tipped into his cup.

'Come on, come on! Coffee's getting cold. Where've you all got to?' he yells. He hasn't finished with them yet. Adam takes another deep breath and stares at his fingernails, but there isn't much left to bite.

Michaela is last in; she immediately notices that Mick's suffering social distancing like he's a confirmed coronavirus carrier. With the exception of Will, nobody's close enough to make conversation with him comfortably. She drags a heavy oak chair, there's no way it's from IKEA, next to him.

'So,' she says, as brightly as she can, while wondering what she'll say next. 'That was a bit of a surprise.'

'It's what I want,' he asserts. He doesn't need to say, *and what I want, I usually get,* but the thought goes through Michaela's mind with the inevitability of the last car on a speeding roller coaster.

'I can plan now,' he says. 'It's the not knowing that makes everything so difficult. Don't you see that?' Michaela shrugs a shrug that could mean anything. Mick ignores her.

'Everybody comfortable?' he bellows, standing again and silencing the murmured conversations. 'Lovely grub, eh? Great spread. And wonderful company. I want to thank you all again for making this day so special. I am now full of enthusiasm to make my plans and enjoy my retirement – which will start as soon as I can find a locum.' He laughs. There are a couple of muted attempts to join in, but who laughs at jokes when somebody in the room is dying?

Mick reaches behind his chair, lifts out a colourful paper bag and plants it ceremoniously on the sturdy wooden table in front of him. He positions it so that the large LT logo, printed in gaudy red, white and blue letters, is clearly visible. It's not a big bag; it's the sort that would hold, what, four packages, each the size of the one he's just opened? In fact, it looks suspiciously like there's one poking out from the top. Had he pulled a knife, or stripped to his underwear, he couldn't have grabbed everyone's attention so fully, so immediately, so easily. It's the sort of hush you'd probably get if incoming ICBMs were to appear over the horizon from behind the oak trees.

'Now, I know it's not usually the custom for the birthday boy to be the one giving out presents, but I'm convinced that LifeTime membership is going to change the way we all think about death. Rather than death being a shock, something to be feared, I truly believe that in the future – well, *now* actually – it's something we can embrace.'

Embrace? Michaela is jolted by such a word coming from Mick's lips. She stares at him, checking that he's not visibly swaying, or drooling. Whatever next? She wonders if she might be on the verge of hearing him utter *OMG*, or even, heaven forfend, *WTF!*

'I won't say we'll look forward to it,' he continues, an English country gent chatting merrily about death at a family luncheon, 'but we can be ready for it. We can turn it into an opportunity. What was it that Kipling said? If you can face those two – you know, disaster and the other one...' He looks around for help, finds only blank stares. 'Well, whatever...'

Whatever? Michaela contemplates, thoroughly bemused. *WTF?*

Steve stares at the bag like it's timed to explode. He shoots Adam a look that says, *That's not full of what I think it's full of...?*

Adam shrugs his reply: *You ever try to talk Mick out of something?*

Michaela's on that tipping point when something's so outlandish that it's almost unbelievable, then it pales into insignificance beside something unfathomably worse – the way Reagan's cartoonish presidency became a benchmark for normality with the coming of Trump, or how Brexit suddenly seemed a relatively reasonable idea when the UK's subsequent decision to apply to become an 'Associate State' of the USA was announced. Looking at the bag, its size, its shape, the logo on the side – all her concerns about *Mick's* LifeTime membership quickly lose their importance: fragile eggshells underneath dancing presidential, or prime ministerial, feet.

Mick, meanwhile, is in smashing form. 'I've decided to give LifeTime memberships to each of my immediate family members, that's Michaela, Steve, Paula and, of course, Will. I know this will allow you to plan your futures using the most up-to-date information available. So, my beautiful daughter, Michaela...'

Michaela experiences a paralysing jolt of numbness surging through her body. She knows what he's saying, understands it perfectly, but can't rid herself of the feeling that she's performing in a bizarre play written by an LSD addict. Mick drops a package into her lap, as her hands don't seem to be working. She stares at it like it's a gift from a stage magician, which might change into a rabbit, most likely a dead one.

'My gorgeous grandchildren, Steve, Paula...' He's forced to cross the room with two more packages as Steve and Paula sit dumbstruck on their sagging sofa. They accept their gifts with the hands of automatons and a stupefied silence, small children finding the complete works of Mao, or toilet brushes, in their Christmas stockings.

'And, of course, my great-grandson, Will.' Will has miraculously retained all his faculties – well, maybe all but one.

'Wow, GG! Thanks. Is it a new *Star Wars*?' he gasps, as he bundles past the ancient furniture and stunned adults. He hugs Mick then starts to rip at the packaging.

'Woah, hold on there, soldier,' Mick snaps, grabbing the envelope from Will's hands and holding it above his head. 'There's a condition attached to my gift. None of you can open it until your next birthday! Call it *my* birthday present to each of *you*.'

Will's arms drop to his sides in what looks like temper, but he's well trained: his head slumps onto his right shoulder in a faux fit.

Mick smiles and hands Will his package. Will studies the exotic stamps, clutches it to his chest, then turns and beams a proud smile to the rest of the room. He's met by stony stares and blank faces.

There are awkward silences, and there's the lounge of the Sacklow Hotel currently hosting the awkward silence to silence them all. Anyone entering might think it was a séance, or a prayer meeting, or seven English strangers sharing a large lift heading for the top of the world's tallest building at half speed. Mick sips his single-malt coffee and tries to empathise. The trouble is he's got Will gleefully investigating the American stamps and postmarks, and stroking the holographic LT logo. Then he's got the rest, staring at their packages like they've ordered *Fifty Shades* on Amazon – but received *101 Dalmatians* by mistake.

'Let me tell you a story,' he says suddenly, seemingly apropos of nothing, an unscripted diversion in response to the distinctly *un*celebratory atmosphere. 'Some of you might have heard it, but it will help explain what I've done if I tell it again now.' He fishes a large Havana out of his breast pocket and makes a show of cutting and lighting it. One of the first acts passed after joining the USA was the repeal of all anti-smoking legislation, making the UK the eighteenth state to allow smoking in bars and restaurants. Adam stands and pointedly opens a couple of windows while Mick pointedly ignores him. Mick was anti political correctness before it went mad. Come to think of it, he was anti political correctness before anyone had ever heard of it.

'As most of you know, I was born in Oz and spent the first few years of my life there. When I was a kid, one of my best friends was a guy called Ted. We kept in contact when I came over here, not easy in those days, a letter a fortnight was our version of Facebook or Tweeter.'

There's an almost inaudible sigh from someone, maybe more than one, but clearly nobody is in the mood to correct him this time. Mick puffs on his cigar and basks in the limelight: an attention-seeking child with a captive audience, a badly tuned violin, and a dozen numbers in his repertoire. 'Ted spent much of his working life saving so that he and his wife could go on a world cruise when they retired. They talked about this cruise endlessly; every year they'd get the latest brochures and dream. Thailand was Ted's main target because his favourite James Bond film, *The Man with the Golden Gun*, was filmed there. Anyway, Ted reaches sixty-five, they get the brochures for real this time, pick out a boat, select an itinerary, Thailand included.'

Mick reaches for his coffee, drains it, pours himself another from the pot, nods surreptitiously at the waitress who's standing guard at the door. His nod might be surreptitious, but it's also laser-guided and nuclear-tipped. Mick's mixer is safely on its way.

'I mentioned I knew Ted in Australia, didn't I? You'd forgotten that, hadn't you? Not relevant, you thought. I'll tell you how relevant it was. Back in the fifties, when we were kids, it was the custom in Oz to let babies sit out in the sun. Then, when they were a little older, they'd play out in the sun. The sun didn't cause skin cancer back in those days, like cigarettes didn't cause lung cancer and asbestos was a perfectly fine building material. So, unbeknown to Ted, he became a time bomb. Sometime in his childhood, he started ticking. And when did the bomb go off? Six weeks before he and Raquel were due to depart, he scratches a spot on his back, and it starts bleeding. Won't stop. Doc sends him for tests and instead of a cruise around the world, Ted starts a trawl around the oncology departments of Australia's finest hospitals. He dies around the time they would've been in Thailand. Will said earlier that I had a golden ticket? Well, I'm happier with my golden ticket than my mate Ted was with the golden bullet in his golden gun. It made me think that nobody should miss the opportunity to know if something like that's on the cards. It's everybody's chance of a lifetime.'

The waitress, in black skirt and white pinny, returns with a whiskey glass balanced on a silver tray. She goes to pour the contents into Mick's coffee cup, but he stops her, takes the glass out of her hand, and drains it in one. Then he motions to her for another.

Chapter Four

'Being wealthy adds nine more healthy years of life, says study.'
—*The Guardian*, 15 January 2020

'I'm going to bin it, sod him, stupid old git. Yeah, bye, Dad, see you in the week. Bye-eee... *Shit!*' Michaela continues to wave and smile at the receding boot of Mick's Jaguar MK2 as it growls down the gravel drive bleeding a thin wisp of dark smoke. 'Bloody, bloody bastard! Stupid, stupid idea. What was he thinking?'

Steve puts a consoling hand on her shoulder. 'As usual, Mum, he was thinking of himself. When does he ever think of anyone else?'

Michaela sighs. She knows that isn't fair. Not entirely, not on the small things. But when it's something big? Then, yes, Mick does only think of himself. 'But what does he think this is going to achieve? Does he really believe this is accurate? He's a bloody doctor, for God's sake. He *has* to know better. You remember that *Guardian* piece you showed me? What was it called? "The Last App You'll Ever Need"?'

'Oh, don't call it that, Mum,' Steve says in a stage whisper, looking over his shoulder as if LifeTime lawyers might be hiding amongst the trees.

'What are you talking about?'

'It's *Life*Time. *Life* this, *life* that. The LifeTime lawyers get itchy fingers if anybody calls it something they don't like. They took some blogger to court for calling it the Death App.'

'Oh, nonsense.' She muses for a moment as she remembers one of LifeTime's cloying TV ads that have been airing in the run-up to their imminent UK launch. She's heard them in practically every ad break for the past month: *Imagine you could find out how long your life was going to be... What would you do if you could plan your life to the minute?* Her mind is then hijacked by the slo-mo, soft-focus couple running along their idyllic white-sand beach, wearing their idyllic designer clothes, and smiling their idyllic smiles as they open their LT envelopes to a rising crescendo of idyllic music. They stare at each other, with quite unbelievable delight, as they evidently discover that they each have plenty of idyllic years left to live. Then they twirl in each other's arms, not caring that their designer jeans are being soaked in the surf, as thought bubbles of newborn babies, fast cars and business-meeting handshakes float behind them across the idyllic blue sky. Certainly not much talk about death. Michaela wonders if her vegetarian coq au vin and apple cobbler might be on their way back up.

She snaps out of her reverie. 'The article said a lot of it was dodgy, didn't it?'

'Well, they quoted some people who suggested it might be a bit dodgy, but they certainly didn't want to risk being hauled through the US courts by the LifeTime Corporation's lawyers.'

'But Dad must know this is all very new, untested. You can't trust it, surely.'

'I think he's got a bee in his bonnet. He probably saw the

Guardian article and dragged poor old Adam into a dark alleyway. I felt a bit sorry for Adam today. The last few weeks must've been a living hell for him, poor sod. Mick's secret brainstorm in his pocket; he must've known it was bound to cause a bit of a flap, and he couldn't tell anyone.'

'He should have told Paula.'

'Yeah, and Paula would've told...'

'Me! Of course. I'm her mum! Of course she would've told me.'

'And you'd have told...'

'Well, you...'

'And...'

'Well, for the sake of Will you would have had to tell Cathy...' They look across the lawn where Will is throwing sticks into the lake. 'We could have stopped this whole bloody farce if Adam had told Paula!'

'What? You'd have arm-wrestled Mick into submission? Like to have seen that on the news.'

'Oh, be serious, Steve. What *are* you going to do about Will?'

'What do you mean? Will's a healthy lad, he does sport, eats well.'

'But what if it *says* something – you know. Not quite right. It'll scare the life out of him.'

For the first time Steve looks less sure of himself.

'Maybe we'll open it first, before he gets a chance to see it, and change it to whatever date we fancy. He'd be happy living to a hundred, I think.' He looks sideways at Cathy who has her eyes locked on Will.

'You can't do that!' Michaela gasps.

'Why ever not? If you think it's all such rubbish that you're throwing yours in the bin, where's the harm in embellishing the crap so that Will lives happily ever after? Job done.'

'That would be dishonest.'

'But if you really think LifeTime's predictions have no merit, then playing along with them is dishonest too. Why allow their dishonesty free rein? Fight back. Or are you not so sure after all?'

'Oh, I'm sure. Absolutely bloody sure. Mine's heading straight for the bin. But the problem's really someone like Will. He's so young, and so impressionable! God, he'll take this as gospel, course he will.'

'I'm not so sure. We'll find a way to short-circuit it before it does too much damage. Don't worry about us. Look, here's Adam and Paula, better dash. Will! We're off!'

Paula negotiates the gravel in her high heels while apologising for the queue in the ladies. She and Michaela swap kisses, promise to call soon, assure each other that it'll all be fine. Believe none of it.

Paula and Adam climb carefully into the back of Steve and Cathy's ageing people carrier. They live in the village so have cadged a lift off Steve and Cathy who are on the other side of it in a dilapidated farmhouse, which they are slowly, and unsuccessfully, trying to renovate. Paula and Adam's entry is 'careful' because while Steve and Cathy's house is awaiting improvement, their car only features on their 'to-do' list if it stops moving.

The manufacturer might have advertised it as a 'people' carrier, but Steve and Cathy use it to carry a few 'non-human' things as well: damp logs with loosely attached bark, infested with enough insects to attract a wildlife film unit; ripped-out Formica kitchen units of 1950s vintage; weekly lawn and hedge clippings from a 'garden' the length and breadth of a mid-sized

IKEA car park; the sodden brick and rotten timber detritus from a hundred-year-old barn which collapsed in a recent storm; oh, and three excitable (but un-house-trained) piglets. Luckily, the piglets are at home today, probably in their own little straw, stick and brick houses, if Steve has been busy with his DIY obsession. It also seems as though the nearest Starbucks and Pizza Hut are using the footwells as recycling bins. Steve and Cathy might think they are living *The Good Life*; Paula and Adam see it as more akin to a rerun of *Steptoe and Son*. To be fair, Steve's DIY skills have made him the go-to odd-job man for miles around; earning them enough to allow Cathy to 'work' on her novel.

As a special treat Will is allowed to ride one of the jump seats in the back (accompanied by a large sack of damp and smelly shrubs, which Cathy grubbed up a fortnight earlier) instead of squeezing in between Paula and Adam. He's also allowed to pop in his earbuds and listen to some music rather than join in the conversation, which is the usual rule. And, for some reason, Steve forgets to remind him not to play his music too loud.

'Anybody find Mick's marbles back there in the lounge?' Steve asks in a carefree tone, as Cathy negotiates a badly parked Range Rover while cursing under her breath.

'You should have warned us, Adam,' Paula groans, as she smiles breezily and waves to Michaela who is struggling with the lock on her rusty hatchback.

'Yeah, sure, Mick asks *you* to keep his birthday surprise a secret and you'd immediately tell everyone in sight? I'd like to see his face after that.'

'But it's not any old birthday surprise, is it? He's bought LifeTime memberships for us. *LifeTime!* The day you're going to die in a golden envelope?' Paula stares at Adam who's fascinated by the local hedgerows, so she changes tack. 'What are you going to do with Will's?' she half-whispers, leaning forward behind Cathy.

Cathy studies the rear-view mirror to check that Will has left planet Earth, then she glances at Steve. 'I don't know,' she says out of the side of her mouth. 'Steve, are you serious about checking it first to make sure what it says isn't going to scare him to death?'

Adam glances at her, wonders whether she's deliberately trying to be funny – decides she isn't.

Steve sighs heavily. 'Of all the people to give one to! We're adults, fair enough, we can take care of ourselves. I think Mum's already thrown hers on the fire. But a *child*? *My* child? What makes him think he's got the right?' He turns around and checks on Will, who's drumming on his thighs with the palms of his hands and nodding like their very own dashboard bobblehead dog.

Cathy stares at the road ahead. 'Maybe we can simply forget it?' she says, without much conviction. 'I mean, his birthday's not for months. Couldn't we play it down as some sort of a joke or something? He's bound to forget; you know what he's like. Maybe we could get him some really special present that'll take his mind right off it?'

Steve smiles at her optimism. 'And what? We get Mick a massive bottle of ten-year-old Bushmills so that he forgets too?'

Steve puts his hand on Cathy's knee and raises his eyebrows in a look that Alfred Hitchcock spent his career attempting to achieve. It succeeds in telling Cathy that she's driving much too fast for the narrow country lane they're on. She smiles a fraught apology, and eases her foot off the accelerator.

There is a lull in the conversation; every comment is such an obvious grenade, and nobody wants to start a war. With the possible exception of Mick, who's recently let off his own private collection of nuclear-tipped cruise missiles. Finally, Adam concedes defeat.

'Look,' he says, like he knows they're all waiting for him to say something, 'I feel responsible for this, I really do. I honestly did try to talk Mick out of it, but there was nothing I could do to stop him. I suggested he asked each of you in turn, before your birthday, whether you wanted a LifeTime membership or not. But he was adamant, said he'd go direct to my head office if I didn't sort it all out for him. He even threatened to forgo the staff discount and buy direct from the internet with a letter of complaint to my bosses to boot.'

'So, how much is the staff discount?' Steve asks, before another lull leads to a change of topic.

'Fifty per cent,' Adam replies quietly, regretting ever having mentioned anything to do with the cost.

'I read in the *Guardian* that membership is a thousand dollars,' Steve says to the bushes that are flashing past his window.

Cathy gives the ABS of their ageing jalopy the most serious workout it's ever had. The car slews through the loose gravel at the near side of the road, spraying it noisily under the front wheel arch, before juddering to a halt with one wheel buried in the grassy verge.

'Wow! Way to go! Cool skid, Mum!' Will yells, as he straightens himself up and gazes admiringly towards his mother, the secret rally driver.

'Sorry, Will,' Cathy gasps, trying to keep her voice even. 'Rabbit ran out in front, managed to miss it, silly bunny.' She restarts the car and pulls off again at a pace usually reserved for royal wedding carriages.

'I didn't see a rabbit,' Steve remarks, sotto voce, a few hundred metres later, having checked that Will has plugged himself back into mission control.

'Oh, shut up!' Cathy responds. If she'd been sure that Will had his earbuds back in, she'd have told Steve to piss off. 'Did you say a *thousand* dollars? What's that in pounds?'

'It'll be about the same, won't it?' Steve asks.

Adam gives the merest hint of a nod at a passing oak.

'A thousand quid?' Paula squeals. '*Each?*'

Adam wonders, rather hopefully, if another rabbit might be due. Or, better still, a horse. Maybe a herd of unicorns would do the trick? In lieu of rescue, he digs beyond the regulation six feet. 'There's a special offer for the first six months of our UK opening, eight hundred pounds and Mick got the fifty per cent staff reduction *plus* I managed to squeeze a bit more off by taking no commission at all.'

'So, what's that? Fifty per cent of eight hundred is four hundred and he bought five? Two thousand quid?' Any incredulity that Cathy is feeling is masked in her voice by a tone of carefree indifference, like she's showing off how easy GCSE maths is. It's a tone Paula can't imitate.

'You're joking! He's spent two grand on this?'

'A little under,' Adam says, almost to himself, while studying the surrounding countryside with intense interest, like he's some kind of botanist, or wildlife enthusiast – which he isn't; his interest in the outdoors is limited to yomping through the foliage and scattering any wildlife with his tuneless singing.

Another lull takes control: Adam's damned if he's going to put his neck in the noose again. The atmosphere is as dark as the inside of an overcrowded, leaking tent in the middle of a midnight hailstorm on Dartmoor.

'You got one, Adam?' Steve asks finally, like he's enquiring about a new steering wheel cover.

'Everyone at LifeTime gets a projection,' Adam replies blandly.

The silence stretches beyond the polite. It's an *I'm not*

telling if you're not asking kind of silence, which only the strongest can tolerate: Paula isn't the strongest.

'You've got fifty-something more years, haven't you?' she says, knowing full well that he's got fifty-six years and change. She grasps his hand tightly, safe in the knowledge that she's got him for another 'fifty-something' years. That's assuming her own projection...

'So what's with the snail-mail delivery, Adam?' Steve asks.

Adam sighs. 'Marketing. They say it adds suspense, gravitas. And most of our customers are elderly; they love getting a package to open. You can get the news on the App if you want.'

Cathy pulls the car up outside Paula and Adam's 1.5 up 1.5 down shoebox in what used to be a smallish field of sugar beet but is now a very cramped development of eight identical Lego homes, each with a garden the size of a table tennis table at the back and one at the front no bigger than a beach towel.

'Pop in for a cuppa?' Paula offers, more to break the train of the conversation than to invite it to resume inside. To her relief, Cathy and Steve both demur, citing the need to *chat* with Will and *sort something out*. Paula and Adam nod understandingly.

'Fifth of February,' Will shouts to no one in particular.

'Say what, Chief?' Adam grasps the lifeline of a change of topic, maybe even the introduction of a hint of childish levity.

'Fifth of February,' Will repeats, making it obvious that he thinks they're all deranged for not knowing.

'What is?' Steve asks, no hint of trepidation.

'The day GG's gonna die.'

Chapter Five

'Eating Meat "Raises Risk of Heart Disease, Diabetes and
Pneumonia".'
—*The Guardian*, 2 March 2021

Before even removing his coat, Mick picks up the telephone
and puts in a request for a part-time locum to start
ASAFP. Then he pours himself a generous Bushmills and scans
the music on the shelves. He's got vinyl, cassettes and CDs, but
never went further. MP3s? Spotify? You'd as likely find a pink
tutu in his wardrobe. He's in a vinyl mood, the beginning. He
knows it was the sight of Paula at the end of the dinner table,
hair down...

The *very* beginning? That was 1970. Not long after
Christmas. He pulls the LP from its place, alphabetically
ordered by artist's surname, and lays it carefully on the
turntable. Two pairs of eyes stare from the album cover, one pair
gazes into the middle distance, the other looks straight at him.
He'd just finished a night shift in casualty with that Geordie
twat, what was his name? Steven? Shaun? Whatever. It was he

who'd suggested the café, said the nurses all went there for breakfast. And there she was. Standing in front of him in her uniform at the counter, humming. So, he'd joined in, singing the chorus of 'Bridge Over Troubled Water'.

And she'd turned, and she'd smiled, and he'd known. Straight away, he'd known. The connection was instant. She obviously loved the song; he obviously knew it. It was like a scene from a film, what did they call them nowadays? A romcom? But without the com. But more important than his knowing, he'd known that *she'd* known too.

He slugs from his glass then tops it up, shrugs his coat onto the sofa and lays back on top of it, closing his eyes. *Good day*, he thinks. Although his prediction – sorry, *projection* – was a bit of a surprise. No matter, there's leeway, Adam says. *But still, two hundred and seventy days*, he thinks. Slightly less than an average pregnancy. One out, one in.

He opens his eyes and sips his drink, allows his mind to drift. Where have the years gone? Did he ever formulate a plan that ended up here? Plan? No. But most of the decisions he's taken have pointed him here. The house, his work, the decision to stay in the village after Celia's death. He resents how his small life has slowly got smaller. He used to enjoy his position as the village doctor: dicky bow, respected, driving his maroon MK2 Jag long before Morse had been invented. In fact, when Morse did emerge, he took such pleasure in quipping, *I've said to Morse: never follow fashion, old chap, always lead.*

His bookshelves catch his eye. Has he really read all of them? He studies the spines, standing tall and straight, except the ones that have fallen in battle and are now carried shoulder high by their surviving comrades. He's a literary man, so he likes to think. He's well read; he imagines people would say that about him. His books are his pride and joy. Floor to ceiling and door to bay window. He used to have them arranged alphabetically, when he was younger, when he had fewer. As he aged, and his collection continued to burgeon, making a space for the next acquisition, especially one that needed to go near the start, a Dan Brown or a Martin Amis, created such a knock-on effect of book shuffling along already overfull shelves that he eventually gave up. So, his oldest books are alphabetically stacked (sort of) while the latter ones are chronological by date of purchase. It irks him to have half his le Carrés on the second shelf of the first bookcase over by the door, between André Brink and Catherine Cookson (he's read pretty much everybody once, you can't trash someone if you haven't read *any* of their books), and the rest on the latest IKEA jobbie under the window mixed in with Nick Hornby and Zadie Smith. He'd counted them once. Then bought more and couldn't remember the tally.

He marvels at how much of his wall space is taken up by books and music; it's like a Bayeux tapestry of his life. No wonder Paula's and Steve's places are so drab and empty-looking, what with their *Kindlings* and *Eye-Pobs* – his memories are there in front of him every day. Even Michaela has stopped buying books, now that she's got one of the reading thingies – he's not sure which is which, cares less.

He hauls himself up and slides an André Brink out from near the door: *A Dry White Season.* He remembers considering it the best book he'd ever read when it came out, when was it published? He flicks the pages. 1979. Thatcher comes to mind like a slap on the back. *Christ!* What was it about? South Africa? Apartheid? Can't remember. Maybe about a journalist? Maybe not. He puts it down on the small side table next to his armchair. There's a pile of other books there. He glances idly through them: *Tinker, Tailor*; *Catcher*; *Angela's Ashes*; *Frost in May*... Yes, he'll have to read all those again – and soon!

He sits back down on his coat, rummages beneath himself, yanks out the golden envelope, tearing it slightly in his contortions. He opens it and stares at the gaudy numbers: 270 days. The music works its way into his thoughts, if that was the beginning – is this really the end?

'Tea?' asks Adam, heading quickly for the kitchen. It's three strides from the front door, three and a half for Paula.

'Talk,' she replies, sitting heavily on the sofa and kicking off her shoes. She's not really a high heeler. She can do them for an event like today, likes the feel of them with a pretty dress. But, having to *walk!* Gravel car park? Jesus!

Adam flicks the kettle on and stares out of the window at the already tiny garden, made to seem minute by the smallest garden table-and-chair set known to IKEA. If Paula had kept any of her childhood Barbie collection, he'd have been tempted to search for a smaller set in her toy box.

'I know,' he says, answering her radar and talking at his own reflection. 'I know, and I couldn't, and I'm sorry. What can I say? These last few weeks have been a nightmare for me, you know?'

Adam knows Paula's rarely able to feel anger towards him. No matter what he does, and it's never much, his sad brown eyes and floppy mane of uncontrollable hair give him a boyish appearance that softens her anger every time. She creeps into the kitchen and feeds her arms around his chest.

'I know,' she says, breathing in the smell of woodsmoke that has clung to his jacket. 'I don't know what we could've done if you'd told me.'

'Mick swore me to absolute secrecy. *Especially* you. I don't know if you've ever seen him when he's deadly serious, you being his golden girl an' all, but I can tell you, he's a mean piece of work. Said he'd call head office and make an official complaint about my conduct if I breathed a word to anyone, you especially, particularly, above all and bar none. What could I do?'

'I know,' she murmurs. 'I understand.'

He turns around and folds her up in his arms. He tugs her sleek blonde hair into a tight ponytail in his fist. She pulls him closer, rests her head against his chest and lets out a long sigh.

'Oh, he can be a bit of a pig when he wants his own way, I know.' She strokes his arm, pulls a loose thread from his jacket. 'You said you took no commission from the sale? I didn't know you were on commission.'

Adam smooths her hair back down, starts curling a few strands round his finger.

'I've been looking for a way to tell you, but with all this stuff in my head about Mick's birthday, I haven't been able to think straight. They're cutting my salary but giving me commission on any sales I close in the UK.'

Paula pushes herself back, stares up into his face.

'Cutting your salary? By how much?'

Adam glances behind her into the lounge where his Springsteen collection includes his favourite, 'The Promised Land', and their wedding photos threaten him with promises about to be broken.

'Fifty per cent,' he says starkly, not taking his eyes off his untidy stacks of CDs.

Paula's blue eyes widen, Disney-cartoon-like – the look of shock, fear even, is what he's dreaded more than anything. He knows she won't get angry, knows she'll *understand*, but for all that, he feels it's his fault, his side of the bargain falling apart.

'Jesus,' she gasps, hugging him again. 'Can they do that?'

He smiles bitterly to himself, now there's a question from the last century.

'Yes, they can.'

'So how much commission did you give up for Granddad?'

He returns her grip, doesn't want her to look into his eyes again.

'A couple of hundred, before tax.'

She breathes out; he feels her deflating and wonders if she might cry. He doesn't deal well with her crying. It doesn't happen often, which, like death, only makes it worse when it does.

'It'll be okay,' he whispers. 'If this takes off in the UK, I could make more than I was on before, but it's not as secure and I wasn't given a choice.'

'Do you want to be involved in sales? I thought you were a statistician?'

'I am – well, I was, but they see the UK as a growth area and think that as I'm on the ground I'm best friends with half the population. They don't really understand. They think the UK is like a small town, about the size and importance of Homer.'

She smiles at the reference to Adam's Alaskan birthplace, bringing back memories of her one and only visit, when it had rained constantly, forcing them to hole up in their clapboard hotel almost the entire trip. Her smile fades ever so slowly, as she loses herself in the memories.

'Listen,' she says, pushing herself away again, locking onto his reluctant eyes. 'Could we get a refund on *my* LifeTime membership? I don't really want it; couldn't we give it back? I haven't opened it and–'

He's shaking his head before she's finished the question. 'Absolutely not, they don't entertain the option; it's clear in the contract, in the largest print imaginable.'

'Worth a try.' She sighs.

'I would never have bought you one if Mick hadn't insisted.'

'No?'

'No. I'd have asked you. Would you have wanted one?'

She shrugs slowly. 'I don't know. You say they come with a pretty big margin of error. Is it worth the money?'

'Probably not for you,' he says. 'I mean, you don't smoke or drink heavily, you exercise, eat sensibly. I can't see you having a projection too far from the average.'

'Are you calling me...?'

'No, no, I didn't mean that.' He sees she's joking, they smile, neither wants to argue about this: they'd submit voluntarily for root canal, walk barefoot over hot coals, anything rather than argue. Adam suddenly looks excited. 'Got some news,' he says, pulling her close again, running his fingers through her hair. 'They've lined me up for a few days of training. They say if I can make things take off here, there might be a promotion from the *only* salesman in the UK to head of a small team, then I might get some of my salary back.'

'A few days?' She groans. 'You're not usually gone that long. It's usually an afternoon.'

'I know,' he says blandly, 'but this is at HQ, in Utah, and here's the good news, you get to come too!'

'You're kidding!' She pulls away, stares excitedly into his eyes with a look that takes him back to their wedding day. He can rerun it at will, but there are moments, like this, when it hits him like thunder. They had so little then: him a part-time lecturing job at the university on a forty-mile-each-way commute; she was earning less than him, full time at a small chemist shop a long bus ride away. They made it through that – it was wonderful – they'll make it through this, he decides.

'Will there be much for me to do if you're in training sessions all day long?'

'I've seen the schedule, I've got a bunch of spare time, plus it's SphereCity, there'll be loads for you to do. You've never been, you'll like it, it's a free vacation.'

'When? I'll need to give the shop a day or two to arrange cover.'

'Beginning of next week, it'll be great: hotel food, pools, cost us nothing, unless you go on a spree in all the designer shops while I'm being taught how to stuff and seal envelopes.'

'Adam Collingworth, you smooth-talking salesman, you got yourself a deal!' She squeezes him as tight as she can. 'We can put a bit of extra effort into our baby-making programme, if you're going to be such a hotshot salesman.'

'Don't have to wait for Utah for that,' he says, smiling his best wedding-day smile.

The kettle starts to boil, sending hot steam into his back.

'Tea on hold?' he quips, leaning behind and switching the kettle off.

Paula arches her eyebrows and pulls him towards the stairs.

Michaela fires up her ageing laptop. Where to start? If she hadn't been a primary school teacher she'd have let the whole computer, internet, dongle – whatever you call it – revolution pass her by. But her job had forced her to get online and teach her young charges how to do the same. It wasn't really *her* though. Surfing the web? She'd be keener to surf off the North Norfolk coast, although her lack of anything that could be called 'fitness' and her middle-age spread, which seemed to be spreading at an increasing rate, made that an unlikely option.

So she types *How accurate are the LifeTime Corporation's predictions?* She deletes *predictions*, replaces it with *projections*; she can't go upsetting Adam now, can she?

Chapter Six

'Two diet drinks a day could increase risk of early death by more than a quarter, WHO warns.'
—*The Daily Telegraph*, 3 September 2019

Michaela dumps a sagging set of maths books onto the staffroom table before optimistically choosing 'coffee' from the vending machine. The plastic cup is filled amid a gasping fug of steam, which reminds her, bizarrely, of *The Railway Children*. She lifts a heavy bag of books off a chair and drops it onto the floor under the window. Then she pushes away another couple of random piles to make herself some elbow room. *Now, what have year four made of adding hundreds, tens and units with carrying?* She dares not imagine. A sip of what she'll loosely call coffee – bloody machine's run out of sugar again. She hunts for the packet and shovels two spoonfuls plus assorted light-brown lumps into her cup. Somebody's brought doughnuts for their birthday, she lifts one with pink icing, knocks the cap off her green BIC, and she's away. None down, twenty-six to go.

The staffroom fills: break is twenty minutes long. Even allowing for the usual two or three interruptions, she should be able to crack these in time to avoid a heavy bag slicing through her shoulder on the way home tonight.

Seventeen minutes later and she's looking at a satisfying pile of corrected maths books. No interruptions, a world record. She contemplates the staffroom. There was a time, she remembers it well, when it stank of tobacco. Nowadays the stink is instant coffee. There might also be a hint of some cheapo fragrance if one of the younger teachers is nearby – or the reek of abandoned cheese or yoghurt if the fridge door is open. She picks a couple of Ferrero Rochers out of the large box left over from last week, and vows (again) that they'll be her last. *Willpower*, she mantras silently – as she pops one of the chocolates into her mouth.

Is Fiona away today? She nearly always has a word to say about her year twos, even if it's only a knowing *wait till you get hold of this lot* raise of the eyebrows. But no, she's in conversation with some 'consultant' or 'adviser' who's visiting for the day.

Michaela's never wanted to leave the classroom and teach teachers how to do it. It's hard enough working out how to do it yourself (without it killing you), while avoiding all the visiting wonks trying to offer you 'helpful' advice from a place as far away from a child as possible. She also genuinely enjoys the company of a classload of junior children. She has enough experience to know how to nudge even the most contrary child onto her wavelength by Christmas. After that, her philosophy is simple: *Treat them like kids, behave like a teacher, laugh like a drain when anything goes wrong.* If she could spin that out into 80,000 words she'd have a bestseller for the university bookshop, but she thinks it would more likely end up on some motivational poster, with a waterfall in the background – or maybe a pride of lions savaging an antelope.

She smiles at the thought, gives Fiona a cheery little wave. If she wasn't such a good friend, she'd swear she pretended not to notice her. Odd. Also odd, she now thinks, how empty the staffroom is and how many backs are facing her. And how people are starting to leave even though the bell hasn't gone. She gives Fiona a quizzical look, which is met with a waxwork stare.

The bell goes and the stragglers almost sprint for the playground. What is going on? Fiona intercepts Michaela at the door and touches her arm gently.

'Listen,' Fiona says, in a tone she'd probably use if she was about to tell Michaela that her blouse was open, and the adviser had been gawping. But, mercifully, it's not that. 'I wanted to say how sorry everyone is. It must be such a shock. If there's anything we can do...'

Michaela's known Fiona for twenty years, the time they've shared at Little Wixlow Primary. Younger staff call them 'the telepaths' as each always seems to know what the other is thinking. So, what the hell is Fiona talking about?

'What do you mean?' Michaela asks tentatively.

'Your *dad*,' Fiona replies, looking shocked at Michaela's question. She knows as well as anyone how the hurly-burly of primary school life can clear your mind, even of the machinations of *Coronation Street*, but this is stretching it. 'Your *news*. Everyone's so sorry. Some of the younger staff don't know what to say to you.'

'My *dad*?' Michaela can't quite grasp how everyone might know about yesterday afternoon's dinner antics, if that's what Fiona is referring to. And if she isn't, then what the hell *is* she talking about?

'His news, his illness!' Fiona's eyes plead for Michaela to understand.

'How on earth do you know about that?' Michaela gasps, now as sure as she's ever going to be that yesterday's birthday 'surprise' is, bewilderingly, the talk of the staffroom at Monday breaktime.

'It's in the paper,' Fiona replies.

'The *paper?*'

'Well, it's online; it'll be in this evening's print edition.'

'Which bloody paper?'

'The *Wix'n'Dist*. It's a nice piece. Your dad sounds pretty matter-of-fact, stiff upper lip and all that. Are they sure there's nothing they can do?'

'Who?'

'The doctors.'

'The... look, no *doctors* are involved in this. It's a stir-crazy American website taking Mick's money and telling a seventy-five-year-old man that he's probably going to die in less than a year. Nostradamus would've been cheaper and probably as accurate. I could've done it myself for a fiver with a deck of cards and the dregs of a cup of Earl Grey.'

Michaela takes a breath. Is *she* the one out of step here? Is this her dad dying before her very eyes and she's refusing to face it? How on earth has the paper managed to get hold of Mick between Sunday teatime and Monday morning for a stiff-upper-lip quote? And what the hell is she meant to be teaching year four after break? She quietly lifts the last doughnut out of the box and waddles towards her classroom.

Little Wixlow Primary School is a Victorian treasure. Built in 1899, when the village had pretensions to being a town, it has high windows, a slate roof and red-brick walls. These are all prominently displayed in the glossy school brochure and on its slick website. What is not so evident in the output from LWP's publicity machine are the mobile classrooms that house half the classes, the buckets that have to be strategically placed when it rains, and the smell from the toilets when it rains heavily. It's also not unknown for the occasional stray pig to escape from the farm next door and cause havoc at playtime.

Cathy pulls the car up at the school gates at three thirty-three. Will opens the passenger door and climbs in. Something's wrong. She checks the after-school kickabout on the far side of the field: yep, in full swing. Something's definitely wrong. Normally, she'd have to start yelling uselessly through the window; often, she'd have to high heel it to the far edge of the playground where she'd wave like she was trying to scare crows off a newly seeded lawn; and occasionally, especially if she was more than ten or fifteen minutes late, she'd have to delicately negotiate up to half the length of the pitch on her toes before she'd be able to attract his attention.

But not tonight.

'How was your day?' she opens, quite brightly, an innocent pawn to queen-four.

'S'okay,' he mutters, which she translates as: *you'll probably be able to drag it out of me before we reach home if you try really hard – and offer Coke and a doughnut at Sandy's tea shop in the town as a bargaining chip...*

'Fancy a Coke and a doughnut?' she asks, in a *don't mind if we do, don't mind if we don't* tone.

He shrugs, like he really couldn't give a shit.

Cathy nods sagely to herself: Martini for me; shaken, not stirred.

Checkmate.

Michaela rumbles her hatchback over the cattle grid at the gate to the Manor House. The gravel drive snakes up towards the house, which sits proudly on its own little hillock. The Manor House is what an estate agent with a degree in psychology might call 'an opportunity'. The six bedrooms could be deemed to have 'potential', some more than others, depending on how much damp you could tolerate. The kitchen fits the 'tremendous scope for improvement' adage, with most emphasis being placed on 'tremendous'. If you could find an honest agent, they'd describe parts of the roof as 'a sieve', while no dictionary definition of 'back garden' would be deemed applicable by any professional gardener who didn't want to be sued. Michaela calls the place a 'mistake' behind Mick's back, and has been describing it as 'lovely when you've finished it' to his face for the past thirty years. She only discovered that double glazing, central heating and fitted carpets had been invented when she moved out to go to university in the early 1990s.

There's no evidence it ever really was a true 'manor' in any historical sense of the term. It doesn't look anything like you'd expect a manor house to look, but when he and Celia acquired the place Mick was determined to use the nickname as fact and invent a history if he couldn't find one. He used the name as his address from the first day they took the upper-floor flat as tenants of old Lady Cage. The local postie was willing to indulge Mick's fantasy, so the name stuck. Mick even had a rather splendid rustic-looking wooden sign made and planted down by the front gate, but Michaela notices that it's no longer visible, either hidden by the grass or, more likely, rotting below it. Nobody was ever convinced that Lady Cage was even a real 'lady', but Mick was happy to take it as more evidence for his claim.

Michaela notices the weeds are making further progress in their battle with the front lawn, which they now seem to be winning, even though Mick is fighting them gamely with the help of a ride-on motor-mower, which keen advertisers could market as *Makes Napalm Look Sissy*. She's suggested that some expert botanists should visit to identify some of the weird-looking spiky plants that are moving surreptitiously, and rather threateningly, towards the front door. She's told Mick he needs a gardener (or a battalion of Royal Marines), but he gives her short shrift whenever he thinks she's suggesting that he can't manage, which, it's becoming abundantly clear, she is, because he can't.

She raps the knocker (electric doorbells being another of her student-era discoveries) and listens, because if he's out on the back terrace (contemplating a nuclear strike, his best option there) he never hears it. But the shuffling sound on the floor tiles, and the muttered *no need to break the door down* tells her that he's within range.

'Dad!' she greets him, mustering as much *joie de vivre* as she can after a long day's work. He edges the door open enough to hustle her in before what little heat there is inside escapes.

'Thought I'd pop in and see how you are after yesterday's do. Lovely day, thanks so much. Did you enjoy it?'

He nods and mutters to himself again as he heads back across the hall towards the kitchen. 'You'll be wanting tea,' he says, by way of a greeting.

'Oh, that would be lovely,' she replies, pulling her cardigan tighter as she follows him into the gloom. The black and white chequered-tile floor in the hall would be fine in a bigger (even a manor) house, Michaela always thinks, but Mick has been adamant it was 'what the place needed' when Lady Cage had died and given him and Celia first option. He hadn't been daft enough to try to install oak panelling, but she knew his budget choice of dark brown wallpaper was his nod in that direction, even if everyone else thought it looked odd. The grandfather clock from the local antique (read *junk*) shop has never ticked or tocked since he bought it, and is yet another of his faux-heirloom touches.

She'll allow him the stairs, mind. The staircase is straight from *Gone with the Wind*, or some other film with a big staircase. It's a dark wood, twisty affair; she's no idea what style it might be. Her favourite touch is the yellow duster draped over the banister: Mick sweeps it up the handrail whenever he goes upstairs, sweeps downwards on the other side when he returns. Hence, it's constantly dusted. The only thing in the house, she thinks, that ever is.

There'd been talk that Lady Cage had done some sort of special deal with Mick and Celia as the house, with six bedrooms and two receptions, was ridiculously big for the pair of them. Still, Mick convinced Celia that it would be a *sound investment*. And, although it was clearly being allowed to go to seed at an accelerating rate, Mick was still here, what, fifty-odd years later?

'You drank the last of your funny teas last time and I haven't been to the supermarket, so PG Tips okay?'

'Lovely, builder's is fine.'

The kitchen's another nod to a much grander house, and a scream for a health and safety inspection. You expect to see a cook and a maid responding to bells while bustling around the rectangular oak table, pulling the pots and pans from their hooks on the tiled walls, and distributing them over the Aga that takes up half of one side of the room. But the Aga hasn't been used since Celia passed away, and there are no bells, cook or maid, so Mick fills the electric kettle and plugs it into the least dangerous-looking socket in the room. Michaela's running joke (out of Mick's earshot) is that the place was wired *before* they'd invented electricity.

She opens a cupboard for his sugar and smiles at all his tins standing to attention like guards on parade: she knows they're in date order. The Cornflakes packet brings to mind one of his many pet hates: the 'serving suggestion' on food packaging which nobody else in the world notices. Shopping with him is a nightmare as he pulls packets and tins off the shelves and rants: *Put 'em in a bowl and pour milk on 'em? Throw a bit of lemon on the side of the plate? For fuck's sake!* She also remembers the day she came home from school (she was about nine) and tried to tell him that Kellogg's was American. Trump might have patented the skill of manufacturing truth by willpower, but Mick had beaten him to it by decades. Ah well, at least it's not a weekend morning, and she doesn't have to relive his only religious observance: half a grapefruit with a glacé cherry in the middle and grapefruit juice squirting into her eyes.

He's always espoused a buy-British policy: Mother's Pride; gold-top milk – damn them for getting rid of the glass bottles *and* for halting deliveries; British lamb and beef; British fruit 'n' veg – he's never bought a pineapple in his life. Won't touch mangos either. His only deviation from his buy-British crusade (apart from the Cornflakes) is bacon, which always has to be *Danishhhh.* Oh, and his New Zealand butter, but that still counts as they're part of the Commonwealth. Nobody mentions his baked beanz – Heinz, of course, but shhhh... She picks up the pack of sugar, Tate and Lyle – natch.

'Seen the paper?' Michaela says brightly, dropping it onto the table. Mick picks it up, surveys the headline, smiles in appreciation.

'Not a bad piece, although I never said anyone was distraught. I'm going to have a word with Bob, get that reporter disciplined or fired or something.'

'They were quick off the mark, we only had the celebration yesterday,' she fishes.

'Gave Bob a call when I got home. He was keen to get it in

for today's run, so he sent one of his hacks along for a chat straight away.'

Michaela knows she should probably keep her mouth shut.

'You called them? Do you really think that was wise?'

'What?'

'Telling the press?'

Mick turns and glares at her. Always a contrary girl, since the first squawk came out of her. Always has to voice an opinion, usually in a minority of one.

'Don't see why not. LifeTime's the future. I know you're not keen on the idea, but things change in this world, my dear, and we must change with them.'

Michaela bites her tongue, physically. She clamps it between her upper and lower incisors and locks it there, concentrating on the discomfort, instead of the instances when Mick has railed (usually loudly) against change. She can think of a few right off the top of her head: decimalisation, for one. He never agreed with that. Ballpoint pens was another, he's always used a fountain. Plastic carrier bags, the Common Market, ring pull cans, compulsory seat belt wearing, having to pick up dog shit from the pavement (even though he's never owned a dog), credit cards, the EEC, Velcro, the Sony Walkman, barcodes, mobile phones, Rubik's cubes, grocers' apostrophes, ATMs, the EU, people who *don't* pick up dog shit, Facebook, Brexit, driverless cars... It seems to Michaela that Mick has suffered from the grumpy old manopause probably since he was old enough to wonder if his Corgis and Dinkies were made in GB or (heaven forfend) Hong Kong – but then wasn't that another colony, or used to be?

Mick's all-time hate programme on the TV, when she was a child, was *Tomorrow's World*, a weekly round-up of the latest scientific gadgets and inventions, which were predicted to change the world they lived in. She loved it but couldn't now think of it without recalling his constant tutting and sighing that accompanied nearly every item. She wonders how he's survived as a doctor; was there any job that had changed more than his over the last half a century?

'I thought it was a bit, you know, of a private thing. A family matter?'

Mick sighs contemptuously as he carries the tea tray through to the lounge. 'I screwed a hundred quid out of Bob for that, he was only offering fifty.'

'Oh, Dad. You can't be that desperate for money.'

'What do you know about what money I might need?' he snaps.

'Just don't drag the rest of us into it, will you? Not everyone wants to be on the front page of the paper. I'm sure Steve and Cathy won't want Will plastered all over the dailies.'

'It's the bloody *Wix'n'Dist*, love, circulation a dozen if you don't count the chippy. I didn't phone the bloody *Sun!*'

'And I'm not sure buying one for Will was such a bright idea, not without asking Steve and Cathy first.'

'Oh, poppycock!' he snarls. 'Didn't you see how thrilled he was?'

'Yes, but the date he's meant to *die*? Don't you think he's a bit young for that?'

'Nonsense! You mollycoddle him too much! He's got his head screwed on, it'll encourage him to look after himself, not start smoking, do drugs, you wait and see.'

She raises her eyes, fumes inwardly at the lifelong smoker pontificating on the health benefits of not smoking. Why did old age make people think they had the right to be so bloody cantankerous? She muses on it as Mick sets the tray down on a large, low table and leaves her to be mother. Young people were never cantankerous. She can't imagine writing *Jenny is a cantankerous little thing*. No, Jenny wouldn't actually say boo to a gosling, but it was true of any child, you'd never describe them as cantankerous. Or was it simply that we wouldn't use that *word* with younger people? Was the word *cantankerous* reserved for old people? Along with *old* (obviously) – and *git?*

'A little milk?' she offers, knowing that he hates it in tea.

Chapter Seven

'Book Up for a Longer Life: Readers Die Later, Study Finds.'
—*The Guardian*, 8 August 2016

'So, what's bothering you?' Cathy asks, as she drops a sugar cube into her tea, bugger the diet, then starts to redistribute the butter on her toasted teacake, sod the diet.

Will takes a huge bite of his doughnut, and chews. He's a happy-go-lucky boy, gets on with everyone, but has a soft centre that can be easily hurt. Or so said Michaela (that's Ms Strong to you, between 9.00 and 3.30), when Will was in her class the year before last. Cathy can sense considerable bruising of the soft centre, enough for a late fitness test to rule him out of tonight's kickabout, so that's considerable.

'Somebody said something?'

A nod, another bite.

'Bobby "Basher" Baines?'

He almost smiles, she nearly got him: Bobby Baines being as much of a 'basher' as a three-day-old kitten.

'Jenny?'

'Oh, *Mum!*'

'Well, *who* then? I'll have to ring school for the register in a minute; I don't know everyone in your class.'

'Josh,' he says to what's left of his doughnut lying on the plate in front of him.

Josh. Who else would it be?

'What did he say?'

A slurp of Coke.

'He said GG was gonna die!'

Cathy sips her tea. The temptation to say, *He is seventy-five years old, so sooner or later Josh's going to be proved right*, is strong, but resistible. Another tack might be better, she's sure.

'So, why did he say that?' Cathy probes, mostly for her own curiosity.

'He saw it on the internet, on the *Wix'n'Dist*.'

'He–' Cathy stands and heads for the counter, where the *Wixlow and District Gazette* tends to reside, always third choice behind the *Mail* and the *Express*. She sits back down a lot slower than she stood up, her eyes locked on the front-page headline.

Local Doc Faces Death Sentence

She skims quickly, her jaw dropping in tandem with her eyes as they pour down the page.

Popular local doc... months to live... shady American deathday website... 1,000 pounds... family distraught...

'So, what do I say?'

'What?'

'To Josh. What do I say?'

'Oh – tell him his own granddad's gonna die!'

Cathy knows as soon as she says it that this is a bad idea. She has no clue how bad...

'Josh's granddad's already dead. Both of 'em.'

'Right. Look, shall we talk about this at home? With Dad?'

Michaela concentrates on pouring and stirring, rattling the cups and saucers loudly, then takes refuge in a sip of tea. She sinks into the creaking velveteen sofa (he has his *own* armchair), carefully avoiding contact with the antimacassars that seem to turn a deeper shade of brownish yellow every time she visits.

'What are these?' she asks, pointing at the pile of books next to his chair.

He stares at them like he's never seen them before. 'Oh, them? They're books that have meant a lot to me when I read them. Now I can't remember what happened in them. If you'd asked me a couple of weeks ago to name some of the best books I'd ever read, these would've been in the frame.' He holds up the curling copy of *A Dry White Season*. 'I'd have told you this book changed my life, changed the way I saw the world.'

'I know,' she says, 'you've told me often. I've heard you tell other people.'

'Yes, well, here's the thing, I picked it up yesterday, and I couldn't remember the story. Couldn't name the main character. Couldn't remember any other characters. Was there a woman in it? I knew it was about a South African journalist, that it was set in South Africa during apartheid. But that was it. Nothing of the story which I say, have said for so many years, changed my life. But now, I've no idea how.'

'It probably woke you up to the horrors of apartheid.'

'I'm sure it did, but I can't remember how, what was the story that fired my response?'

'Does that really matter?'

'You know, that's a really interesting question. Instinctively

I feel it does. It matters a lot. This was an event, a story that affected me deeply. So where is it now? In the sense of being a part of who I am now?'

'Well, you're vehemently anti-racist.'

'Yes, but I'm vehemently lots of things that don't have a single incident as a cause. My love of the NHS, for example. But this book, *this* book is part of me like a football team is part of other people. Yet I can't remember the main character's name. You get these football people who can tell you who scored a goal in a match they attended in the 1970s. Who was it? Nick somebody. Wrote a book about following the Arsenal when he was a kid. *Fever* something. Quite good, actually. Where is it? I might give it another read.' He gets up and starts scanning the shelves like he's browsing in Waterstones.

'But people who follow a football team go again and again. You read *Dry White Season* once. Years ago. Are you worried about Alzheimer's?' She gasps as the words leave her lips, an involuntary intake of breath follows them, like she's trying to catch them, suck them back in before he hears them. But she's pulled the pin, tossed the grenade, she waits for the explosion.

'Not particularly.' He shrugs, pulling *Fever Pitch* off the shelves and riffling the pages. 'It's more, I don't know, a sort of disappointment, that my past isn't as important as I always assumed it was. I feel all these books have been a waste of time if I can't remember what's in them.'

The silence hangs like a developing fog between them, every second adding to the mist of misunderstanding as it thickens and obscures. She could probably think of a dozen ripostes, each aimed to ease his worry, but she can't trust herself to word them in a way that he will understand; a part of her wonders if he even wants it (whatever *it* might be) eased or explained away.

'You know,' he continues, dropping the book next to his

other to-be-reads and slumping back into his armchair, staring at the ceiling like he's forgotten she's there in the room with him, 'there are moments when I read a particular sentence or paragraph, that I can feel, I can really *experience* where I was, who I was with, when I first read it. It's like the words are stored in my brain somewhere, and the rereading of them accesses that little box and opens it. But it's not just the words that are inside; it's everything else that was going on at the time. I read some of *Catcher* last week and suddenly I remembered Bill Bailey, I was sharing a flat with him at the time, and I could smell the curry he used to cook. I almost went out into the kitchen to check I hadn't left something on, burning. Isn't that remarkable?'

She watches him as he talks; it's as if he's not talking to her, she imagines he'd carry on the conversation even if she quietly left the room. His eyes don't seem to be focused on anything, like he's got some internal vision of Bill Bailey cooking curry while he's reading *Catcher in the Rye*.

'So, I'm going to read them all again, remember what it was that meant something!' He's got a note of triumph in his voice, like he's solved a particularly vexing problem.

'Aren't you afraid you might be disappointed, second time around? I mean, we change, the books don't.'

'What's the problem?' he demands. She wonders if he's afraid he's gone too far, opened up too much, *navel-gazing, can of worms* and all that. It's certainly an unusual conversation, for him. All that introspection. 'I want to read. You're a bloody teacher; I thought you'd be pleased, setting an example for Will. We could read together.'

'What? *Tinker, Tailor*? He'd love that!' She's instantly aware it's a ridiculous jibe to make. What is she thinking? She hunts desperately for a question to grab his attention, prevent him from responding. 'Isn't it a bit obsessive?'

'What do you mean, fucking obsessive? What about all the

time you spend in your fucking church praying to your fucking ghosts. Is that not obsessive?'

Michaela backs off, knowing that the use of the F-word is a signal. She should have heeded the warning of the B-word, but she didn't. Once Mick's introduced the F-word into a debate, he'll never back down. Like a rhino lowering its horn, there's never backward movement after that. She sips her tea.

'Want a top-up?' she offers, desperate to change the subject. Why do conversations with her dad always turn into a fraught, final set at Wimbledon? They used to play tennis when she was a child, there's, well, there *was*, a grass court out back, now in the jungle, so the analogy seems appropriate to her. Every comment is like a forehand that has to be parried, or a backhand that needs to be fended off. Why can't they simply discuss something? She reaches for a biscuit, hides behind her crunching and crumb catching for a few more precious seconds.

'So,' she says finally, deciding to change tack a fraction. 'How do you feel about *your* news?'

'My deathdate?' Mick says, apparently keen to smack Michaela's euphemism into the back of the net. Love–fifteen. 'Pretty much what I was expecting. Average life expectancy for men in the UK is about eighty. I haven't done too badly.'

'Yes, but what do you *feel*? Do you think it's right? Do you really believe it?'

'I'd hardly have forked out the money if I wasn't going to believe what I'd paid for. Tell you what though, the bloody form on the internet was much too long, asking loads of daft questions you couldn't possibly answer, lots more were utterly irrelevant. Give me five minutes and I'd have cut it down to size for them. Must have a word with Adam about that.'

Michaela breathes deeply, sips more tea, nibbles her biscuit. Love–thirty. 'What I mean is...' What does she mean? She has no idea. 'What I mean is, do you really think you're going to die, in two hundred and seventy days?'

'Two hundred and *sixty-nine* now, actually.' Love–forty.

'Yes, I know.' She did know. She can do two hundred and seventy take away one, even if half her class of eight-year-olds can't. She didn't do it because – well, because it felt like she'd be starting a countdown if she had.

Mick shakes his head. 'Adam's told me there's a bit of leeway either way, a few days, weeks even. Says if I give up smoking, I could count on a few more weeks. Cut out the booze, another couple of months, maybe. It's not a prediction, you know. It's a... the other thing.'

'And are you going to?'

He shrugs. Sips tea, picks up a biscuit. She notices that he hasn't really considered this before. He's considering it now.

'I mean–' she knows she's risking a McEnroe tantrum now, '–if you had a day to go, and they told you that if you stopped smoking you could have another week...?'

'That's ridiculous,' he snaps. *You cannot be serious!*

She wants to shout *none of this is bloody serious!* but that might be overstepping the mark at this stage. She leaves him to brood on it for a bit. Maybe, with a bit of luck, she might have planted a seed.

Fifteen–forty.

'You know, some people are saying that LifeTime are a bit fast and loose with their figures, to cash in before the regulators can take a proper look, not that there's much regulation left now. They say their algorithms are still pretty rudimentary, that the margin of error is much bigger than they're willing to admit.'

'That's good for me then, isn't it?'

'Depends on whether it makes your projection too long or too short...'

'Where are you getting this nonsense? You been on the interweb again?'

'I'm just saying.'

'Bloody American conspiracy theories probably. Tin-hat cranks, you can't believe any of that non–'

'*American?* LifeTime's American, Dad. You can't defend an American company by criticising all things American.'

'Fake news,' he taunts, shaking his head. The end of all arguments.

Game, set and match. He lifts his cup.

Steve picks up the TV doofer and presses the *off* button.

'Hey!' Will pleads. 'I'm watching that!'

'Dinner time,' Steve insists, then meaningfully adds, '*family* dinner, c'mon.'

They've made his favourite, to soften the blow to their usual *dinner in front of the telly* routine. Will stares suspiciously at the sight of spag bol piled high on his plate, a mound of grated cheese in a bowl, and (especially) the two-litre bottle of Coke on the table: it's *diet*, but hey...

'There's apple pie and custard for afters,' Cathy says as she sits. 'Well, this is nice!'

Will picks up his fork, eyes them both, like he's expecting his mountain of spag bol to explode.

'We wanted to talk to you about Great-Granddad's party,' Steve starts, somewhat obliquely, like he wants to raise and avoid the issue of the projection.

Will negotiates a forkful of spaghetti into his mouth and nods vigorously.

'We don't want you to worry about it,' Cathy adds, although

they had agreed while cooking that Steve would lead. 'It's a lot to face up to.'

Will swallows. 'It's okay,' he says, twirling his fork inexpertly, flecking his shirt with spots of tomato sauce. 'It's not a problem.'

'What do you mean?' Steve asks.

'Well,' Will says, concentrating on a huge roll of spaghetti, dripping Bolognese sauce, now on its way to his mouth. 'Mum's sorted it.'

Steve gives Cathy a confused glance while Will chews. She shakes her head.

'What are you talking about?' Steve asks, as they wait for him to swallow.

'Mum said I should tell Josh that *his* granddad's already dead!'

'I didn't say that!' Cathy splutters.

'No, you said that I should tell him his granddad's *gonna* die, but seeing as he already *is* dead, I can tell him that. That'll shut him up!' He smiles a huge, Bolognese-stained smile.

Cathy sighs, shakes her head at Steve, *let's not go there now.* 'No,' she says calmly to Will. 'We're not talking about that. We're talking about the present Great-Granddad gave you. We don't want you worrying about that.'

'Why would I worry about that?' Will sounds completely mystified.

Cathy looks at Steve. Steve looks at Cathy. Why would he worry about that? Cathy takes a deep breath.

'We're not sure that a LifeTime prediction is the best idea for a boy of your age.'

'Why not?' Will asks, shrugging. His mouth drops, as does a dollop of sauce onto the table. 'And Uncle Adam says it's a pro-*jection.*'

She glances at Steve, but he's chewing slowly. 'Well, they're really quite new, and they're not that reliable yet, their accuracy is pretty questionable.'

Every reason she gives sends Will's face further into gloom.

'But GG gave it to me. *He's* got one.'

Cathy looks at Steve again. How do you construct an argument against undeniably true statements of fact? She now knows how Kirk felt, arguing with Spock.

'We thought you might want something nicer for your birthday,' Steve eventually weighs in. 'Something you could play with. I mean, what can you do with a LifeTime prediction – *projection* – at your age? We thought you might like a droneboard?'

'Wow! *Would I?*' Droneboards had recently appeared on the market: small platforms, the size of a dustbin lid, with six, high-torque propellers that lift you a few centimetres off the ground and travel at slow speed using a handheld controller.

'So, that's settled,' Cathy says, sighing with relief, but wondering how the hell she's ended up agreeing to Will smashing himself straight into a wall on a flying bin lid.

'Thanks, guys,' Will gasps, forking more spaghetti into his mouth and chewing excitedly.

'And we'll get rid of the LifeTime stuff,' Steve mumbles.

'What?' There are more blobs of spaghetti and sauce on the table in front of Will.

'For the droneboard. You get the droneboard *instead* of the LifeTime. That's what we agreed.'

'But GG gave me the LifeTime.'

'Yes, we know, but we thought you'd prefer a droneboard.'

'But why can't I have a droneboard *and* keep GG's present?'

'Well...' Steve tries to buy time by filling his mouth with spaghetti. Neither he nor Cathy had seen this coming. The promise of a droneboard had seemed a sure-fire bribe. 'A droneboard is quite expensive. We'd need Great-Granddad to share the cost, and we wouldn't be able to afford that *and* a LifeTime membership.'

Will turns his fork slowly in the remains of his spaghetti. His brow furrows. Then he looks up.

'No, I wanna keep my LifeTime. Like GG.' He scrapes his plate. 'Can I have my pud by the TV, please?'

Cathy shrugs, defeated, or scared to take it any further, she can't be sure.

'Go on.' She stares at Steve, who's concentrating on his spaghetti. She wonders what's lying in wait in *his* golden envelope, but decides she can't fight both fronts at the same time.

Steve continues twirling spaghetti around his fork, but his mind is obviously somewhere else.

Chapter Eight

'Cutting screen time lowers risk of early death, study finds.'
—BBC News Online, 23 July 2020

The drone hangs in mid-air about four metres off the ground, like a giant insect hunting a flower to drink from, or some skin to sting. It's completely silent, not that you'd know it – the noise of the chattering crowd waiting at the arrivals gate of Terminal One at Salt Lake City International Airport would drown out the planes were they to test their engines outside on the taxi rank. There's the usual collection of courtesy-car drivers with scribbled name cards; tearful parents with expectant eyes; and singletons – probably harbouring more expectations than anyone else.

Adam and Paula step swiftly through the US & UK Citizens Welcome Corridor – a post-Brexit arrangement introduced after the UK closed its borders and submitted its citizens to Department of Homeland Security vetting as part of a trade agreement, which included free movement of labour (and chicken) between the two 'equal' partners. The left wing in the UK ridiculed it loudly as the birth of the fifty-first state; the right wing in the US privately boasted of their first twenty-first-century colony.

The display screen on the drone starts to flash and scroll a *Welcome to SLC Adam and Paula* message as soon as its facial-recognition camera picks them up.

'Look! Adam, look! There we are! On that drone! Look at *that!*' Paula points and grips Adam's arm.

They're led to a parking lot where shiny cars are spaced a couple of metres apart. The drone settles on the roof of a sleek, silver-grey executive model with the LT logo flashed down the side in a colourful hologram that twirls and twists as they approach. The door and boot hiss open, and a welcoming voice invites them to stow their luggage, Paula emitting little gasps of surprise at every interactive response to their presence. Adam wonders if the wilds of north Norfolk, with all their advantages, might be getting left behind in the previous century – maybe even the one before that. They collapse into leather armchairs as the gentle voice encourages them to face the internal camera for another facial recognition check, before alerting them to the drinks available in the fridge. The door slides shut and the air-conditioning envelops them. Paula spins and giggles wildly as Adam pours the cold drinks. Yes, much too long out in the wilds.

'Wow! Is this driverless?' Paula asks; she's noticed that aside from the four swivel armchairs around a small coffee table, there's no driving seat, no steering wheel. They're on their own. 'I've never been in one.'

'Hold tight,' Adam says, smiling. He knows the sight of a driverless vehicle in north Norfolk is still rare enough to attract excited children to point and squeal.

'Where's it taking us?' she asks, without looking away from the window.

'HQ, I hope. We'll follow the freeway most of the way.'

They drive for less than an hour, before heading out over a barren, desert wilderness, leaving the freeway behind. The ground is rocky, but the road is smooth tarmac. There are mountains in the distance, but it's hard to tell if they're monstrous peaks half-a-continent away, or mid-sized hills in the middle distance.

The sense of the machine being in complete control of their destiny always spooks Adam. What if it malfunctions? What if they crash? Who would come and rescue them out here? Who would know they were here at all? He assures himself that some all-controlling computer will sound an alert in some hi-tech control centre should anything go wrong.

Adam points out a series of what appear to be transparent domes in the near distance, interlinking like a small mountain of soap bubbles nestling together on the ground. As they approach, the curved structures turn pastel green and then more verdant against the mountainous background and the scrub desert floor. Three immense domes dominate, with maybe up to a dozen or so more of varying, smaller sizes.

They approach one of the smaller domes on the outskirts of the ensemble. Paula's head shakes slowly in disbelief, as the distance they still have to cover, and the size it's going to be when they arrive, become apparent. The biggest buildings she's ever entered, the Royal Albert Hall and Carrow Road Stadium, would look like Lego bricks beside the construction that continues to grow as they approach. It's like The Eden Project, but on steroids, huge quantities of them. Adam has told her the whole of downtown Manhattan could fit inside the footprint of SphereCity, but it meant nothing to her, having never visited NYC.

They enter the first bubble. The sides are sheer and sleek, the sun glinting brightly off the smooth surface. Behind it, the larger bubbles march into the distance, now obscuring any view of the mountains behind. They're sealed and wrapped against the blistering desert sun. A cocoon of safety.

They drive into a short tunnel before rolling through a series of barriers that lift, swing or drop silently as they approach. Armed guards in sentry boxes on either side wave them on with cheery looks and steady eyes. Adam muses, correctly, that the thick steel arch of the tunnel contains enough scanning and surveillance equipment to keep out anything it is hunting. Once again, as it has done in the past, the level of security gives him an unsettling sense of unease; he's not used to seeing so much firepower carried openly. They pass, unhindered, and their vehicle accelerates away from the entrance.

Paula, meanwhile, is gazing at the inside of the first dome with a tourist's eyes, studying details, pointing them out to Adam without turning to look at him. She's seen this type of construction in sci-fi films, portraying colonies on other planets, hundreds of years into the future. The change in scenery is stark: from barren scrub desert on the outside, to a lush green carpet of grass with flowering shrubs and full-sized trees.

'It's enormous,' she gasps, finally breaking away and smiling at Adam.

It's his third visit to HQ but it still impresses, like he's on a film set but taking the tour rather than acting the part. The idea that he works for this company still hasn't fully penetrated his mindset. He's only been on board fifteen months and still feels like an imposter, likely to be unmasked and ejected. His sudden pro– or is it a demotion, to salesman is almost unsurprising. He needs to see Ron, his immediate superior in InfoDiv where he used to work.

They sweep through the boundary between the first two

intersecting domes and Paula's mouth opens without releasing any sound. The roof of the second rises upwards until it's invisible against the blue sky. The only hint that they are indoors comes from the distortion of the mountains, once again visible, away in the distance. They appear slightly hazy, like peering through the bathroom window of an exhibitionist.

The roof of their car suddenly slides backwards, and Paula looks up instinctively. 'Where's the heat gone? It was roasting when we left the airport.'

'SphereCity is climate controlled. We'd bake in it if it wasn't. It'd be the world's biggest greenhouse. They can add more domes at any time so the city can grow. Amazing, but what with the climate going to hell, it's probably the future.'

They pass several futuristic-looking buildings as they cruise through the rolling hills and lush vegetation. One, a four- or five-storey glass block, reflects the surrounding countryside so perfectly that, at times, it's practically invisible as a building. Then, moments later, it starts to reappear as the reflection changes slightly. It's hard to tell how tall it really is, there are no floors visible on the outside. For all he knows, it could be a hollow glass cube.

Cyclists, bladers and hoverboarders wave and smile from the tracks, which sometimes parallel the road, but often disappear behind screens of flowering bushes or small hillocks. Every now and again, they spot what look like hamlets: half a dozen low-level houses, aquamarine pools, a tennis or paddel court.

'Do people *live* here?' Paula asks, absent-mindedly, staring at a game of doubles tennis going on in the distance.

'Sure,' Adam replies. 'You fancy it?'

'Maybe...' She shrugs, following the game until it disappears behind a bank of pink azaleas in full bloom, '...in a few years?'

They feel the soft pull of the brakes as they turn towards a building a few hundred metres away. It appears low-rise, but as they get closer, it becomes clear that behind the façade of flowered terraces it gets taller.

'Welcome to the Hitñon Hotel at Babylon Dome,' the on-board computer purrs as they glide to the entrance and three top-hatted doormen circle their wagon.

Chapter Nine

'Adding Salt to Food at Table Can Cut Years off Your Life,
Study Finds.'
—*The Guardian*, 11 July 2022

Adam's first meeting in the morning is with his new boss, the director of MarktDiv at LT. He has no idea who this person is; the message has only given him a job title and instructions to arrive by ten. He leaves Paula by the infinity pool and hops onto a Segway, speaking his destination into the docking station.

Paula's last instructions echo in his ears: *Tell them what you're worth; don't let them bully you; demand to be put back on your old contract.* Yeah, sure, and a massive pay rise – easier said.

Adam glides off in the direction they arrived from the night before, and he spends his time going over his options – yet again. Can he turn down this move from stats to marketing? It didn't sound like a request or a suggestion when MarktDiv initially messaged him. He knows he's a small fish in this ocean, but he feels insulted to be shunted without so much as a *would you mind?* Which he does, but doesn't feel he can say.

LT has never felt like a company open to negotiation. This was confirmed when he called his (now, ex-) boss in InfoDiv to ask him what was going on. Ron Rubenstein, good friend and confidant from way back in grad school, confessed the same sense of annoyance because he hadn't been consulted about Adam's change of role either. He'd tried to dress it up for Adam as an opportunity, with the UK market promising to grow rapidly, but he hadn't hidden his fear there were things going on at a high level that he himself wasn't privy to. Adam has some time in his diary to have a chat with Ron: find out if he's discovered some beans that he might be willing to spill, maybe a whole load of vegetables as well.

So, option two? Take it on the chin. He wonders if this is his only option, so better to concede without much fuss? The cut in basic salary is a worry, but losing his job completely would be a disaster. The job market for statisticians in the UK is relatively flat, and neither he nor Paula are keen to move at the moment. Can they really do this to him? He knows they can. They have.

The sight of the mirrored cube building he'd noticed the evening before breaks his train of thought. *So this is MarktDiv,* he thinks to himself. *Impressive.* He parks and makes his way inside.

The lobby area takes up close to half the building. There's no desk to report to, no receptionist to tell him where to go; it's completely silent, totally deserted, except for a cyclopic camera eye staring at him from a far corner. He wonders if there are a team of people somewhere, watching him, assessing him against a checklist of MarktDiv goals, or targets, or whatever the latest nonsense is. The sensation of being totally alone while closely monitored is completed when a soft melodic *pling* draws his attention to a door-sized opening in the wall, which he takes to

be for him. He searches in vain for a metal plate engraved with
the names of the architects, but he knows who they'd be: Escher,
Kafka, Blaine & Associates. It was probably there once, but now
it's disappeared. He steps inside, turns around, and the floor lifts
him. Like everything else in the building so far, it's as close to
silent as a great white shark browsing for a light lunch.

He steps out into a lavishly enormous, yet spartanly
minimalist, office. The sky is visible through the high, slightly
darkened ceiling, and both side walls are full-length picture
windows larger than juggernauts. Near the right-hand window,
a white leather sofa-and-armchair arrangement surrounds a low,
black coffee table, like a family of polar bears stalking a small
seal.

'Coffee?' The voice jolts his head around and thumps his
heart against his ribcage. She's black and white: her blouse is
white silk; her skirt charcoal black; her hair a matt ebony – solid
as a cap; her skin, polished porcelain.

'Um, yes, please. White, no sugar. I, um, didn't mean to–'

But she's already turned, her highly polished black high
heels ticking like a small metronome with the volume turned
down to minimum. He tries to smooth down his red-checked,
open-necked shirt, wishes he'd worn a jacket and tie.

He watches people down below on bicycles and Segways,
all moving silently like characters in a video game. There's a
toytown appearance to them all, like someone's tilt-shifted the
world into a Legoland of unreal people in an unreal place that
now controls his future.

A smart suited man appears carrying a silver tray with a
coffee pot and cups. He nods a greeting, sets the tray onto the
table, places a cup and saucer in front of Adam, the other in
front of the armchair with its back to the window. He's dressed
for a high-level business meeting: black suit, crisp white shirt,
and a silk tie, so close to black to fit in with the rest of the

surroundings, but not close enough to be funereal. He pours two cups, nods again as a farewell and leaves.

The woman reappears instantly, the idea of AI androids flashes into his mind. He studies her as she approaches, no hint of make-up on her face. She's concentrating on a sleek tablet that she's carrying in one hand. To his surprise, he thought she was a waitress, she sits in the armchair by the window and makes a couple of last decisive stabs with blood-red fingernails, the colour seeming all the more audacious for its rarity in the room. With the exception, of course, of his shirt.

'So good to meet you at last.' Her voice is clipped, like she's reading a script in a foreign language for the first time and is taking care not to make a mistake. She offers her hand almost halfway across the coffee table, and he ends up shaking her fingers with his own, noticing how cold they are, feeling his shirt tug out of his trousers as he crouches and stretches. She looks briefly into his eyes and smiles, friendly, open and welcoming, but somehow infinitely practised. Her eyes flit to his shirt and he feels himself flinch, like she's touched him, felt the quality of the fabric, and not been impressed. He resists a strong temptation to apologise, to explain.

She doesn't introduce herself. Should he know who she is? Did he not read the message carefully enough? He doesn't want to reveal his stupidity by asking her. Now he feels rude, ill-educated, a spotty schoolboy with shirt tails flying awaiting a dressing-down in the headmistress's office, but also confused. Is she the head of MarktDiv, one of the most important roles in LT? Or is she an assistant of some sort, here to put a few of his details onto the system in preparation for his real meeting? He's about to try to clarify this, without actually asking outright, but she's talking again.

'We're extremely pleased with how you've run with the marketing ball in the UK. Five sales before we've even officially

launched? Cheeky, but I have to say, impressive. I like initiative.'
She taps and scratches on the tablet. It could be his personnel
file she's amending; it could be a transatlantic flight she's
checking.

'Oh, they're all family,' Adam says, and she stops tapping
and looks up at him again, this time with genuine interest and
not a little disdain: the butter-wouldn't-melt girl with the large
magnifying glass scrutinising an ant on a sunny day.

'Oh, don't undersell yourself. Never do that. Not in your
job. Not now that I've promoted you.'

He doubts that this is the time, or the place, and she
certainly isn't the person he should attempt to collar with gripes
about his 'promotion'. Although, calling it a promotion does
seem to be excessively creative, even for a marketing
department.

'Now listen,' she says, before he has time to reply. 'We're
expecting the UK to be big. Huge. I'm confident that you are the
right man for the job. You've got your feet on the ground, you're
embedded, you know the country, you know the culture, you've
been there a couple of years, right? Married to a local.' She
doesn't wait for an answer. 'Your new role is head of UK sales;
shortly, we'll be appointing four regional deputies who will lead
teams working to your direction. Your gross salary will be a
hundred and sixty-five thousand pounds plus five per cent of all
your own sales and one per cent of the gross sales of your team.
Your minimum annual bonus will be fifty per cent of your gross
salary paid in stock. You'll receive the usual package of private
health insurance for you and your family, and a generous
company car allowance although you're free to choose your own
wheels. You'll be able to get something nice; make sure it's
appropriate for an LT exec. Let us know when you've got it, and
we'll get the LT livery done. We're also going to be giving you a

dedicated publicity team to work directly with the British media.'

Adam tries to keep his face from looking like that of a five-year-old who's had a knickerbocker glory plonked down in front of him. Problem is, the five-year-old fears it's been delivered to the wrong table; he distinctly heard his mother ordering him an egg sandwich. Adam wonders if his Segway has malfunctioned, and taken him to the wrong building, making this the wrong meeting, someone else's meeting – someone else's hundred and sixty-five thousand pounds. He's acutely aware that she hasn't actually used his name.

'We need to move quickly. Our operations in the UK have to expand rapidly before the British decide they want to scrutinise the regulatory framework. You understand what I'm saying? Unless and until they decide to amend the regulations in place as a result of our post-Brexit agreement, they'll be accepting US rules which suits us fine. You've already demonstrated that you can use your initiative and act decisively without waiting for clearance from above. I like that very much. Now I need you to sign your contract, then go straight over to Jaz Forrester who'll be your immediate manager at MarktDiv. You'll be reporting directly to him; he'll be keeping me up to date with your progress. I expect his reports to explode onto my desk. He's expecting you in about twenty minutes; his office is in Halicarnassus Dome, that's the next one north from Babylon.'

She hands him the tablet, stands up, and offers her hand to shake again. He hesitates, shocked that their meeting seems to be over.

'You can read the details at your leisure, I'm quite sure you'll find them acceptable. Sign the screen when you've finished and leave the tablet on my desk. And something to bear in mind, Jaz doesn't like lateness. It was a great pleasure to meet you. I'm expecting great things – I hope you won't disappoint me. Now, if you'll excuse me, I have a meeting with the directorate. I also like to be on time.'

Her hand is still out ready for him to shake. A box on the tablet is open ready for him to sign. He stands and shakes her hand, wondering if the handshake outranks the signature he's yet to put in the box. Then she turns and walks away like an expensively dressed magician's assistant – except, she's clearly nobody's assistant.

Adam slowly sits back down into the soft leather. He's never had a meeting like it. Calling it a 'meeting' seems a linguistic fraud of Ponzian proportions. Did he speak? He can't remember. He wonders if there's been some sort of error. Did he mishear? A hundred and sixty-five thousand? That's four or five times his old salary *before* they cut it in half. He scrolls down the contract on the tablet, and there it is in figures: £165,000. He even checks it's per annum and not for a fixed term, say three years – or a decade. They can put a good mortgage on a house with that. They can choose a house big enough if Paula falls pregnant with triplets with that. Private health, company car? What's he missing? He scrolls down and down, skim reading as he goes, but it's pages and pages long, small print followed by smaller print. A hundred and sixty-five thousand pounds. A hundred and sixty-five thousand *fucking* pounds!

He flashes back up to the signature box and signs. Well, he tries to: his haphazardly manicured nails producing a dark blob on the screen. Next to her razor slash of tight lines at forty-five degrees to the horizontal, his looks like a three-year-old's attempt to paint a large black (slightly deformed) teddy bear. He tries to rub it out, succeeds in making his bear appear pregnant. Sod it – he'll take that as an omen.

He places the tablet on the desk and half turns to head back to the lift, but he picks the tablet up again. Underneath the razor-sharp signature there is a name. Ms H.D. Lennox, Director MarktDiv (LT Global).

Thank you very much, Ms H.D. Lennox, he thinks as he steps into the lift, which drops as smoothly and as quietly as snow does – just before the storm rolls in.

Chapter Ten

'How to Live Longer: The Optimal Amount of Fruit and Veg
You Need Daily to Live Longer.'
—*Daily Express*, 8 March 2021

'Jaz Forrester's office,' Adam barks, stepping onto a free Segway. He straightens his back, rolls his sleeves up higher, tries to grow into his new role. Were he to call Paula now, and tell her what's happened – a hundred and six... Christ, sixty-five thousand would've sent her over the moon and back. A hundred and...? But he'll tell her face to face. He wants to see her reaction.

The sun is high and bright, but the air is still comfortably cool. He drives down a curving path before joining a wider track and accelerating into the flow of traffic. Adam mulls over his new position. They can afford a house now; they can afford a bloody mansion! He has to stop himself from yelling or screaming out loud, for fear of causing another passenger to swerve into a tree.

Twin signs, *Leaving Babylon Dome – Entering*

Halicarnassus Dome, announce the boundary. He heads down a small grassy path towards a lake. There's a house on the near side, flat and modern, mostly polished stone from what he can see, straight out of some fancy, glossy coffee-table hardback. The path clearly goes nowhere else.

Jaz Forrester appears at the heavy wooden front door. They shake hands, but Jaz seems to have no desire for small talk, beckoning Adam towards the house and striding off slightly ahead of him so that he almost has to trot to keep up. Jaz is head and shoulders taller than Adam, his legs seem to make up more than half his height, given the speed he's able to cover ground. Adam silently bets: *college basketball.*

They enter a parqueted hallway, a large comfortable-looking lounge opens directly off, and Adam can see the lake beyond a sizeable deck through dark-wood French windows. But Jaz turns left and leads the way into a smaller office, which is still larger than Adam's lounge – maybe even with the kitchen included.

'Have a seat,' Jaz says, indicating an upright chair in front of an imposing hardwood desk: possibly teak, Adam muses, what would he know? The desk is almost certainly bigger than Adam's front garden; it could conceivably cost more than his car. Jaz closes the door, rounds the desk and settles himself into an expensive-looking swivel chair, all chrome and leather.

'So,' Jaz says, eyeing Adam carefully, like he's wondering if his valuables will be safe. Adam feels underdressed again; Jaz's dark suit and silk tie trumping Adam's dress-down Friday getup.

'You're expecting me, I assume,' Adam opens, when it begins to appear obvious that Jaz isn't going to.

'Oh, yes,' Jaz replies with a weary laugh, suggesting clearly it's not the sort of knowledge that got him out of bed with much of a spring in his step.

Adam glances around the room, clocks a couple of fancy-looking framed certificates, which he can't read, and notices college football photos on the walls. Football? Basketball? All the big guys. Adam was a soccer player, so there's clearly no conversation to be found there, not unless he wants to start a fight. He wonders if all staff in MarktDiv receive extensive training in *putting a visitor in their place*.

'Can I ask...?' Jaz finally begins, as if there's something truly stupid, which he's been told, that he feels the need to have confirmed before they *really* start. 'You didn't apply for this transfer, did you?'

'No.' Adam smiles, shaking his head.

Jaz doesn't smile – he simply shakes his own head. 'And you're not trained or qualified in marketing or selling – in *any* way?'

'Well, no. I guess not.'

'So why do you think you're here?'

Adam ponders for a moment. The phrase, *welcome aboard*, enters his head then swiftly exits. 'I was hoping you might be able to tell me,' he replies, but immediately regrets it, as Jaz shakes his head again and shrugs a *don't ask me*.

'Listen,' Jaz says, sitting forward and bouncing the tips of the fingers of one hand against those of the other, as if he's put Adam sufficiently in his place to feel able to move on. 'I'll level with you. I've had you parachuted into my team, over the heads of some highly qualified and professional people here. Hannah Lennox is clearly expecting big things from you, and she usually knows what she's doing. I argued against your appointment. So, if you prove her wrong, she's big enough to ride the punch, but I'm not too convinced that you've got a lotta backup here, except her.' Jaz speaks like a sports commentator: fast, authoritative, completely uninterruptible. Adam takes a breath to break in more than once, then slowly lets it out as Jaz drives his soliloquy as if addressing a live microphone as the leading pack of an Olympic 5000m final hears the bell.

The phrase *I'll do my best* comes into Adam's mind but doesn't come out of his mouth. He's quite sure this is a good move. Jaz continues into the very short void.

'All the LT advertising materials, TV, print and digital, will be organised from here, so you and your team will be mostly involved in day-to-day matters rather than strategy. I – well, *we* – want you to take a particular interest in this doctor fellow, what's his name?' He picks up a sleek tablet and starts prodding it with a strong finger that looks like it's used to gouging eyes.

'Dr Michael Strong,' Adam says quickly, relieved to be able to demonstrate that he's an on-the-ball type of guy, with one finger on the pulse and the others in every pie, and not the useless klutz Jaz seems to think he is.

'Yeah, that's the guy, Strong. Great name, don't ya think? Can't wait to see what your tabloids will make of it. Listen, we think he's ripe to be a sort of poster boy for the UK drive. We want him on national TV as the first British LT member, a hundred thousand Facebook friends within the month, Twitter, Instagram, TikTok, the works. You think you can handle that?'

Adam wonders how Jaz is even aware of Mick's existence. And as for Mick on TikTok? He's certain Mick is as au fait with TikTok as he is with the surface of Saturn. Wouldn't know Twitter if it shat on his head. And Mick? Poster boy? About the only thing he can imagine Mick being a poster boy for is Swan Vesta matches – or maybe Bushmills whiskey.

'How do you know about Dr Strong?' he asks, more as a way of buying some time than anything else.

'His article in the – what's that newspaper called? The Wiki something? Hannah spoke to me about it.'

'*Wixlow and District Gazette*,' Adam supplies seamlessly, again relieved to have facts at his fingertips (any spare ones that aren't on the pulse or in the pies) before Jaz can use his own to prod them out of his tablet.

'Yeah, that's the one. Anything referencing LT gets flashed straight to us here so we can assess its value and then push it or pull it, depending on how it fits into the growth strategy. It was quite a nice piece as far as an initial splash went, apart from the slight negative spin the locals put on it. That was quick work, Adam, I'll give you that. But you gotta get a grip on them editors fast. I know all publicity is good publicity, but good publicity is better than iffy publicity. That paper got a good circulation, has it, Adam? Lotta Britishers read it?'

Adam's quite sure the entire readership of the *Wixlow and District Gazette* would all fit into Jaz's house leaving ample space for dancing on the lakeside decking, so he changes tack quickly.

'I'm not sure Dr Strong is as media savvy as you might think, I'm sure he's not actually on Facebook, you know? He's a seventy-five-year-old country doctor. He's twentieth century. Just.'

'Well, drag him into the twenty-first century before he dies!' Jaz snaps, shaking his head dismissively. Adam isn't sure if the gesture is dismissive of Mick, or himself. Probably both. 'We need his face everywhere. He's the first LT member in the United Kingdom; we want him to lead the way so others will follow. You get his profile sky-high. I'll put you in touch with some Fleet Street editors I've got contacts with, and we're accelerating preparations for the reality show—'

'The what?'

'The TV show. You caught us a bit flat-footed by your move on the press before release date, Adam, I'll admit that, but we'll make it up. We want your Dr Strong on the first episode.'

'The first... what TV show is this?'

'Not sure what the working title is at the moment. Where is it?' He swipes and scratches on his tablet.

'Look, Jaz, I can't say I'm convinced that Mick's going to be up for a reality TV show.'

'Oh, he'll be up for it when he sees how much money he's going to be winning,' Jaz replies, his brow furrowing as he pushes down on the screen like he's pressing the doorbell of an unresponsive host.

'He's *dying!*' Adam cuts back. 'What does he care how much they pay him? He'll be dead in a year.'

'What did that Warhol guy say? Everyone wants their couple of hundred days of fame, or something – ah! Here it is: *How Long is Your Life?* You wanna see the opening credits?'

Adam waves his hand against the offer. 'How's it gonna work, this show?'

'Oh, I'm not sure, the production company's still working out the details. Shooting starts in London in a couple of weeks, I'll get them to give you a call. We want your boy on there. In fact, they were wondering at top level how your man would take to wearing a bodycam?'

Adam sits back in his chair and tries to prevent his expression from alerting Jaz to the fact that he thinks he's mad. He rubs his chin, buying time, hopefully creating a sensation that he's considering the idea seriously.

'To be honest, Jaz, I can't see Dr Strong finding a bodycam acceptable on his deathbed. Nor can I imagine him keen to spend his last moments tweeting his farewell to the rest of the world. That's not his normal way of doing things. And as for a reality TV show...'

Now it's Jaz's turn to sit back. He puts the tablet down on his desk. There's a silence, but it feels like a countdown to Adam.

'Listen, Adam, can I give you a friendly piece of *welcome to MarktDiv* advice?'

Adam nods silently, almost tears a muscle trying to suppress a shrug.

'Whenever you attend any MarktDiv meetings, that's *any* meetings, if you bring a problem, then make sure you also bring two solutions to said problem. Secondly, marketing isn't about imagining what might be acceptable or normal. Marketing is about shaking the tree, chopping the fucking thing down, getting some attention. You don't get attention by doing things that are acceptable. And especially not if they're normal. Now, I'll be honest with you, as far as I can see, the only reason you landed this gig on *my* team, is cos you're big buddies with this guy, Dr Strong. You got him signed up and in the media before we even launched in the UK. You managed to convince Hannah Lennox that you're some kinda hotshot, maverick, British media left fielder who'll drown us all in his wake if we don't swim faster. She sees you as someone who *gets things done.*' He makes air quotes with his fingers to emphasise the final three words, the clear implication being that this is how Hannah Lennox has described him to Jaz.

'Now, I've read your file, so I can't say much at this moment cos Hannah Lennox has got your back, but from where I'm standing, it don't seem to me that you know jack shit about marketing. But despite this, despite what I said earlier, I want you to succeed, Adam. We're gonna get one chance at this UK launch so I'm gonna help you all I can with solutions. What I can't do, is solve any of your problems for you. Bottom line, we want Dr Michael Strong trending by the end of next week.'

Jaz leans forward on his desk and stares hard into Adam's face.

'So, if I were you, Adam, the man who gets things done, I'd get *this* thing done – fast.'

Chapter Eleven

'Michael Caine, 90, says "younger wives" are one of three
"secrets" to a long life.'
— *The Independent*, 24 September 2023

P aula's white bikini is only a shade lighter than her pale
English skin. She's realised that the sun isn't going to tan
her through the domes, so at least she doesn't have to bother
with sunscreen. It does kind of beg the question as to why she's
lying out in a bikini at all. She could easily sit on her lounger in
shorts and a T-shirt. She'd be equally as comfortable. The pool
looks beautiful but she's not that keen a swimmer, and the
temperature isn't so hot that she feels the need to cool off. Ah
well, what else is there to do with Adam out fighting dragons –
and (hopefully) slaying them?

She might have used the gym, which she can see through
the plate-glass windows on the first floor of the Hitñon Hotel.
However, if she were completely honest, the squadron of Barbie
look-a-likes pounding the treadmills without squirting a micron
of sweat out of their perfumed pores has intimidated her a

smidgen. She's had breakfast in the morning room, elevenses in the tea room, lunch on the terrace, afternoon tea in the Rose Garden Café, and now she's having a pre-dinner cocktail on her lounger by the pool.

Her phone rings: R-E-S-P-E-C-T... now who else can that be?

'Hi, Mum.'

'Hi, darling, just a quickie, everything okay?'

'Yeah, great. I'm lounging by the pool with a Tom Collins in one hand and a Jackie in the other. Adam's off at a big meeting with his bosses, fighting to get some of his salary back.'

'Oh God, I hope he succeeds. It's really not fair the way they've treated him.' Paula has apprised Michaela of Adam's situation, but sworn her to secrecy to save his blushes.

'I know. He works so hard.' She sips her drink, puts it down and plays with her wedding ring – an automatic tic she has whenever she thinks about Adam, not that she's aware of it. 'How's Gramps?'

'Oh, the usual: grumpy. Although he's got a part-time locum organised so he's a bit more free and easy now, playing extra golf and making dates for interviews with all sorts.'

'Hah! Gramps the media celebrity, who would have thought it?' There's a pause, and she senses her mum is weighing up whether she should broach a subject. It's usually Mick, something he's done to upset Michaela, but she knows how close Paula is to him. Although it doesn't usually stop her.

'I'm concerned about Steve and Cathy,' Michaela kicks off. 'I think they're worrying about Will, you know, about his prediction, what it might say.'

'Have they said anything?'

'No, but they probably wouldn't, would they? You know what Steve's like.'

'Yeah,' she says, not really knowing what Michaela means. 'I'm sure they'll talk to you if they're worried.'

'We'll see,' Michaela says, obviously not convinced. They chat about the weather, the soap opera episodes Paula's missed. 'Got anything special planned while you're there?'

'Yes, we're going for a fancy dinner here in the hotel. Although, to be honest, everything is fancy. It's really plush. They do that funny thing with the towels on the end of your bed, you know, swans I think they are. I almost didn't take a shower this morning, didn't want to ruin it. And chocolates on the pillow.'

'Sounds lovely; you have a great time. Hope Adam gets what he deserves. Look, I'd better go. I've got a stack of books to mark and this call is costing more than I'll earn in a week. Just wanted to say hello. Better rush. I'll see you.'

'Okay, see you.'

Paula sits and mulls over the conversation. There was something else, she's sure of it. Something Michaela was considering bringing up but didn't. She knows her mum well, can always tell when she's brooding over some family issue, Mick's purchase of LifeTime memberships being up there with the biggest of them.

She glances up for a sign of Adam, returning with the head of a dragon over his shoulder. She wonders again what chance he's got. He's not a go-get-em type, she wouldn't have fallen for him had he been. She spent half her year at Yale fighting off the loud-mouthed jocks who clearly thought an English rose should swoon at their oversized feet. It was Adam's genuine, self-effacing ordinariness that had attracted her to him. He didn't assume she'd think him an irresistible prize. He didn't throw snide, disparaging comments at any sign that she might have a mind of her own. He was a nice guy. This is what worries her now.

LifeTime wasn't academia. They'd known that when he'd taken the job there. But the money was better and there were promises of quick promotion and more money. No one had said then that he could be transferred from stats to sales like he was moving from the stockroom to stacking shelves in a supermarket. If only he would stand up for himself. Deep down, she knows this isn't altogether fair, but she can't think what else to suggest. They both know that his heading back to academia is an unlikely option now. He could teach maths in a secondary school – well, maybe not. And as for his chances in a primary classroom – he'd be more likely to win the Champions League as manager of Norwich City.

She spots him striding across the lawn, drops Jackie and picks up Tom. Adam only ever strides when he's happy and purposeful, so that's a good sign. She gives him a little wave, which he returns, another good sign. If he's low, he shrugs or hangs his head. Often both.

He sits on the side of her sunlounger and stares at her.

'And?' she says, after a few seconds. She's sworn herself to keep calm, not appear disappointed if he's had no success. The last thing he'll need is for her to make it worse. 'What did they say? Did you tell them you wanted your salary back? Did you tell them how hard you work? How good you are at your old job?'

He nods slowly, still staring at her expectant face. Then he picks up her hand in his.

'Listen, we need to make a baby, and buy a house. In that order. I thought we could go upstairs and start on the baby now...' A smile breaks out on his face; all the little creases beside his eyes turn upwards.

'You what? Tell me, *tell* me!'

'I'm back on salary.'

'Oh, Adam, did you tell them, did you–?'

'Ask me how much.'

'Wha–?'

'Ask me.'

'Wh... How much?'

'A hundred–'

'A what?'

'...and sixty–'

'Sixty?'

'Five.'

'What?'

'Thousand.'

'Sixty-five thousand?'

'A *hundred* and sixty-five thousand.'

'You're joking.'

'Would I?'

She looks like he's told her he's been given a hundred and sixty-five thousand years to live on one of his golden tickets. Something this good can't simply fall out of a clear blue sky. She hoped he might come back with a little more of his salary reinstated. She hardly dared hope they'd give him all of it back. But this? A hundred and sixty-five thousand? It's outrageous. She's no clue how much money that really is. She knows nobody who earns that much. Are they now rich? Rich like a bank manager? Or a footballer? Is she now a sort of non-footballing WAG?

'What did they say?'

'It's a promotion. I'm *head* of UK marketing, I'll have a team working under me, and they're paying me a hundred and sixty-five thousand plus bonuses and commission on sales.'

She sits upright and faces him, taking both his hands in hers. 'You're not kidding me on this, are you? Don't joke about this.'

'I'm not joking,' he says, shaking his head and smiling. 'We can make babies. As many as we like. We can buy a house. A big one.'

He doesn't lie to her. He wouldn't. He simply doesn't correct her when she makes assumptions. *I knew they'd listen to you. I knew they'd be reasonable when you explained everything. They could see how important you are to them, couldn't they?*

People often hear what they want to hear.

Especially when you let them.

It's a thirty-minute car journey from Babylon into Rhodes, the third bubble, and the views of the mountains are a little more distorted, less sharp, slightly faded. Rhodes Dome is older than the other two. The further you head north into SphereCity the older the bubbles are; all the expansion takes place on the southern end, and Adam always feels more isolated the further he travels into it. Isolated from the 'real world' is over-egging it, this *is* the real world. It simply seems a little more detached from – everywhere *else*. Like maybe the phones won't work this far in.

There is a sensation of travelling *in*, like some cave system, deeper and deeper, farther and farther away from civilisation, from normality, from reality. He can imagine the rest of the world being destroyed by some natural catastrophe, and nobody in SphereCity would know anything about it. Until, maybe, they tried to leave.

Ron's office is clearly a couple of rungs down the LT property portfolio compared to the ones that Adam visited the day before. And then a couple more. To tell the truth, it's a turntable ladder down. Plus, a couple of fast-moving escalators – and maybe even a freefall skydive. The block is perfectly functional. Its concrete slabs and glass windows are newer than a sixties London office block, but that's probably where the differences end. While it might not, technically, be brutalist – it's still pretty brutal. The usual office paraphernalia is visible through the windows: computer monitors with their black spaghetti entrails; jackets or cardies slung over office chairs; a few glum faces staring out, maybe wondering how to escape. It's an office block. What would you expect?

Ron never complains. He doesn't seem to worry about décor, as long as he's got the tools to do his job. But Adam isn't sure that Ron has ever visited the office of the director of MarktDiv. He wonders what Ron would make of the chasm between Ms H D Lennox's enormous space and his own hutch.

Ron is standing with his back to the door as Adam enters. He's rearranging three columns of Post-it notes on the wall, using his own, slightly idiosyncratic, coding system. Pink is 'important'; red is 'emergency'; green is 'yesterday'. Adam remembers Ron's system from the time they studied together at Yale. A year older than himself, Adam saw Ron as almost another species. While Adam plodded his way through an idea, Ron would snap his fingers with Eureka-style inspiration. Adam sneaks to the desk, takes a green Post-it, and writes *coffee* on it. He then reaches over Ron's shoulder and sticks it at the top of the green column. Ron spins round and beams at him.

'Bastard! Why didn't you tell me you were coming?'

'Thought you'd tell me you were too tied up in meetings for a coffee.'

'Get away. Your shout.'

They take the lift to the atrium café on the ground floor: the only part of the building, in Adam's view, with a hint of style. Its high glass ceiling fans out, accommodating perfectly half a dozen large palm trees that mask another concrete-and-glass monstrosity next door.

To Adam's dismay, however, it's clearly had a takeover and a makeover (there should be one word for that, he thinks, wearing his new marketing hat, but he fails to come up with any ideas). He winces as he recognises the ubiquitous light, dark, and forty other shades of brown livery, and dreads a repeat of the experience he endures, in any one of half a dozen Norwich city-centre branches, whenever Paula needs a break from shopping: competing groups of loud Gen-Zedders, each re-enacting their favourite scenes from an episode of some years-old sitcom, and all convinced that every other customer has purposely chosen that particular branch to catch their 'performance'.

Mercifully, this place is two-thirds empty, although he still suffers a ten-minute wait as three smartly dressed execs spend more time itemising the lurid ingredients of their bespoke coffees than they'd probably spend drinking them. He wonders, while he waits, how many additional flavours it would take to eliminate the chance of tasting any coffee, or even fitting any into the cup. There's probably a PhD thesis in there somewhere, something with a marketing slant. Could you actually market a coffee with no coffee in it? Almost certainly. Adam's a traditionalist when it comes to the hot drink: he prefers it in the size of cup his grandmother once had in her cupboards; and he doesn't feel the need for the person making it to possess a diploma or a degree to manage the task. He breathes a sigh of relief as he takes his small black coffee – *no, really, no milk with my black coffee, thanks all the same for asking...*

'So what's this move over to the dark side all about?' Ron asks as they sit in a couple of soft springy armchairs by a window.

'The email was the first I heard of it. I thought you'd be able to tell me?'

They look at each other. 'Is this Popeye?' Ron asks, sipping his decaf, non-fat, extra whip caramel macchiato with chocolate sprinkles.

'Who?'

'Lennox?'

Adam nods, while watching Ron's face. 'Who is she?'

'Head of global marketing is what it says on all her emails, I calls her Popeye.' He does a passable imitation of the rogue sailor, complete with trademark chuckle, causing Adam to smile against his better judgement.

'Why?'

'Well, she came aboard a couple of months ago. Got an email from her not long after, asking me to tweak a couple of algorithms that didn't need tweaking. Told her so, and the next thing is I'm on the carpet with the head of strategy telling me that, from now on, marketing is four queens, stats is a pair of jacks. Since when did that become law?'

'What was the algorithm?'

'Converting food intake into LT outcome.'

'We worked on that for months.'

'Close to a year, with teams of doctors, researchers. But Popeye knows better.'

'How'd she want it tweaked?'

'More time added per can of spinach, basically. All the LifeTime range of so-called "health foods" and "life-lengthening" supplements that they're launching as we speak. Wanted their impact on life expectancy practically doubled across the board. A LifeTime own-brand apple pie a day now keeps the doctor away forever, according to Popeye. It's a wonder they're not prescription only.'

'Based on what?'

Ron places his cup carefully on the table.

'Based on more people will want an LT membership if they can see their life expectancy increasing dramatically in real time every time they drop a LifeTime-branded snack down their necks while lying on the sofa watching baseball. That's my own personal take on it. You got a better one? Course, it could also be that the mainstream health food lobby are secreting brown envelopes stuffed full of nuts and tofu into Popeye's office after dark, all in return for permission to place an LT sticker on their own range of products. But my money's on the own-brand LT miracle supplements as a faster way into Joe Public's pockets. But then that would be a conspiracy theory, so probably the correct explanation.'

'There must be some science behind it. She can't simply tell you to change what took months to calculate, argue over, agree. We had bloody medics on the team, serious scientists, nutritionists...'

'You think I didn't say? I dropped so many names with Nobel prizes that I gave up bothering to mention PhDs. I had this argument for an hour and a half in strategy: no dice. If Popeye says LifeTime's own-brand spinach has magic powers beyond any scientific study on the planet, then we have to jemmy it into the algorithms. It was made reasonably clear that if I didn't comply, I'd end up making the coffees and serving doughnuts down here. Say nothing, but I'm mapping a route out.'

'Where to?'

'Civilisation. Only trouble is, I'm never gonna find a salary like the one I got here. I simply don't like throwing everything I learned in college into the bin in exchange for flavour-of-the-month policy decisions based on the corporate bottom line. It's dishonest. It's unprofessional. So what's Popeye got you doing? Snake oil massages using fake snake oil?'

Adam sighs deeply, shakes his head. 'It's madness, really. Paula's grandfather, you know, Mick Strong?'

'You mentioned him. Crazy old dude. Doctor?'

'That's the guy. Mick strong-arms me, 'scuse the pun, into getting him membership ahead of the launch date in the UK.

Wanted it for all his family members, five in total, including himself.' He raises his eyebrows in a *see how crazy he is?* stare, to which Ron shakes his head slowly. 'What can I say? Threatens to complain to mission control if I don't get him signed up. Wants to be the first Brit on board. So, I sort him out. Before I know what's happening, he's got himself on the front page of the smallest newspaper on the planet. This paper has a lower circulation than the Pentagon-Peaceniks' Newsletter. Mick plays golf with the editor, so he's instant front-page news, pushing the largest marrow of the year and a pile of dog shit outside the village hall onto the inside pages. According to my new immediate boss, Jaz Forrester, Popeye, as you call her, spots this on her radar and promotes me to be Mick's publicity agent on a salary of a hundred and sixty-five K.'

'A hundred–?'

'Wait, there's more. Mick Strong was born in the last century and never agreed to there ever being another one. He thinks Facebook is a photograph album, TikTok is what his grandfather clock does, although it doesn't, and Twitter is the sound a certain type of bird makes. He probably knows which one; no doubt he can do a perfect imitation using nothing more than a blade of grass and a deep breath. My new boss, meantimes, wants me to get him, Mr Birdsong, onto some new reality TV show in the UK for people racing to the grave. Also wants him trending with half-a-million TikTok dance partners by the weekend.'

Ron's eyes are now popping, and he starts to laugh. 'The only thing I can say to that pile of horseshit is that I *know* you're not kidding.' He splutters as he starts shaking and holding his sides.

'Yeah, you can laugh,' Adam sneers, draining his cup. 'I gotta make it happen – yesterday! Stick that on one of your Post-its!'

Chapter Twelve

'How to Live Longer: Raspberries May Hold Anti-Cancer
Properties to Boost Longevity.'
—*Daily Express*, 11 March 2021

Babylon Dome's Hanging Gardens Restaurant occupies the
ten terraces that form a chain of steps down the west side
of the Hitñon Hotel building. Starting at the ground floor, each
higher terrace is smaller than the one below until you reach the
top terrace, which has only one table. Adam and Paula have that
table on the prized Level Diez terrace on their last night. This is
courtesy of Ms H D Lennox, Director, MarktDiv (LT Global),
which they, and everyone else, discover on the swirling, fit-
inducing LCD screen at reception.

They ride the glass elevator to the top floor and climb a
short flight of steps to the extra level where they discover their
own, very private, dining area. There is a 360-degree view, and
a careful placing of plants and flowering hedges makes it feel as
if there's no building beneath them, and no other diners either.
There's just the sky, glimpses of mountain, and even a crescent

moon. Adam doesn't want to spoil the evening by suggesting that it might be a projected hologram – but he has his suspicions.

The sky is cloudless and turning darker. The inside of all the domes is coated with a non-reflective film so, at night, you'd swear you were in the open air. Only the temperature suggests otherwise, it's barely changed since mid-afternoon.

The menus are sleek tablets, showing short videos of a sumptuous selection of dishes from across the globe. They both order halloumi-stuffed peppers to start, while Adam chooses a lightly grilled salmon fillet with a lemon, tarragon and garlic sauce. Paula selects chicken breast with a spicy peanut sauce. They choose a Chablis, but as Paula taps to order it, the tablet emits a little bleep and a message informs them that Jaz Forrester has provided a magnum of Krug Brut Vintage 1985, to celebrate Adam's arrival in MarktDiv. Adam spots the jaw-clenching price on the menu but hides it from Paula, fearing she'll suggest attempting to cash it in. There's even an option to watch your food being cooked on a live stream, but they swipe left.

Adam is gearing himself up to reveal to Paula the true extent of his new role, and the one soon to be expected of Mick. He decides to wait until their first course arrives before he raises the subject. As he's pouring their first glasses of champagne, a soft trilling sound alerts them to a square of undulating lights in the floor. The square rises slowly, revealing a dumb waiter beneath, carrying their food. He postpones his announcement as Paula is so thrilled by the high-tech machinations, which have yet to arrive at the Fish and Anchor, the local pub back home. He postpones again so as not to spoil their main meals. It's not until they've practically finished that Adam chooses a moment that isn't right, but he knows he has very few left.

'TikTok? Granddad? Didn't you tell them he still uses Swan

Vestas to light his cigars?' Paula blurts, her last spoonful of tiramisu stalled halfway to her mouth. 'Granddad?' she repeats. The prospect of having to teach Mick to hang glide or belly dance would've produced no greater expression of disbelief on Paula's face.

'I know,' Adam says. 'I've tried to explain to them what Mick's like.'

She giggles helplessly, and Adam congratulates himself, somewhat sardonically, on his timing.

'They're talking Twitter as well,' he says, now on a roll, smiling bitterly. 'And Instagram.'

Paula's mouth gapes, but her horror is tempered by champagne-fuelled sniggers, as she taps the table with the flat of her hand.

'They're also planning a reality TV show,' Adam says quickly, going for broke while she's finding it hilarious as opposed to completely fucking ridiculous, which she no doubt will in the morning, when she's sober – and hungover.

Her eyes widen as she snorts helpless laughter. Her last spoonful of tiramisu is still in a holding pattern, denied landing permission due to her evident inability to close her mouth around the spoon.

He's relieved he's caught her in this mood, and even he can sort of see the funny side, although with almost half their magnum gone it isn't that surprising. But he's aware of the implications for him, for *them*, if he can't pull this off. It almost feels like *he's* the one in the reality show, given an impossible task to perform, in the full glare of a braying audience and a giggling wife.

'Why don't you bring him out?' she says, after she's finally recovered the ability to eat. Adam's been over-egging his Chaplinesque role of hapless marketer, suggesting ever-more ludicrous dances that Mick might learn – the Macarena (too complicated), Gangnam Style (too likely to land him in an ambulance). But Paula stops laughing suddenly.

'I'm serious. Bring him out here, introduce him to this Jaz guy, let this place get under his skin. It's infectious. The easiest place to sign him up to Facebook would be here. Imagine! Jaz sounds like the type to impress Granddad, and if he suggests friending him, Granddad'll be flattered and feel like he's being invited to join some exclusive club with funny handshakes. You know what he's like, he'll love it. Flatter his ego and he'll have a hundred friends before the end of the month.'

'They're talking in the region of a hundred *thousand* friends.' Adam's expression tells her that this isn't a joke; he's deadly serious about it. They really do want Mick to have a hundred thousand friends on Facebook. More, probably. But Paula's positivity makes him think there is a way.

They've polished off the bubbly, kissed under the moon, then stumbled back to their suite for another, this time rather drunk, baby-making session. Paula now sleeps silently beside Adam, but his mind is electrified as it churns through the pros and cons of bringing Mick out to Bubbleville.

He wills himself to sober up. Only then will he know if Paula's idea to bring Mick out is beginning to look like a brilliant solution to an apparently insoluble problem. Ignore the fact that Paula was under the influence of enough alcohol to render her unconscious when she came up with the plan. Is it a goer – or is it a wildly drunken, frat boy prank, along the lines of a kidnapped sheep in a friend's bedroom?

Would he come? Of course he would. As Paula implied, flattery will take him anywhere, he'd be hypnotised by his status here. They'd have to lay it on with shovels. Paula's promised to help convince him, but what if she decides in the morning that it's a sheep-in-the-bedroom idea? He'll *have* to keep her onside. If she falters, then it's a non-starter.

What about Mick's tendency to open his mouth and walk down his own throat, especially where the more woke niceties of expression are concerned? Nobody could call Mick a racist, but he'd never really caught up with the full range of expressions that were now commonly deemed to be offensive. Would he clumsily offend any one of LifeTime's numerous Black or Latino staff with a loose comment? Would he launch off with his half-baked understanding of woke pronouns? On the other hand, Mick would surely respond to Jaz's gravitas, his job title, his lodge on the lake.

Adam starts to write Jaz a text, but decides he'll wait until morning when he finds that he's completed the whole explanation without using any commas or full stops. He doesn't want to send Jaz a sheep at three o'clock in the morning, and even he can see that the one he's composed is bleating. He'll talk to Jaz. Yes, better idea. Dress it up as the only way to drag Mick into the twenty-first century. *Come to me with solutions*, Jaz'd said. Well, this is the solution. At least it is now. Until he wakes up.

If he ever gets to sleep.

He starts counting sheep.

———————

In the morning, Paula, incredibly, miraculously, is still of the view that a trip for Mick to Utah is the best idea since the invention of the tiramisu-Krug cocktail. It surprises Adam, as he's woken up with a head stuffed full of sheep's wool. He's half a mind to bin the idea as the worst plan he can imagine, but Paula pushes it enthusiastically over a tsunami of black coffee.

'Try it,' she pleads, as Adam shakes his head as slowly as he can, a futile attempt to prevent the room from rotating. 'What's there to lose? We all thought Granddad going to the *Wix'n'Dist* was crackers, but your publicity lot see it as a stroke of genius. Who's to say they won't think the same about this?'

Adam nibbles at a corner of dry toast. Is it possible that she might be right? Is he so ill-suited to this role that he's the only one who can't see what a brilliant move this would be? He's not keen on making a complete fool of himself – especially not in front of Jaz – but the alternative, trying to convince Mick on his own and on Mick's home ground, seems the absolute worst option. He glances at his watch, ten twenty-five.

'I'll call Jaz. See if he can give me twenty minutes this morning.'

By eleven o'clock he's making his pitch. Jaz nods, not unenthusiastically, while slicing his way through two fried eggs, a couple of sausages, a mountain of back bacon, toast, tomatoes, baked beans, hash browns and fried mushrooms. Adam refused the offer of a spot of breakfast on arrival and is now hugely relieved that he did. He looks everywhere but Jaz's plate as he first paints Mick as accurately as he can, a seventy-five-year-old man who's firmly set in his small-town ways – a weekly half a bitter in his local, a round of golf, a scone and a coffee in the tea shoppe. He moves quickly through to the solution, arguing how Mick will be flattered by the scale of the LT organisation, keen to feel even more a part of it all.

'Mick's not immune to flattery,' he argues, stopping for a second to sip his third cup of very strong black coffee. 'Once he sees the scale of the LT operation, how he could occupy such an important role in its international development, I'm sure he'll follow our lead.'

Jaz lays down his knife and fork, slurps coffee, smiles reflectively.

'Yeah, it's good,' he says after a long, scary pause. 'I'm impressed.'

Adam's guilt, at not confessing that it's all Paula's (drunken) idea, is buried beneath his relief that, between them, they might have found a way to achieve the seemingly impossible. There's also the bonus that if Mick does say *You must be bloody joking!* then at least Jaz will be implicated in the failed strategy. Or, even if he doesn't admit this, at least he'll see up close how unlikely a customer Mick always was, thereby confirming Adam's initial judgement.

'Get him out here next weekend,' Jaz says, draining his cup and pushing his chair back. 'All expenses paid, honoured British guest, blah-de-blah. What'll we say? Three, four days? There's a medical conference next week we can tie him into, a Q&A, something like that. I'll arrange a few treats for him at this end, soften him up, then reel him in. Yeah. It's good. What's he like? You said he's a golfer?'

'Well, he's got a set of second-hand clubs, but I don't think he's good enough to have a handicap. I think he hacks around the local links with a few small-town bigwigs.'

'Great, I'll book some time at the country club here, get him all the gear, let him pick a set of clubs, wine and dine, then we'll hit him with Facebook. I'll get Ralph from Tech to set up his phone.'

'Er, he doesn't have a mobile – not what we'd class as a mobile.'

Jaz is mid-pour of coffee, which is black as crude oil and almost as thick.

'No phone?' he says, like he's sympathising, *no legs* or *no arms.* 'Right, so this guy really is last century. Okay, we'll give him a phone. I'll get Ralph to get him one ready, child's-play buttons, point-and-shoot set up, the sort you'd give to a five-year-old. Christ, I wish you'd said he was that Neanderthal. But no matter. Putty in our hands. This'll be fun. I'll look forward to this. Good work, Adam. You're surprising me. I like that.' Jaz stands and strolls towards the lake, coffee in hand.

Adam follows, relieved that Jaz has found his proposal a surprise. It could've been so much worse, he thinks. He could have thought it insane. Then he starts to imagine how much worse it might still be: decides those are thoughts best left for another time. He's completely unaware how quickly that time is going to arrive.

Part Two

<u>The End of the Beginning</u>

'...the law is the first thing that is crushed under the rubble of transformation... Those who positioned themselves well in the first three years... were often in a position to make up the rules of their brave new world as they went along.'
—Misha Glenny, *McMafia*

Chapter Thirteen

'Eat fish for a longer life, study suggests...'
—Medicalnewstoday.com, 22 July 2018

'Open it,' Steve urges, gently nudging Cathy's elbow. 'Go on!'

'I'm not sure this is right.' Cathy fingers the golden envelope, turning it over in her hands, alert for any hint of sound from Will's bedroom door.

'It'll sort everything,' Steve coaxes. 'As long as it gives him sixty or seventy years, we seal it up again and let him have it on his birthday. Job done.'

'But it's not right. Your granddad gave it to *him*.'

'Yes, silly bastard had no right to. All we're doing is preventing the worst possible eventuality of his stupidity. You don't want Will opening it and getting any unwelcome shocks.'

'No, but it's not likely, is it? He's fit and healthy. Why would there be any unwelcome shocks?'

'No reason that we know, but what *do* we know about this LifeTime nonsense? From what Adam says it's a load of baloney mixed with a little bit of science and a hint of maths. Who's to say they know what they're doing at all? Anything to do with computers involves glitches, they're forever patching bugs. We're simply making sure there are no bugs waiting to bite Will. And if there *is* something unwelcome, whether it's true or not, isn't it best if we know about it and Will doesn't?'

'But it's dishonest, it's like we're lying to him.'

'So was Father Christmas and the tooth fairy, but we never had a problem with that pair.'

'This is different.'

'How?'

'This is *serious*.'

'No, it isn't. It's another internet fantasy that some people might take seriously while other people get very rich.'

'How do you know it's fantasy?'

'How do you know it isn't?'

Cathy sighs. 'I understand everything you're saying, and agree Mick should never have bought it for Will in the first place, but this doesn't feel right.'

'Do you want to take the risk?' Steve says, looking grave.

She shakes her head. 'You do it. Mick's your grandfather.'

Steve takes the envelope and examines the seal. Luckily, Will made quite a bit of excited progress before Mick rescued the package from his scrabbling fingers. Steve's able to stretch the tear in the wrapping and fish out the golden envelope without doing much extra damage to make it look suspicious, especially as Will's not going to see it again for another few months. They examine it carefully. There seems to be a layer of gum, which, if he can peel it open without damaging the envelope, he should be able to reseal afterwards. He slides his finger underneath the flap and starts to work it. The gum stretches and gives way, piece by piece, until finally he can open it up. So, not Fort Knox standard by any stretch. He stares at Cathy, she nods, he unfolds it carefully. They stare at the figure together.

'Look at this, look at *this!*' Mick points at the *Daily Mail* lying on the coffee table between them. Paula picks it up and frowns at the headline: *Crazy Rejoiners Demand Referendum*. 'No, at the top,' Mick coaxes excitedly, leaning over and tapping at a multi-coloured banner below the masthead. Paula and Adam's eyes widen simultaneously.

'It's you!' Paula gasps, hardly able to credit her grandfather's face on the front page. Mick sits back in his armchair and grins proudly, sips his whiskey.

'Country doctor faces date with death?' Adam reads in a quizzical tone, over Paula's shoulder.

'It's on pages seven and eight,' Mick prompts, leaning forward, watching Paula's face as she flicks through the pages.

'Wow!' she squeals as she sees the half-page, full-colour photo of Mick looking every inch the country doctor; crisp, white open-necked shirt, couple of biros in the breast pocket, leaning on a gatepost with his stethoscope draped around his neck. 'How did you get in the *Mail?*' she gasps, skim-reading the rather flattering article which paints Mick as a pioneer, an explorer, confronting his 'destiny' as bravely as Columbus in the Americas, Neil Armstrong on the moon, or CR7 in Saudi Arabia.

'Bob at the *Wix'n'Dist* put me in touch. I'm on local radio next week.'

Paula looks up, turns to Adam. 'Can you believe this?'

Adam smiles, calculating silently that Mick's sudden love affair with the media might make his own Augean task slightly more doable, especially with Mick already wallowing happily in bullshit.

'Reads well, really flattering,' Adam says, feigning deep concentration on the article, but secretly composing an email to Jaz, asking him what he thinks of *his* decision to get Mick on the front page of the highest circulation daily in the United Kingdom.

'And they paid me,' Mick preens, 'four figures!'

Better and better. Adam nudges Paula: isn't there some quaint English phrase about *hitting hot irons* or something? Paula straightens up.

'Oh yeah, listen, Granddad, when we were at LifeTime HQ in the States, Adam's bosses were really keen to invite you out as a sort of special guest, you know, the first British member and all that? They were desperate to meet you, show you around, answer any questions you have. They'll pay all your expenses; put you up in the five-star hotel where Adam and I stayed. It's really plush. All your food will be on the house. And drinks. Granddad, you'd love it.'

'Two thousand, one hundred and sixty-two days,' Steve says, slumping back on the sofa and leaving the envelope in Cathy's hands. He pushes his hair back with his palms and breathes out the sort of sigh he usually reserves for his monthly games of squash – when he remembers to book them. 'Thank God for that,' he says to himself.

Cathy continues to stare at the figures. Two thousand, one hundred and sixty-two days? How many years is that? How does she work it out? Does she have to multiply it by three hundred and sixty-five? Yes, she's sure she does, she's usually quick with maths, but she's in a bit of a panic, she struggles with the calculation, concludes that Will is going to live for another six hundred years. That can't be right. Steve stands up.

'Cuppa?'

What's she doing wrong? She can't think straight.

'Do you want a cuppa?'

'This isn't right,' she says. 'Help me work it out.'

'Course it's right,' Steve says.

'How many years is it?'

'What?'

'How many *years* is it?'

'Loads.'

'It's not.'

'Let me get my phone. Here we go, what do you want to do?'

'Two, one, six, two, divided by three, six, five,' she says, voice trembling.

'There...' He stares at the display. Cathy stands beside him. 'Five point nine something. Is that years? Can't be. Let me do it again. Two thousand, one hundred and sixty-two days divided by three hundred and sixty-five will give us how many years, won't it?'

Cathy's crying openly; Steve punches the numbers again.

'Shit! This can't be right. Jesus, Steve!' She grabs at his arm, tries to get him to look at her. But he's shaking his head, staring at the numbers on the screen.

'It's rubbish,' he mutters grimly. 'Like I said, complete bollocks. How can anybody predict an eleven-year-old will be dead in five years' time? It's not scientifically possible.' Now he looks at her. Tears are pouring down her cheeks, making two rivers of mascara on her skin which itself has turned an unearthly white. 'It's rubbish, Cathy. This is crap!'

'How do you know?' she whispers, smearing mascara over her cheeks. 'What if he's got–'

'He hasn't *got* anything!' Steve snaps. 'This is crap! It's all crap!' He tears the card in half. Cathy moves to stop him but she's too late, he's too angry. He tears it again. And again. He crushes the pieces in his fist, the knuckles whitening as he squeezes tighter. A tear starts to roll down his own cheek.

They've already softened Mick up with a couple of dozen photos on Adam's tablet of their recent visit: Paula by the pool with cocktail in hand featuring prominently, plus a short LifeTime promo video of the Bubble Campus, including a flyby over its eighteen-hole golf course. Adam takes his turn and moves from soft to hard sell.

'They're really keen to meet you, Mick. They see you as a bit of a trailblazer, especially as we haven't even launched officially in the UK. Want to chat to you about the British market, get some tips from an expert. I told them how you were keen from the start; you could see the potential on your own.'

'You see!' Mick says, wagging an admonishing finger in Adam's direction. 'There you were, trying to put me off, and now here come your top brass to shake my hand. Really, Paula, he tried to stop me buying the LifeTimes, any of them, I'm not joking. Really gave me a hard time. I had to threaten to write to his bosses before he finally agreed.'

'Yeah, I admit it,' Adam replies, rolling his eyes, as Mick leans back and puts his hands behind his head. Adam's not entirely unhappy to have Mick chide him for attempting to put him off. The fact is, he's quite pleased that Paula can hear his defence coming straight from Dobbin's mouth. Having let him run long enough, he reverts to enticing Mick; homing in on what he's sure is a weak spot.

'The American press will be keen to chat to you as well, we

might even pull in some radio and TV appearances, seeing as you clearly handle the media so professionally.'

Mick appears interested; he scratches his chin as though considering if he could fit an all-expenses-paid trip to the US around his hectic schedule of lawn mowing, golf and general grumpiness.

'When would this be?' he asks casually, like he's opened a multi-coloured spreadsheet of his appointments and engagements covering the next eighteen months.

'Whenever you like really, but they want to get you fast, before any other Brit is picked up by the media. You might be the first, but if someone appears with a shorter projection, they might appear a bit more interesting. They'd like you and me to fly out Saturday, they'll send a car to us here to take us to Stansted, then we'll be first class direct to Salt Lake. There's going to be a conference, experts in health from across the States: if you were agreeable, they'd like you to do a Q&A on the British experience, you being in the profession, your expertise would be much appreciated. Come out with me for four or five days. There'd be time to relax as well, meet a few people, enjoy yourself at LT's expense.'

'You could call a full-time locum in for that, couldn't you?' Paula coaxes. She knows he only does a couple of hours of surgery a week; most of his other patients opted to join the new health centre in the town when it opened a few years back. What she doesn't know, and neither does Mick, is that quite a few of those patients were relieved when a convenient alternative to Dr Mick Strong opened up in the locality – Dr Strong's reputation for being up to date with the latest research and training not being as highly regarded as Mick might have thought, or indeed wished.

'We'll cover the cost of that, of course,' Adam adds, as if Mick's joined some gilded elite whose appearance at prestigious international conferences is essential: Greta Thunberg, Mark Zuckerberg, Mick Strongberg.

'I saw on your video they have a nice golf course out there. Any chance of a round?'

'Sure. You'll have plenty of free time. I can get Jaz to book some tee times, I know he's a player,' Adam says.

'Is he good?' Mick asks, suddenly wary. 'I'm no Tiger Woods.'

'Nah, nah, he's a weekend hacker, but he loves the game, can talk about it all day. He was only saying to me last week he never has the time to play; you'd be doing him a big favour if he could claim to be "working" by taking you out. We could get you some free time with the club pro as well, if you'd like.'

'Why not?' Mick says, shrugging, as if he's decided that a pub lunch would be a good idea. 'Why not indeed!'

Chapter Fourteen

'Savour Your Steak and Cheese – They Won't Take a Bite Out
of Your Life Expectancy.'
—*The Daily Telegraph*, 7 July 2023

The clifftop path between Little Wixlow and Happisburgh is one of Michaela's favourite stretches of the north Norfolk coastal path. Starting on the beach, the grassy land rises quickly so that a brisk thirty-minute walk takes you to the top of a two-hundred-foot cliff overlooking the North Sea. A rough sea at high tide takes periodic bites out of the cliff face, altering the route of the path as walkers move in response, and making attempts to erect fencing a fool's errand long since abandoned by the local council. Occasional *Beware of the Cliffs* warning signs are the only sop to a previous era when sensible health and safety concerns had not yet been downgraded to the status of *'elf'n'safety gone mad* meddling. So, when Cathy calls and suggests a stroll, including a stop at the Watch Café (where Michaela's stock order is a hot chocolate and an eclair), she doesn't meet any resistance.

'How's Mick?' Cathy asks, as they make it to the clifftop and recover a bit of puff. 'Any comeback from his *projection?*' She says the word slightly under her breath, like it's an obscenity.

'Oh, I don't know. He seems okay with that; he is getting a bit obsessive with other things.'

'Like what?'

'He's decided he needs to reread most of the books on his shelves cos he can't remember the stories.'

'You're joking; he's got thousands of books.'

'Well, maybe not all of them, but a good few. The important ones, the ones he says changed his life or made a big impression on him when he first read them. He says he can't remember anything about them now so he's going to read them again.'

'So what's the problem? He has to do something with his time.'

'I know. But it's like he's trying to recapture his past.'

'So, what if he is? What would you prefer him to do? Buy a motorbike?'

Michaela gives her a *don't ever suggest that within his earshot* glare. 'Travel a bit?' She shrugs. 'He's been nowhere but here and Oz, where he was born, but he was too young to remember much of that. He was only five or six when his family emigrated here. None of them ever went back.'

'So, what if he says he's going to visit every capital city on the planet? Would that please you?'

Michaela sighs, picks up a stray tin can and detours towards a bin.

'I was thinking maybe a couple of city breaks: Prague? Vienna? Maybe a week in Majorca with his great-grandson – me taken along as babysitter.'

They laugh, although not very loudly, and it doesn't last long.

'Nothing he'll do will ever please you, will it?'

Michaela sighs, knows there's truth in it. 'Look, don't get me wrong, I don't think he's going to die when Adam's company says he's going to die, but it does make you think: he can't have *that* many years left, why not do something with them? He doesn't seem to have any vision. He rattles around that old house as it collapses around his ears. Why doesn't he see a bit of the world? He can't be short of a bob or two.'

'What've you done with your projection?' Cathy asks in a by-the-by tone, like she's wondering what happened to an old pair of trainers Michaela used to wear.

'Oh that? I chucked it somewhere, hoping never to see it again. What was he thinking?'

'Didn't you even look at it?'

'No, it's a piece of rubbish, best place is *in* the rubbish.'

Cathy laughs lightly, steers the conversation carefully, expertly, an MI5 spook working over an unsuspecting Joe.

'You weren't tempted to take a peek? Come your birthday?'

'Christ, no! Why encourage the old fool? As far as I'm concerned, if it wasn't so expensive, it'd be the sort of thing you'd buy a mate as a silly birthday present. You know, like some Viagra-flavoured chewing gum, or a heated bra. Everyone would have a good gin-soaked laugh, it'd sit in the bottom of a cupboard for a few years, then you'd throw it out. What really gets me is that he bought one for Will. I mean, we're grown-ups; we can make up our own minds about this kind of thing. But Will? I'm really sorry he did that. It wasn't fair. I told him, but he simply said I mollycoddled him.'

They walk on in an increasingly uneasy silence. Eventually, Cathy presses on, tentatively, before Michaela changes the subject.

'What do *you* think we should do about Will's?'

'What do you mean?'

'Well, we tried to get him to swap it for a droneboard, but

he's dead keen to have LifeTime. You know how much he adores his great-grandpa. So, we were thinking of maybe opening it without Will knowing, before his birthday, to check that it doesn't say anything, you know?' She leaves the question unfinished, so her voice doesn't betray what she *really* means.

'Seems a sensible compromise. Mick's put you in an impossible situation.'

'It's just that – what would we do if it does say something bad? What if it says he's only got a few years to live? You know, like Mick? What would we do then?'

Michaela veers slightly off the beaten path and walks down a shallow slope towards the cliff edge. Cathy follows but stands behind her, listening to her catch her breath.

'I used to come up here a lot as a kid,' Michaela says, looking out to sea rather than down at the beach. 'We'd come up as a family, for walks. Mum was never keen, she'd be forever warning me about the cliffs, keep away from the edge, all that. But Dad always encouraged me to defy Mum's warnings about the fencing that was invariably missing or in disrepair. He belittled her actually, called her a sissy, although I didn't see it like that at the time. I always thought he was funny; I loved his derring-do. There's a phrase you don't hear anymore. He's always had that in him. Never wanted to be mollycoddled, as he puts it, especially by busybody politicians and the like. Course, in later years, it came back to bite me, when Mick encouraged Steve and Paula to run as freely as I had done. It was only then that I could understand how Mum had felt. Funny how time can change your perspective.'

Cathy takes a breath, but Michaela carries on without a pause.

'I guess you'd have to take him to a doctor, wouldn't you? Will, I mean. To get him checked out. In case the bloody thing had happened to pick up something. You know I think the whole predicting your death date is a load of cobblers, but if there *is* something in his medical data that the docs have missed, you know, some test result that they didn't look at carefully enough, sitting in his file, you'd be silly not to get it checked. What does Steve say?'

'Oh, he's put his head in the sand. Won't discuss it. Says it's all nonsense.'

Michaela studies the sea. There's something about Cathy's voice that nags at her. She wouldn't call them close friends; Cathy and Paula are close friends. They occasionally go out for a girls' night, the three of them, but she knows Cathy and Paula often chat together. She turns and looks at Cathy; she isn't that surprised to see her face wet with tears.

'What did it say?' Michaela says. Cathy covers her eyes. Michaela takes a step and wraps her arms around her. Now the tears are joined by a shuddering release as Cathy weeps openly.

'Does Steve know?'

'He... he won't talk about it. He... he simply refuses.' Cathy gulps as she nods.

Michaela resists the urge to ask again. Cathy will tell what she wants to tell when she's ready. Cathy pulls away and finds a handkerchief in her pocket. She blows her nose, wipes her eyes, takes a couple of deep breaths.

'Oh, Michaela, it's dreadful. He won't talk about it. He's torn the card up, thrown it away, says it's all rubbish and won't discuss it anymore. I don't know what to do.'

'He's afraid,' Michaela says quietly. 'I'd feel the same.'

'But you think it's all rubbish, same as him.'

'Yes, but if it told me something – something *unwelcome* – there'd be part of me that wondered what if? I couldn't ignore it.'

'Oh, that's exactly how I feel. In my heart of hearts, I think it's bunkum too, but what if Will *has* got something, and this computer has picked it up, and we ignore the warning?' She starts to cry again, wringing her handkerchief as if she's trying to cleanse it of some dangerous virus. Cathy stares into Michaela's eyes; steels herself to say the words she's afraid to utter. 'Two thousand, one hundred and sixty-two days,' she says flatly, like it's the answer to some mildly interesting quiz question. 'It's less than six years.'

Michaela keeps her face impassive. In her mind she says, *fuck!* Screams it. *Fuck!* Can't believe Cathy can't see it printed on her eyeballs. *Fuck!* She clenches her teeth, works desperately to keep her lips steady and hold the tears back. *Fuck!* She turns away, shaking her head. *FUCK!*

'I'm sure it'll prove to be an error, some glitch in the software, something incorrectly entered in a database. They can't have had time to build up enough case studies to be able to predict that much, I'm sure there'll be some technical explanation. Remember, didn't Adam say the younger you are, the larger the margin for error. What if LifeTime's algorithms aren't that accurate yet? The margins of error could be bigger than they're willing to admit. They'd still release it, purely to make money, you know what these big businesses are like. They probably publicise all the projections they get right, or even close, and hide the ones they don't. You know LifeTime refuses to make public all their results? I bet they cherry-pick what they release. Exactly like petrol companies denied climate change for long enough, tobacco firms did the same with cancer. They're all the same.' Michaela bites her tongue. She wants to tell Cathy more about what she's found on the internet. She's tried telling Mick; he calls her a crank. She can't tell Paula; she doesn't want to cause problems between her and Adam. And now, much as she agrees with Steve, she doesn't want to put Cathy off taking Will to a doctor. She can't say anything to put her off. Because – what if?

'But?'

Michaela turns again and looks Cathy straight in the eye. 'But you *have* to take him to a doctor.'

'Mick? Mick's his doctor.'

'No, not to Mick. You have to go private. I can't see the NHS doing any serious investigations without more to go on than a LifeTime projection. You're going to have to pay. I can help you with that if cash is tight.'

'But Steve won't even discuss it. He's adamant that it's all rubbish, end of.'

'I think he might change if you give him some time. I'm sure he's afraid to confront it, even the possibility.'

'Please don't tell anyone I told you.'

'Of course I won't.' She waits a beat. 'Why *did* you tell me?'

Cathy takes another deep, shuddering breath.

'I wanted to tell Paula, but it would be awkward for her, with Adam, you know. I felt you'd understand – and that I could trust you. I know it puts you in an awkward situation with Paula. I didn't know what else to do. With Steve refusing to discuss it, I had nobody else I could turn to.'

'I wish I could help more,' Michaela says, shaking her head.

'You have. You've told me I'm not being stupid. I know you think it's all rubbish, so do I, but for you to say he should see a doctor means a lot.'

'When Steve's less angry, I'm sure he'll come round. He's not stupid. He'll see the sense in checking things out.'

She stops herself from adding, *Just in case.*

'Radio Wixlow at twelve minutes past the hour and our first guest tonight on The Jim Price Evening Show *is Dr Mick Strong, local GP for over fifty years and now famous for being the*

first UK member of LifeTime, the American company that predicts the day you're going to die. Dr Strong, welcome!'

'Thank you, Jim. Good to be here.'

'So, Dr Strong, tell us for openers, what made you decide to join the LifeTime programme?'

'Well, Jim, when I first heard about the scheme, I must admit I was a bit sceptical. There's a lot of snake oil out there if you're not careful, but I investigated how LifeTime were doing their predictions, and there's a lot of good science and mathematical modelling going into it.'

'So, let's move on to your own prediction, Dr Strong. Am I right in saying that your prediction was for two hundred and seventy days? Did that come as a bit of a shock?'

'Not really, Jim. I'm seventy-five-years old, I like the odd cigar and a wee dram. So, if you remember that the average life expectancy for a male in the UK is just under eighty years, then I'm not doing too badly.'

'But were you shocked to see the figure, two hundred and seventy days? Didn't that seem a bit, how shall I put this? Final?'

'You have to remember, Jim, this is only what they call a projection. They say that if I give up the booze and quit smoking it could give me a bit more time at the end.'

'And are you going to do that?'

'We'll see. Maybe.'

'What are your plans for the future?'

'I've recently been invited to the United States to address a conference on medical aspects of the LifeTime programme, and after that I'm going to arrange a couple of trips to visit a few parts of the world that I haven't managed to see yet.

'And I've got a few offers for interviews and the like from the media, plus I'll be spending some time with the family.'

'It sounds like you're going to be busy. Dr Strong, we wish you all the best, and thank you for joining us on The Jim Price

Evening Show. *Up next, our final guest, farmer Pete Miller tells us about the mystery of his missing pigs.'*

Jim Price hits a key on his laptop and removes his headphones.

'Thanks, Dr Strong, great performance.'

Mick appears surprised.

'I thought we were going to have a little more time; there are a couple of things I haven't mentioned yet.'

'Oh, I'm sorry, you won't keep an audience on a news show for more than five minutes in the evening, and Pete's pig story came in late. Tell you what though, if anything else develops over the next few weeks, let me know. We might get you to come in and do the phone-in. I'm sure we'd have a lot of people wanting to hear how you're coping.'

'Great,' says Mick, brightening instantly. 'I'll call you.'

Large, fenced landscaped front garden with drive to double garage and path through lawns to front door

Entrance hallway laid to parquet with understairs storage and closet-style toilet with sink

Through lounge from front bay window to French doors leading onto fully landscaped garden including large terrace laid to tiles and space for swimming pool

Modern, open plan, hi-spec kitchen/diner with walk-in pantry and door to back garden

4 generously sized bedrooms, bedroom 1 with en suite

Family-sized bathroom/toilet with hi-spec, stylish fixtures and fittings including massage-shower closet and separate spa bath

Set in a small development with communal children's

play equipment, central community lake and nearby
woodlands

Brand new, available for immediate purchase

Paula parks her shiny new Clio cabriolet in the drive and cuts
the music. Since marrying Adam, she's had to develop a taste for
Bruce Springsteen and, to be fair, she does like 'Thunder Road',
especially now that she's got a soft top and the wind can really
get to work on her hair. She turns and stares at Adam, who's
stowing his air guitar on the back seat.

'Do you think I need to close the roof?' she asks.

He shakes his head. 'It'll be safe here.'

'No, I think I'll close it,' she says, flicking the switch and
watching, spellbound, as what looks like a giant black butterfly
opens its wings and covers the two of them.

'Better?' he says, smiling.

'Nah. I think you were right, leave it open.' She flicks the
switch again and shivers with pleasure.

'Come on,' he says, opening his door and hauling himself
out. 'We've come to make a decision on this house not play with
your new car.'

She bleeps it locked and skips up next to him, feeding her
arm inside his as he unlocks the front door. She takes the keys
and opens the French windows, stepping out into the garden
where a path squirms away off the terrace towards a small
ornamental pond in front of some mature trees that mark the
boundary. The curve of the development means the garden isn't
overlooked from any side.

The sun has come round to give them perfect afternoon and
evening sunlight, another selling (or buying) point they hadn't
twigged on their previous visits. Paula imagines dinner parties,
spreading out from the terrace.

'What do you think?' he asks.

Paula wrenches her wind-blown hair into a fist then locks it with a scrunchie; she glances back at Adam. They've been married nearly two years, but she sometimes still gets the same tingles she got when they first met. Now they're about to buy the type of house she'd always assumed only existed in the magazines on rich people's coffee tables. She hadn't married Adam expecting this; his time at Yale was probably what got him his sixty per cent teaching job at the University of East Anglia, which allowed him to follow her back to the UK. Then LifeTime had made him an offer that promised so much, briefly took it all away, and have now given it back again – with a certain amount of interest.

'I can't believe we can afford this,' she whispers. She doesn't know why she whispers; the agent was busy so trusted them with the keys.

'Easily,' he says, 'if it's what you want.'

'But what are we going to do with four bedrooms? Won't we struggle to pay such an enormous mortgage?'

Adam shrugs. If he's honest, it might have been sensible to go for one of the two- or three-bedroom properties, but they've hummed and hawed for so long they've all gone. They're sold on the development now, with its community lake and forest walks, so it's four bed or camp bed.

'So, what'ya think?' he says again.

'I love it!' she says. 'But I loved the first one we saw. Shouldn't we look at more?'

'As many as you like, but remember, if we come back here in a couple of days this could be gone as well.'

'I know. It's so hard. What did the agent say, he had three of these left?'

'Yeah, but only one with the double garage. Why don't we put in a cheeky offer?'

She nods, heading back inside and climbing the stairs. She

tours the bedrooms. The smallest is bigger than either of their current two-ups. The master bedroom – with en suite – is bigger than their bloody lounge. It's a lot of money, but Adam's salary covers the projected mortgage payments with a shave to spare. Adam moves in behind her, leans over her shoulder.

'So?' he asks.

Paula turns to face him, clasps her hands around his neck. 'So, let's put in your cheeky offer and if they turn it down, let's pay the full price!'

Chapter Fifteen

'How to live longer: Eat one tablespoon of olive oil a day to increase your life expectancy.'
—*Daily Express*, 21 June 2018

M ick steps on the thing that he doesn't know the name of – the escalator that isn't an escalator because it doesn't go up or down. It simply goes along, and you only ever see them at airports, or in shopping malls the size of airports. Some people call it a travelator, or a walkalator, but they're not real words so he certainly won't be using them. He likes the thing itself; he's whizzing along at close to twice his usual walking pace without expending any extra energy at all. This is lucky as he's exhausted from the ten-hour flight and rather out of it from the amount of complimentary whiskey he's put away in first class. Why don't they install these things on pavements? He soon finds out.

A young family who are standing still blocks his way. The man is dressed in hiking gear while the woman is trying to control two young kiddies. They each have a pull-along, including the children!

'Excuse me!' Mick harrumphs. The man starts to move their bags into a more orderly pile at the side, while the woman attempts, rather unsuccessfully, to herd the overexcited children behind her. Mick marches through the gap. Adam follows, apologising with a half smile and raised eyebrows.

Twenty paces later Mick's stalled again, this time behind a group of tanned teenagers on their way back from Hawaii or some similar hellhole. Not only are they standing still, but like most youngsters, in Mick's view, they are conducting their conversation in loud voices, as if they think their fellow arrivals passengers are desperate to hear their exploits. Why does everybody stand still on this thing? He can understand the couple with the two young kids and four cases. But he's now travelling even slower than the people who decided not to step on what is now a stand-still-alator! Did the inventors mean for it to slow you down? He thinks not. He glares at Adam, indicates the group with his eyes, then rolls his eyes heavenward. *Idiots!* He fumes silently for a few moments, until they are all overtaken by an elderly man (not on the walkalator-thingy) pushing a woman in a wheelchair.

'Oh, for pity's sake!' Mick explodes. 'Excuse me! These things are meant to speed you up! Could we get through, please?'

The youngsters move to the side, shrugging in bemusement, as Mick steams through – followed by Adam, his apologetic smile, and his embarrassed eyebrows.

Mick's mood improves when they reach the arrivals hall, and he spots the drone with his name on it hovering above the crowd. Paula's told him how she was greeted, and Adam knows, *boy* does Adam know, Mick is expecting no less. He preens as he reads the screen that tells anyone who cares to look that he is *Dr*

Michael Strong, British Guest Speaker, LifeTime Medical Conference.

'There we are,' he shouts to Adam, who is standing next to him, his voice loud enough to alert the gang of young Hawaiian sun-lovers who have yet to catch them up in arrivals. 'Come on, no time to lose.'

Mick's spirits lift. He's determined to be positive while he's in the States. He's well aware of his default tendency to disparage a few choice aspects of American culture: specifically, the accents; the spelling; the grammar; the food; the television; the dress sense. Those for starters. And maybe also the false *Y'all have a nice day* politeness; the giant billboards at the sides of the roads; the churches with platitudinous messages displayed outside; the oversize cars; their ludicrous presidents... But he's going to be positive this week, a bit more *American* even, he thinks, with a wry smile.

It's his first trip stateside and he's hoping that maybe all the TV programmes and tabloids have exaggerated, or are out of date, or have lied. Oh, that's another thing, the lying politicians: don't get him started on Trump or DiCaprio.

Mick's mood dips, however, when the reception-desk staff at the Babylon residence (sponsored by Hitñon Hotels) are forced to break the news that SphereCity is a smoke-free zone. Still, he's treated with more than the extra reverence he was already getting, with everyone on the front desk wanting to make sure his stay is something he'll remember for – well, close to three hundred days, with a bit of luck, although nobody is tactless enough to say it in so many words. Mick's particularly impressed by the LCD display panel behind the receptionists that welcomes *respected visitor Michael Strong MD*. It's the MD which tickles his pride sensors the most, being (as he is) an ardent fan of medical dramas with the complete collection of *Marcus Welby MD* DVDs on the shelf back at home.

The next morning causes Adam some headaches. Mick oversleeps, although Adam should have predicted the effects of so much first-class whiskey mixed with jet lag and a bottle of Chablis Grand Cru with dinner. Adam enters Mick's adjoining suite to shake him awake when his increasingly frequent phone calls go unanswered.

Mick reluctantly resists the champagne on offer at breakfast but insists on ordering a full English even though it's not featured on the menu, his server assuring him the chef will know what it is. The coffee pot is refilled twice with the strongest blend they have, nicknamed Mule. He's clearly thrilled by the news that unlimited refills are free – although the shine is slightly taken off his glee when he's reminded that LifeTime are picking up the tab anyway.

Adam orders one of the hotel's driverless cars to take them to Jaz's place, but Mick has already spotted the majority of people scooting around on Segways and is keen to have a go himself, having learned from his server that, as a guest, he can use any of them whenever he likes for no charge at all. *Yes, really!* They waste another age while Mick struggles with the basics of a Segway before they (finally) stutter away from the hotel, fifteen minutes behind schedule.

They eventually cruise down the slope towards Jaz's house and park up, only for Adam's relief to be curtailed by a crowd of elderly folk in tracksuits who are limbering up for a jog.

'Look, that's Dr Strong,' shouts one – Mick's face is twinkling on any number of digital display boards they've passed, advertising his upcoming appearance at the conference. The tracksuited group surrounds Mick, hands are shaken, backs are slapped. Adam is surprised that no autographs are sought. As he watches this impromptu display of hero worship, he notices Jaz gazing out from his front door. Adam catches his eye, gives an exasperated and apologetic *what can I do?* shrug, only for Jaz to shake his head vigorously, clearly telling Adam to leave Mick and his elderly groupies exactly where they are.

It transpires that the jogging group is from one of the SphereCity hospitals and that they're all booked in to hear Mick speak. Offers are made for him to visit the hospital to see their facilities. As the meeting starts to break up, there are several requests to swap details on social media, which Mick has to deflect. The joggers move slowly away around the lake, Jaz walks jauntily down the steps from his front door, as if on cue.

'Dr Strong, I'm Jaz Forrester,' he booms, striding across the lawn to greet them. Jaz is dressed with enough style for a business meeting, enough class for a London club, and enough cool to raise the eyebrows of both sexes. 'Such a great pleasure to meet you; Adam has told me so much about you, but I also can't miss you in the media. Most impressive.'

Mick shakes hands and nods his appreciation of the surroundings and of Jaz.

'It's kind of you to invite me,' he replies, the epitome of English politeness and reserve.

'No, an honour, I assure you. Our first British member. You are history in the making, sir.' Jaz moves a half step aside and indicates the way to the house with an open palm and the slightest bow, which only Mick would notice.

Mick smiles modestly, accepting the praise as due. Jaz rises in his estimation. At last, someone who can see what's plain to see. Jaz escorts them up into the lounge then towards the terrace overlooking the lake.

'Wow!' Mick gasps at the vista. 'What a view.'

It's hard to tell where the inside ends and the outside begins. Immediately ahead of them, through the large doorway more than twice the width of a normal French door, is the polished deck, the size of a tennis court. Sturdy cane furniture with pastel-coloured cushions invites relaxation and contemplation of the lake, which stretches away into the distance to where pine trees creep up and over a hillside. The water is the crystalline blue you only find in Scandinavian eyes and in-flight magazines. The trees and sky on the far bank are reflected in near-perfect symmetry. The joggers appear as a multi-coloured snake slithering through the greenery. Mick stops on the threshold, clearly stunned by such a sight.

'This could be *On Golden Pond*,' he muses.

'You fish?' Jaz asks, as he points to a couple of luxurious wicker armchairs with deep, beige upholstery set facing the water in the far corner. Adam's toes curl, memories of Mick's distaste for the idiosyncrasies of American modes of speech. But this time, Mick isn't itching for a fight.

'Sure do,' he replies, Adam smiling to himself at John Wayne's sudden appearance in the conversation. Here's the pedant, who pulls Will up if he stops a glottal or splits an infinitive, using 'sure do' instead of a good old-fashioned English 'yes'. Adam remembers vividly his first torturous months in north Norfolk. Practically everything he said had incited a forensic quality control comment from Mick.

Sure, said Adam, when offered a drink – *Do you mean 'yes'?*

Math, said Adam, when explaining his job – *Do you mean 'maths'?*

When he'd described a sudden rainstorm as a *bummer*, on the day of a planned picnic, Mick stared at him with an expression that Adam wished forever after he had been quick enough to photograph. Whatever next? He doesn't have to wait long.

'We got some time in the schedule for a bit-o'-fishin'?' Jaz asks, glancing at Adam, who has little clue what's in Mick's schedule. 'That settles it,' Jaz continues, 'we got nothin' on for most of the morning tomorrow so let's settle back and see what we can pull outta the lake.'

'What you got in there?' Mick asks, dropping effortlessly into the truncated American grammar he's usually complaining loudly about.

'Mostly trout, you catch a big 'un, easily feed the three of us.'

'Really?'

'Sure. I got lots o' spare tackle. Adam, you join us?'

'Love to, but I can't promise to be as good at it as Mick.'

'That's a date, then. Now, I understand you've had breakfast, so let me get you fellas a couple mid-morning drinks. Dr Strong?'

'I'll have a whiskey, if I may.'

'Any particular brand?'

'You got Bushmills?'

'You kiddin' me?' Jaz says, smiling. 'I drink nothin' else. Ice?'

'No, thanks.'

'Me neither. Adam?'

'Okay, the same for me,' Adam says, nodding at the smoothness with which Jaz's email earlier in the week, asking for Mick's favourite teas, coffees, drinks and idiosyncratic food preferences, has effortlessly turned into a male bonding session to rival Butch and the Kid.

'Two ticks – you make yourselves comfortable and I'll get María to fix the drinks,' Jaz says, and Adam listens in vain for Mick to ask what's wrong with them.

As Mick wanders onto the deck to take in the view of the lake, Adam heads inside to check out the ground floor. There are three separate areas to the living room: a polished hardwood table surrounded by eight matching chairs dominates a large corner with picture windows showing off the lake; on the opposite side, a four-seater corner sofa and three sumptuous armchairs in a rich red leather surround a low glass coffee table, itself strewn with glossy magazines and books; straight ahead of him on the far wall is a massive TV, silently showing CNN, faced by a couple of modern, leather and wood reclining chairs.

They take their drinks on the spacious back deck, which overlooks where the lake ribbons away through a valley. A morning mist has almost risen, and the sun plays on the glass-smooth water. Mick takes his drink to the edge of the deck and looks out, sips his whiskey.

'I hear a whisper you're a golfer?' Jaz says as he sidles over next to Mick. At this, Mick turns, looks at Adam who shrugs innocently. Jaz glances at Adam as well and smiles. 'I got good sources. We got a helluva course here; I don't play nearly as much as I'd like. You'd be doing me a huge favour if you gave me an excuse to take you out?'

'Fantastic,' Mick replies, genuinely pleased. 'Of course, I haven't brought any clubs or shoes...'

'No problem. There are a dozen bags in the clubhouse for guests to choose from – although I've already secreted away the best Titleist set – just in case. And I'm sure the budget we've agreed for Adam's new UK marketing department will be able to cover some appropriate shoes and clothing. You might need to grab another bag out of the shop to get it all back to the UK with you. Tell you what, if you like the clubs, and I'm sure you will, we can ship 'em home for you, as thanks for helping us out at the conference at such short notice.'

'That's very generous,' Mick says, glancing across at Adam who nods nonchalantly. 'Sounds great.'

Adam grudgingly marvels at the ease of Jaz's courting, and the elasticity of his own marketing budget. He feels slightly out of the loop. Fact is, he's not sure it's a loop at all: more like Jaz is wrapping Mick in a double helix of marketing sorcery while he's been left to amuse himself with a fraying rubber band.

Jaz refills the drinks while quizzing Mick about his experience of LifeTime so far, and Mick chats modestly about discussions he's having with the editor of *The Times* about writing a weekly column. Adam has no idea if this is true; Mick hasn't mentioned it before. They chat on: fish, golf, the weather, all the while Jaz busies himself 'refreshing' their drinks. The level of whiskey in the bottle is dropping like a freefall skydiver in a hurry to get home. Adam has long since covered his glass with his hand, but Mick is made of sterner stuff. The bottle on the table is close to half empty as they ease themselves into the comfortable chairs. Adam feels his head swim slightly; Mick revels in the attention; Jaz prepares to strike.

'We'll want you to do a little bit of light work while you're here as well,' Jaz opens.

'What you got in mind?' Mick asks casually, shedding verbs alongside his jacket.

'You're good for the conference Q&A tomorrow night?'

'Yep, ready to go.'

'We've got a couple of media interviews lined up for the day after. You okay to speak to *The Salt Lake Tribune*, local TV and radio, *CNN*, maybe a few others?'

'Yeah, fine.' Mick fires a nonchalant glance at Adam, raises his eyebrows. '*CNN*?' he says, proudly. 'We're in the big league now.'

'Oh, I got a question,' Jaz 'remembers'. 'Nothing important, I nearly forgot to mention it. We've had so many people here in SphereCity trying to friend you on Facebook, follow you on Twitter, especially once they saw you were speaking at the conference, but there's been a bit of trouble finding you. *CNN* were the first to ask, actually...'

'Ah.' Mick colours slightly, leans over and tops up his glass.

'Don't tell me – you never bothered signing up with all this new-fangled stuff. Am I right? Too busy saving lives and playing golf? Can't say I blame you.' Jaz shrugs. 'Not a problem, don't use it much myself. But – a pity...'

Mick looks worried. 'It's not something I ever got involved in. I live in a small community, my family all live nearby, I've never really felt the need.'

'Entirely up to you,' Jaz says dismissively. 'We can get away without it. It's just that here, things move in and out of the news cycle so quickly, you never know, Kate Bolduan, Wolf Blitzer – they wanna get a hold of you pronto, they'll probably come that route. But no matter, they might find other ways to get in contact.'

Adam sneaks a glance at Mick's face. In normal times, he'd imagine him telling Jaz it's not pronounced *rout*. Or maybe he'd be wondering who the hell Kate Bolduan was – and whether he really wanted to be friends with someone called Wolf? But the doubt etched on Mick's face is the type usually worn by children who've said they're not hungry, before spying the takeaway pizza menu in Mum's hand.

'I imagine if you were to join, you'd have close to ten thousand friends, or followers, or whatever they're called, by the time you've finished your publicity tour here. How many friends you got, Adam?'

'Um, I think I got two or three hundred on Facebook, less on Twitter.'

'Yeah, me the same.'

'Well, I don't really know much about them, to be honest,' Mick admits. 'I've lived long enough without feeling I need them; I guess I'd want to know what I'm missing.'

Jaz nods. 'That makes sense. I guess I'd say it's not a case of what you're missing; it's more a case of what everybody *else* is missing. Everyone will want to know what you're thinking, and the easiest way for them to find out is to follow you on social media.'

'Will I have to do a lot of twittering and the like? I'm quite a busy man.'

Jaz expertly suppresses a grin under a sudden cough; Adam decides he's in desperate need of a long pull from his glass, as he tries to figure out how a couple of rounds of golf and a spin on his ride-on mower take Mick anywhere close to 'busy'.

'No, not at all, not at all,' Jaz continues. 'In fact, we have a team here in the secretarial division who do a lot of the donkey work for our busy people. Long as you can take a couple of photos every week of whatever you're doing, they'll pad out the text and suchlike, deal with all the fan mail, so to speak.'

'Really?' Mick sits forward. 'They'd do that for me?'

'Sure, no big deal.'

Mick stares at Adam who smiles. 'It's a piece o' cake, any issues you hit, you can always give me a call and I'll sort you out in no time.'

'I tell you what...' Jaz says, 'suddenly' having an idea... 'Why don't you give it a go while you're here stateside, and if you don't like it, you can drop it when you leave? How does that sound?'

Mick looks like he's trying to feign a relative lack of interest. 'Would it take long to set up?'

'Are you kidding? You got ten minutes?' Mick appears dubious. 'Gimme your mobile.'

Mick passes over his phone. It's clearly not 6G. It might not even be G. It's probably an F. The screen is the size of a postage stamp and the buttons each have three faded letters, now almost invisible, above the numbers.

'Wow!' Jaz gasps. 'I seen more functions on a pair of sunglasses! Boy, you sure are the country doc, aren't you? Look, I'm sure I've got a couple of old things I don't use anymore; you can have one of them, gimme a sec...' He heads into the lounge and rattles the drawers of his desk, returning with a sleek-looking model. 'This'll do, I upgraded a few months ago; this is actually quite a nice phone,' he says, sliding Mick's SIM into it.

'Are you sure? I don't want to be any bother.'

'No bother at all. Come and sit down over here,' Jaz says, pulling over a spare chair so the lake provides a cooler-than-cool background.

'Hang on, hat!' Jaz says, returning indoors while still punching the screen and grabbing a hat. 'You do a nice panama?' he shouts over his shoulder at Mick. Jaz places a two-hundred-dollar panama hat on Mick's head then fires off a dozen shots. 'That'll do for your profile. Nice wide angle for your background?' he asks, not expecting Mick to know what he's talking about and not waiting for confirmation. He shows them to Mick who nods appreciatively.

'They're great.'

'Right, you can do the rest, I think, full name, choose a password, blah-de-blah, don't forget to include the *doctor*, adds so much gravitas.'

Mick takes the phone and pudges in his email and other details. 'It wants date of birth, here. Is that it?'

'All done,' Jaz replies. 'Let me show you how to get the photos in the right places.'

Mick sits forward and watches as Jaz opens the pictures. 'Great shots. This one for your profile, Mick? What do you think? You can always change it later.'

Mick points at another head and shoulders portrait.

'Yeah, better,' Jaz agrees. 'And one for the background. How about that one? Lovely view of the lake and the valley.'

'Okay, let's go with that.'

'Right, there's a whole load of other stuff you can go over later with Adam if you like, otherwise we're ready for your first status, let's tell the world what you're up to.'

Jaz steps back. Mick shrugs.

'What do I say?' he says, looking from one to the other.

'Something meaningful,' Adam says. 'If you're going to be an infrequent poster, then you'll need to make them interesting. How about mentioning the conference tomorrow evening?'

'Good idea,' Jaz says.

Mick stares blankly at the screen. Jaz continues without a stop.

'How about, "Greetings from SphereCity, Utah. I'm looking forward to the FutureMed Conference tomorrow night," then we can add a link to the website and the live stream.' He helps Mick draft the status, and then shows him how to add a selfie.

'Hey, what's that?' Mick says, sitting back, startled, as a melodic *ping* emits from his new phone, which is also buzzing in his hand.

'Friend request!' Adam says, sitting forward. 'That was quick!'

'It's Paula!' Mick gasps. 'How the hell does she know?'

Adam waves his mobile in the air as he sips his drink.

'Bloody hell!'

As Jaz shows Mick how to accept Paula's friend request, the phone pings another couple of times.

'Who's this? I don't know a Mary West.'

Jaz glances at Mick's mobile.

'That's *Doctor* Mary West, look what it says there, she's a heart specialist at a SphereCity hospital. She was one of the runners you met this morning.'

Mick accepts the request and starts to scroll through her profile. Jaz and Adam sit back, smiling, and silently raise their glasses.

By lunchtime, Mick's on Insta, TikTok, Twitter – has over a hundred friends, followers, hangers-on, mostly SphereCity medical workers, and he's glued to his phone like an average sixteen-year-old on Christmas morning – well, *any* morning.

Every time his phone pings, Mick announces the new request without looking up, the unconscious running commentary of the seriously self-absorbed, oblivious that there's no response to his torrent of auto-babble.

Jaz works his tablet, feeding the flow; Adam wonders silently what they might have unleashed, and whether any of them will come to regret it.

Chapter Sixteen

'Balancing on one leg may be useful health test in later life, research suggests. People who cannot stand on one leg for 10 seconds are found to be almost twice as likely to die within 10 years.'

—*The Guardian*, 21 June 2022

The SphereCity theatre holds 2,000. It's full tonight. Jaz has suggested collars and ties and the three of them spend a happy hour in the bar beforehand, which quite by chance, has had a recent delivery of a twenty-one-year-old Bushmills Madeira which Jaz is 'dying to try'. By the time they leave for the event, Mick has decided that it's his favourite.

Jaz leads them down the centre aisle, shaking hands, waving, high-fiving, air-kissing. He introduces Mick to a dozen or more names and faces, all delighted to see him, can't wait to hear him, congratulations. Adam brings up the rear, shaking the odd hand offered to him from faces he can't always quite place.

They take their seats in the front row as the curtain rises to reveal a pair of armchairs and an enormous plasma screen.

Welcome Dr Michael Strong, it screams in glitzy lettering that twirls and glistens and should carry a health warning for people with epilepsy and anyone of a sensitive artistic disposition. Mick beams and nudges Adam. One or two whoops accompany the applause, which intensifies as Mick's Facebook profile and Twitter handle replace the on-screen pyrotechnics. There's a rustling as phones are retrieved from bags and pockets, closely followed by Mick's mobile starting to dance and sing in his jacket until Adam urges him to switch it to silent.

A modicum of order descends until Jaz stands and trots athletically up the steps and onto the stage. More applause, even more whoops and whistles. Jaz calms them with raised hands. Mick admires the panache that Jaz exudes onstage. Once again, he seems to have hit the fashion tone perfectly without seeming to try: his jacket says Clooney in a coffee ad, the open-necked shirt is all Gosling gone La La, while the delivery is Obama in playful mood – when you think he might be about to sing.

'Thank you, thanks so much. You're very kind. Thank you for coming tonight, we have an extremely interesting evening planned for you. I've been told today has been a successful day at the conference, and to round it off I've brought a special guest to share the experience and maybe answer a few questions. He's spent the day making me sweat on the golf course and he still has enough energy to talk to you tonight. He's come all the way from Blighty.' Muffled laughter from some in the audience, shrugs and looks of confusion from others. 'Our first LifeTime member in the U-ni-did Kingdom, will you please offer an almighty SphereCity welcome to Doctor... Michael... Strong!'

The noise is thunderous. Mick has attended one or two BMA conferences but has never seen anyone received in such a fashion. It's unthinkable. Quite ludicrous. People are standing, cheering, waving at him. He waves back, does a little bow, isn't quite sure what to do in the face of such unbridled enthusiasm.

Jaz shakes his hand and leads him to the armchairs. A young, clean-cut man in beige chinos and a navy-blue polo shirt appears from the wings carrying a small movie camera attached to a tripod. He sets it stage left, hits a couple of buttons, and adjusts it as Mick and Jaz appear on the screen behind.

'It's a bit like *Parkinson*,' Mick quips, realising immediately that nobody here will have any clue who he's talking about. Jaz lets it pass and takes control.

'Welcome, Dr Strong, can we call you Mick?'

'Of course you can. It's great to be here.'

The whooping and applause starts again, but Jaz calms it quickly and easily.

'Now, Mick, I must explain to our audience here how you really jumped the gun in the UK ahead of our British launch, joining LifeTime before it was even officially available, with a little help from our man on the spot in the UK, Adam Collingworth. Big hand for Adam, everybody.'

There's a polite round of applause for Adam, who stands, half turns and acknowledges the audience with a wave and a couple of short nods.

It's a free-flowing discussion, lots of scope for Mick to build his reputation as a far-sighted medical expert on all things British. He's stoical about his own projection; Adam's insistence that it is a projection rather than a prediction finally sinking in as he refers to it as such all the way through. Mick slips into a passable impression of Dr Finlay, and his audience responds by drifting him a flood of folksy questions about how many house calls he usually makes and whether he has a dog. The slot is scheduled to last an hour, but after forty minutes, Jaz stands and heads for the front of the stage.

'Now, ladies and gentlemen, I have a small confession to make. I hope you and Mick will forgive me. You see, having seen how proactive and enthusiastic Mick is in his commitment to

LifeTime membership, I put a proposal to our directorate earlier this week, that we should reward him with the opportunity, if he so desires, to extend his membership, at no extra charge, to include one of the latest developments we have, which will be officially available in the not-too-distant future. Dr Strong, I believe, might be up for an even bigger leap of faith than hijacking a LifeTime membership before it's legally available in the UK.' There's a buzz of murmuring through the audience, which Jaz does nothing to quieten.

'As a lot of you are aware, we are constantly working to improve the efficiency and functionality of the LifeTime service. And there's been one development above all others–' The murmuring is now a not-so-quiet hubbub as audience members swap quick conversations with each other. '–which we've been working extra hard to bring to fruition. Now we're ready!' The applause starts again, then quietens as more conversations begin.

'We have been working on a project called LifeBuddy for the best part–' At this point his voice is drowned out by a cacophony of cheering and clapping, people are standing again, a rhythmic *thud-thud-thud* starts as the vast audience stamps its approval on the polished wooden flooring. From stage right, a pair of chino- and polo-clad young people wheel on a stainless-steel trolley, followed by another cameraman whose pictures take over the large screen as the stage lights flash blue and white, ambulance-style. Jaz fights to control the noise, decides to shout over it.

'So, what we've got here this evening, ladies and gentlemen, is the very first LifeBuddy, which we think it appropriate to offer to Dr Mick Strong, if he's willing, and we think he might be. Dr Strong, come to the front, would you?'

Mick stands and the cheering intensifies. He joins Jaz at the front of the stage. Jaz holds his hands aloft, pats his fingers down a few times in the universal signal for quiet. He nods his thanks left and right as an uneasy silence allows him to continue.

'You okay, Mick?'

'You tell me,' Mick replies to a burst of nervous, expectant laughter from the crowd. Mick exudes youth, until the camera close-up appears on-screen. Here, his face betrays him. Beneath the sheen, if he stays still long enough to allow close study, his skin reveals an intricate delta of ruddy lines, like a windscreen that's been hit by a stone.

'Now, Mick, what we propose is to offer you our first LifeBuddy. It's entirely up to you whether you accept it or not. However, it'll be difficult for you to decide if you don't know what it does. So, we'd like to put one on you, show everybody how it works, then we'll leave it on and you can make your decision over the next few days before you fly transatlantic again. How does that sound? Are you game?'

Mick nods sagely and receives more deafening applause for his decision.

'Okay,' Jaz shouts again, beckoning a smartly dressed woman out from the wings. 'Let me introduce Dr Sandra Pereira to everyone, she's head of the LifeBuddy project of the LifeTime organisation, and she's going to explain this sensational new piece of kit. And, I think I can also add, can I?' He looks offstage for confirmation. 'Yes, I can, I can announce that we're now live on *CNN*. Dr Pereira, would you like to take over?'

Dr Pereira approaches the front of the stage as if she's deaf to the applause. Her hair is out of a salon catalogue, make-up from one of Fifth Avenue's most exclusive stores, clothes an aquamarine two-piece with matching kitten heels that nobody in the audience will see in the shops they usually patronise, nor the magazines they usually read. So far, she could be straight off a Parisian catwalk, except she's demoted it all beneath the crispest white lab coat, killing frivolous fashion with a prescription of science and brains. Experience floods from her very presence, an aura of authority cascades off the stage, she drips gravitas. The only aspect of her that one might dispute is her age: she's obviously a fair few years out of college, but were she to ask Mick to guess how many, for once in his life he'd duck the question, afraid to offend her by guessing too many – or even too few.

The noise evaporates to silence without a word or gesture from her. She shakes Mick's hand warmly. The two exchange a few private words, smile and nod; her pats linger on his shoulder as if she's transferring some kind of magic curative powers from her to him. He seems to shrink as she commands their muted conversation like a stage hypnotist. The silence concocts an uneasy feeling of intrusion into an important doctor–patient consultation. Dr Pereira shakes the room to attention with a final smile and a turn of her head.

'Thank you, everybody,' she announces as she faces the front. She has the hint of an accent, unplaceable but precise, correct, making what she says seem completely unchallengeable. The applause begins again, nervously. She waits as it subsides, then waits some more as the whispered chatter dies, then waits again, until the final few voices are identifiable and shushed by those around them. 'Thank you,' she says eventually, to sepulchral silence. The lights dim, evoking a sense of expectation, like a magician is about to attempt a unique and quite dangerous illusion. Dr Pereira picks up an A4-sized plastic envelope from the trolley and holds it above her head.

'Fellow LifeTime members, I have here a piece of technology that is going to revolutionise the way we live our lives. I am fully confident that this device will have as significant an effect on our future well-being as the invention of the hypodermic needle.' There's a smattering of polite applause from the back of the auditorium, as if those nearer the front are afraid to displease Dr Pereira and are fearful that she'll be able to identify them even in the muted glow from the stage lights. Dr Pereira waits for the applause to die, which it does – quickly.

'Now, if you think about it, you will no doubt recognise that the hypodermic needle, while allowing us to do many marvellous medical things, is also capable of being used for some less wholesome activities.' She pauses for a few moments to allow her words to sink in. 'And if you think about it some more, you'll realise that this is true of quite a few medical inventions and innovations over the years. Medicines can relieve or heal our maladies, but some of them, by misuse, can kill us. Too much of the radiation that we use to kill cancerous cells, for example, can indeed kill the patient if we don't monitor and control its use carefully. The simple scalpel, which in a skilled hand can excise a tumour and save a life, can also, in malevolent or disturbed fingers, cut through an artery and end a life. There are few medical tools that cannot be put to an ill purpose, and it's with this warning that I offer you all the LifeBuddy.'

The applause is light, thoughtful, and brief. Dr Pereira puts the plastic envelope down and slips on a pair of latex gloves. She indicates for Mick to remove his jacket and roll up one of his sleeves while she busies herself with a packet of surgical wipes, ripping it open, unfolding a small white sheet.

'You're going to be needing a scalpel this evening?' Mick enquires, with a glint in his eye as he scans the contents of the trolley in front of him. The laughter pops a bubble of tension, which has quickly built under the low light and the serious demeanour of Dr Pereira. She smiles at him, a teacher amused by a small child's exuberance, shakes her head briefly, and dabs at his arm.

'The LifeBuddy attaches to the inside of the forearm, here,' she says, pointing. She lifts the A4 envelope again and carefully rips off the seal. From inside, she extracts a black container, about the size of a slim case for a pair of extremely expensive spectacles. She opens the lid and presents the contents to the cameraman who is hovering like a greedy but indecisive insect surveying a full-bloom flowerbed but fearing a squirt of powerful insecticide. 'Here is the LifeBuddy.'

The audience erupts like she's scored the winning goal in a World Cup final. The cameraman crouches in and the screen shows what appears to be a wafer-thin plastic rectangle. Dr Pereira reaches inside the case, pinches a corner of the sheet between her thumb and forefinger before lifting it up into the air. She lets it twirl in the lights, where it sparkles and glistens like ripples on the surface of a shallow river.

'Ladies and gentlemen, there is more processing power in this little device and the computers that it is served by than there was in the entire Apollo 11 mission to the moon.'

There is a gasp from somewhere in the middle of the audience before the applause explodes. Dr Pereira waits patiently for the noise to die again before she continues.

'Now, Dr Strong, I'm going to put the LifeBuddy in place, for demonstration purposes, with a temporary glue which we'll be able to remove later in the week. Okay?'

A chant from one or two over-excited spectators begins at the back of the auditorium. But in seconds, it moves like a living being across the hall.

'Fu-sion, fu-sion, FU-SION, FU-SION!'

'Please,' Dr Pereira says, in a quiet, controlled voice, while lifting one gloved hand. The noise disappears like smoke up a papal chimney. 'You okay?' she says quietly to Mick, and he feels nobody else hears her but him.

Mick nods and swallows; he feels strangely cowed by the lights, the excitable crowd, and probably most of all, by Dr

Pereira's sedate manner, cool efficiency and apocalyptic commentary.

'Now, if you'll lay your arm out flat on this part of the trolley.'

The lights on the stage now dim further, all except a pair of spots, one on Dr Pereira and one on Mick's arm. The cameraman flits left and right, hunting for the best sight line, and Dr Pereira waits, almost imperceptibly, for him to settle. The screen now shows Dr Pereira laying the sheet of shiny plastic onto the inside of Mick's forearm. She lifts a slightly wrinkled corner and smooths it flat again.

As she tinkers and fusses, squeezing ever closer, Mick realises that he's holding his breath. He breathes out slowly, then breathes in and is immediately aware of an intense perfume, a whole hillside of orange blossom under a warm Valencian sun suddenly making him heady. He grips the side of the trolley with his free hand. Her hand is on his shoulder in an instant. Their eyes meet, and he feels a powerful, almost overwhelming sense of trust, as if he'd give this woman permission to do whatever she pleased with him without any fear of harm.

Dr Pereira steps closer. 'Comfortable?' she asks him, almost in a whisper, so close now he can hear her starched coat rubbing against his shirt.

'Very,' he says. It feels like they're alone; the spotlights mask everything except the two of them. She holds his stare for too long, then longer.

'Can we activate, please?' Dr Pereira snaps, straightening up and stepping back into the darkness. 'Stand still, please, Dr Strong.'

He stares at the sliver of transparency on his skin. It's so thin, so lightweight; he could almost believe she's painted it on with a soft brush. Suddenly it flashes, the reflection of sunlight in an inquisitive schoolchild's mirror, except there's no sun, no mirror. He's aware of an intake of breath from somewhere in the darkness, a murmur of startled conversation. Then he sees the pale skin on his arm disappear behind another glint of colour, and the space on his arm is filled with scrolling colours. There are more gasps from the darkness as a digital display solidifies in the rectangle on Mick's arm, as if someone has cut a hole using a sharp scalpel, and implanted the most up-to-date HD colour monitor. The swirling settles into a LifeBuddy logo, in the trademark LifeTime red, white and blue colours, with a smaller LifeTime logo visible in the bottom corner.

'Beautiful,' he hears Dr Pereira murmur, almost to herself, from behind his left shoulder. The scent of her perfume is there again as she says, 'Welcome to the future of life monitoring.'

Bedlam. People are on their feet instantaneously. The house lights go up like they've exploded; people are cheering and clapping, waving and smiling. Mick turns to see his arm filling the screen behind him, and in the top corner, *We're live on CNN*. He notices the cameraman stepping away from him, so he turns to face him head on. As the cameraman backs down the steps, Mick follows like a child in a trance, but he stops at the top, front and centre. He soaks the applause; the lights in his eyes make it impossible for him to see anyone so he simply absorbs the sound. Slowly, he lifts his arms, palms open, and spreads them to the side, holding the pose, looking for all the world like he's been crucified.

Chapter Seventeen

'New war on cancer aims at long term survival, not cure.'
—*The Guardian*, 16 May 2019

They give the audience a ten-minute break knowing they'll be uncontrollable without it. Mick is ushered backstage where a team of chino-polos fuss and test and express delight with the connection. Dr Pereira reappears and takes his hand, lifting it so that she can see the LifeBuddy, view it from every angle. Her fingers are smooth and cool, her touch firm and steady. He sucks her perfume in and senses a potent combination of white blossom petals on a warm breeze. She nods slowly, as if she's looking at a row of precious stones in a 24-carat necklace. Then she smiles at him, a radiant smile.

'It looks good,' she says, 'everything working, are you ready for the demonstration?'

Back on stage, Dr Pereira sits next to Jaz in the armchairs. A fixed camera is trained on Mick's LifeBuddy, his arm resting on a tall table as he stands at the front of the stage. Behind him, the monitor is displayed like a giant electronic scoreboard at a football match. The audience are back in their seats, eager to see what's going to happen next. There is an air of expectation, as if a historic event is unfolding before them: penicillin is about to be discovered again; Einstein is shuffling E and MC^2.

'Welcome back, everybody,' Jaz opens, approaching the front of the stage. 'We've been running through some checks backstage and Dr Pereira is happy with the way the LifeBuddy is working. She's now going to explain exactly what it can do. Dr Pereira, please.'

Dr Pereira moves towards Mick's side and lifts his hand into hers. 'There is a press pack available on our website for anybody who wants the detailed specs; I'm going to run through the basic features that should function relatively well without full fusion.

'Now, Dr Strong, can I ask you to swipe the LifeBuddy screen, like you're cleaning a speck of dust from it.'

Mick swipes across the colours on the inside of his forearm and the logos disappear and are replaced by a column of green numbers on a darker green background. There are gasps in the crowd, which are quickly silenced by Dr Pereira.

'Can you see these figures running down the left-hand side of the LifeBuddy? I'm sure you'll be able to work out what they are, Dr Strong?'

On the big screen, Dr Pereira's fingers are visible pointing at the column of figures, but it's her blood-red fingernails that dominate the picture in Mick's eyes. They take on an unearthly power when they're reproduced at such huge magnification. He finds it hard to reconcile the hand that is pointing at the inside of his forearm, right in front of his face, with the enormous blood-red shapes hovering above his head.

'Dr Strong?'

'Sorry?'

'These figures here, can you work out what they are?'

'Oh, right, sorry, yes, ahh, vital signs, I'd say.'

'Of course. There you have your heart rate, blood pressure, oxygen saturation, respiration and temperature. You appear to be in very good shape for your age, Dr Strong. All seventy-five years, sixty-one days, two hours, four minutes and twenty-five seconds.' A ripple of laughter spreads across the audience.

'H-how did you know that?' Mick stutters, looking from the screen to Dr Pereira.

'Right there.' She points at a miniscule row of scrolling figures at the bottom of the display.

'That's my age?' Mick gasps, wiping his finger over the smooth plastic. 'You programmed it in, right?'

'No, the monitor is doing a full check on you at this moment; one of the first things is an age calculation. It's correct?'

Mick does a few quick sums in his head.

'Seems so,' he says, smiling. The laughter returns for the briefest moment, but the audience is spellbound by what it's watching.

'And over there on the right is your projected LifeTime: two hundred and ten days. Now, I must explain, over the course of this trial, the LifeBuddy will tick down one day every twenty-four hours. If we were to fuse it on permanently, which will be an option for you to consider at the end of the trial, it would start recalculating your projection in real time, taking account of your ongoing lifestyle choices. So, for example, if you started exercising more, your *fused* LifeBuddy would add an appropriate amount of time onto your projection. If, on the other hand, you started taking harmful drugs, it would sense that and subtract time from your projection. At the moment, because it's not fused on, during this trial period it will tick down one day each day.'

'But it's wrong to start with.'

'Excuse me.'

'It's wrong. Sixty-one days ago, my projection was two hundred and seventy days, so it's now two hundred and nine days, not two hundred and ten. It's wrong.'

There is a slightly embarrassed murmuring; Adam is gesticulating from the front row.

'The smoking?' Adam shouts. 'Maybe the Buddy calculated his projected LifeTime taking into account the fact that he's not been smoking for a couple of days?'

'You've stopped smoking?' Dr Pereira turns to Mick, a look of surprise and approval on her face.

'Well, while I'm here, I can't,' Mick replies, to another ripple of laughter from the audience. 'Can't buy a packet of ciggies for love nor money here.'

'That'll be it,' Dr Pereira announces authoritatively, nodding at Adam. 'The LifeBuddy will have sensed that you've been smoke-free for a couple of days and will have adjusted your projection accordingly when it did its start-up assessment.'

'You mean, I'm going to live an extra day?' Mick asks to more laughter.

'Of course,' Dr Pereira replies. 'It's probably only a couple of hours, but even that could flip your projection over to show an extra day. We don't display the projections in units of less than a day unless the monitor is fused on; we don't really want casual members to think they are on a countdown.' Dr Pereira waits for the laughter to subside before continuing. 'Of course, if you were to give up smoking *completely*, your projection would rise even further, and, more importantly, you'd live longer.' A huge round of applause follows this news.

'How much?' Mick says, as the clapping calms, replaced by a curious silence.

'How much longer?'

'Yes. How much longer would I live if I never smoked

again?' There's a murmur in the crowd as he looks at Dr Pereira and she returns his stare.

'Well, our algorithms are based on an assumption that each cigarette cuts an average of close to fifteen minutes off life expectancy. You obviously included your smoking history when you filled out the application. You wouldn't gain exactly fifteen minutes for each cigarette you don't smoke in the future, as some of the damage to your heart and lungs will already have been done by the years that you have smoked. But if you give up now, you'll still see some benefit in your LT projection.'

'How much?' Mick repeats.

'If I were to change your settings to that of a non-smoker as of now, we'd see. Would you like me to do that?'

'Okay,' Mick replies.

'You want me to change your smoking status to new non-smoker?'

Mick nods. The auditorium is ghostly quiet. Somebody backstage – almost certainly a huge fan, or a distant relative, of Alfred Hitchcock – lowers the lights so slowly that nobody notices it happening, but they all feel the effect: there's a chill in the air, people shift in their seats, the glow of the spotlights on Mick and Dr Pereira seems all the more intense. They look like they're encased in some space-age tubes, about to dabble in the alchemy of life and death.

'Okay, hold on. Charlie?' she calls, her voice authoritative. 'Have you got Dr Strong's details available there?' Dr Pereira walks towards the back of the stage and shouts again towards stage left. 'Charlie?'

'Yes, I've got them here,' a disembodied voice cracks through the air, as if someone has made contact from the beyond.

'Could you change his status from smoker to new non-smoker, effective as of now, please?'

'As of *two days* ago,' Mick cuts in, provoking a burst of

nervous laughter and enthusiastic clapping from sections of the crowd.

'As of two days ago,' Dr Pereira repeats slowly, nodding appreciatively.

'Okay, all done,' the voice from afar reports, 'updating now.'

There is a collective gasp and cries of 'holy shit' as Mick's LifeTime projection flips from two hundred and ten days to two hundred and thirty-seven.

'How does that look, Dr Strong?' Dr Pereira asks to a shocked background murmur.

Mick's mouth opens, but he seems unable to say anything. He nods instead, wiping his hand across his lips, giving him an expression of bemusement.

Dr Pereira moves slowly away from him and stands still.

'Now, of course, as everyone here will understand, I have an important question for you, Dr Strong.' If all eyes hadn't already turned to her, they have now. Even Mick turns his head slightly. 'Because obviously, your LT projection isn't accurate anymore if I don't change your status back to that of a smoker. Would you like me to do that, Dr Strong? Would you like me to switch your status back to smoker – and take those twenty-seven extra days away again?' Her voice has lowered almost to a whisper, as if what she is suggesting is somehow clandestine, stealing time from some universal vault, undiscovered until now. The quiet in the auditorium is almost unearthly. If this were a game show the lights would be flashing, the music would be building to a crescendo.

Mick's face goes blank, like he's lost consciousness, and his eyes will roll in a second and his legs will give way. Then his bottom lip moves. It's the slightest tremble, but unmistakable to Adam and those sitting in the front row. As Mick appears to be losing it, Adam starts to stand. The big screen flashes to a close-up of Mick's face, pinpricks of sweat glistening on his forehead, and the trembling lip now clearly visible to all.

A shout from somewhere near the back of the hall shatters the silence. It's a young girl's voice, maybe seventeen- or eighteen-years-old, obviously someone Mick's never met before, but there's real emotion in it. It's not loud, it's quite frail, but the deep silence means everybody hears it clearly, as if she's shouting it in their faces. It cracks with a raw, heartfelt plea.

'Say no, Mick!'

Mick's lip wobbles as if the muscles have been cut. Tears stream instantly down both cheeks. He claps his hand over his mouth, like he's holding the muscles in place, and the tears wash over it. There's a gasp from the crowd, a shriek from somewhere up back. Suddenly it doesn't feel at all like a game show.

'Say no, Mick!' Another voice, young again, but male this time. A gentle voice, but carrying enormous power in the near silence, now punctuated, as it is, by other urgent pleas from the darkness.

Mick's crying openly, one hand on his knee as he stoops lower, almost bending double, tears plopping loudly onto the stage. Dr Pereira moves to go to him, but Jaz catches her arm, shakes his head minutely but firmly: *Leave him*, he mouths.

'No,' Mick croaks.

'Louder!' someone shouts, female, older, mature. 'Say no, Mick!'

'No!' Mick responds, his voice stronger, straightening up, holding himself steady on the table.

The applause starts in scattered locations. There are more shouts, then cheering, thunderous applause and stamping. Mobile phones are out and recording, cameras flash. Mick's legs buckle and he half-drags the table over. Adam leaps up the front steps, Dr Pereira and Jaz get to Mick first, Jaz's armchair scattering backwards as he races to keep Mick upright and help him offstage. The crew lower the curtain, raise the house lights, one or two from the audience try to mount the steps, a couple of security guards convince them to retreat before the stage is swamped. More mobile phones and tablets appear like spring flowers in time-lapse, brightening worried-looking faces.

Within minutes, Mick has a quarter of a million friend requests on Facebook, nearly a million followers on Twitter, the CNN phone lines are jammed and #SayNoMick is trending ahead of any other topic.

The share prices of all the major tobacco companies fall precipitously.

———

'I'm fine!' Mick snaps as hands offer him water, towels, steadying pats on the shoulders. 'Really, it simply got a bit hot out there, a bit overwhelming. But really, thank you, I'm fine.'

Dr Pereira crouches beside him; he's no idea how long she's been holding his hand. 'You did well out there, Michael; it's understandable you got a bit emotional. I'm sorry if I–'

'No! Not at all,' he butts in, covering her hand with his own, squeezing it tightly. 'Don't think that for a minute. I knew exactly what was happening out there, and I'm happy with it. You didn't change my status back to smoker, did you?'

'No, I didn't, but I can alter it at any time, well, you can yourself.'

He stares into her eyes, and notices that they are a little reddened, slightly puffy. 'Don't do that,' he says softly. 'I'm grateful for those twenty-seven days. Thank you. There aren't many people who can conjure up twenty-seven days.'

———

They hit The Town: Mick, Dr Pereira, Adam, Jaz, his wife Yolanda in a long night-blue satin gown, and twenty-something daughter Jazelle in a short red lacy dress and pin-thin red Jimmies. The Town is the top-floor, five-star restaurant in Ephesus Dome, three bubbles north of Babylon, where the champagne flows and Mick draws numerous requests for selfies, Facebook friendships, and handshakes. Everybody wants to know how he is. He raises his champagne glass in what becomes a trademark response that's photographed, uploaded, and shared around the world. The *Daily Mail* follows him on Twitter, and the other British dailies are not far behind, plus two dozen from the States including the *New York Times* and *The Washington Post*. Nobody complains as Mick spins from his phone to a phone-toting admirer, to his champagne glass, then back to his phone. By midnight, the traffic is tidal, so Jaz links Mick's accounts to the LifeTime support centre, where the social media team will handle his day-to-day activity.

They move on to Snatch, a high-class jazz bar in Giza Dome, another bubble north, where Mick orders a bottle of sixteen-year-old Bushmills for the table. A three-piece plays cool background music, although the saxophone's swirling low notes soon pull Jaz and Yolanda out onto the small dance floor. Dr Pereira leads an unprotesting Mick out in response, and after a short, ultimately futile attempt at resistance, Adam is taken in hand by Jazelle.

'I haven't danced like this since my wife died,' Mick says, almost to himself, after the first two numbers. Dr Pereira – *Sandy, please* – lifts her head from his shoulder, leans back slightly and looks up into his face.

'I'm sorry, I didn't know your wife had passed,' she replies softly.

'It was a long time ago. I've been a widower for forty-odd years.'

'You never thought to remarry?'

He shrugs. 'I've had a few, what do they call them nowadays, relationships, in my time. But I guess in the early years I felt guilty, and as time went by, I sort of missed the boat. You know, work and stuff...' He trails off, leaving it to sound like he's regretting missed opportunities. Sandy puts her head back onto his shoulder.

'You be ready for dozens of marriage proposals now you're on social media and trending, Michael. You'll need to take care; there'll be alligators in that swamp.'

Mick smiles. 'I've already had three propositions, with photos, you wanna see?'

It's Sandy's turn to smile. 'How sure would you be that any of those photos are going to be genuine?'

'What? Are you suggesting...?'

'I'm not suggesting, Michael, *everybody* knows! Half the photos on DateMe are AI deepfakes.'

'What's DateMe?'

'Oh, Michael!' she gasps, straightening up again. She explains how the in-bubble dating app works for the half-a-million (and growing) residents of SphereCity.

'But how do you know that half the pictures are fake?'

'*Mine* are!' she quips, laughing.

'You're not on DateMe!'

'Sure I am! Wallflower is *so* last century, Michael.'

He shakes his head. 'You'll never be a wallflower.'

The music ends, polite applause replaces it. She takes his arm and steers him back towards their table.

'C'mon, Michael, I think there might be enough left in that sixteen-year-old bottle of Bushmills for us to squeeze out two nightcaps, don't you?'

'That sounds like a wonderful idea, but only the one, I've drunk so much.'

Chapter Eighteen

'Viagra could help men to live LONGER: Blue pill prolongs life
and prevents heart attacks in males with coronary artery disease,
study finds.'
—*Mail Online*, 22 March 2021

H is eyes open and focus on the ceiling fan swirling lazily
above his head; his stomach responds by copying the
motion, so he closes his eyes again. His headache is
monumental; he hasn't suffered one like this since he was a
student. He fights to slow the movement in his stomach, which
stops swirling like suds down a plughole and starts lurching like
a small boat on the high seas in a force-ten gale. His head feels
as though a wooden stake has impaled it deep into the mattress.
Voluntary movement of any kind seems inadvisable, probably
perilous.

But his mind is working sluggishly on a problem. He's no
idea why it's fixated on this issue, it's a minor one, but that's
where his brain has decided to slump: he's certain his room
doesn't have a ceiling fan.

He knows this because he couldn't get to sleep after the flight from the UK and remembers studying the complex design of glass triangles that made up the lampshade above his bed. There was no ceiling fan. He opens his eyes again. Ceiling fan, whirling lazily, producing hardly any draught at all, but whirling nonetheless. Eyes closed again, brain racing – but with little progress towards any sort of sense.

There's water running somewhere. It's the sort of water that takes your mind off a mysterious ceiling fan, he notices. Why would he hear water in his hotel bedroom? For a while, he thinks it's in his mind or maybe in his ears – some hangover after-effect of all the drinks he downed last night.

Last night? What does he remember? Drinks, sure. Lots of drinks. An empty sixteen-year-old bottle of Bushmills. What was he playing at? The water is close. A waterfall? Can't be. A tap? Sounds more like a shower. A shower? There's a shower running. He moves his head, slowly, painfully, feels like it's wrapped in a heavy blanket; the door to the en suite isn't where it was yesterday.

He then notices something else that's in the wrong place: the lacy black brassiere draped over the back of a Regency-style chair in front of the desk. He sits up, his head tries to force him back down onto the pillow, but he resists. Next, he clocks his trousers and underwear on the floor in the middle of the room. Also, panties, the same black lace, right next to the bed, as if they were the last item to be discarded.

'Shit!' His head is in his hands. His memory is a soufflé of empty glasses, bright lights and a smoochy saxophone refrain.

He scrambles from the bed and stumbles across the room, knocking into a heavy armchair on the way. He can't bend to pick up his underwear, afraid the pain in his head will pull him to the floor. So, he sits, arthritically, hauls on his underwear and trousers, cursing quietly as the sweat starts to baste his ribs. He finds his shirt, two buttons missing, damp with sweat and the smell of stale booze and an intoxicating perfume. His jacket is nowhere. Shoes and socks are on the floor in front of a small sofa and coffee table ensemble by the window. On the dainty glass coffee table, there's a half-empty bottle of champagne and two glasses, but it's the mess of discarded white powder that pumps his heart up another gear. He doesn't bother tasting it to see if it's clumsily spilt talc, or something more sinister; he's never tasted either in his life so he probably wouldn't know the difference.

'Jesus!' He smooths his hair back and tries to get some sense out of his muddled brain. Pacing the room is evidently what he should do next as his legs respond to some unconscious instruction and take him, metronome-like, to the window and back. Each time he completes a circuit his eyes pick out the bra, panties, champagne bottle, white powder... After a couple of laps his stomach threatens to empty itself, so he sits on the bed, head and heart pounding like that washing-machine music Will sometimes plays. The shower goes on and on.

'No!' He tries to concentrate, tries to put the jigsaw of last night's memories back together to complete a picture that makes sense. He can get the auditorium, champagne at The Town, with salmon, or was it tuna? All he can taste now is fermenting alcohol of some sort, it could be ethanol, it could be paraffin. There was a band. Was there? No, that was later. Did they go on somewhere else? Was there dancing? Yes, he remembers dancing, slow dancing. He hasn't danced for so long. They were a big group; he cranks his brain – it's like wringing an almost-dry sponge, the memories coming in meagre droplets. He remembers the doctor, Pereira? *Please, call me Sandy!* And a friend of Jaz? His wife? He can't remember her name, something unusual. There were more than that, he's sure.

He gets up, approaches the bathroom door, shower still

running like a late-summer storm out of looming dark clouds, threatening thunder and lightning, uprooted trees, and untold trouble later. His hand is on the handle, but he can't turn it. No idea if it's locked or not, he can't bring himself to try it. Back to the bed. Head in his hands again, as if he might be able to squeeze the things that he's almost remembering out of it, angrily wiping the sweat away like irritating flies.

'Shit!' He takes long breaths, concentrates – he needs to remember. Dinner, they ate dinner. Then they went somewhere else, that was where the music was, and the dance floor. The saxophone refrain invades his concentration and wipes it like a wave over a name drawn in the sand. He tries to see the name again; another wave takes it away before he can make it out in his mind. He tries to hear someone saying it. Jaz introduced her. His wife? Daughter? Similar name to his. Jazzy, or something?

There's a noise in the far corner of the room, like an alarm sounding at the bottom of a deep well. He knows he recognises the sound but can't remember what it signifies. Is it a TV theme tune? No, it's his phone, at the bottom of that deep well. His jacket: his phone's in his jacket. Somewhere over by the picture window – which also wasn't part of his room yesterday. And this view certainly isn't his view, he had mountains yesterday, a metropolis today, mid-sized tower blocks, the one he's in is one of the tallest, he must be ten floors up – although he daren't look down for fear of starting his stomach on a rinse-and-spin cycle. The phone continues to ring. He finds his jacket on the floor behind the curtain. Then he sees the dress. Small, red and lacy, enough material to make a skimpy bikini – at a push. And the pin-thin high heels, the same bright red, discarded carelessly, as if they've been kicked off in a frenzy.

He fumbles for the phone, eight missed calls, all Paula.

He pings it on.

'Adam?' she blurts.

'Yeah, hi,' he gasps, failing miserably to sound calm, relaxed, even pleased to hear from her.

'Adam? I've been calling, why weren't you answering?'

'Oh, I'm sorry, we had a big night last night, Mick was a hit at the conference; we went out for drinks, back late, overslept...' He starts putting his shoes on, stuffs his socks in a pocket, quickly crosses the room and stands by the door, ready to exit into the corridor if the shower stops.

'I called you a dozen times.'

'I'm sorry, I think my battery died. There was a lot of action yesterday with Mick joining Facebook and Twitter and stuff.' He wipes sweat, a thick sheen on his pasty brow, scans the room to make sure he's got everything – watch, wedding ring, his phone? His phone? He can't see – it's in his hand.

'Oh, right, all going well then? Mission accomplished?'

'Yeah, great, he's like a sixteen-year-old with a new phone.'

There's a pause as he waits for her to reply, and she waits for him to continue. Then they both start to speak together, and they play *you go first, no you*, then they speak together again.

'Adam...?'

'Yeah, you go...'

'Any idea when you'll be back?'

'A couple more days, maybe, it's taking off a bit faster than I'd expected. I think Jaz has got plans for Mick to do a bit more media stuff...' The silence lengthens, he's about to break it, but she starts.

'Adam?'

'Yeah, go on.'

'I wanted to save it, Adam. I wanted to tell you when you got back...'

He knows exactly what she's going to say.

Chapter Nineteen

'Every Hotdog Eaten Shortens Life by 36 Minutes. Experts
Have Assessed Which Foods Add and Shorten Life Spans –
Nuts Add 26 Minutes and Salmon 16 Minutes.'
—*The Daily Telegraph*, 19 August 2021

Ten minutes later, Adam ends the call and throws his
phone onto the bed. The tears begin immediately; he
shudders and gulps with his hand clamped over his mouth. Is it
all guilt? Are there no tears of joy? It was hard enough trying to
make his voice portray the unbounded joy he knew he would
have felt had Paula not told him today, now, here – amongst this
garage sale of assorted lingerie and drugs scattered around his
room – *not* his fucking room – and the shower in the bathroom
still running. Now he leans against the wall feeling desperate.
He fights the tears. He and Paula have been married nearly two
years. The most blissful time of his life. Hers too, he's positive.
What the hell has he done? He can't make his brain reconstruct
any memories beyond some club, a dance floor, a bloody

saxophone. What the hell happened? He can't have. He wouldn't. He simply wouldn't!

'Jazelle?' he shouts, knocking the door – where did *that* name come from? The shower's relentless. 'Jazelle? You in there?' He tries the handle, it gives; he pushes the door slightly, that gives too. 'Jazelle? You in here?' Steam starts to seep out of the crack between door and jamb, inside it's a sauna, clouds billow past him as he edges the door wider. 'Jazelle?' He steps inside, eyes averted for modesty, although God knows why?

The sound of the water now drills into his hangover headache; steam wafts past his face; condensation rolls down the walls and the enormous mirror, and drips like tears from the fittings and the ceiling – but beyond that, the bathroom is shockingly empty.

Adam jumps a cab back to his hotel fearing a ride on a Segway would result in a cocktail of sixteen-year-old whiskey and salmon (or tuna) spraying into the bushes at high speed. His head pounds but, like a loyal friend, refuses to reveal the end of last night's movie.

He sits on the bed in the sanctuary of his room: all doors in their rightful places; spare lingerie absent; likewise, powders, running water and ceiling fan.

And he cries.

'The prodigal!' Jaz beams as he opens the front door, ushering Adam inside and through towards the terrace. 'Some night, huh? You get back okay?'

'Yeah, sure,' Adam replies, not wanting to reveal what Jaz, hopefully, doesn't know. 'You?'

'Well, maybe a few too many champagnes, a few too many mojitos, a few too many shots of Mick's Bushmills, and it got pretty outta hand by the end. Last thing I remember is Mick and Sandy jiving in the street then we sorta lost 'em. I think Sandy might've whisked him off to hers for a nightcap; he's a bit of a sly old fox, isn't he? Jazelle did well, we don't usually socialise together, so she was happy when that pack of her mates showed up to give her some breathing space – no idea where you disappeared off to, or when. You know you left your tie in Snatch?'

'Where?'

'The club. We brought it back for you; it's on the table there.'

'Oh, great, thanks.'

'Helluva night!'

They reach the terrace to find Mick dozing in one of the armchairs, tie askew, white shirt less crisp now, jacket auditioning for a charity-shop rail.

'You wanna coffee?' Jaz asks Adam, with a sly wink towards Mick. 'We bin drinking nothing but, and a fat lotta good it's doing him!'

'Love one,' Adam says, flopping into an armchair and gazing out across the lake, his eyes seeing nothing.

'So, where *did* you get to?' he hears Jaz yelling from the kitchen.

'Oh, I always flake early when the booze starts to flow,' he replies, stepping into the living area so he won't wake Mick, but not entering the kitchen to avoid a face-to-face inquisition. 'I was wasted, so I headed off, didn't want to party-poop. I could see Mick, especially, was having a good time, he's not really a party animal, you know.'

'Get away, he was the life, soul and probably corpse, 'scuse the expression. He was havin' a ball. He's a great guy. Bowled up here about an hour ago and been asleep in that chair, on and off, ever since.'

Adam creeps back onto the terrace and tries to contemplate the lake. The water's still as an ice rink; he wishes his stomach was the same.

'You had some breakfast?' Jaz asks as he puts a pot and a fresh cup onto the table.

'Couple of pastries, I'm fine,' Adam lies. The likelihood of anything other than coffee remaining in his stomach for more than twenty seconds isn't promising; he's not that convinced about the coffee's chances.

'Listen,' Jaz says, sitting on the sofa next to Adam's armchair and lowering his voice. 'That thing yesterday with Mick, it's gone enormous, the internet, international press, TV, radio, everyone's after a piece of him. I was half expecting it to be press at the door when you rang.'

'Really?'

'Yeah, it's fantastic. He's the British doc tugging the heartstrings of everyone. Couldn't have planned it better if we'd tried. That thing with the extra twenty-seven days? Pure marketing gold. All we've got to do now is nurse him through the frenzy, then help him drip his social media with tidbits and the rest of it will take care of itself. That okay?'

'Sure, no problem.'

'Great job, Adam.'

'You too,' Adam replies. 'You were very smooth with him over the social media sign-up. I was nervous about how he was going to react.'

'Lamb to the slaughter?' Jaz says, smiling. 'If he ever wakes up, I'm gonna take him golfing today, maybe fishing if he prefers. I'll put out a bit of it on my social media and to the news hounds, so we don't end up with a paparazzi stakeout. You think Mick'll be good for that?'

'I should think so, he seems to enjoy the limelight, let's make sure we don't let it overwhelm him.'

Jaz nods, pours coffee for Adam and himself, leans forward again, whispering now. 'You don't think there's a problem, do you? I mean, that little hiccup on stage yesterday. I know it ended up all's well and all that. But you don't think Mick's got an issue buried somewhere that we might be about to uncover?'

'Meaning?'

'I'm not sure, I'm no psychoanalyst, but, you know, is he handling all this okay? He's ending up way out front as far as the British wing of LifeTime's concerned, kinda superstar status all of a sudden, and not only in the UK. He's trending throughout the States as well; everybody seems to be on his side. Is he going to be able to handle the exposure?'

Adam sips coffee, wonders why nobody, himself included, has bothered checking the locks on this stable door until now.

Mick revives shortly before lunchtime, and with more of a headache, and worse memory problems than Adam. His LifeBuddy, however, soon takes centre stage. Sandy has apparently spent half the night giving him a crash course in how it works. First thing it does is tell him he's dehydrated, and he needs to drink water. Nothing but. So, Mick drinks water like it's Cask Reserve at a rich cousin's wedding. Lunch? He checks his LifeBuddy. A grilled or poached salmon seems to be exactly what he needs, promising to add another thirty minutes to his projection. Some lightly steamed broccoli and a little rice will add another thirty minutes or so. Pudding? Maybe some fresh fruit, another thirty minutes. And afterwards, fishing or golf?

Golf wins hands down, eighteen holes is worth another hour or so, fishing is negative an hour: Mick vows never to fish again.

Over lunch, Mick pours forth like an evangelical preacher with not long to live, Sandy having been elevated to the status of biblical prophet.

'Look, Sandy says if I tap in here six ounces of salmon, grilled, it'll show me it's worth thirty minutes. Then, if this thing was fused on, once I'd eaten it, it'd automatically add the time to my projection, the bloody thing would *sense* that I'd eaten grilled salmon, or gone for a walk, or whatever, and add it onto my projection, and show it to me on my wrist. Can you believe that?'

Jaz and Adam shrug. Yeah, they suppose they can. Mick barely registers them; he's in six-year-old mode, showing a Lego Technic model he's made at home to his teacher. *And if you push this button, the missile will fire from under the wing, watch.*

'Sandy showed me how the LifeBuddy will suggest diet, exercise, rest, everything. I can do it or not, it's not in control of me, but I can see which options are good, and how many minutes they'll add to my projection. Then, if I want to go with the suggestions, I can. It's amazing. I've told Sandy I'll be up for the power walk tomorrow morning, that's worth another hour. You should come too, Adam. You don't get nearly enough exercise.'

Adam tries to make a joke, says he's fit enough, but he's not fit enough for Mick. Does Adam know about microlives? No, he doesn't. Well, Mick'll tell him (whether Adam wants to know or not). An average adult life is roughly half-a-million hours long. This time can be split into one million half-hours, each one called a microlife. So, every day is forty-eight microlives long. This isn't some harebrained theory; the guy who worked it out is a professor at Cambridge. But here's the thing! Here's the secret! You listening?

They're listening, but only just.

You can *waste* your microlives faster than that! You can use up more than forty-eight in a day. How? Easy. Smoke twenty cigarettes in a day and that's ten microlives thrown away. That day won't use up forty-eight of your microlives; it'll use up *fifty-eight*! That's twenty-nine hours used up in a twenty-four-hour day. Mick's decision not to smoke any more still stands after three days and is now inviolate. Same with booze (he's given that up as well). Glass of whiskey? Pint of beer? One microlife, that's thirty minutes off your life, *gone!* Steak? Another microlife, thirty minutes off your life. Steak is *off!* Two hours in front of the TV? Or behind a fishing rod? Another microlife gone. He'll play some golf instead, three or four extra microlives *added* to his life, depending on how many holes he plays. Another hour or two! He also needs statins; they'll add a microlife a day, the list goes on and on apparently, as does Mick. He's on his high horse; he's taken the high ground; Adam thinks he's as high as a kite.

Adam passes on the golf, promises he'll walk back to the hotel instead of taking a hover, or a Segway, or a cab. *Yes, I promise! Jeez!*

Adam doesn't walk back to the hotel: as soon as he's sure Mick's out of sight, he sneaks back to the lot and takes a cab to Ron's office. On the way he ponders last night again, although it's not through choice, his brain is binge-playing one episode from the boxed set of his life: it's *The One Where Adam Wakes Up In Someone Else's Bedroom* – not one of the funniest. In the cool light of a sunny day, nothing seems to have changed, but his memories from this morning's rude wake up, those that he can get to, drag his heart into the pit of his stomach. Earlier, he'd checked his wallet in his jacket pocket. Nothing stolen he was relieved to find, at least that was a silver lining. But the receipt for a three-pack of condoms stopped him in his tracks like a stone under his Segway.

Suddenly, even his silver lining has a cloud.

Chapter Twenty

'How Humanity Gave Itself an Extra Life. Between 1920 and 2020, the average human life span doubled. How did we do it?'
—*The New York Times Magazine*, 27 April 2021

'What happened to you?' Ron's expression is that of a witness at a particularly gruesome road traffic accident.

'Oh, late night with Mick and Jaz after the thing at the theatre. Bit of booze flowed.'

Ron smirks; he knows Adam isn't a big drinker.

'Bit of booze? You look like you been hit by the beer truck. Black coffees on me, then?'

They sit outside on one of the tasteful wooden tables near the trees. Adam cradles his coffee and stares into it like he might be able to see his future, or maybe his past, in the steam.

'Something the matter?' Ron says eventually, after they've sat and ignored each other for a couple of minutes. 'It's like chatting with a corpse.'

Adam seems to come out of a trance, sucks air deeply.

'What d'you know of Jaz's daughter?'

'What? You mean *apart* from the fact I never knew he had a daughter. Why?'

'Oh, this is really fucked up. She joined us last night. We ended up in some club. There was some dancing, some drinking, nothing sensational–'

'And?'

'And the next thing I remember, seriously, *the... next... thing*, is waking up in the morning in some strange hotel suite, naked in the bed, with all her clothes scattered around the room. *All* her clothes. There's a bottle of champagne, half drunk, two glasses, what appears to be coke on the tabletop...'

'And Jaz's daughter?'

'Well, that's the strangest thing. The shower's running, so I sit there panicking and waiting for her to come out. So, I wait, and I wait. Finally, I go into the bathroom and it's empty. Shower's running, no one inside.'

Ron makes a *weird* face. 'So... what do you reckon?' he asks tentatively.

'I have no idea. I can't believe I don't remember anything. *Anything*. From the dancing to waking up in that bedroom. Nothing. Not one word, not one image. I can't believe I cheated on Paula, but I can't understand what happened.'

'So, how did this girl disappear without her clothes? She run out the hotel naked?'

Adam shrugs, shakes his head, decides that's not a good idea.

'Search me. It was some kind of penthouse suite. Maybe she lives there? I didn't check the wardrobes. Maybe she'd gone out in a dressing gown for coffees or something and was coming back. I didn't hang around.'

'And the shower?'

'Again, who knows? Maybe she turned it on, then forgot it, or panicked, threw some clothes on and fled? Once my brain stops pulsating, I might be able to think, but at the moment it's all such a mess. I've no clue what happened.'

Over the next couple of days, Mick's LifeBuddy steers him towards the microlives to be gained on the golf course. The golf buggy also gets a rest as Mick insists on walking. Jaz muses (but doesn't say) that it would be even healthier were they to ditch the pull-along trolleys and carry their clubs on their shoulders. He doesn't voice this because he's afraid Mick might think he's taking the piss – but his bigger fear is that Mick will think it's a good idea.

Mick develops a sudden taste for fresh fruit juice, raw vegetables, grilled chicken, while his interviews with the media turn into evangelical sales pitches for a return to simple living, healthy eating, and the purchase of ten-thousand-dollar LifeBuddies. You'd think he was on commission, but it's simply the genuine goodwill and acute tunnel vision of the recently converted. Some of the journos even develop the fixed stare usually found on those who answer the door to the God squad, but he gets good write ups from all of them. He's flavour of the month, untouchable: the Ponzi-scheme godfather, riding high before anyone dares voice concern.

Mick's final appointment of the trip is another appearance in the auditorium, to give his considered opinion on his LifeBuddy. They start again in the bar where the atmosphere is akin to backstage at a rock concert: Mick signing autographs; posing for selfies; offering snippets of wisdom to adoring faces; drinking only mineral water.

Adam and Jaz stick to beers unless Mick's up for another bottle of the Bushmills Madeira – but he shakes his head, points at the inside of his forearm: *Nah, mineral water for me thanks, microlives! Imagine how many hours I'm adding to my projection!*

They're on time into the auditorium, although they're late to their seats as Mick is swamped by well-wishers he doesn't know from Eve – eighty, maybe ninety per cent of his well-wishers are female. They stroke his shoulders with the studied disinterest of professional pickpockets; stare into his eyes with the pointed concentration of stage hypnotists; hang on to his jacket like pilgrims in the presence of a holy man. He takes it all like he's Bruce Springsteen on his valedictory tour rather than Mick Strong, virgin celebrity.

A single spotlight picks out Hannah Lennox as she walks to the microphone from stage right to reverential applause. Gone is the black and white piano-keyboard outfit she adopted for her meeting with Adam, tonight she's in business grey, everything: jacket, blouse, pencil skirt, shoes.

'Good evening, everybody, and welcome to tonight's event, a chance to hear Dr Michael Strong's opinions on his trial with our brand-new LifeBuddy, followed by a Q&A where you'll get another chance to quiz the good doctor. I won't keep you from tonight's event, ladies and gentlemen, please welcome Dr Strong.'

The applause is enthusiastic as Mick climbs the steps while fixing a loose cuff then pointing into the crowd, appearing to recognise someone, a long-lost friend, maybe. He repeats the pantomime point and wave, point and wave. Adam sniffs a Jaz-inspired *how to mount the stage like a politician* tutorial, it could be Obama, it could be Trump. Mick shakes Hannah's hand and moves to the lectern, pointing and smiling at yet another ghost. Adam's mind drifts to the afternoon at Sacklow Hall where all this kicked off. He's not sure whether wildest dream or worst nightmare is the most appropriate way to describe his amazement at how they've got from there to here.

Mick takes a folded sheet of notes from his inside pocket and flattens it out on the lectern.

'I feel like the best man at a wedding,' he begins, to generous, supportive laughter from around the auditorium, the goodwill pouring towards him would halt a charging elephant. It's packed again, but this time there are people sitting in the aisles and standing at the back. Jaz has told Adam that they're live streaming on Facebook and *CNN*, and that the BBC are taking a recording and have a reporter waiting for an interview afterwards.

Everywhere they've gone over the last couple of days, posters and adverts for this event have been appearing on billboards, digital displays, Facebook ads, tweets and the rest. It's like their whole trip has been leading up to this moment – and Adam has a sneaking feeling, no, it's more than that, Adam has a premonition, a foreboding, that Jaz has one last, bigger than the unveiling of the LifeBuddy, surprise to round the show off tonight with something of a bang. He wouldn't expect anything less from him.

Adam feels embarrassed that Jaz keeps congratulating him on how well he's promoting Mick, that the week has been an outstanding success. In his own mind, Adam knows that most of the success has been generated by Jaz's initiatives. He wonders if it's all been a clever ploy on Jaz's part: pull out all the stops here in the States, then sit back and watch Adam carry on the good work when they return to the UK. Jaz is clearly at ease with all his publicity and marketing tricks; he's got an enormous team behind him who he's been constantly calling and messaging to *set this up* and *have a word with* X and *start something on Facebook*. He's even confided proudly to Adam that the ambush of Mick by the hospital joggers on the first morning was exactly that – an ambush, orchestrated by him. Meanwhile, Jaz has spent his own time golfing with Mick, while this publicity blitzkrieg has exploded around them. Adam's acutely aware that he'll find it a tricky Broadway show to take on tour to the wilds of north Norfolk.

Mick speaks for about ten minutes. Jaz's team have written his script after a short conference call where Jaz and some of his media people have guided Mick through the features of his LifeBuddy, so that they can cull a selection of complimentary quotes. It's polished; Mick has no trouble delivering it. He'd make a decent salesman, Adam muses somewhat jealously.

Jaz joins Mick on stage to more applause. Again, his clothes tell everyone else not to bother in the cool-class category. He takes a microphone and comperes the Q&A, running through a string of questions that are clearly designed to allow Mick to sing the praises of his LifeBuddy. *What do you think are the main benefits of having a LifeBuddy? It looks really cool on you; do you agree that the design is especially well done? We know that it's a very high-spec piece of kit, designed by a team of specialists in health, computing and mathematical modelling; can you think of anything that they should include in future models?* Er, no, not really.

The lights dim, Dr Sandy Pereira enters stage right to loud, respectful applause. Her walk is purposeful, her nod to the audience is perfunctory: she has important business to conduct, dressed in the sort of understated designer trouser suit and trademark white lab coat that would convince you to put your life in her hands – and maybe your life savings as well. It certainly says *don't mess with me* with all the authority of a scientific paper chock-full of complicated equations and long Latin words.

An air kiss for Jaz. Two for Mick, plus a hug, and an elongated *let me take the measure of your health with my superhuman powers of observation* stare, as she keeps her hands on his shoulders and looks him up and down a couple of times.

Yes, you're fine, I can see it. She smiles, everybody else seeming to let out simultaneous sighs of relief. Then they all clap again – like seals waiting for food.

Jaz hands the mic to Dr Pereira who faces Mick.

'Dr Strong, you've had your LifeBuddy for a few days now. Would you like to hear what the medical team have made of the data it's collected from you?'

Mick nods, sure, why not? He's at home with these people. One of them.

Adam glances at Jaz, who at that exact moment is staring straight back, nodding a conspiratorial little nod. *You wouldn't expect anything less of me, would you, Adam? Watch and learn.*

'We have some amazing figures for you, one of the headlines being your blood pressure. Do you know what your blood pressure usually is?'

Mick shrugs an apology. 'I think it's usually a little high, not too much, but a little.'

'Yes, that's right, the LifeBuddy picked that up right at the start. But let me tell you, over the days that you've been wearing it, we've detected small, but measurable indications that it's starting to fall slightly. What do you think of that?'

The applause sweeps his answer away as Mick smiles his appreciation. Adam can't help but wonder what they'd expected was going to happen to his blood pressure after he'd arrived soaked in Bushmills and then spent the best part of a week lounging around the pool, sipping juices and buggying (then walking) around the golf course. It was hardly a recipe for an aneurysm. There's more good news about his cholesterol, step count, vitamin levels – who's to say, he might even be able to remember the plot of *A Dry White Season*, which is his poolside pal.

'We've also been monitoring the oxygen levels in your blood, Dr Strong, and they too are showing improvements over the past few days.' More applause, some whooping, which Mick would usually frown at, but here, it seems to please him. 'Have you any ideas why that might be?'

'I imagine it's because I've stopped smoking. What do *you* think? You're a doctor.'

This nearly brings the house down; even Jaz, Adam and Sandy Pereira join the laughter.

'Well, *Doctor* Strong,' Sandy says, eliciting more laughter, 'I absolutely agree with you, but tell me, we know you stopped smoking because you weren't allowed to here in SphereCity. You're still sticking to your decision to stop for good. Is that right?'

'Yes, it is.' The cheering is instantaneous, a standing ovation.

'Can you tell me why you've made that wonderful decision?'

'That's simple. I stopped smoking because of this.' He stretches out his arm, shows his LifeBuddy, and the room explodes. People are on their feet cheering; phones are up filming; cameras are flashing. Dr Pereira has to struggle to make herself heard. She's swimming out as the tide is coming in, but she's a strong swimmer – and she has science on her side.

'Now, we've got a mountain of data out of your LifeBuddy over the past few days, and I'm delighted to tell you that the vast majority of it is positive, but I suppose the figure everyone's waiting to see is your projection.'

A ripple of anticipation moves through the crowd, more people are pinging their phones into life and nudging each other. Adam hears his phone trilling in his jacket pocket and mutes it.

Jaz has told Adam earlier that there was a sweep on how many days Mick's projection would rise by. Adam had felt a wash of distaste at the idea. Effectively, they were betting on when Mick was projected to die. He wonders if Mick's aware of the reason for the increase in interest.

'So, Dr Strong, let's show the audience how many days you've added to – or lost from – your projection over your time here.'

The lights dim, the giant screen descends like a ghost so that it's right behind them, directly above their heads. It's showing the data from Mick's LifeBuddy: heartbeat is 82bpm; blood pressure is 135 over 92, but, given the circumstances, respiratory rate is steady at twenty-two breaths a minute, respiratory effort mildly increased, on and on it goes, temperature, blood oxygen level, Adam's surprised he can't see Mick's bank balance and credit rating.

'Obviously, this is the standard data available through the unfused monitor, but we are able to show you Dr Strong's precise microlives balance, one of the features of the premium service available if the LifeTime member chooses fusion–'

Near the back of the auditorium, a low chant starts up – *Fusion, fu-sion* – Dr Pereira talks over it.

'So, let's check out Dr Strong's microlives balance over the time that he's been wearing his LifeBuddy.'

The screen behind flickers, numbers scroll, Adam's surprised there's no drum roll and cymbal crash as the final figures appear. The audience erupts.

'Dr Michael Strong, since you started to wear your LifeBuddy, your microlife balance has increased by one thousand–' The noise is unbelievable. Dr Pereira has to wait a full minute before she's able to continue. 'Your microlife balance has increased by one thousand four hundred and ninety-six microlives.'

Now the rafters are at risk. There are only a couple of thousand people in the auditorium, but they are making enough noise to rival a last-minute winning goal in a Manchester derby.

Amid the camera flashes and whooping, the chant starts again, *Fu-sion, fu-sion!* This time more people join in, clapping along to the syllables like a heartbeat at the end of a marathon sprint finish.

Dr Pereira manages to quieten them, but not silence them, as she shakes Mick by the hand.

'That's fantastic news, Dr Strong. Can you remember what your projection was in days when we put the LifeBuddy on earlier this week?'

'It was two hundred and thirty-seven days.'

'That's correct. Can you show the audience what it shows now?'

Mick taps and strokes his LifeBuddy, the screen flipping to the main display of his projection. A camera operator moves in, and the figures appear on the large screen.

'Your LifeTime projection is now two hundred and thirty-two days, that's the five days you've been wearing it. But what I can do is recalculate it to show the effects of all your golfing and non-smoking.' Dr Pereira taps on a small tablet and the numbers change. 'Your projection is now two hundred and sixty-three days. An increase of thirty-one days since you arrived, Dr Strong.'

The crowd roars, Mick beams, Dr Pereira waits for calm.

'Now, obviously, you understand that this sort of huge increase in projection can't be achieved every week. You can only give up smoking once, you can only radically change your diet once. But, as we all can see, you can make a difference to your projection, and although you can't gain thirty-odd days every week, if you keep up your healthier lifestyle you will continue to add some time.'

FU-sion, FU-sion, FU-sion.

'But now it's time to end the trial, unless, of course, you've decided—'

FU-SION! FU-SION!

'Dr Strong?'

'I-I don't know–'

'It's a big decision, Dr Strong; it's irreversible if you decide–'

FU-SION! FU-SION! FU-SION! FU-SION!

'It only takes thirty seconds; we could do it right now if you want–'

He looks her in the eyes, she returns his stare, smiles. He gives the slightest nod of his head. The big screen has closed in on his face, so everybody sees it. The response is delirium in the hall. Seats slam up as people swarm to the front, leaning onto the stage, setting up their phones to record the moment.

'Are you sure, Dr Strong?' Dr Pereira says, still smiling at him.

'Of course he's sure!' someone yells from the front. The entire hall is now chanting – *FU-SION! FU-SION! FU-SION!*

With Jaz's help, Dr Pereira manages to quieten the noise enough to speak.

'You must be sure about this, Dr Strong. Once fused, it can't be removed, but it will give you instant data on your current projection as it increases and decreases in response to your behaviour. It will analyse every mouthful or sip you swallow, every cigarette you smoke, every step you jog, every drug you pop, snort or inject and then calculate its effect and register it positively or negatively on your LifeBuddy in real time. Eat an apple and you'll see your LifeTime extend by, what, twenty seconds, I think? Take a drag and watch it decrease by nearly a minute. Snort a line and see your life expectancy fall by twenty minutes. Eat a healthy meal or take a brisk walk and your projection on your monitor will change instantly, and these changes will be calculated in minutes and seconds, so you'll see the impact of every piece of fruit you eat, every round of golf you play. Are you absolutely sure, Dr Strong? There's no going back if we do this.'

Adam keeps his face straight but wonders if he's gate-crashed the Mad Hatter's tea party. *Could I have a cup of tea?*

One minute, Sir.

Is that plus or minus?

Mick gazes out at the faces, all trained on him, filled with expectation and hope. He searches in vain for Adam, who was surprised by the surge to the front and is now squeezed behind the first four rows of the throng who've invaded the space in front of his front-row seat. It happened so quickly; it was almost as if the move to the front had been planned.

'Let's do it,' Mick says.

Chapter Twenty-One

'How to live longer: Positive people more likely to live past 85
years old, study says.'
—*Daily Express*, 15 March 2021

The arrivals hall reminds Adam of film he's seen of the Beatles arriving at some airport, but without the screaming. Mick spends over an hour answering questions, submitting to selfies, signing autographs, and miming his champagne-toast celebration to anyone who shouts *I'll drink to that!* before embarking on a series of interviews with the UK press and a news conference for TV and radio.

This strategy had been agreed by Mick and set up by Jaz and Adam. The argument was: try to hide from the interest and Mick'd face a paparazzi siege at the Manor House that would swamp the village. So, a deal was struck: as well as the touchdown commitments, Mick would contract to a series of regular media interviews and photo opportunities, TV specials and newspaper exclusives – all in return for a moratorium on the doorstep treatment, as much to save the village as Mick, who would pocket a tidy sum for fulfilling his ongoing part of the deal.

Jaz's thinking is that if they try to restrict access to Mick too tightly, then every gold nugget that the journos or snappers managed to pan, would only increase the value of the next. Guarantee them a regular flow and the snappers won't need to climb the trees at the back of the house or park their vans on the village green. Any enterprising minnows, tempted to step out of line, are promised a quick duffing up by the heavyweights in the pack, fearful that a rogue hack or pap will threaten the free flow to everyone else. The agreed thinking, as Jaz had predicted, is that it'll be so much easier for the journos to sit in the offices waiting for Adam's call, than it will be for them to hang out in the bushes on a wet and windy north Norfolk clifftop. So, it's past midnight before Adam drops an exhausted Mick off at the Manor House, before heading home.

Paula sleeps on the sofa, one hand protectively draped over her midriff. He stares at her in the moonlight that streams in through the French windows – his fairy-tale princess. He tumbles his options for the twentieth time, wheels spinning like a fruit machine promising pleasure or heartbreak at the pull of a handle. His gut reaction was to tell her the truth, that'd he'd been so out of his head that he's no idea what really happened. But that makes him look, and feel, like some shallow kid, no backbone, no integrity. How could he ever expect her to look at him the same way again? And, as much as he hates the idea of lying to her, the thought of breaking her heart doesn't compete.

He sits softly on the sofa and puts his hand on top of hers. He can't. He can't destroy the happiness he knows she's feeling as she sleeps, blissfully unaware of his torment. The pain of carrying his secret will be a price he'll suffer and pay alone. It's his heart that's been broken, and by his own stupidity. He vows to make sure it remains the only one. A penance, his secret atonement. She'll never suffer it.

He picks her up without waking her and carries her upstairs.

Family tradition, first Sunday of every month: lunch at Mick's. It began years ago, when Michaela started worrying about Mick's state of mind after she and Steve had moved out of the Manor and Mick began to look increasingly isolated. She twisted Steve's arm until it nearly popped out of its socket and, as the family grew, she co-opted every new addition with an expectation that they would attend whenever possible. Over the years, rather surprisingly, it started to work (despite Steve's initial fears that it would become *Christmas, every bloody month*). Mick's house was big enough to host the initial 'impromptu' Sunday share (with Mick taking responsibility for providing all the booze), and a mixture of guilt and pleasure has kept it going with surprisingly few absentees.

Over the years, the Sunday share has played host to announcements of family news. So, nobody is surprised when, after an eclectic mix of vegetarian falafel (Paula and Adam); two takeaway pizzas (Steve and Cathy); and a two-litre tub of Death by Chocolate ice cream (Michaela), Paula and Adam stand up and call (rather unsuccessfully) for silence.

Paula, who has spent days planning her speech, catches Michaela's eye, starts sobbing uncontrollably and sits down again. Adam is left holding the embryo, as it were.

'She's pregnant,' he announces to cheers and shrieks, and the uncorking of some of Mick's champagne horde.

'When's it due?' Mick asks as he half fills Paula's flute – he's stoically sticking to mineral water.

'Seventh of April,' she replies with a teary smile and a signal that she won't be drinking too much bubbly.

'Oh, that's a shame.' Will groans loudly, as Steve calculates likely Cup Final dates.

'Why's that?' Mick asks, continuing around the room with the bottle.

'Cos you'll be dead by then,' Will replies glumly. He's spent the morning pressing the touchscreen buttons on Mick's wrist, so he's best placed to know these things.

'Don't count on it,' Mick says breezily as he completes the circuit. 'As Adam has said, there is a marginal something. What is it, Adam?'

'Margin of error.'

'That's the Johnny. There's a marginal error, which means you can't count on it happening on the day, so to speak. It's a guide, not a countdown to a nuclear attack. That's what Jaz told me. That not right, Adam?'

'That's right, Mick. It's only a general guide.'

'Plus, all my healthy eating is adding days to my *projection*.' He nods pointedly at Adam, who smiles at Mick's perfect command of the appropriate terminology. 'I wouldn't be surprised if I didn't live another year or so.'

'Really, GG?'

'Really. And I have to say, I'm feeling better for the change of diet, especially. Should've done it years ago.'

'You serious about all this, Granddad?' Paula asks, now recovered from her tears. 'All this healthy eating lark? No more booze? No more ciggies?'

'Absolutely,' Mick replies, completely straight. 'And I might have a few more reforms in the pipeline. You wait and see...'

Michaela picks up a book from the sofa, flicks through the pages. She's always the last to leave; she can never work out why. Is it to make sure everyone's tidied up properly? Steve often leaves his empty cans or bottles next to wherever he's been sitting. Is it to let Mick down slowly? Save him from going from full house to busted flush in the starting of a couple of cars? Or, is it maybe to have one last row with the old bugger?

'You should give that a read,' Mick comments from the high horse which is his habitual armchair. 'It's written by a professor from Cambridge University, tells you how to keep yourself healthy and add time to your life. Give up all those cream cakes and rubbish you eat.'

'Good, is it?' Michaela responds, settling herself on the sofa as if she's preparing for the Le Mans 24.

'Very,' Mick replies. 'Very clever bloke.'

'It says here...' Michaela reads, pointing at the page so Mick knows she's quoting, '...that having a religious belief adds time to your life. That mean you're going to be joining me in church?'

Mick scowls. The idea that he would voluntarily enter a church is as likely as him taking up pole vaulting. He's read this bit in the book and has dismissed it as poppycock. However, he's not keen to surrender the high ground or his high horse.

'I know,' he says, thoughtfully. 'I've always felt Celia would be waiting for me somewhere. I've got quite a spiritual side, you know.'

'I don't think that counts,' Michaela grumps. 'I think you have to actually *believe* in God, maybe even step inside a church.'

'Nonsense. Is it only *your* church that counts? The happy clappies? What about Hindus and all them? It says they get the same effect, and they don't even have churches.'

Michaela sighs, wonders what they can chat about next. She's been digging a bit more on the internet; there are a few slightly unsavoury articles about LifeTime doing the rounds. The problem is, the articles are mostly about how their marketing and legal departments are hugely active in shutting down (actually, shutting *up*) any kind of criticism long before it reaches the mainstream. So, the more she searches for information about LifeTime, the only things she finds are cases where they have managed to gag whoever it is who is trying to investigate them.

LifeTime apparently use things called SLAPPs, Strategic Lawsuits Against Public Participation, with huge enthusiasm and against the smallest critics: bloggers, journalists, campaigners, whistleblowers, anyone who asks awkward questions. Or even ordinary questions like, *How accurate are your projections? Can we see the data they're based on?* It's quite difficult to get to the meat of the criticisms as the SLAPPs close the debate with threats of defamation, which are hugely expensive to defend against. All that's left is a mountain of these lawsuits but little detail on what's being alleged or denied. She remembers scoffing when Steve had told her that LifeTime were even attempting to stop people calling their product *the last app you'll ever need*, or the Death App. But it's true. Against her usual judgement she decides not to raise the issue with Mick, not now, anyway. Maybe after she's done a little more digging. But that's the problem with these SLAPPy things: there's nowhere to dig, because every criticism has been SLAPPed.

'Just off to the tip,' Steve yells into the house.

'I'll come with you,' Cathy shouts back. He'll be in a good

mood; he's wanted to dig up those brambles for a while now. Plan in motion.

They chat about his ideas for expanding their allotment and she agrees (after long consideration) that the bottom end of the lawn can go. He's probably been building up to ask her that, so now's the perfect time to concede it, as it means he owes her.

She suggests the long way back and *how about a coffee?* as they pass the Watch Café on the clifftop. As the sun comes out coffee morphs into a light lunch, she's going to have a beer, why not? He decides to join her.

The girl from the café comes out and puts up their parasol. *It is getting warm, isn't it? Lovely!*

Dessert?

Why not?

Coffee?

Actually, I fancy another beer...

Yeah, go on then, me too.

Ducks in a row, locked and loaded, ready to rumble.

'Steve, I've had an idea about Will.'

'What about him?'

'This thing that Mick's bought him...'

Silence.

'I was thinking, why don't we get him checked out? Full medical, and if it comes up with nothing, I'll accept what you're saying. It's rubbish. Forget it.'

Steve mines the last thin seams of apple crumble and custard.

'To put my mind at rest. If the doctor says he's fine, then I'll trust the doctor over this American rubbish. Deal?'

He shrugs. 'We'll probably have to pay. Waste of money.'

'It'll put my mind at rest.'

He breathes deeply, threatens the integrity of the bowl as he goes for the last bits of custard. 'If it makes you happy.'

She smiles, leans over and kisses him on the cheek. Now, all she has to do is convince Michaela to come with her; make sure Steve agrees not to; and deal with the small matter of the four-hundred pounds the Davidson Clinic on Harley Street has quoted.

She scoops the last of her ice cream with her finger, notices Steve looking pensive. She's been so wrapped up in Will, she hasn't really thought about Steve that much.

'You thought about your projection? Intrigued to see what it says?' she asks, absent-mindedly licking the ice cream off her finger.

He snorts, shakes his head slowly. 'Not really. If I was that interested, I wouldn't wait till next January, I'd open it now. I can't give it that much thought. I'll open it if you want me to.'

This rocks her. She hadn't intended to go down this track, but if she thinks about it, it's only logical: she agreed to open Will's projection; isn't she worried about Steve? But she doesn't want to say yes, not quite now, she's got enough on her plate with Will. He's looking at her, waiting for an answer. She can hardly say *no, I'm not worried about you at all.*

Chapter Twenty-Two

'How to live longer: Walking every day promotes longevity –
the amount you need to do.'
—*Daily Express*, 5 February 2021

Can't be! Michaela thinks to herself, as she drops her Fiesta into second to take the hill up towards the clifftop. She slows as she overtakes and almost collides with a lorry coming the other way as she confirms the impossible. She parks in the lay-by at the top, gets out, and waits.

'What are you doing?' she shouts, incredulous, as Mick, in shiny purple tracksuit and fresh-out-of-the-bag-for-life supermarket trainers, crests the brow of the hill and passes her at a brisk pace, arms pumping like a small child in a big huff.

'Power walk,' Mick calls into the air, head held high like he's searching for something in the sky.

'What?' Michaela squeaks, hurriedly locking her car and hobbling after him as he steams onward, a metronome set to samba pace. She wishes she wasn't wearing Crocs.

'Power walking,' he repeats, louder, as if he's hailing the gods. 'Keep up if you want to chat.'

She takes twenty metres to catch him up but is then too puffed to talk. She tries to settle to his rhythm but he's too fast for her fastest walking pace, so she ends up shuffling along behind him like a small child begging a hurried parent for sweets.

'Since when... have you... done *this*?' she gasps, finally able to gather three breaths for a question, but only too aware that she won't be able to manage many more.

'Since Utah,' he barks. 'Opens the lungs, relaxes the shoulders, strengthens the legs, exercises the heart. Adds time to your life, it's all in the book if you'd only read it properly. You should join me; listen to your breathing. And you're carrying far too much weight, not good for your old ticker.'

She's forced to concede, to herself at least, that she's surprised how fast he's going and how well he seems to be coping. As for how he's managed to get up the hill to the top of the cliff – she often struggles to do that in her car!

'How often... you doing... this?'

'Every day, five miles, it's worth two microlives, you know, an extra hour onto your life expectancy. Join me whenever you like.'

He surges on; she's convinced he's speeding up to show off and will probably collapse within twenty metres of her running out of puff – which won't be long. A car passes them, tooting its horn like it's a charity race.

A dog is yapping beside them, prancing and hopping. 'Get away!' she snaps at it.

'Leave him!' Mick yells. 'That's Lucky Boy. He's mine.'

'He...?' Michaela has neither breath nor brain-width to formulate a response. As a child, she'd begged for a dog: promised to walk it, bath it, pay for its food from her pocket money. She might as well have asked for a nuclear weapon. Dogs were dirty; dogs were expensive; dogs tied you to the house; dogs had fleas.

'Where'd... you get... him?' she gasps, unable to believe she's heard right.

'Dogs' home, Norwich. Very good tempered.'

'Why?' she bleats, unable to come up with a single logical or coherent idea as to why Mick, dog hater for seventy-five years, would have gone out and bought a mongrel.

'Microlives,' he shouts. 'Having a pet adds half an hour to every day you have him. Cats the same apparently, but I don't believe that. You go for a walk if you've got a dog, exercise, see? Nobody walks a bloody cat.'

Michaela feels the strength draining from her legs, the air seeping out of her lungs, the sense disappearing from her world.

'You got a bag... to pick up... its do-dos?' she gasps.

Mick waves a hand blithely towards the sky.

'Not here.' He shrugs. 'It's common land.'

She has no idea what that's supposed to mean. More importantly, she has no strength to find out.

'You know that super food you were going on about a few months back?' Mick shouts.

'Quinoa,' she yells, relieved he's asked a question with a one-word answer, she's slowing rapidly.

'Can you write that down for me?'

'Course.'

'Can you get it in Tesco?'

If she wasn't rapidly losing consciousness she'd laugh, take the piss gently. Not going to happen, the state she's now in.

'Think so.'

'Will it be with the meat?'

'No... with the rice... or pasta.'

'Wha–?'

'Pasta!'

'Faster? Okay.'

He speeds up noticeably.

'Wha–? *No!*'

'I'll take you this afternoon; show me where it is.'

She stutters to a halt, gasping and heaving, and watches him marching away, arms pumping, legs pounding, head back. Her own heart feels like it's smashing her ribs apart like skittles, her legs are wobbling like a newborn giraffe's, she wonders if she might have pulled a hamstring. She'd noticed, the last time she'd visited, his Bushmills had two fingers remaining, same as it was a week previously. Either he's getting through exactly a bottle a week, or his claim to have given up the juice is true. She hobbles painfully towards the café as Mick disappears round the bend.

Cathy drives them home in silence, not knowing how to pull back from the decision to open Steve's projection.

'You remember where you put it?' she asks with a hopeful laugh, as she opens the front door; last chance for Steve to say he can't find it, or that he threw it out.

'It's in the bureau,' he says.

'You don't *have* to open it if you really don't want to. If you feel you should respect Mick's wishes...' She's nearly out through the bottom of the barrel now, and she'll know that he's only looking for an excuse if he plays that card. He riffles through the paperwork in the bureau drawers, then turns, holding the LifeTime package.

'Here we go, rest of my life.' He slits through the seals with a paperknife.

Chapter Twenty-Three

'Every year spent in school or university improves life
expectancy, study says. Analysis also says not attending school
is as deadly as smoking or heavy drinking.'
—*The Guardian*, 24 January 2024

Mick unhooks a trolley and manoeuvres it down the first aisle.

'Lead the way,' he commands, but then sets off at a brisk trot. Michaela hobbles behind. If it's not a hamstring, it's her Achilles, she's sure, plus there's a blister; she can feel the strap cutting into her heel.

'Turn right, it's with the pasta, I think,' she calls as he ups the gears and swerves out of sight.

'This it?' he says, squinting at the label on the packet he's pulled off the shelf. 'Kwin-o-ah? That's not what you said.'

'It's pronounced keen-wah,' she says, like he's a six-year-old trying to read *knowledge* or *thorough*.

'Ridiculous!' He tuts.

'It's from the goosefoot family, originally from the Andes,' she patters, deciding to go the whole hog. He's wrecked her Achilles; she'll sour his temper.

'Mother of God,' he hisses. 'What do you do with it? Sprinkle?'

She smiles, wonders if he's taking the mickey back, doubts it. 'No, you boil it in water, like rice. The instructions are on the side.' She refrains from saying *a child could do it*.

'Okay,' he says, pleased with himself. 'Now, watch this.' He rolls up his sleeve and lays the packet across his LifeBuddy, QR code down. There's a small flash of redness on his arm, then he lifts the packet. 'Not bad,' he says, nodding, showing his arm to her.

'What does that mean?'

'It means the whole packet is worth six microlives. It'll add three hours to my lifetime. Hardly a superfood, but I'll give it a go.'

They continue to tour the store, every now and again Mick's LifeBuddy flashing to alert him to certain foodstuffs with high microlife values. Michaela says nothing, but one of the SLAPP orders concerned certain companies 'agreeing' (the suggestion was 'bribing') lucrative marketing and advertising contracts with the LifeTime Corporation. A jigsaw starts to piece itself together in her mind: companies bribe LifeTime, LifeTime promotes products on a private screen embedded in your arm... What the actual...?

They continue their spree, Mick sighing as Michaela adds chocolate biscuits and crisps to her own trolley, scanning them across his arm and scolding her when they reveal less than optimal scores.

'You really should be taking better care of yourself,' he mutters, as she adds a tiramisu out of pure spite. 'That sort of crap is killing you.'

'You want to pick up some whiskey while we're here?' she ripostes.

'No thanks,' he says airily. 'Cut that out a couple of weeks ago.'

Michaela decides their regular tandem shopping habit might be past its sell-by date.

'So? What does it say?' Cathy pulls the golden envelope out of Steve's hands.

Steve stands, raises his hands in FA Cup triumph, and breathes a quiet sigh of relief.

'Twenty-six years?' Cathy says. 'So, you'll be fifty-seven?'

'Well, you know, give or take, like Adam said. Plus, Granny died from a heart attack, so it's probably factoring that in. I look after myself though, all that work in the garden, all the veg we eat.'

'If we weren't always too tired to cook it, and order in pizza instead.'

'Yeah, well, we can stop that. Plus, I've got my squash.'

'You play once a month and spend more time in the pub than you do on court.'

'There's a league, I've been thinking of joining, strengthen the old heart muscles.'

'I thought you didn't believe this stuff.'

'I don't, but you've got to look after yourself, don't you? Nothing to do with this crap.'

'So, you'll be giving up the ciggies as well.'

He moves to the window, stares out at the half-dug vegetable patch, the strip of lawn that grows faster than rabbits breed.

'We'll see,' he says.

Meaning no, she thinks. She watches him. What's he thinking? What's he planning? What would she do if she'd recently discovered she had two-dozen years to live? Almost half her life gone? On the way out instead of on the way in? She thinks she'd take up marathon running. Buy a bike and cycle to Wales and back every morning. Damn! Fifty-seven? Damn Mick!

They share the silence, neither quite sure what's been revealed: the chance of a lifetime or a death sentence.

'I'm delighted to tell you that your son is in perfect health, Mrs Strong, passed every test with flying colours: blood, urine all normal, cholesterol levels good, strong heart, lungs, kidney function, liver, all the scans are normal, vital signs are tip-top, his medical records show he's had all his jabs, even his fingernails are neat and trim. You have a very healthy lad there, congratulations.'

Cathy's face drops.

'Are you sure?' she says, shaking her head in disbelief.

'Quite sure,' the doctor replies, looking at her as though he thinks it might be Cathy who's in need of a check-up, not Will. 'You seem a little surprised?'

'Well, I–'

'Tell him,' Michaela urges, nudging Cathy with her elbow, steel in her voice. 'Just *tell* him!'

So, she does, alternating between fits of tears and rage. She tells the whole story, including the blazing row with Steve when he discovered how much the full check-up was going to cost. She'd organise it; she'd pay for it; she'd take him – but she wouldn't tell Will why. And neither would Steve. They'd tell him it was a normal thing to do when you were getting ready for secondary school. She'd bluff it, take him to London, treat him to Madame Tussauds or the London Dungeon, whatever he wanted, a ride on the Eye, as long as the check-up was part of the day (in the end they needed two days). She and Michaela are back for the results. Without Will. Without Steve.

Roger Morris is an experienced doctor, eighteen years in the NHS before moving to the private Davidson Clinic four years ago. So said the website that looked more appropriate for an upmarket spa hotel than a doctors' practice. His reputation as a cardiac specialist is among the best. He listens attentively until Cathy's tears finally silence her monologue.

'Hmmm, this is a strange case,' Dr Morris begins, as Cathy makes another raid on the tissue box on his desk. 'I've heard of LifeTime, and I have to say, this is a very new... I'm loath to call it science, although I suppose all science has to begin somewhere. If you want my honest opinion, I'd say there should be a lot more regulation on this type of *medical* activity.' He makes air quotes with his fingers to show that he's not convinced that the work of LifeTime is worthy of the description medical. 'Have they told you why they think he's got such a short projection? Is it a heart issue? What?'

'No, it doesn't say.'

'You'd think they'd be obliged to give their reasons, wouldn't you? And even so, if we find a patient with a hole in their heart, we don't simply give them a countdown to death, we treat them. This is most unusual. Why hasn't this been regulated properly before people are put in such an awful position? The government should be all over this *before* it's on sale.' He looks at Cathy, shakes his head. Michaela bites her tongue, unwilling to undermine the doctor's arguments with internet tittle-tattle, but resolving to dig further.

'Listen, you want my honest opinion?' Dr Morris continues.

Cathy nods bleakly, dabbing tears and wiping her nose.

'Number one, I think this is pseudo-science, at least at the moment. While you might be able to make general statements about how long groups of people might be likely to live given their lifestyle, smoking habits, exercise, et cetera, I honestly don't think you can give an *individual* person some kind of a specific life expectancy figure without diagnosing some medical issue. If he's dying of something, tell us what it is, and we'll try to treat it. It's common sense, isn't it?'

Michaela squeezes Cathy's hand but resists the urge to agree with Dr Morris openly. She's said similar to Cathy enough times, the more the doctor tells her this time, the better.

'Number two,' Dr Morris continues. 'In my view, the most likely explanation for this is error. Some data wrongly entered, some box incorrectly ticked or not ticked. But as for me, I can find absolutely *nothing* in any of the tests we've done, and we've done everything available. It all suggests a long and healthy life for your lad. I cannot imagine what extra tests this LifeTime organisation could have done to have come up with a different conclusion.'

'They haven't done *any* tests,' Cathy sniffles. 'As far as I know, it's an online questionnaire about your lifestyle, plus access to your medical records.'

Cathy starts to cry again. Dr Morris sighs.

'You know I really think this is a most irresponsible activity for this company to be undertaking. I wonder if your best line of action now would be something legal. Maybe you should try pursuing some kind of claim for damages against this firm, negligence possibly. I could put you in touch with a firm of solicitors who specialise in medical negligence who might be interested in a test case against LifeTime. I would certainly have no hesitation in giving any help you or they might need regarding the tests we've done here.'

Cathy's tears fall unwanted, like raindrops at a wedding.

Michaela pulls her close and nods at Dr Morris to tell him that she agrees with him, and that he should go on.

'I know it's difficult at this moment, but my honest advice to you is go home to your family and enjoy your lives. You have a fine, healthy son; there is nothing wrong with him that any modern medical test wouldn't find and nothing I can see that could lead anybody with an ounce of sense to feel they can predict that he's going to pass away before a ripe old age. I don't want to appear hard or uncaring, Mrs Strong, I sympathise completely with your situation. But I really feel the problem here is with LifeTime, and not with your son's health.'

———

Cathy and Michaela sit near Regent's Park boating lake and eat the sandwiches they've bought, life as normal going on all around them: office workers out to lunch, kids feeding ducks, tourists enjoying the sunshine.

'So unfair,' Cathy whispers. 'I could kill Mick. He has no idea what he's done to our family. I promised Steve I'd accept what the doctor said, but I can't. What if something happens and we haven't done anything? Thank God Will knows nothing of it. If it wasn't for him, I'd take that doctor's advice and sue the bloody pants off LifeTime. But I can't put Will through that. Imagine the publicity, the time it would take? There'd be no way to shield him from it. I can't put him through that. God, what a mess. What am I going to do?'

'It won't be easy, but I think you're going to have to try, ever so slowly, to start believing what Dr Morris, and Steve, are saying. This doesn't make sense, Cathy. It's a quick-buck, moneymaking company playing fast and loose with people's emotions. Don't get me wrong, I love Adam, he's a great guy, but this company he's working for? They're a bunch of shysters. I can't think of any other thing you can do.'

'But it's so unfair. The doubt. The worry. The *what ifs?* Oh God, and the thought of Mick going from one TV studio to the next waxing lyrical about how wonderful it all is. I mean, no offence, I know he's your dad, but is there something wrong with him? Someone tells you you've got a year to live. Do you really start a tour of the TV stations as the best way to spend your last months? Are we all missing something here? Has he talked about this since he got back from the States and turned into Mr Media?'

Michaela covers Cathy's hand with her own.

'What? Spoken about his impending death? Jesus, Cathy, we're British, we don't talk about death! We talk about football, or *EastEnders*. But I have been thinking similar myself, that he's flown straight down to the wrong end of the sane to insane continuum. If he really does believe that his LifeTime projection is accurate, you're right, why would you spend your time pissing about with the press? It's madness. He's either in some sort of denial, or he's quite seriously taken leave of his senses. Some sort of mental breakdown making him incapable of thinking sensibly.'

'Are you worried about him?'

'I might be, if he allowed me to. Do you know he's also started a health kick? He's power walking to the top of the cliff every day.'

'You're joking?'

'I nearly crashed the car when I spotted him the other day. Then, like a fool, I tried to ask him about it, but I couldn't keep up with him. No way was he going to stop for a chat. I nearly pulled a muscle before I ran out of puff.'

Cathy smiles weakly. She throws her last crust to the least

bossy duck she's spotted, but it's instantly mugged by a gang of foul-mouthed drakes.

'But it's good he's thinking about his health, isn't it? It might give him a longer life, whether or not you swallow all this LifeTime crap.'

'I suppose. The thing is, you never know what's coming next with him. He's got this new phone now, got it in the States. I went up to watch some DVD drama with him the other evening. Trouble is, he spent half the night on his bloody phone. He sees someone he recognises, and he pauses the show, gets his phone out and starts working through the names on the DVD case, to see what else they've been in that he might have seen. He sorts it out, seen him on *Frost* or something like that. Off we go for another couple of minutes before he pauses it again: *Who's that? Where have I seen him before?* Trouble is, he's forgotten which names from the DVD case he's already looked up, so he starts again from the top of the list. He's like a teenager with Alzheimer's. I feel like I'm living in a dream.'

And I feel like I'm living in a nightmare, Cathy thinks, but doesn't say.

Chapter Twenty-Four

'Coffee drinkers may be at lower risk of early death, study suggests.'
—*The Guardian*, 30 May 2022

'Mick Strong.' Mick holds out his hand.

'Yes, I've seen you on the telly, pleased to meet you. Margaret Wallace.'

'How long have you got?' Mick points towards the LifeBuddy poking out of the sleeve of Margaret's mauve dress.

'Oh, a couple of years.' She reveals the shiny display flashing *766 days*. 'You've got a little less, I seem to remember?'

Mick slips off his jacket and undoes his cufflink.

'A hundred and eighty-one days,' he says, before uncovering the display, wanting her to know that he doesn't need to check. 'But I've changed my diet and started quite a rigorous exercise regime, so I'm slowing the countdown significantly.'

'Yes, I'm doing a bit more exercise myself, and eating better. You were the first, weren't you?'

'That's right. I could see the potential immediately. It's a great invention. Changes the way we think about death.'

'It certainly does,' Margaret replies, without making it clear whether she thinks that it changes things for the better.

'So, what do you know about *this* programme? They were a bit vague when they first mentioned it. They're not going to make us eat caterpillars, are they?'

Margaret appears shocked. 'Goodness me, no. I've heard it's highbrow: *LifeTime Challenge*. They say they've modelled it on *University Challenge*, very cerebral. I mean, the amount they're charging for LifeTime membership, and then the LifeBuddy, they'll need to aim way above the riff-raff.'

Mick feels relieved. He'd heard spine-chilling stories of the antics they got up to on some game shows, often with people who should know better, politicians and the like. Ten thousand pounds was ten thousand pounds – but he had his dignity. Also, some good news had been announced a few days earlier: they had managed to get Tony Trent to front the show. Trent had class; Trent had gravitas; Trent is one of Mick's TV heroes.

The door opens, a woman dressed for an executive meeting steps in. She's carrying a clipboard, has headphones slung around her neck. She smiles.

'They're ready for you.'

Mick and Margaret stand and follow her towards the studio.

She introduces herself as Roxy and chats non-stop as she leads them through a series of plasterboard passageways, squeezing past painters and carpenters as they go.

'They're putting this show together very quickly,' Roxy says, as they step over pots of paint and toolboxes. 'Everybody's really excited. Have either of you ever been on TV before?'

'I was on *CNN* in the States,' Mick says with cut-glass casualness, making it sound like he had his own show sandwiched between Kate Bolduan and the Wolf fellow.

'That's cool,' Roxy replies, narrowly avoiding a collision with a woman in overalls carrying a tray of pastel-blue paint. 'They're saying this show could be groundbreaking,' she says, glancing back over her shoulder and nodding seriously. 'They paid a lot of money to get Tony Trent. And what about you, Margaret? Have you been on television?'

'I was on *Countdown*,' Margaret replies.

'Oh, I love *Countdown*. Never miss it. Okay, nice and quiet from now on, we're nearly there. I'll send you on when it's time.'

From the wings of the studio, they can hear the audience being given last-minute instructions. Mick knows that the whole family are out there to see him. They've come down on the train and are going to spend the night in a small hotel near Golders Green. He breathes in and out a couple of times but he's not really nervous. He doesn't know enough about the show to be nervous. There's been a splash of publicity over the last ten days, but no details have leaked ahead of this, the first edition. He had been relieved to hear that he'll only have one rival contestant for the ten grand prize.

The studio is smaller than Mick had imagined. He can see a pair of cameras trained on a couple of dark-wood daises and a backdrop which looks like a cross between a Gothic cathedral and an Oxford college. The audience are sitting in seats resembling choir stalls that surround the daises on three sides. The lights dim. Roxy puts her finger to her lips. The theme music starts. There are clear echoes of the bells from the *University Challenge* intro.

From the far side, Mick recognises Tony Trent striding onto the stage dressed in his trademark dark suit and bright silk cravat. Trent reaches his spot right on cue as the music stops; Mick would've expected nothing less.

'Good evening, ladies and gentlemen, and welcome to the first edition of *LifeTime Challenge*, the show that will teach you how to live a longer life.' The applause is gentle and respectful. Mick is pleased with the tone; he's going to enjoy himself.

'So, let me explain how the show works: each week we invite two members of the LifeTime family to compete live on stage. Their task will be to demonstrate that they have the best knowledge of two things. The first is healthy living, and the second is a sound understanding of how their LifeBuddy can help them to extend their projected LifeTimes. You see, ladies and gentlemen, it is this combined knowledge of healthy living and LifeBuddy functionality that is the key to a longer life. Whichever of the two contestants demonstrates they are the most knowledgeable and the most skilled will walk away with our weekly prize of ten thousand pounds.'

Mick glances at Margaret, wonders how good her knowledge of a healthy lifestyle and the functions of her LifeBuddy will be compared to his. He feels quietly confident.

'So, let's bring out our first contestant. You'll all know him; he was the first British LifeTime member. Ladies and gentlemen, an enormous hand for Doctor... Michael... Strong.'

Roxy gives Mick a little thumbs up and he steps onto the stage, the lights blinding him momentarily. Tony Trent takes a couple of steps towards him and shakes his hand warmly. He leads Mick back to centre stage and joins in the applause as it dies.

'So, Dr Strong. Can we call you Michael?'

'Friends call me Mick,' Mick replies, smiling.

'Very pleased to meet you, Mick. Tell us where you've come from today.'

'From Little Wixlow, in Norfolk.'

'Along the coast from Cromer?' Tony asks.

'Yes.' Mick nods, surprised and delighted at Tony's knowledge.

'Family holidays as a child,' Tony reveals. 'Wonderful part of the country. So, what do you do in Norfolk, Mick?'

'I'm a GP, have been for fifty-odd years.'

'A GP? That bodes well for our healthy living questions, I'd say. Do you keep yourself in good shape?'

'A bit of golf, lots of walking, you know.'

'Very good. So, to business, as they say, Mick, how much have you got on your LifeBuddy as of this moment?'

'A hundred and eighty-one days,' Mick replies proudly.

'Okay. And are you already using your LifeBuddy to monitor your projection, trying to extend it a little through diet and exercise?'

'Oh yes. I'm very diligent. I've recently taken up power walking, quit smoking and alcohol.'

'That's marvellous, Mick. Exactly how we'd hope the LifeBuddy would help people to take care of themselves. So, what I'd like you to do now is go up to your podium where one of our LT crew will check that our wifi is picking up a clear signal from your LifeBuddy. Ladies and gentlemen, please give a big hand for our first *LifeTime Challenge* contestant, Doctor... Michael... Strong.'

The applause is enthusiastic and expectant. Tony Trent continues as it quietens.

'Yes, ladies and gentlemen, the LifeBuddy, the unique invention of the LifeTime Corporation that can show you, in real time, how the decisions you make on a day-to-day basis impact on the length of the rest of your life.'

There's a lull in the studio as a glitzy LT advert plays for the viewers at home. It sells the advantages of the LifeBuddy as much as the LifeTime projections, advising people to *take control* of their lives and *Don't let the state nanny you!* Mick tries to spot his family in the audience, but he can't see beyond the curtain of darkness created by the bright lights. He inspects his LifeBuddy: pulse and blood pressure are up a bit; he breathes deeply to try to settle them. A twenty-something, dressed in the LifeTime T-shirt and chinos, helps him to prepare and adjusts a little gizmo so that his LifeBuddy is visible on a big screen behind him. The advert ends.

'Let's meet our next contestant, Margaret Wallace!' Tony Trent shakes her hand as she comes onto the stage. 'And where are you from, Margaret?'

'I'm from London, Tony,' she says, looking slightly nervous.

'And what do you do for a living?'

'I'm a wellness consultant and nutritionist.'

'Very impressive,' Tony replies. 'We could have quite a battle on our hands this evening, with Mick being a GP and you being a nutritionist. We could be in for a high-scoring contest.' There's a hum of chatter in the audience.

'So, tell me, Margaret, what's your LifeTime projection at the moment?'

'Seven hundred and sixty-six days, Tony.'

'And are you using the LifeBuddy to help you make healthy-living choices, maybe slow the rate that your projection falls?'

'Oh, absolutely, Tony. Although I've always eaten healthily, I haven't in the past done as much exercise as I should, so the LifeBuddy has really helped me to concentrate on upping my step count.'

'That's wonderful news, Margaret. Please take your place at your dais beside Mick and let our LT crew member check your LifeBuddy is displaying on our big screen.' Tony Trent walks to the front of the stage.

'Okay, ladies and gentlemen, our two contestants are ready for the first round, which is about choosing healthy food. This is a round where each contestant must use both their own knowledge of healthy food and the power of the LifeBuddy.

Each contestant will have a selection of six foodstuffs to consider. They each need to choose the *healthiest* of the items before them, that is, the item that will add the most or subtract the fewest microlives were they to eat it. So, they can use their own knowledge to discard four of the options, and then consult their LifeBuddies to analyse the last two of the options, before making their final choice. Understood?'

A couple of camera operators glide their machines into position as a man and a woman, dressed in chefs' uniforms complete with tall white hats, push out silver trolleys from either side of the stage. Tony Trent ushers them into position. A third LT worker slides an opaque screen between Mick and Margaret so that neither can see what the other is doing. Tony indicates for the first 'chef' to reveal the food in front of Mick by lifting the silver dome off the platter.

'Now remember, Mick: not a good idea to give Margaret too many clues regarding your thinking, so we'll talk about this or that food item rather than naming them. Make your first choices by pushing the foods you are rejecting to the front of the tray.'

Mick studies his choices, and immediately concludes that this is an easy icebreaker round to put the pair of them at ease. His choices are a chocolate eclair, an apple, a banana, a Mars bar, a packet of cheese and onion crisps, and a glass of full-cream milk.

Mick studies the six choices then pushes the eclair, the Mars bar and the crisps forward. Then he slides the milk to the front.

'So, you now have two foods left, are those the two you'd like to analyse with your LifeBuddy?'

Mick stares at the apple and the banana and nods happily.

'Right. So, hold fire there for a moment, Mick, while I walk Margaret through her first four rejections. Margaret, let's look at your options.' He nods at the second 'chef' who lifts the silver dome with a flourish. Mick is unable to see what Margaret is doing, but he listens carefully in case she lets slip any clues as to her thinking. He's sure that, being a nutritionist, she's going to be able to make a good choice, but he's also convinced that his knowledge of microlives is excellent, having spent weeks studying the tables in the book by the good professor from Cambridge.

Mick listens as Margaret makes her choices, but she gives no hint as to what they are. Finally, Tony Trent announces that they are ready to analyse their chosen two foods, and asks the stagehands to remove everything else. Mick glances across and sees that Margaret has chosen a satsuma and a pear.

'I said this would be close, ladies and gentlemen. You can see that both Margaret and Mick have chosen the fruit, sensibly rejecting the other foods on offer. But this is where the LifeBuddy comes into its own. You see, while a lot of you will know that a piece of fruit is worth one microlife, that's half an hour added to your life, what you might not know is that's only an *average*. You see, each piece of fruit is unique, this apple is bigger than that apple, so do all pieces of fruit save you *exactly* one microlife? The answer is no. And that is where the LifeTime LifeBuddy can help you find out which piece of fruit is the best. Are you ready to analyse your fruit, contestants? Off you go. The results will be shown on the big screen for all to see.'

Mick knows that the score of one microlife for each piece of fruit is only an average, that's common sense. He picks up his apple and rests it on his LifeBuddy. The Buddy glows as it analyses the fruit then stops when it has finished. His LifeBuddy, also projected up on the giant screen, shows the apple to be worth 0.97 of a microlife. He scans the banana and sees that it's worth 1.13 microlives.

'So, how are we doing? All finished?' Tony asks.

Mick and Margaret nod.

'So, Margaret, let's start with you. Which food have you chosen?'

'The satsuma, Tony.'

'And you, Mick?'

'The banana for me, Tony.'

'Okay, now let's have a look at the correct answers.'

The studio lights dim, the large screen splits in two with Margaret's satsuma visible on one side and Mick's banana on the other. Both fruits are replaced by giant green ticks. The audience applauds.

'Well done, the pair of you, you've both selected the best food from your available choices, so you both score one point.'

There's a lull in the proceedings as the TV viewers are treated to a five-minute ad break. LifeTime have bookended the first and last thirty seconds for hard-sell ads about the benefits of membership in general, and LifeBuddy ownership in particular; the rest of the time has been allocated after a bidding war, the intensity of which was almost as frantic as what's usually experienced during World Cup finals.

Chapter Twenty-Five

'Physical inactivity directly contributes to one in six deaths in
the UK, the same number as smoking.'
—Everybody Active, Every Day (2014): *Public Health England,*
Department of Health, UK government, 23 October 2014

'Welcome back, ladies and gentlemen, to round two of
LifeTime Challenge. Now, round two is our quick-fire
Take a Risk round in which our competitors will have to choose
the *safest* out of a pair of activities. There are five pairs and for
each one you choose we'll add the appropriate gain or loss of
microlives to the master scoreboard here.' He points to the giant
screen above their heads, which now shows a cartoon figure of
Margaret on the left wearing a sleek aquamarine tracksuit, while
on the right is a picture of Mick in golfing attire, leaning on his
golf bag. Each contestant shows a score of plus one microlife
from the first round.

'Now obviously, contestants, the microlives you win in the
show will not be added to your real LifeTime calculations. Even
we can't give you more life simply for answering questions in a

quiz, now can we? So, let's get started. You each have a keypad on your podium with two buttons, option one and option two, and you will have ten seconds to make your choice each time. Longer than that and you'll score the worst option. Ready?'

Mick and Margaret nod.

'First question, fingers on your keypads.' The lights dim further until Mick and Margaret are each encased in a tunnel of light falling from above, a drum roll patters in the background. 'Remember, you must choose the *best* activity, the one that would add the most or subtract the least from your LifeTimes. Here we go, first question.'

The question flashes up on the giant screen: *Which would you choose to eat? A portion of red meat or two servings of bacon?* There is a buzz through the audience as a melodic voice starts to count down the seconds. *Ten seconds... nine... eight...*

Mick's confused. He looks around, it's clear the audience are reading the question from the giant screen. He's slightly behind it so he can't see. He suddenly notices that the question has appeared on a small screen on his podium.

Seven... six... five... The writing is small; he can't quite make it out. He scrambles for his glasses and fumbles to put them on.

Four... three... two... He reads the question as quickly as he can – *Which would you choose to eat?*

One... A portion of red meat...

Zero! A buzzer sounds as Mick hits the second button on his keypad; he knows red meat is a no-no – that *has* to be the worst option. The crowd applauds.

'Time's up!' Tony says. 'Let's look at your choices. Margaret, you've chosen the portion of red meat.'

There's a murmur from the crowd as people discuss the best option.

'And Mick, you've chosen... two servings of bacon.' Mick's mouth gapes; he knows he's made the wrong choice. Tony continues with a tone of expectation. 'So, let's see the correct answer, shall we?' The drum roll returns, the giant screen flashes, and Tony announces, 'Red meat is healthier than two servings of bacon, so, Margaret, you've lost one microlife, while Mick, you've lost two!'

The scoreboard flickers and shows Margaret now with zero and Mick with minus one. Mick's sorely tempted to call foul. If he'd been told he was going to have to read the questions, he'd have had his glasses ready. If he'd had his glasses ready, he'd have got the right answer. Any fool knows how bad bacon is for you. He's been revising the LifeTime statistics ever since he'd heard the show was in the planning. He's on the verge of complaining, ten thousand pounds is ten thousand pounds, but he hesitates. Does he *really* want to reveal how seriously he's taking all this on live TV? The idea that he might look and sound like a spoiled schoolboy shouting *it's not fair* isn't that appealing. Tony Trent moves quickly on anyway, and Mick resolves to catch Margaret up as soon as he can.

'Second question, ready both of you?' Mick gives a curt nod as he squints at his screen. The lights dim, the drum rolls, the question flashes up; he's ready and waiting this time.

Which would you choose to do? Eat a serving of vegetables or walk a kilometre?

'Your ten seconds starts *now!*' Tony announces, and the voice starts to count down.

Ten seconds... nine... eight...

This is an easy one for Mick, he knows the vegetables will give him four microlives, while the walk will give him less than half a microlife. He presses the first button.

Seven... six... five...

Margaret is clearly in a quandary, she's rubbing her chin, throwing quick glances at Tony as if she's angling for a clue.

Mick thinks she might know her nutrition, but hopes she isn't as sure about the effects of exercise.

Four... three... two...

Mick drums his fingers on his dais, willing Margaret to choose the walk.

One...

Margaret slaps a button.

Zero!

'Okay, everybody. Time's up. Let's have a look at what our contestants have chosen. We'll start with you this time, Mick. You've chosen the *vegetables!*'

Polite applause from the audience.

'And Margaret, you've *also* chosen the vegetables. Let's see the correct answer... It's the vegetables! That's *four* microlives each! Walking a kilometre will give you less than half a microlife. Let's check the scoreboard again.' Once again, the scoreboard twirls and settles, leaving Margaret still in the lead, now by four microlives to three.

They break for more adverts.

The next two rounds fail to alter the distance between Mick and Margaret. In the first, they each gain a microlife, Mick for choosing a dog over a cat as a pet, and Margaret for choosing the cat. It irritates Mick that they've included a question that doesn't give him a chance to gain ground. He's already complained to the LifeTime Corporation about the cat and dog thing, arguing that anyone with a dog will walk more than someone who owns a cat, so the two should have different microlife scores. He'd chosen the dog in the hope that the corporation might have listened to his argument, and maybe changed their weighting, but no, Margaret scores the same for sitting on her sofa all day with a moggy, as he does for walking Lucky Boy up the cliff road.

In the next round they tie again, both scoring four

microlives for choosing an active mind over meditation, which was worth only three.

'So, the *last* question in this round, and then we'll move on to the third and final round. Only one microlife in it. Are you ready, contestants? Here's the last question in round two.'

Which would you choose to do? Cycle twenty kilometres or run a marathon?

'Your ten seconds starts *now!*'

Ten seconds... nine... eight...

Mick hits the marathon button grumpily. He knows it will gain him two microlives, but even if Margaret chooses the cycling, she'll still gain one point nine microlives, leaving him trailing into the last round by point nine of a microlife.

...seven... six... five... four...

Margaret is rubbing her chin again, snatching furtive glances at Tony; she clearly isn't as secure in her knowledge of exercise as she is on nutrition.

...three... two... one...

Margaret hits a button.

Zero...

'Time's up! Let's have a look at your answers. Mick, you've chosen the marathon!'

The audience applauds.

'And, Margaret, you've chosen the cycling! Ladies and gentlemen, the correct answer was the marathon! And so, with the scores showing Margaret on ten point nine microlives to Mick's ten, let's go for another break. And when we return, the final round, and a sudden death end to tonight's contest. Back in five.'

The ads roll, the audience chatters noisily. Mick feels disappointed that they've reached the last round already. He thinks they've spent more time showing adverts than they have on the contest. Tony Trent has been having a little chat with

Margaret and now approaches Mick. Mick puts a smile back on his face.

'Very close contest, Mick. Are you enjoying it?'

He nods graciously, decides not to voice any of his complaints. 'Very educational,' he says instead. 'We're really showing people how to live healthier lives, aren't we?'

Tony nods. 'I saw you on the TV, getting your LifeBuddy fused on. Great moment. I bet it's fantastic out there at LT HQ.'

'Most impressive,' Mick says. 'It's an incredible organisation, and SphereCity's a great place.'

'Just outside Salt Lake City, yes?'

'That's right.'

'I must visit one day.' Tony then steps a pace closer to Mick, lowers his voice.

'Do you have a lucky number, Mick?'

Mick shrugs; he's taken by surprise by such an off-the-wall question. 'Not really.'

Tony Trent moves even closer. 'Mine's number *four*,' he says with a conspiratorial wink. 'It never lets me down...' He gives Mick a hard stare.

The adverts finally end and the theme music starts up again. Mick stares out into the audience and spots Will, jumping up and down and waving madly in the front row. Mick waves back and sees the rest of the family.

'Okay, ladies and gentlemen,' Tony says as a hush descends. 'We couldn't have a tighter contest, zero point nine of a microlife in it and one microlife to play for in the last round, winner... takes... *all*!

'Right, Mick and Margaret, this round is called the Circle of Life. Could the LifeTime team members bring out the Circle of Life, please?'

Two stagehands wheel out what looks like an oversized

dartboard attached to a door-sized frame. They place it between Mick and Margaret before leaving the stage.

'Okay, everybody. Now, I'm sure you'll agree, our contestants have expertly demonstrated their knowledge about living healthily. They've also shown that they know how to use their LifeBuddies to help them in that quest. But, as I'm sure we all understand, sometimes life doesn't go as we expect. Surprising things happen, we are sometimes rewarded with good luck, and we are sometimes penalised with bad luck, without us having any say in the matter. We could lose our job, and not be able to afford our gym membership. We might be involved in a traffic accident and be unable to exercise for a long period of time. So, our last round includes a healthy dose of luck, just like in life. Behind me is our Circle of Life, and as you can see there are twenty boxes on the circle. Each one contains a question. Each question is worth one microlife, but not all questions are the same level of difficulty. We have some ridiculously easy questions and some devilishly hard ones, so that's the element of luck in the game. So, I'm going to ask Mick to choose first as he's trailing by point nine of a microlife. Get your question correct, Mick, and you will go into the lead by point one of a microlife. Then Margaret will have *one* chance to retake the lead and win. Get your question wrong, Mick, and the contest is over, Margaret will be the winner. Do you understand?'

They both nod.

'So, Mick. An important choice for you to make here. You must choose one number. You're going to need some good luck. I hope you've got a *lucky* number, Mick, a number that has *never* let you down. Which number would you like to choose?'

Mick almost gasps. He stares at Tony Trent, who has a look of innocent curiosity on his face. But he'd used the exact words, a number that had *never let him down*.

'Number four,' Mick says hesitantly, hardly believing that he's saying it, and not entirely knowing why.

'Number four,' Tony repeats, reaching into box number four on the Circle of Life and pulling out a card. 'So, has your lucky number brought you an easy question? Here it is: where is the headquarters of the LifeTime Corporation?'

Mick's mind blanks for a moment, as he realises that he knows the answer: he visited with Adam, had his LifeBuddy fitted there. He can picture the bubbles, the Segways, Jaz's deck, but he can't for the life of him bring the name of the place to the front of his mind.

'Is it a difficult question for you, Mick? Would you like me to repeat it?' Tony offers, looking slightly nervous. 'You need to get this question correct in order to make Margaret answer one more. Where is the HQ of LifeTime located?'

Mick tries to clear his mind as sweat prickles out onto his brow; he's feeling giddy, unsteady, he grips the sides of his dais, stares into the audience, the lights are up for this last round. He spots Will, waving furiously, and wearing a sweatshirt that Adam had bought for him for his last birthday, it has SALT LAKE CITY emblazoned across the front in red capitals. Next to him sits Paula, wearing a T-shirt, another gift from Adam, bearing the legend UNIVERSITY OF UTAH. Mick smiles.

'Salt Lake City, Utah,' he says with a sigh of relief. 'They call it SphereCity.'

'The correct answer,' Tony responds instantly. 'You earn a microlife, putting you in the lead by zero point one of a microlife.'

The applause is loud, but brief, before Tony continues.

'So, Margaret. You have one chance to overtake Mick and take tonight's prize. You have nineteen numbers left to choose from, some of them holding easy questions, others not so. Make your choice.'

'I'll have number eight, please, Tony.'

'Number eight,' Tony repeats, reaching into that box on the Circle of Life. 'So, the final question of tonight's competition, Margaret. Get it correct and you are tonight's winner. Get it wrong, and Mick will be going home with ten thousand pounds. Here we go. Question eight: What is the name of the current Governor of Utah?'

Chapter Twenty-Six

'Behind the Wheel, Women are Safer Drivers Than Men.
Compared With Women, Male Drivers of Cars and Vans Were
Involved in Twice as Many Fatal Accidents.'
—*The New York Times*, 27 April 2020

'I 'll get these. Pint?'

Adam nods, surveys the bar. You'd call the Fish and Anchor a nice little pub if you didn't want a selection of 'fine ales', nor a range of wines from around the world. Neither would you be hungry for anything other than pork scratchings, nor looking for a table outside in a large, shady beer garden. Any of the other usual pub décor: brasses, dusty library books on wooden shelves, parchment scrolls, pictures of the locality from the last century? You wouldn't be in search of these either. In fact, drop the 'nice'. The Fish and Anchor is a little pub. Grubby little pub, actually. Best if you brought your own newspaper too.

They take the corner table by the window: the seats are torn like those jeans that cost more than the ones that aren't. Maybe it's a sign of class, Adam muses, realising once again what little understanding he has for the world of sales, or marketing, whatever it is he's supposed to be doing. The table is scratched and stained; the beer mats seem to have been doused in beer and dried half a dozen times without ever leaving the table. As they walked from the bar, he'd mistaken them for dead leaves. The ashtray is erupting cigarette butts, which is strange really, seeing as they're the first customers of the day.

'I'll come straight to the point,' Steve says, after having drunk a quarter of his pint in one swallow. 'I need to ask you a favour, maybe a big one.'

Adam tenses. He's been on edge since Steve called him last night. They're not drinking buddies, so the invite was a surprise – an ominous one. It's almost certainly something to do with LifeTime, Adam has assumed. So, he's pleasantly surprised – absolutely ecstatic, in truth – that Steve is almost smiling rather than wringing his neck in the toilets.

'Go on,' Adam says, hedging still.

'It's Will's LifeTime projection.' Adam takes Steve's use of 'projection' as opposed to 'prediction' as a peace offering. 'I know we shouldn't have, but we opened it.'

'And...?' Adam's insides are all in the down elevator, sinking fast, producing that queasy feeling you get when you mix grape and grain, a lot of both, bolt a quick kebab, and then pile onto the dodgems.

'It says five years, just over.'

'Five–' Adam resists the temptation to complete the sentence.

'Cathy took him to a specialist, I was against the idea, you know what I think about this stuff. Huge margins of error, right?'

Adam consciously decides not to remind Steve that it isn't a prediction.

'They did everything: blood, urine, X-rays, CT scan, ECG,

more initials than I know what they stand for, they gutted his medical records, they've obviously got his genome, they probably did an MOT as well.' Steve laughs. But it's a nervous laugh, the one you use when you're afraid you're going to cry. 'Promised us there was nothing else we could pay to get done if we were royalty.'

'And?'

'Nothing. Couldn't find a thing wrong with him. He's fit and healthy. I want to know if you might be able to help...' His voice lifts as he says the last word, as if he might have been intending to say more but now isn't able. Takes a pull of his pint instead.

'Does Will know?'

Steve shakes his head, keeps his eyes down.

'Cathy's in bits. She promised she'd accept the doctor's decision if I agreed to send him to one, but she can't. If I'm honest, I'm more worried about her than I am about Will. Does that seem stupid to you?' He looks up now, eyes ruddy and moist, lips tightly drawn.

'No, it doesn't seem stupid. If the doctor says there's nothing wrong with him and the doctor's seen all his medical records, then it's impossible for our computers to come up with a different conclusion. The projection is based on data. I don't know how Mick sent the data, whether his medical records are digital, whether he's filled in the forms personally on our website. It's a big process, lifestyle, diet, all that. Does he run often? Keep fit? To be honest I can't imagine how Mick could have filled it all in without speaking to Will, or you.',

Steve shakes his head. 'Not a word. Nor for mine, he doesn't know how much effort I put into a game of squash; he's never asked how often I play, what I eat...'

'Look, I don't want to disparage Mick to you—'

'But you think he's fucked this up.'

'It's more likely than anything being wrong with Will. He'd *have* to have asked you some questions. He couldn't have filled the applications in accurately otherwise. But how could he then have surprised you all if he'd peppered you with questions beforehand?'

Steve shakes his head slowly, looks steadily at Adam.

'You want me to check it out?' Adam asks.

'Would you?'

'Absolutely. Look, I'm sorry. Personally, I'm sorry. This is awful. I really don't know what to say. If you want me to talk to Cathy.'

'No, not yet. She wasn't keen that I spoke to you today, but let's see if you can get some answers back from LifeTime.'

'I'll get on to them straight away; this is obviously a serious issue for the company as well as you. I'll call them this morning and tell them what's wrong. I'm actually flying out tonight, so I'll follow it up personally tomorrow with people I know in the right departments. Would you be able to give me copies of everything: medical records, the doctor's report? I don't know whether...'

Steve fishes a microdrive out of his pocket.

'I imagine this cost you a fair bit?'

'The receipt's on there.'

'Good. I'll get that sorted for you. You shouldn't be paying to solve our problems. They *will* sort this out, Steve.'

'I hope they can,' Steve says, standing up. He drains the dregs of his pint.

Adam stares at the bubbles rising in his glass. He's a statistician; *was*. His work was mostly to do with studying the data and helping with the calculations to turn it all into positive or negative microlife measures. He worked as part of an enormous team: doctors, physiologists, psychologists, nutritionists, researchers, Tom Cobley... If this doctor has seen all the data that Mick has put into the LifeTime application, then they should come to similar conclusions. LifeTime doesn't add anything to the data that Mick's provided. If a doctor has said that Will is fine, then the algorithms should produce a similar result. They have to! Even if Mick hasn't asked for some details from Steve and Cathy, even if he's answered each question with an average, that's no reason for the algorithms to give Will such a short projection.

This is his problem.

Michaela realises she's speeding and eases back on the accelerator. She checks her mirror for blue flashing lights but is blinded by the setting sun behind her. Her brain is in overdrive as she goes over the permutations of what she's learned this afternoon. Although the bigger problem is what she should do with the things that she's discovered.

Michaela had known that Fiona's son worked with computers. Fiona had never been sure what he did, but it was that thing where the screen is dark and filled with lines and lines of small white type, numbers and letters scrolling down towards oblivion, making no sense to anybody except those who understand the code. And usually wear hoodies. Even indoors.

So Michaela had probed, casually, and then offloaded over afternoon tea about Mick and LifeTime and what she'd discovered on the internet about doctored margins of error and toothless regulators and SLAPPs.

'Gordon will find out whatever you want to know,' Fiona had said. 'He's always on the thingie, what does he call it? The black web, no, the *dark* web. That's it.'

So, she'd called Gordon down and he'd shrugged, *piece o' piss*, and they'd followed him back up to his den where he had more screens than your average multiplex, and larger speakers than Coldplay, and a space-age leather swivel chair and blackout curtains. Most of the screens were bigger than Michaela's telly and seemed to have more colours than the LSD trips she'd experienced in her youth.

But Gordon had one smaller, darker screen that he pulled close and he started rattling the keyboard, which brightened it – a little. Yes, Gordon had reported, as he clicked and scrolled through a part of the internet unknown to Michaela, there was a lot of unease about LifeTime and what they were all about, or rather what they *claimed* to be all about. Which wasn't always the same as what some people, some very clever and well-informed people, were sure they were actually all about. 'But,' he'd said ominously, 'there's an awful lot of *lawfare* going on...'

Lawfare, Gordon had explained patiently, was the street, or dark web, name for SLAPPs, the expensive defamation lawsuits, often used by the rich and powerful, to shut down wannabe investigators. LifeTime were active against any snooping around their algorithms or finances. Gordon had confirmed the accusations that LifeTime's margins of error were almost certainly much larger than they claimed. There were other little pieces of tittle and tattle, he'd said, concerning younger LifeTime members in the States receiving worryingly short projections. Michaela had asked him to dig further on that topic. It was then she'd discovered that while she had been digging with a teaspoon, Gordon seemed to have a JCB at his disposal.

'Hackers,' he'd said, as if that explained everything, after a few minutes of rattling and reading. He said there was clear evidence of a running battle between a group of hackers and LifeTime. Every now and again the hackers broke through LifeTime's digital defences and altered the projections of a number of younger members, making them much shorter. LifeTime always responded by pretending they were data glitches, and buying the family's silence. At the same time, they were enthusiastically SLAPPing the journos with lawsuits so they couldn't report on the issue without incurring huge financial costs. LifeTime would then patch the breach, and start all over again as if nothing had happened. The hackers want money, essentially, millions, but embarrassing LifeTime is another of their aims when they refuse to pay up. LifeTime seems happy to play cat and mouse instead, and pretend nothing's really wrong, minor glitches, that sort of rubbish. The last thing they want to admit is that hackers have got into their servers and altered their projections.

Michaela had asked Gordon if Will's name had cropped up in any of the reports about younger members who'd had their data hacked and changed, but he hadn't been able to find a trace of him.

The speedometer rises without her noticing as Michaela desperately decides what to do. Cathy and Steve. She *has* to tell Cathy and Steve. If Will's projection is the result of a hack, then there's nothing for them to worry about. And Adam. Adam needs to know, if he doesn't already, which she doubts. Adam will be able to find out if Will's projection has been hacked. And Mick. Mick needs to know. His projection could be years out. At the very least, it might not be worth the expensive paper it's written on.

Michaela's mobile rings. She must get one of those hands-free gizmos. She pings it on to speakerphone and drops it on the passenger seat.

'Hello?'

'Am I speaking to Michaela Strong?' An American accent.

'Is that you, Adam?'

'You're putting your family in danger.'

'What? Who is this?'

'You're interfering in matters that don't concern you, family

235

members could suffer. Jobs could be lost, houses also. You'd be wise to back off before you do real damage.'

'Who is this? Are you threatening me?'

'Just some friendly advice. And some information. If you attempt to communicate any allegations in the public domain, then we will take legal action against you. This legal action will be expensive for you to defend...'

Distracted for the moment, she's travelling very fast into the bend.

Chapter Twenty-Seven

'Your children and my grandchildren will live to be 150.'
—Nicholas Negroponte: *El País* in English, 21 June 2019

'Hi, Adam. You okay?' It's clear Ron is concentrating on another screen as he takes the seecall on his mobile.

'Yeah, fine. You?'

'Oh, you know, busy busy. How can I help?' There's the rattle of a keyboard in the background.

'I've got an issue with one of the memberships Mick Strong has given out.'

'Oh yeah? What sort of issue?'

'Eleven-year-old boy, projected five years...'

The rattle dies; Ron faces his phone and sighs deeply.

'Shit! They going to the media?'

'God, no! They've come to *me*. Want us to check out the data. They've taken him to the doc, full medical, CT scans, everything. Can't find a thing wrong with him.'

'Okay, send me his details. Can you get hold of the doctor's report, all of it?'

'Already in your inbox.'

'That's great. We've had cases like this before. If the medics have done their work, it's going to be a GIGO: your doctor guy cocking up the input, garbage in, garbage out.'

'That's what I'm hoping. I'm at the airport now, so see you tomorrow.'

'Yeah. And thank God it's a Brit and not a Yank. Legal-wise, I mean.'

Mick turns off the TV and sits back on the sofa, smiling. *What a performance*, he thinks. The way the camera caught him as he remembered Salt Lake City was fantastic. He's watched that bit four times. He wishes the cameras had picked out Paula, Will, and the rest of the family at the moment of his triumph, but he can't spot them. No matter. He did it. And ten grand in the bank. He did a dozen media interviews afterwards in the studio; he now has a pile of papers on the sofa to go through. But there's something nagging at him. Why?

Why had Tony Trent given him such an obvious clue so that he chose the easiest question in the world? Why? Mick would bet his ten thousand pounds that every other question on the Circle of Life had been a stinker, equal to Margaret's choice. Governor of Utah? And it was as if Tony had *wanted* Mick to know that he was giving him the clue – asking him about Salt Lake City just before. Why?

Lucky Boy sits loyally next to Mick's chair like he's guarding a royal tomb in Thebes. Every now and again, he glances lovingly up at Mick. Mick leans over and refreshes his glass from the drinks cabinet, another chock of ice in his water. He ruffles Lucky Boy's ears. He gets up and surveys his music collection for something appropriate. Lucky Boy follows him silently. Something upbeat? Let's see. He pulls out an album. The cover brings back memories of Celia; she seemed to play it all the time that year. Was that their wedding year? Yes, it was. He remembers it being played at the disco afterwards, him propping up the bar, she (still in her wedding dress) and her mates all waving at him from the dance floor. He smiles. Doesn't think he's played it since. He didn't really like the music, not his sort of thing at all, but it was a favourite of hers, so... He slips it out of the cover, which shows a motorcyclist heading into the sunset, drops it on the sofa and puts the record on the turntable, then sits back down again, Lucky Boy following him. What was that group called? The Rolling something, not the Stones. He can't remember, and can't be arsed to get up and check the sleeve. He hums along with the chorus, only now, years later, realising how morbidly appropriate the title has become.

'Bye Bye Baby...'

Chapter Twenty-Eight

'My Ultimate Goal? Don't Die: Bryan Johnson on his controversial plan to live for ever.'
—*The Guardian*, 14 September 2023

Cathy thinks he'll survive now. His breathing has returned to something approaching *normal for your average OAP who's due a triple bypass*, although he's only been slumped in the deckchair for five minutes, so give him time.

'Good run?' she ventures, calculating that he'll surely be able to give her one word by now. But her diagnosis is obviously off; Steve simply nods like it's going to be his last act before he pops them. At least the ground's prepared, she thinks sardonically, looking over at the mud heap that was once lawn.

'Go far?' she probes, after another few minutes listening to his wheezing turning into the sound a car makes just before you flatten the battery completely while failing to start it.

'Across the rec...'

She waits. He's still pointing. Like he's building up to a change of direction before he goes off the cliff.

'...and back.'

His hand flops into his lap. That was it? Across the rec and back? Less than a mile, she guesstimates. She could walk it in the time he's taken to jog it: probably be able to talk afterwards – maybe even sing and dance. So now Mick's gone mad and so has Steve.

'I've been thinking,' she starts, secure that he'll let her finish. 'I might get myself one of these LifeTime thingies.' His expression doesn't change. She wonders if he's died. She knows what he thinks of them. *Complete crap.* Yet here he is, transformed from Allotment Man into Marathon Man at the opening of an envelope. He didn't even need to step into a phone box. Shazam! If it wasn't so real.

She's not sure why she's had the thought. She's the sceptical agnostic to Steve's devil-worshipping atheist. Will's disaster should have put her off, but Steve's reaction to his own projection has got to her. He's taken a positive step in response. In contrast to what he says, he's trying to change it. If it doesn't kill him.

Whatever her projection says, she reasons, she'll respond. If it's short, she'll join Steve in the Lycra club. If it's long, she'll probably join Steve in the Lycra club or she'll never see him again now that he seems to have divorced the allotment. There's an argument for not bothering, simply bite the Lycra bullet as the best thing to do in every circumstance, but there's something about the fact that Will has one and Steve has one. She wants one. Call it jealousy. Call it whatever you want. It's simply a feeling. She wants one. End of.

Steve's expression still hasn't changed. Maybe he really has died! That would truly bugger LifeTime's reputation.

'Latte and an espresso, please. To go.'

'We not sitting down? I like it here,' Adam says. Ron shakes his head. Adam quizzes him when they get outside, strolling down one of the tarmacked paths between the skate and bike lanes and the lawns.

'So, this your new fitness regime? Coffee on the go?'

'They listen,' Ron replies, glancing over his shoulder.

'What do you mean?'

'What I say, they *listen*.'

'Who listens?'

'Who do you think? *Them!* The ones who might fire you.'

Adam sips his coffee, wonders if he's in the lead-in to a punchline.

'You serious?'

'You think I *like* walking? You ever see me walking anywhere I don't have to?'

'What makes you think they listen?'

'Couple of things happened, couple of things other people said, couple of people lost their jobs. Most of these things, the only explanation is that they listen.'

'What? You mean seecalls?'

'I would guess *everything*. I would guess they read our emails, bug our offices, tap our phones, suck data out of our tablets, read our coffee dregs. I speak to the dudes in DataDiv a lot. These are the best computer minds in the country, except for the people who *they're* convinced are hacking into their data and watching over their shoulders. I mean, these guys, they really think they're the best, so when *they* start telling you, and they'll only ever tell you outside or off campus, when these guys start telling you that someone is hacking *them* and they can't quite nail them down, that means they're admitting they're no longer top dogs of Cyberlandia. If those guys get paranoid, then I get paranoid.'

'You are serious.'

'Last week, I went for a drink with Sal, one of our newbies. She's good; her mind pushes envelopes into origami animals. We were chewing the fat and she says, wouldn't it be wild if we could get the LifeBuddy to check air quality as it was breathed, factor it into the projections. We were shootin' the breeze, you know, end of the day whack-job chatter. It was interesting; imagine if you *lived* in a poor-quality air area, interesting. Two days later, I'm called to see someone I've never met before, in an office the size of Manhattan, asking me if it would fly. Could we do the stats? I checked with Sal, was this something she's discussed with people? She thinks I'm nuts. We were just joking around, she says, we'd had a couple of beers. You know, Adam, I think they *want* us to know.'

They stroll on, Adam wondering if Ron has lost it or if he is simply naive.

'So, my eleven-year-old nephew with five years on his LifeTime, have you been able to find anything in the data to give us a clue?'

Ron shakes his head. 'I gave it to MedDiv, priority, they've been right through it from top to bottom, there's absolutely nothing in the health data you sent over this morning to suggest he's going to die anytime soon. He's a fit lad, hasn't been in hospital for anything major, and that check-up the parents paid for was bloody thorough. My mate in MedDiv went through it first thing, couldn't find a wart. So, if we rule out the chance that there's anything wrong with the boy, which I'm happy we have, the only explanation left is the elephants.'

'You've lost me.'

'The elephants in the room. That's us. If there's nothing wrong with the boy, then we've got a problem with the data.'

'Such as?'

'I did wonder if your old doctor friend might have put something fizzy in the application process, so I checked.'

'And?'

'Well, there's nothing in there saying the boy'll be dead in five years, but, tell you the truth, it was a bit sparse. He hit every *average* button going in the lifestyle survey, your boy does everything averagely, according to the doc. Running, swimming, everything – average.'

Adam sighs, shakes his head. 'Steve, the boy's dad, told me that Mick didn't ask him one thing before applying for a LifeTime for him or the boy.'

'Right. So good old Dr Mick has flashed through the application process with minimal fuss.'

'But that shouldn't give Will a death sentence.'

Ron takes a deep breath. 'You ever heard of Lozenge?'

'Like the throat sweet?'

Ron smiles. 'No, Lozenge was a massive digital patient record system the Brits tried to put in place at the end of the twentieth century. I got involved in the last few months as it collapsed. It wasn't good. Between ten and twelve billion pounds down the toilet; they're still counting. Twenty thousand of it went into my pocket, but they got their money's worth there. Since then, I don't really know what's happened, a lot of local initiatives instead of an over-arching system, I think.'

'You think that's gonna explain it?'

'It's possible, but it's difficult to prove it. We've got an increasing number of these odd projections in the data that's coming from the UK. My guess is there's some incompatibility between their records system, whatever it is, and ours. Our quality assurance flags up certain things for checking, people with very short projections is one, obviously. We don't really want to send someone a golden envelope that tells them they have less than a week to live, or the Apollo 13 scenario, we send out a projection that has passed by the time it arrives. Imagine the publicity on *that* one.'

Adam smiles weakly.

'Another of our flags is younger people with relatively short projections. This hasn't come up often, until we started to get British data. Now, there's so many flags, it looks like we're standing outside the United Nations.'

'It *has* to be computer error?'

'Unless British kids are unhealthier than children from war zones, refugee camps, or famine areas. You notice British kids dropping dead in the streets over there? No? So, it's the elephants. It could be a small thing, but we can't find it as yet. We had a persistent number of cases in the US, can't find a reason for them, according to their projections those children should've died a couple of years ago. They're all still alive and kicking.'

'Was there any comeback?'

'LegalDiv changed our terms and conditions to make sure there wouldn't be, and I know they've tried to bury the stories when the parents started going to the press or the law. But I'm surprised to see this one has slipped through the net, our QC should have picked it up, might be because your doctor nabbed one before we'd completed the full roll out.'

'So, what can we do about Will?'

'Same as we do with all these problems. We'll change it.'

'You'll what?'

'Change it. When do you want him to die?'

'You–'

'Average life expectancy for a male in the UK is, what now, seventyish? I know it used to be more in the UK, until you went all loopy economics this last twenty years or so. What was that truly daft prime minister's name? Blonde, scary eyes?'

'Trussed, I think.'

'Should've been. Anyway, shall we give your boy eighty-five years? Ninety?'

'You can't do that!'

'What do you mean, *I can't do that?*'

'It's fraud, surely?'

'This isn't *fraud*. This is *business*. Did you sleep through Dieselgate, Adam? Cheating emissions tests so that cars could pour umpteen times the permitted levels of pollutants into the air? *That* was fraud. Tobacco company bosses swearing nicotine wasn't addictive? Et cetera, et cetera, since the dawn of capitalism?'

'But we put months into getting the math of this right, you can't simply change a date. What if he really is sick?'

'The kid ain't sick. They've been through every line of his medical data, same as the American kids, there's nothing else to explain early death dates, our top minds have been all over this. They haven't got leukaemia or cancer; the computer can't say they're dying if we haven't put something in to justify it. It doesn't have any secret tests. It's our old friend GIGO.'

'Garbage in, garbage out.'

'But we still can't find the garbage *in*. If it's not in the data, it's in the programming or some data-transfer gibberish. We simply can't find it. But the kid ain't sick. I'll change his date.'

'But you can't do that!'

'Listen, since Popeye took control all our work has been trashed, most of our data has been so squeezed and bounced, you wouldn't recognise it. But give her her due, at least she's also changed our terms and conditions, there is now not a single sentence, not one, in any of our literature that promises any of the projections we make are any nearer to the truth than your average daily astrology chart. It's quite brazen. Have you read our stuff? It's all *it depends on this* and *it depends on that...* Have you watched the adverts? They're the real genius. What do they say? *Imagine you could find out how long your life was going to be... What would you do if you could plan your life to the minute?* That's it. *Imagine! What would you do if...?* Nowhere do we say we're going to *tell* you! It's all *suggested*. We no longer promise *any* level of accuracy at all. My guess is we've got a linguistics department hidden away in some bunker somewhere, with more people in it than the math, programming and medical Divs combined.'

'But it must be illegal.'

'Hell no, we're in the digital Wild West now. Although, this time we're moving east, so it's the Wild East. Lotta Brits to flog stuff to. But the sheriff's now on a horse, bit of a nag, actually, especially since they had their Brexity brain fever. He won't be here for years. We've got the plains to ourselves. Anything goes over there, now that they've chosen us over the other Europeans for spiritual guidance. And by the time the sheriff arrives, what can he do? If someone dies before their LifeTime projection, they won't be alive to complain. If they live beyond it, what's their complaint? We tell 'em they probably ate too many apples, kept the doctor away, what're you complaining about? We edit the rulebook as we go along. The papers lap up the "accurate" stories we feed 'em, and occasionally run a piece on somebody who *cheats the grave*. People love that stuff. It's a perfect money printing machine for everybody, now that Popeye's in charge.'

'I can't believe there's no comeback.'

'Not anymore. If we took out all our math, everything, and simply spun a wheel every time we got a new member, we've got no legal obligation to get it right. Or even close. Pure chance is all we promise now, so how can we ever be wrong? And even when we are wrong, you wanna sue? Okay then, prove to us how many burgers you've eaten in the last thirty years. Prove you've never smoked. Prove you run every night.'

'So, how come people are still paying for this shit?'

'Oh, Adam! You're not seriously asking? You might as well ask how come people read horoscopes? How come they gamble? Use dating apps? How come people are still paying for this shit? Because they're people. *Why are you surprised?* is my question.'

'Are you serious?'

'Am I serious? You ever buy a computer?'

'Of course?'

'And then what? You get a virus, so what do you do? You spend hundreds more bucks on anti-virus protection. Then what happens? They hack your internet banking. You lose thousands, then you spend months trying to prove to the banks you didn't tattoo your password on your knuckles. Does anyone – ever, in the history of the world – take their computer back to the shop and say *this is a piece of shit? Gimme my money back.* Do they?'

Adam stares like a child who's recently discovered that Santa's a fence and the tooth fairy's been short-changing him for years – selling his teeth at a two hundred per cent markup to some aphrodisiac potion-blender in the Far East.

'But we worked our butts off to make this work...'

'Yeah, and they decided astrology would sell better. Actually, there's a rumour, only a rumour so don't go saying this to anybody, but the rumour says they've passed it all over to some AI system that now controls everything: the projections; the pricing; the marketing – everything's geared to profit. The word says the AI profiles the customer, then gears their projection around how much healthy food supplements and magic potions they'd be likely to buy. Men respond to a low projection with their wallets much more than women do, I've heard said. I mean, let's be honest, it makes a lotta sense, doesn't it? What else would they do with all this data and an AI bot? It's all rumour, but who knows anymore? So, get over it. What does your boy deserve? Shall we say ninety-two? Go on, play God.

I'll get it packaged up and sent over. Wish him my best. Seriously. But tell him it's a game. That's all it is now.'

'And what do I tell his parents?'

'The same. It's a horoscope. Nothing more. The health data we've sucked in is now nothing more than a smokescreen for the money magicians.'

'How can you do this?'

'Oh, I'm not here for much longer, Adam. I've got my exit strategy. Probably won't be here next time you visit, but keep that under your bowler too, will ya?'

Paula's phone buzzes in her pocket. She's not meant to answer personal calls, but the manager is out delivering repeat prescriptions to elderly customers and the shop is empty.

'Hi, Paula? It's Annie, from the school.'

'Hi, Annie, everything okay?'

'Well, your mum hasn't come in today and she's not answering her phone. Is she all right?'

'Far as I know. Ummm, I'm at work, let me check it out. I'll give her a call, and if I get no joy I'll see if Cathy can pop round and find out what's wrong. I'll get back to you, okay?'

'Okay, love. Thanks. Not to worry.'

Paula phones Michaela's mobile. Voicemail. Tries her landline. No luck. Phones Mick. Nothing. Phones Cathy.

'Hi, Paula. Thought you were at work today?'

'Yes, I am, but listen. The school called. Mum's not at work and isn't answering either phone. Would you or Steve have a moment to pop round the house, make sure she hasn't... I don't know? Could you pop round?'

'Sure, don't worry, I'll go now.'

'Will you get back to me?'

'Of course.'

She tries Michaela's phones again. Same result.

As they leave the house, Cathy's phone rings.

'You drive,' she says. 'This might be... oh, it's Adam. Hey, Adam?'

Steve starts the car and listens in as Cathy switches the call to speakerphone.

'Hey, Cathy, everything okay?'

'Yeah, just got an odd call from Paula, Michaela isn't in school and isn't answering her phones. Steve and I are going over to check on her.'

'Right. That's strange. She wasn't going down with anything, was she?'

'Don't think so, we haven't seen her for a couple of days. It's probably nothing. How are you? Aren't you in the States?'

'Yes, that's why I'm calling. Good news about Will, so I wanted to tell you straight away.'

'Go on!' she says, turning to Steve, grabbing his wrist.

'Yeah, it's all good. Everything solved. We checked his medical stuff first and found a lot of corrupted data in the transfer from the UK to us. We've done a complete check through the systems and we're issuing a new projection. I can't give you any details but Will's going to live to a ripe old age. I thought you'd like to know. We've sent a new pack over by express courier; you'll have it in the morning.'

'That's brilliant,' Cathy blurts, starting to cry. 'Are they sure, absolutely positive?'

'As positive as your doctor was; he's a healthy lad. Everyone here's so sorry, me especially. I don't know what to say. I've also got twice the cost of the medical reimbursed to compensate you for the trouble and upset, and I've included a few other bits'n'bobs in the parcel by way of apology.'

'That's brilliant. Thanks, Adam, take care, we'll see you soon.' She disconnects the call and stares out through the front windscreen.

'That's a relief,' Steve says.

Cathy continues to stare impassively through the windscreen.

———

Steve pulls into the drive of Michaela's house. No car. It's a two-up two-down, tidy mid-terrace that Cathy would sometimes swap for their farmstead. The opportunity to sit down and read a book with a glass of wine in the small back garden. She'd maybe have some spare time to tippy tap a few chapters of her novel if she didn't have a field to mow, or the piglets to catch, or the veg to water or collect or, or, or... What she wouldn't give? At times.

She rings the bell as she slides her key into the lock.

'Michaela? You in?' she shouts. No response. 'I'll go up,' she says to Steve, trotting up the stairs. The bed is made, all neat and tidy. Back bedroom, bathroom, nothing out of place. She meets Steve who's been out in the back garden, even checked the small shed, in case. In case what? In case she locked herself in it?

They stare at each other, then scan the sitting room for clues. What do the police search for in the crime dramas? All Cathy can see is a tidy life. Her phone rings. Paula. She puts it on speaker.

'Hi, Paula? Any news?'

'I don't know. I phoned Fiona in Hunstanton, on an off chance, Mum sometimes goes to hers Sunday afternoons. And she was there yesterday. They had afternoon tea together then a walk on the beach. She headed home before it got dark. It means we know where she was yesterday.'

'Right. We're at the house. No sign, no car. And there's a letter on the mat. So, it might be she wasn't here last night cos post is always early. Wait a min, Steve's found something in the kitchen. I'll pass him over.'

'Hi there. Look, I don't want to be dramatic, but you know what Mum's like, anti-germ warrior? Never uses a dishcloth, drain and then away? Well, the crocks in the drainer are from yesterday lunch, there's no breakfast stuff, so she almost certainly didn't have breakfast here this morning.'

Both Paula and Cathy notice Steve doesn't make a 'secret lover' crack, which would be normal for him in any other situation. One by one, they contemplate whether they'd be silly to suggest calling the police. They all wait for one of the others to suggest it, agree to meet at Mick's that evening and make a decision regarding what to do there.

Part Three

<u>The Beginning of the End</u>

'An apple a day keeps the doctor away...'
—Traditional proverb

Chapter Twenty-Nine

'Higher testosterone levels in men linked to greater melanoma risk.'
—*The Guardian*, 31 March 2021

'I think we should call the police,' Paula says finally. She's chewed it over all afternoon in the shop, unable to keep her mind on the simplest tasks: she's short-changed three customers – Christ knows how much money she's *given* away. 'Mum's never done anything like this before. It's so out of character. To *not* go to school...?'

Cathy glances at her and nods slightly but doesn't speak.

Steve looks across at Mick. 'It is out of character. I can't imagine her showing up here with a reasonable explanation, can you?'

Mick shakes his head. 'No, it's not right.'

The sound of a car crunching up the gravel drive sucks attention like a black hole drawing light. Lucky Boy leaps to his feet, barking, but Mick quietens him with a single raised finger. Paula is first to the window.

'Jesus, it's the police!' She starts to cry as she heads for the front door, opening it as a policeman and policewoman approach. 'Is it Mum? Michaela Strong? Have you found her?' She's watched enough TV police dramas to know what this looks like. Steve arrives at her shoulder.

The policeman introduces himself as PC Tommy Bruner, and asks if they can come in, making it infinitely worse. He then makes it worse still, by asking them to sit down.

'You're Tommy from school, aren't you? You were in Mum's class, in primary school. I remember you,' Paula blurts through her tears. She recognises his face. He nods, looks at Steve who nods recognition as well. Still, nobody sits, as if this might stop him saying whatever it is he's come to say.

'This is PC Sofie West,' Tommy continues, obviously struggling to contain his own emotions. 'She's a family liaison officer, her job—'

'Please tell us. Have you found her?' Mick's voice cuts through Tommy's trembling speech like a judge in court. 'You've found her, yes?'

Tommy nods, a tear rolls down one cheek, he wipes it away, opens a small notebook and begins to read, voice that of a six-year-old confessing to breaking a window.

'Earlier this afternoon, following information from a member of the public, we found a car, a red Fiesta, with the body of a woman in—' Again, he stops, sucks air, wipes his face. The liaison officer moves as if to take his notebook, but he regains control. 'The body of a woman inside. Registration of the car and identity documents inside are Michaela Strong's.'

'You know her,' Paula sobs. 'Is it her?'

He looks her straight in the face. Paula was a year above him in school, out of his circle. He nods slightly.

'We'll need to ask someone to do an identification...'

There is a beat of time that none of them will ever forget.

'I'll do that,' Mick says. 'I'll do that...'

'Hi, gorgeous! What's wrong?' Adam's facial expression and tone of voice change completely between the first two words and the last two. It takes that long for his screen to show him something has happened.

'It's Mum,' Paula whispers, desperate at seeing his smile disintegrate in the time it's taken him to greet her. 'I don't know how to tell you. She's dead.'

Adam watches, stunned, as she cries softly. He never had the *everybody remembers where they were when Kennedy was shot* memory, too young, but he knows now what everyone else was talking about.

'What's happened?'

'They're not sure,' she sobs. 'They found her in her car. She'd run off the road into a field. They don't think there were any other cars involved. They think she simply died at the wheel. They don't like to speculate, but we're obviously wondering, you know, Granny Celia, heart attack? They're doing a post-mortem.'

'I'm so sorry. I'm coming home. I'll get a flight first thing. I'll be home soon as I can.'

'Hurry,' is all she says in reply.

It's hard to imagine anything worse than the funeral of a child, but a funeral where the vast majority of mourners are young children comes close. The crying is infused with a sense of absolute shock, complete disbelief that the waking nightmare is continuing, minute after dreadful minute. It's one of life's hardest lessons. *It's not fair*, doesn't get close. Chances are, many of the mourners will lose whatever faith they had, destroyed by a childish feeling of injustice that will never be forgotten.

The town closes. There are only seven shops, including the Fish and Anchor. She wasn't a regular by any means, rarely been in, but even that shuts. There's also a sizeable media scrum outside the church and throughout the town. Michaela's untimely death has catapulted her into the startling position of being the first LifeTime member in the UK to die. Mick has dominated the media's attention for so long, but now the focus is shifting fast. Everybody wants to know the answer to one question. What had Michaela's projection said? The family wonder for a while how the media know Michaela had a projection, until Steve reminds them that Mick had told the whole story of his birthday gifts to the *Wix'n'Dist*.

Mick has a couple of dozen people back to The Manor; he's got the caterers in from Sacklow Hall. He's given the back lawn a once over with his ride-on mower in preparation, in case some of the guests spread outside. Adam's in the kitchen to see if there's any coffee. Steve is pouring himself a cup.

'Hi, Adam, meant to say thanks for Will's new projection, I know we're lawbreakers, but we had a peek, thanks.'

He shrugs. 'I can only apologise again. Anything I can do to put it right. Cathy okay with it?'

Steve takes a breath, glances behind to make sure they're not overheard.

'She's happy, yes. But there's something, I can tell. She's going to keep that first date in her diary or in her mind somewhere, and I don't think she's going to truly believe it was wrong until it's passed. Maybe not even then. She's like that. You know, she used to do the lottery, same numbers every week, my birthday, her birthday, all that. Did it for years. Then she stopped. No reason. But here's the thing... she still checks the numbers.'

'What? That's mad.'

'Crazy, I know. So, you know what I do?'

'You buy the ticket.'

'Course I do! I mean, have you ever heard of anything so crazy? The pair of us?'

They laugh briefly, then Steve moves back into the lounge.

Adam decides to wander outside onto the back porch. It's been a long day. No one's said anything, but the LifeTime projection has hung in the air of every conversation like he's an escaped convict. He's felt people staring at him, thinking he'd got access to some database that tells him what Michaela's projection is. No one's said anything, but the looks in their eyes have been enough.

'Need a favour,' Mick says, appearing from the house, drink in hand, then lowering himself unsteadily into the large double seat, next to Adam. Lucky Boy pads behind him and settles himself on the floor. It's a phrase that sends chills down Adam's neck. He remembers Mick's last favour, where that's led. The moon is fighting gamely against a few wispy clouds; they hear the church clock strike the half-hour. Adam checks his watch, 1.30am. *Christ!* He's got a flight before lunch.

'What?' he says, against every better judgement screaming at him.

Mick belches, makes a gesture with his whiskey tumbler, the words don't come with the movement. He's drunker than he was a couple of hours previously when they last spoke.

'Can't find Michaela's projection,' he says finally, shaking his head like he's trying to lose a loose-fitting hat. He's slurring slightly, fighting to appear more sober than he clearly is. 'Bloody journos are pestering me at the gate and on the phone. Can't find the bloody thing. She won't have opened it, obviously,

259

seeing as her birthday's not for a while yet. I've had a snoop round her house but nothing. Can you organise me a replacement? I understand they'll probably want a reprinting fee or whatever. Just get me another, bloody pronto. Okay?'

Adam calculates. Mick's *wait till your birthday* command is a first as far as he's concerned – so the request for a replacement is equally unusual.

'Can't see an issue,' he says. 'I'm back stateside tomorrow, I'll see Ron.'

'Good man!' Mick says, patting Adam's forearm with meaning, squeezing it to make sure he knows how grateful he is. 'I did warn her, you know? All that crap she ate, she never did any exercise, and the stress at work. She was always stressed. I told her to watch her ticker.'

Adam nods limply; Mick slops whiskey onto his shirt as he tries to take another sip.

'You know, you're the best thing that ever happened to my Paula,' Mick suddenly says, wiping the whiskey away with hesitant dabs of his hand. 'I'd have killed you if you hadn't made her happy. I mean it.'

'I know,' Adam replies, deciding that humour is the best way to handle Mick in this mood.

'You see, I've let her down–'

'Don't be–'

'No, listen. I have. I've let them all down, all my life.'

'Mick–'

'Listen, and you'll understand.' He takes another pull at his drink. 'You like my house?' he asks, waving his half-full glass around like he's acting the drunk in a village hall play.

'It's great.'

'It's not mine. Everybody thinks it's mine. But it isn't.' He shakes his head theatrically, as if the shakes add more words to what he's already said. 'You see, before old Lady Cage died, she gave us the option to buy. But we could never have afforded it, not even with Celia working full time. I loved the place. You can see why, can't you?' He doesn't wait for an answer. 'So, she made some change to her will, said we could continue renting it after her death. Absolute pittance she charged, she liked us, you see. Young doctor and pretty nurse in the village? She wanted us to be here, give the village a bit of something. It left us mountains of spare cash for the Jag and my golf. But I was so ashamed, that we could never afford the house. So, after Celia died, when people started assuming that we somehow *owned* the place, I never set them right. Anybody asked outright, I simply shrugged them off, said the old lady loved us and gave us a great deal. Deal of the century. All lies.'

Adam stares at the moon as the clouds glide by. Why hadn't Mick glided past his chair instead of hooking him into another of his family secrets?

'Anyway. That's why I'm glad you're taking care of Paula, and that's why I'm making a bit of money out of your LifeTime thingy; you see, none of my family will inherit this house, it'll go to Lady Cage's daughter, that's who we rent it off. You might actually have solved a lot of my financial worries, Adam. I want Paula to be all right.' He pats Adam's arm again, best-pals-forever style.

Time passes. Adam wonders if he can stand up and move away, but Mick leans over and whispers.

'You know, something strange. When I was on that TV thingy with Tony Trent. He told me which box to open for that last question. Told me to ask for number four. Easiest question in the world. Where's LifeTime HQ? I mean, what was that all about? Handed me the ten thousand pounds. Don't understand it.'

They sit for longer. Mick doesn't seem to be expecting a reply and Adam can't think of one anyway.

'Look at this,' Mick says suddenly, heaving himself forward and setting his glass on the floor. He half turns in the seat and starts unbuttoning his shirt, pulls it open. 'Know what they are?' he asks.

Adam stares at the dozen or so dark marks splattered across Mick's chest; it's like a child has carelessly flicked a fully-loaded paintbrush. Adam shakes his head slowly, has a feeling of something really bad unfolding. Why didn't he make his excuses?

'You remember the story I told on my birthday? At the hotel? My mate from Oz, Ted? Laid out in the sun by his mum? Well, I was laid next to him.' He slowly buttons up his shirt, lifts his glass up and takes another pull, then settles back in the chair.

More time passes, clouds move. When the clouds pass in front of the moon, it looks as if the moon is moving. Adam thinks his life is moving into a place he had never expected.

'Have you had someone take a look at them?' He wonders what the hell he's doing in this conversation with Mick.

Mick smiles, then chuckles.

'What? You mean a doctor?'

'Well...'

Mick laughs. 'I am a fucking doctor, Adam. It's cancer. Same type Ted had. I don't need a doctor to tell me that.' He breathes in and lets the air out of his nostrils slowly, like the life force is draining out of him here and now. He half turns again, facing Adam. 'So, you see, when your LifeTime show came onstage, I realised immediately it was *exactly* what I needed. A chance to tell them what I wanted them to know, without actually telling them. Do you understand? I couldn't have taken all the pity, you see. All the whispering behind hands, *there's Mick, he's dying, you know, big C, poor bastard.* So, by getting the LifeTime, I've warned them. Got them thinking about it. They can start getting ready without treating me like a specimen in a jar. And without the fucking pity, Adam. You see, the last thing I wanted from any of them, especially Paula, was the pity. I want my life to end pretty quickly one day. Not drag out in a painful tragedy of chemo, hair loss and *fucking pity*. I'd seriously jump off the cliff first. You understand, don't you? And you won't blab a word of this to anyone, I know you won't.'

Adam tries to think of some consoling words that don't sound like pity. There aren't any. 'Why are you telling me this?' he says finally.

'I don't really know. It might be the booze, I've had plenty. But I think it's probably that you're the only one I know who won't tell anybody. I suppose with her mother now gone, I want to make sure you'll take care of Paula. I can't tell her, she's the one I most want to keep this from, and I can't tell Steve cos he wouldn't be able to hide it, and it wouldn't be fair. And Cathy would tell Paula in minutes. I know I can trust you. Although there is another reason.' He drains his glass in a long swallow. 'When I'm gone, I want you to tell Paula that I told you, and I want you to tell her why I didn't want her to know. And ask her this – would she rather have spent the last God knows how long it might be knowing? Or was she happy with the way she and I were cos she didn't know? Cos that's gonna make *me* a lot happier. Am I making sense, I've drunk rather a lot of this?'

'You're okay,' Adam says quietly. 'I understand what you're thinking. It probably is the best way. You can handle it, I know that. And she wouldn't. It would spoil the time you have left. It's a brave thing you've done for her. But I won't forgive you for the hole you've put me in.'

Mick smiles, laughs loudly. If bears could laugh, they'd sound like this.

'Price you pay, my son,' he says as the porch door opens. 'Price you pay.'

'What price does he have to pay?' Paula asks, walking a slightly wobbly walk in her bare feet.

Mick stands, folds her in his arms like that large, hugely amused, gentle bear.

'Ah, now that's me and my drinking buddy's secret, ain't it, Adam?' He looks over Paula's shoulder and winks at him.

Adam smiles a half smile.

'Quiet as the grave, me,' Adam says, which makes Mick roar with laughter again.

'Oh, you've got a good 'un there, lass,' he says. 'Take care of him. You take care of him an' he'll take care of you. Now, I'm off to bed before I embarrass myself. Goodnight, all.'

Having kissed him goodnight, Paula lowers herself down next to Adam.

'What was *that* all about? Price you pay?'

'Best part of a bottle of Bushmills,' he says, almost to himself.

Paula snuggles up against his arm.

'He's not a bad old stick, is he? I know he can be a bit of a grouch, and he dropped you right in it with his LifeTime escapade, but you do get along, you and him? Don't you?'

She pulls herself closer into his embrace and Adam notices how cold it's become.

'Yeah, we do. He's okay.'

'Good,' she says, squeezing herself closer still. 'He needs a few pals to have some man-chats with. Don't you think?'

'Yeah, I guess he probably does...'

Chapter Thirty

'Scientists Have Reached a Key Milestone in Learning How to
Reverse Aging.'
—*TIME*, 12 January 2023

On the way home in the car, Adam tentatively raises the
issue of Michaela's projection, and Mick's wish to see it.

'What does he want with that?' Paula sighs. 'He's been
fretting about it all day. Cathy said Mum told her she'd thrown
it away, but I couldn't tell him that.'

'I'm not entirely sure, but it's a bit of a hot topic now with
the press. They want to see how accurate the projection was.'

'Is *that* it?'

Adam doesn't want to ask her outright to look for it so is
relieved, in a way, to hear that he doesn't need to bother.

'You sure she's thrown it away?' he asks.

'That's what she said. You remember how angry she was on
the day? It doesn't surprise me in the least.'

He drives on. 'I'll ask Ron to reissue it when I get back
tomorrow.'

'Do you have to go back so soon?'

'I guess I could delay it a week, if you want me to.'

She weighs it up. 'It'd be nice to have you here, although I've already made promises to go to Mick's the day after tomorrow and see Cathy the next day. No, you go. Do what you have to do. I'm going to be busy with things. Best you get this done and then you'll be here when I'm on my own.'

He nods, wishing for a moment when at least one of the wheels in his life would slow a little. He thought he'd spend less time stateside now that his job was specifically UK-centric, it's been the opposite so far.

'Where are you going?' she says suddenly.

'*Shit*! Forgot again!' He turns the car, and they smile at each other. If nothing else, their new house has the ability to make them both smile.

'Shall I order those curtains I showed you, for the baby's room?'

He shrugs, unable to remember being shown curtains.

'Yeah, they were nice.'

She puts her hand on his as it rests on the gearstick, speaks quietly, almost to herself. 'I don't know how to behave, you know? There are moments, like now, when I feel normal, happy even. Then I remember, and it feels like I shouldn't be feeling that. Like I should be sad all the time. I feel like I shouldn't be having any happy thoughts.'

'I think that's probably a normal feeling, you can't keep concentrating on sad things all the time. I told you about when my grandfather died? My mum insisted that we tell each other happy stories about him; this was the day of the funeral. I was only ten, maybe eleven, the house was full of mourners and there we were, my mum, my sister and I, telling funny stories about things he'd said and done. We were sat away in a corner giggling and laughing while all around us people had long faces and sad expressions. It was weird, but it seemed to work. I remember feeling thankful that I had some sort of permission *not* to feel sad all the time, as it had become quite a strain and I kept forgetting. Before the funeral, I sometimes had to make a positive effort to *act* sad. It wasn't that I didn't love my granddad; I don't think you can concentrate on one thing all the time. And we shouldn't feel we have to. Our minds wander, we forget, at least for a while. Isn't that how we get over it, in the end?'

Paula rubs the back of his hand. She loves his homespun, slightly off-the-wall philosophy – if that isn't too grand a term to use.

'Granddad will be next,' she says, almost to herself.

'Oh, honey, I didn't mean to–'

'No, you didn't, I've been noticing–'

'I really wouldn't hang on the LifeTime date; you know that's as vague as can be. Don't live these next months waiting for him to die on cue.'

'No, it's nothing to do with that at all; I see it. He's slowing down, even as he tries to outrun his projection, which everyone knows he's trying to do. You know he's power walking every day now? Mum told me. Silly old fool. I think he might be trying to outrun the baby, you know? He's trying to buy time so he's still here when I give birth.' Her hands move instinctively over her bump, caressing it softly.

'You really think so?'

'Put yourself in his position, he's projected to die about a week before I'm due to give birth. Wouldn't you try to race it? I think he's running himself into the ground. He'll either have a heart attack out on the road one day or he's simply going to go downhill rapidly. If I'm honest, God I'm in a morbid mood, if I'm honest, I'd prefer him to go quickly than see him deteriorate and start losing his memory or his health. Does that sound terrible?'

'Of course it doesn't. But you don't really see him going downhill, do you, not with all the power walking?'

'I do really. Look at the house. I know he's spruced it up a bit for today, but it's getting worse. I used the upstairs loo cos the one downstairs was busy, and it's a tip. I poked my nose into his bedroom; he never used to live like that. You know, I came round recently on the way home from work, and he was asleep in the armchair. I rang the bell and banged on the window but couldn't wake him. For a minute, I thought he was dead. He's never done that, doze during the day. I ended up phoning him from my mobile, that was the only thing that woke him, but you should've seen him, he suddenly seemed very frail. I know he's stopped the smoking and drinking – well, excluding today, and that's good. But he's looking old, and all this walking and healthy eating, don't you think that's a sign of a bit of senility?'

'I thought he was simply trying to hang on to life.'

'Maybe, but there's life and there's *life*, isn't there? I'd hate to see him humiliated in nappies and unable to walk or–'

'Has he *said* something to you?'

'God, no! Imagine! I can simply see it happening. It would break my heart and worse, it would break his. He'd be so *angry* if he lost his independence. His pride...'

'I know,' says Adam.

Because he does.

Saturday morning is Big Breakfast. Steve's always up at six and out in the allotment, doing battle with whichever enemy has appeared: weeds, weevils, slugs, greenfly, blackfly, frost, hail, next door's cat, squirrels, seagulls, robins... yes, robins. The gardener's friend? Not when they're tucking into Steve's strawberries before they even reach the size of dice. It's a jungle out there.

Cathy has a lie-in, but her payback is that she'll do a traditional fry-up. It's the one time she dominates the kitchen: Steve is always co-cook, except for Saturday mornings – and whenever the pizza delivery crew come to the rescue. Or the chippy. Or the Chinese. Or the Indians.

There are rules to Cathy's Big Breakfast, two of them. Firstly, Steve has to be in and washed by nine – then finished and back out again by nine thirty. Suits him fine: doesn't want to leave those vicious robins too much time to attack, although today he's gone for a bike ride. Sod the strawberries. Rule two: Will has to be washed, dressed and at the table – *Yes, Ma'am!* – by nine thirty. She finds he's always in the mood to chat during Big Breakfast.

'Mum...?'

'Yes.'

'Can we have a party?'

'When?'

'When GG dies.'

She continues cutting her sausage, but the pace of sawing slows noticeably.

'It's called a funeral, love. Yes, we–'

'I know that. I mean before.'

'Before he dies?'

'Yeah. Sort of say goodbye. The Ancient Egyptians used to do it, we learned about it in history. They gave the Pharaohs presents to take with them into the afterlife.'

She wishes she could get inside his head. It's down at the moment so she can only see his hair, sandy and tousled, he hasn't combed it. Wishes there was an app somewhere, *inhead* or *brainshow*, or something, which would let you feel what another person was feeling: maybe even think their thoughts with the premium version. Is he thinking aloud while chopping and shovelling his breakfast? Half his mind on Michaela's funeral, the first he's ever been to? Or is he really worried about Great-Granddad? Fixating on it? She doesn't dare ask, for fear of feeding the fixation, if that's what it is. And yet, is she wrong to ignore it? Will he go deeper into himself, worry and brood and turn into a recluse, or something? They should talk about it. She wishes she knew how. All the parenting handbooks she used to devour were useless on this point. It was all feeding and teething and potty training. They all stopped before they got to the *How do you bury a great-grandparent* bit.

'You know what?' he says suddenly, holding up a chunk of sausage on his fork.

Cathy braces. What's he come up with now? Is he going to suggest they give him presents to take to the afterlife? She doesn't know if she can indulge that sort of thing. Neither she nor Steve are in any way religious. They're agnostics. Or atheists. The ones who haven't got time to think about it, except when they drop an egg on the floor, or hit their thumb with a hammer, and then shout *God!* or *Jesus!* Doesn't the education department have a psychologist they can contact for this type of situation?

'What, love?'

'These are the best sausages *ever!*'

'That's good,' she says, relief and worry and concern and doubt flooding her mind like a fire hose on full. 'That's good. Fancy another?'

Chapter Thirty-One

'Cost of living worsening health of children in UK, say school nurses. Survey reports increased levels of tooth decay and stunted growth as families struggle to afford nutritious meals.'
—*The Guardian*, 28 June 2023

A dam's car clears the security tunnels in the entrance dome, but misses the turn to his hotel. 'Where are we going?' he asks the on-board support.

'Our destination is the residence of Jaz Forrester, Halicarnassus Dome.'

'Why are we going there now?' Adam asks, perplexed. He's tired and wants to shower and change after the transatlantic flight.

'I do not have that information,' the voice responds.

'Can I at least take a shower and drop my case at the hotel before we head over there?'

'That destination is not on the schedule.'

He watches as the hotel recedes into the distance, its tiers of restaurant decks clearly visible, like a flowered staircase going nowhere except the top, where he and Paula hatched their improbable plan to tempt Mick into the twenty-first century. The lake comes into view, Jaz's lodge a brown patch on the near shore. He sees another cab arrive and Ron exit and head swiftly inside. Interesting.

Adam gives his cab instructions to take his bags back to his hotel after dropping him off. This, it's perfectly happy to do. He's then met at the front door by a flunkey wearing white gloves, and he's ushered briskly inside. Over by the picture window, five people are sitting around the brightly polished hardwood table. The two nearest him are suits he doesn't recognise; Ron is taking his seat opposite Jaz. At the head of the table, dressed in a dark crimson jacket and cream blouse, is Hannah Lennox.

'Welcome, Adam. We're sorry for your loss,' she says. The others murmur their condolences, which Adam acknowledges with a nod. There are six desk blotters placed around the eight places, so he knows he's the last to arrive. He also knows his place, at the foot of the table, like a star witness – or the prime suspect.

'Will you lead, Jaz?' They've either agreed this in advance, or he's telepathic, because he launches straight into what appears to be a ready meal of a speech: it's more of a ready snack.

'Thank you, Hannah. As you all know, events have moved quickly in the United Kingdom. The death of Michaela Strong is already attracting enormous media coverage, as she is the first LifeTime member to die there. We need to have an agreed marketing message ready. Adam?'

Most of Adam's brain is still at thirty-thousand feet, the small portion of it that is attending this meeting goes into shock. He's seen this type of high-level, executive brain-storming session in movies, where sharp-suited execs joust for position using only their wits, a few Machiavellian dark arts, and maybe a line or two of coke snorted beforehand off the top of the toilet cistern. Adam has had a couple of beers on the plane, and is feeling the effects, which are quite the opposite of a couple of lines of coke. He plays the one strategic card his brain is capable of inventing under such pressure: he reaches for the water jug and pours himself a glass to buy himself some time.

He drinks half the glass, slowly, and refills it. 'Well,' he says, finally. This gets their full, undivided attention.

Ron rescues him. 'Before we move on to strategy, could I clarify a minor, but maybe important detail.'

Adam, ever the gent, gives him the floor.

'It's only a couple of facts I need to square that I've got some mixed messaging on.' There is silence around the table, so he continues. 'First thing I heard was that Michaela Strong died in a car accident. This causes us no issues here, as you all know, because this form of accidental death, along with suicides, murders, et cetera, are all specifically excluded from LifeTime projections. We only make projections relating to natural deaths. Fine. But this morning, I got an alert from a small UK newspaper, the um, *Wixlow–*'

'*Wixlow and District Gazette,*' Adam cuts in, a desperate attempt to put some credibility on the table.

'That's the one, *Wixlow and District Gazette*. This report, it's in this morning, says she had a heart attack.'

'That's right,' Adam confirms. 'The post-mortem confirmed she had a heart attack and died at the wheel. The car simply rolled off the road into a field. There was no collision, no other vehicle involved.'

'And there lies our problem,' Ron says solemnly. 'A heart attack is a natural death, therefore our projection applies. Her LifeTime projection was for another twenty-four years.'

'Jesus,' Jaz hisses. There's general movement around the

table, people shuffling position, trying desperately to shed responsibility, maybe. 'How old was she?'

Ron taps his laptop, Adam assumes he has Michaela's details to hand, but he needs every bit of credibility he can scrape off the floor.

'She'd be fifty in a few weeks,' he says quietly.

'So, she was forty-nine with twenty-four more years projected, we said she'd live until she was seventy-three. How does that compute?' Jaz again, eyes switching from Adam to Ron and back again.

The silence returns, more shuffling, responsibility floating in the air like yet another coronavirus on the loose, nobody wanting it to infect them.

'I have to say,' Adam opens, immediately regretting starting the sentence before he has the end of it clear in his mind. 'It's just I'm surprised now to hear that Michaela had such a long projection, given her history.'

'What do you mean?' Ron says, slightly defensive, but then who isn't?

'The family history, heart problems. Her mother died of a heart attack when she was in her thirties, I think. I know medical techniques have improved since then but seventy-three still seems quite a long–'

'What do you mean, her mother had a heart attack?' Ron again, eyes on Adam, fleetingly, hands fluttering as if he's playing a particularly intricate maze game on his laptop.

'What I said, her mother died of a heart attack. You'd have thought that would have brought Michaela's projection down well below seventy–'

'I've got no family history of heart issues in Michaela's data.'

Adam looks stunned. 'You sure?'

Ron nods, eyes stuck on the stats. 'Nothing.'

The silence settles around the table as each tries to calculate the implications of this piece of information, the likelihood of it affecting them.

'So, we're clear,' Jaz says slowly, like he's thinking aloud, waiting to be contradicted. 'Mick Strong ordered all the projections for his family, didn't he, Adam?' He takes Adam's nod and continues. 'So, if he's forgotten, or whatever, to include Michaela's mother's heart issues in the medical history of Michaela herself, the projection is void. Incomplete data. We got no case to answer. Nothing to explain.'

Six pairs of eyes scan the table, all attempting to ascertain where, if anywhere, responsibility might rest while at the same time, desperately trying not to catch anybody else's eye. All except Hannah Lennox, that is.

'But, in that case, we have a different problem,' she states. Scanning the table for anyone who can see what she, evidently, can. When the silence lengthens, she continues.

'Dr Strong, our poster boy for the LifeTime roll-out in the UK, will appear to be a fool. We'll take collateral from that, even though our Ts and Cs give us no responsibility to check the data provided,' she says quietly. Nobody seems keen to contradict her. 'But it won't be a good look if we've let such a high-profile customer mismanage the application process. Even though we won't be, we might still appear negligent, in some way.'

'Any way we can shut down this news that she had a heart attack?' Jaz asks.

Adam shakes his head. 'But there is a way to protect his reputation, and by extension our own,' he says, looking embarrassed, evasive, like he wishes someone else would come up with the idea.

'What's that?' Hannah Lennox again, moving forward in her seat, eyes like lasers on Adam.

'Well, Michaela wasn't impressed with Mick, Dr Strong, buying the projections. She thought he'd overstepped the mark, not asking people whether they wanted them. Especially Steve and Cathy, the parents of Will, the eleven-year-old. Anyway, Michaela was so angry, she threw hers away. We think she didn't even open it. Nobody knows what it said.'

'*What?*' Jaz and Ron chorus. Hannah's eyes narrow slightly, but her focus stays on Adam.

'Dr Strong actually made it a condition that none of the family opened their projections until their next birthdays, Michaela's is still a while off. But she threw it away anyway. Dr Strong, in fact, asked me yesterday if I could get him a replacement. He, naturally enough, also wants to know what it says.'

'I bet he does,' says Jaz.

'So, we can update it,' Hannah says slowly, the thought seeming to occur as she voices it. She takes the silence to indicate confusion, so she clarifies. 'Before we reissue a replacement to Dr Strong, we can correct the error, include Michaela's family history of heart problems. Can you give us an idea of what sort of a projection that would give us, Ron?'

Birdsong filters in from the trees near the lake. Ron covers it with a volley of keystrokes. 'You say she died young, Michaela's mother?'

'Celia was in her early thirties, I think. I can get the details if–'

'I can get that from public records. So, was Michaela having regular cardiac check-ups?'

'Not that I know of. I'm pretty sure she wasn't. Again, I can–'

'Any reason why not? That seems strange.'

Adam wipes away the sheen of sweat that is breaking out on his brow; the last thing he expected fresh off his flight from the UK was a board-level inquisition. 'I can only guess. She was a bit of an "alternative" person, you know, holistic medicine and all that. Plus, there is the issue of the state of the British healthcare system.'

'That's their *socialist* medicine,' one of the unidentified suits comments sotto voce.

'Actually, it's had a bit of a capitalist makeover in the last twenty years, and that's the problem, it's not nearly as good as it used to be at screening and, well, pretty much everything. And add to that the cost of private medical insurance in the UK, and it's not that unusual for people over there to find themselves with insufficient cover. It's a lot more like it is over here, in fact, than it ever used to be when it was, how did you put it? *Socialist.*'

There's a moment when Adam wonders if he might be sent from the room, but Ron drags the conversation back to the immediate issue of Michaela's projection.

'With that data, the projection falls to six years. That might seem quite a big drop, but the British NHS, their... what is it, Adam?'

'National Health Service.'

'That's it, thanks. Their National Health Service, as you've said, isn't what it used to be, they've seen more cuts in the last few years than at your average barber's shop, and my records show that none of the Strong family have private medical insurance. And if she wasn't having check-ups...'

'Can you do any more?' Hannah asks.

'What do you mean?'

'If Dr Strong forgot to include Michaela's medical history, maybe he got some other things wrong. Any way you can get it lower? Did she work? Was she stressed?'

'Primary school teacher,' Adam offers.

'That's high stress. Can you boost that a bit, Ron?'

'It says she's in education here, doesn't say she's a teacher.'

'Add that. How about smoking? Was she a smoker?'

'Yes, but that's included.'

'How many a day?'

'Um, wait a moment, here it is, average,' says Ron.

'What's that? How many a day do we calculate average to be?' Hannah asks.

'Off the top of my head? I think that was set to ten. Adam, do you remember?'

'Ten sounds about right.'

'Does that seem accurate to you, Adam? Was Michaela a ten-a-day smoker?' says Hannah.

'I don't really know–'

'Could it have been twenty?'

'I...' He shrugs, remembers Steve telling him that Mick had asked him nothing about his own lifestyle; Ron said that Will's application was light on detail. And Adam's already concluded that in order to spring his surprise, Mick couldn't really have asked anybody much. He would probably have predicted Michaela's negative reaction, so almost certainly didn't ask her for a full rundown of her habits.

'What would twenty a day give us, Ron?' Hannah asks.

'Let's see. That and the primary teaching, we're down to two and a half years.'

'And twenty-five?'

Ron's fingers tap rapidly. 'Six hundred and twelve days, that's a little under two years.'

'Can you get it under one? How about diet, was her diet good?'

'She was a vegetarian,' Adam cuts in.

'Vegan?' Hannah again.

'No, she ate eggs, cheese...'

'So, high cholesterol?'

'Possibly...'

'Did she have a sweet tooth?'

'Well, yes, she did.'

'Ron, is her diet accurate?'

Ron's fingers play across the keyboard like a concert pianist. 'Again, it's a bit bland. It says average diet.'

'Nothing about a sweet tooth? What did she like, Adam?'

'I know she liked cakes, and biscuits. Ice cream, oh, of course, chocolate.'

'And alcohol?'

'She drank a lot of wine.'

'Any help, Ron?'

He studies the screen, flicks his fingers across the keys. 'I can bump her food from average to sugar heavy, fat heavy, alcohol consumption from average to above. Gives us three hundred and twenty-four days, that's under eleven months.'

One of the suits, who has watched motionless the whole time, stands, rubbing his hands. 'That should save the good doctor's reputation,' he says, sounding pleased with himself.

'Would we want to go lower? A bit nearer her actual date of death?' Ron asks, fingers still hovering over the keys.

Hannah shakes her head. 'It would look a bit suspicious if we nail her death date without there being any regular cardiac monitoring data available. We can nudge the journos to spin that fact to explain why we were a little out on the projection, but not that far. We still have a problem, however. Possibly an even bigger one.'

The suit sits, eyes roam, thirty seconds pass, sixty.

'Can none of you see it?' she continues, almost to herself.

'Shit!' Adam replies. 'It's Mick.'

Hannah Lennox nods. 'It's Mick. If he's mismanaged Michaela's application data...'

'Then how accurate is his own?'

'Exactly. Especially as it underpins the projection he has,

the one we are advertising to the world.' She stares at Adam. 'You came to MarktDiv from InfoDiv, didn't you?'

'That's right.'

'So, you know how this data works and you'll know, or can find out, how accurate Dr Strong's application figures are if we give you access to them?'

'I can go through the data, and I can find out as much as I can from the family.'

'Good. I want you and Ron to study Dr Strong's numbers. Our reputation depends on them being as accurate as possible.'

Chapter Thirty-Two

'Do Pregnancy and Childbirth Accelerate Aging in Women?
Maybe.'
—*The Washington Post*, 19 October 2019

A dam shares a cab to his hotel with Ron. When they arrive, they sit in the outdoor café to chew the morning.

'What do you think about Dr Strong's projection, Adam? Think it could be way outta shape, like Hannah was suggesting?'

Adam shakes his head. 'I kinda doubt it. I mean, we can go through the figures, check out what he's put in, but he's a seventy-five-year-old guy with a couple of hundred days projected—'

'Less now.'

'Yeah, whatever. But I coulda come up with that projection myself by chatting to him for half an hour. It's got to be close to on the button. We don't have to worry about him dying in *less* than his projected time, he's close enough it won't damage us.'

Ron nods to himself. 'Yeah, the only issue would be if he

goes on and on for years, then reputational damage would accumulate. But he's not some superhuman bodybuilder, is he? You said it yourself; seventy-five years so the projection appears sensible.'

'It does. I guess all we can do is go through his numbers, but I can't see how he could have missed out stuff that would give him a longer projection. It's unlikely. In fact, he told me the other day he has cancer, isn't having treatment.'

'You serious? Jesus. Do we need to factor that into his projection?'

'I don't think we can. He told me in confidence, and who knows if he's right? He hasn't even had a proper diagnosis. Imagine if we include it, and his projection drops by half. He'd want to know why we've included something that he hasn't put in the application. It'd be a nightmare legally. Say nothing of the fallout if he went public. Actually, I was thinking on the plane over, wouldn't the LifeBuddy pick it up? The cancer?'

Ron shakes his head. 'It's not diagnostic like that, not yet. The LifeBuddy just adds current exercise and food to the algorithm. I've heard they're working on the next generation. Lots of nano stuff being included. Don't ask me what that means, I'm only a statistician.'

They sit for a minute before Ron breaks the silence.

'How did things work out with that young lad, Will? The one we changed the projection for?'

'Oh, pretty good. His dad's happy, but his mum...'

'She doesn't accept it?'

'Well, it's not that she doesn't accept it. Steve thinks she's going to count down the days to his original projection even though we've all explained it a thousand times. She won't let it go.'

'GIGO the sequel,' Ron says, shaking his head and smiling.

'Meaning?'

'GIGO the original, garbage in, garbage out: you feed trash into your computer, you get rubbish results. Easy. But some people prefer GIGO the sequel: garbage in, *gospel* out. If a computer has said it – or worse still, the internet – then it's true. Truer than true, it's gospel.'

'That sort of sums it up, yeah. Genie out of the bottle. Don't see what else we can do.'

'Pray he doesn't die in five years?'

Adam gives him a *don't!* glare.

'I'm just saying. You wanna take a bet? I'll give you a thousand to one, that boy'll live to get his letter from the king.'

'Telegram, I think.'

'What? Jesus, you Brits.'

'I'm *not* a Brit!'

They laugh.

'It's like playing God, though, don't you think?' Adam suddenly asks. 'What we did for Will? What we did back there to Michaela's projection? Was any of that legal?'

'That's a good question. Technically? Given the way we now write our terms and conditions, it probably is. Morally? No chance.'

'At least your friend Popeye was keen to protect Mick's reputation. Would've killed him if it'd got out he'd fucked up the application.'

Ron turns and stares at him. 'You serious?'

'Yeah. I know it helps LifeTime too–'

'Helps them? That was *gold dust*, Adam. Fucking *diamond* dust. LifeTime are in the death throes of a massive negotiation with the British government. The Brits are bidding for our systems to help them with health service forecasting, pensions, this is top bloody secret, right, the press know nothing of this. I shouldn't be telling you. This is mega money, billions of dollars. If what's her name–'

'Michaela.'

'If her LifeTime projection is accurate, I don't mean to the day, but, you know, within a year, let's say, call it eleven months even better. Shit, Adam, it'll be massive news. *LifeTime predicts death date!* Imagine the headlines when they lean on the proprietors to spin it as *less than a year out* as opposed to *nearly a year wrong*. Leak the fact that she wasn't even being monitored? Appearance is everything.'

Adam nods slowly. 'You know, Mick told me something strange happened on the TV show in the UK. He says the compere helped him to win. Told him which number to choose in order to get an easy question and win the show. Why would they rig that?'

Ron smiles. 'Doesn't surprise me. Think about it, Mick's their poster boy, have you thought about why?'

'He was the first.'

'Yeah, but they really could've chosen anybody. Within a week of Mick, I think we'd sold a thousand memberships in the UK. So, apart from being technically the first, can't you think of another reason they'd want to have, and then keep, Mick front and centre?'

Adam shrugs. 'You got a theory?'

'Sure, I've got a theory. Mick is their "perfect" poster boy for two main reasons: first, because he's going to die *soon*. That much is guaranteed: he's seventy-five, lifelong boozer and smoker. Secondly, and more importantly, when he does die, nobody will be surprised, which will cut down any potentially bad publicity for LifeTime. Mick dies – what did anybody expect? So, I'm expecting LifeTime to lean on all the media to consign Michaela's death to the inside pages alongside the celebrity tattle. It's not a disaster, now that we've given her a projection of less than a year, but there'll still be some sympathy for her: she wasn't that old, primary school teacher, questions to be asked about why she wasn't being monitored. But what LifeTime will want to happen quickly is that Mick dies, so they can splash him across the front pages, bury Michaela, no pun intended, in the ballyhoo of Mick's demise.'

'You serious?'

Ron shrugs. 'If I was on the marketing side of LifeTime, I can't think of a better outcome. Michaela's death causes questions, sympathy, problems – Mick's death is their best-case scenario.'

'Jesus! This whole thing is becoming nothing but a scam.'

'I know; it's why I'm on the way out.'

'But why would the Brits buy this if it's so shot full of holes?'

Ron smiles, then starts to laugh. 'I think that kinda depends on what you mean by "buy". In the strictest sense, the UK government are going to give us a lot of money, and in return, we're going to give them access to our data. That's what "buying" means. It's not quite the same as "deciding" to buy something. I think the deciding bit isn't included in this transaction. I think that's where the accuracy of our projections come in. It's mostly window dressing to make it appear like a "good" buy for home, I mean UK consumption. In reality, the Brits have no choice; the good old US of A is doing a bit of colonial harvesting. It saves the British government a bit of face if it looks like they're buying the real deal instead of a real turkey. Keeps prying eyes away.'

Adam shakes his head slowly. 'You know, I didn't get into stats to do this. I didn't join LifeTime to do this. I thought we were going to be helping people, not tricking them.'

'Sounds like you're starting to think about your own exit strategy, Adam.'

He doesn't reply, stares instead into the trees, as if he's trying to find answers there.

Paula *no comments* the gaggle of reporters at the gate and walks her bike up the gravel drive to The Manor. Like a lot of old buildings, the sun adds charm where the moon (and a little storm) can concoct a horror movie. The lawns to left and right still look good now she's up close, although she can see the weeds winning the battle long term. She doesn't know if the scattered mounds of Lucky Boy shit will fertilise the grass or the weeds more. She passes a deliveryman coming the other way; he gives her a smile and a mock salute. The front door's open, he's expecting her.

'Granddad?' she shouts from the hall when she sees the front lounge empty.

'Out back,' she hears him yell, as Lucky Boy smashes into the kitchen off the back porch, nearly sending the flimsy door into the *firewood* category. She fusses him mercilessly, but after a few moments he turns tail and trots back outside, as if he's afraid Mick might abscond – or worse.

'You on coffee?' she calls from the kitchen, seeing the pot half full.

'No, I'm okay, you help yourself.'

She chooses the cleanest mug she can find in the cupboard – he really should get a dishwasher – and sniffs the milk in the fridge before deciding she'll have it black.

'Enjoying the sun?' she asks, joining him on the large double seat and kissing his cheek, rough bristles telling her he hasn't shaved: a novelty she files in her *Granddad's going downhill* folder.

He hands her a golden envelope without speaking.

'Oh, is this Mum's? Where was it?'

'I couldn't find it; I asked Adam to get a replacement sent over. It just arrived.'

She opens the flap, frowns.

'I don't understand.'

'If she'd opened it when I gave it to her, instead of waiting as I insisted, she'd have known.'

'Three hundred and twenty-four days? That's less than a year.'

'She'd have had time to get seen. She could've had tests. They might have been able to do something.'

Paula shakes her head. 'You can't know that.' She looks at the numbers, doesn't even have to calculate, Michaela would obviously have opened it within three hundred and twenty-four days, but that didn't mean they could have saved her.

'Why didn't I *think*? I'm a fucking doctor! I shouldn't have been so stupid. What's the point of giving it to her and then telling her not to open it for months? It was stupid. Why didn't I *think?*'

'I can't believe it would've made a difference, Granddad. She wouldn't have believed it anyway.'

'I know. All her holistic nonsense. But this would have brought it home to her. Christ, once is bad, *twice!*'

'What do you mean, *twice?*'

He slumps forward, head in hands, grinding his fingers into his scalp as if intent on burrowing inside and pulling something out, some dark secret from the past.

'Oh, what's the point now? I let your grandmother down.' He sighs, head still in his hands; she thinks he might be crying. 'All those years ago. Celia complained of pains in her chest, sickness, cold sweats, shortage of breath, tiredness. Her doctor dismissed it; he said it was all part of the pregnancy. Why didn't I listen to her? Of course, I backed the bloody doctor, told her not to be silly. I thought we were invincible.'

'Granddad! You *can* have all those symptoms when you're

pregnant! I'm getting flushes and sickness; I'm tired all the time...'

Mick's face drains of colour.

'Why haven't you said?'

'Because I'm *pregnant*! It's normal, I'm fine.'

'Have they checked your heart?'

'They took my pulse and blood pressure.'

'Did they do an ECG? An echo?'

'Why would they? I'm not sick, I'm pregnant.'

'Paula! Where's your projection? We need to open it.'

'What? It's at home, but my birthday's not—'

'Now, Paula! We need to open it right *now*!'

'You seen this?' Cathy shouts, marching across the lawn towards the garage. Steve is oiling his bike, preparing for another spin.

'What?'

'It's Michaela. The paper says her projection was pretty much spot on.'

Steve takes the paper in his grubby hands. The headline, over a smiling picture of Michaela that he recognises from the school website, tells him everything.

LifeTime Predicts Teacher's Death!

'Where's this crap come from? I thought she threw it away.'

'She did. She told me she did. Mick was asking me the other day where it was. Do you think he found it?'

'Yeah, and sent it to the press to prove how fucking clever he is. I can't believe he'd do that. Stupid old git!'

'You have to open yours immediately. *Today.* I want to see what it says.' Mick hauls himself to his feet.

'But–'

'Don't you *see*? Your grandmother died of a heart attack; your mum's died of a heart attack. You should be having tests. Steve too. I'll pay for them. Let's get you both under a cardiologist, even if it means going to London.'

She can see what he's saying but can't really match his urgency. He's actually putting his coat on.

'You mean *now*, don't you?'

'I'll drive you over.'

'I've come on my bike.'

'You're pregnant, love, you shouldn't be riding a bike!'

'Of course I can ride a bike,' she scolds. 'Can I finish my coffee?'

He jangles his keys with the patience of a toddler waiting for the ice-cream seller to squirt the ice cream onto the cornet.

'*Come on*, love. Every minute counts!'

She smiles ruefully and gathers her things; small mercy, at least he's not hopping from foot to foot. As Mick opens the front door a couple are about to knock. One's tall with hair from American TV, but her show's a rerun from the eighties. The second looks like she's climbed – or fallen – off a Harley: black leather jacket, red-checked bandana, clichéd skull helmet under her arm. But neither Mick nor Paula takes much interest in their sartorial choices: the microphone and the shoulder-camera have yanked their attention away from any catwalk considerations.

'Hello, it's Dr Strong, isn't it? I'm Emilia from *Norfolk Digital News*; can I ask you about your reaction to the story in today's *Mail*?'

Paula can see that, despite the hair, she's quite young and doesn't appear convinced she knows how to do such a job.

'What story?' Mick says.

The reporter holds up a newspaper. Mick takes it from her, skims the story. Paula reads it over his shoulder. He hands the reporter the paper, then pulls himself up to his full height. Paula winces.

'I find it deeply insensitive that you should come here, camera running, to catch people who are grieving, off guard, with your intrusive questions. Please respect our privacy at this sad time, leave my property and don't bother any of my family members. None of us have any comment to make. Tell the pack at the gate the same or I'll call the police.'

The reporter hesitates, the camera rolls on.

'I wondered if you had—'

'Would you like me to repeat what I've said, in a *remarkably* civil tone, I must say, given the circumstances? I can't guarantee that I'll maintain such a tone if you force me to repeat my response.'

The standoff stretches for a couple of seconds.

'Please?' Mick says quietly, taking his phone out of his pocket.

'W-we're sorry we bothered you,' the reporter eventually stammers.

'Good girl,' Mick says. 'Now, if you'll let us pass.'

'You were brilliant!' Paula hisses as she eases herself into the battered front seat of Mick's Jag. 'Although I think you might have ended her career.'

'I thought I was quite gentle with her,' Mick says, fiddling with his keys.

'I'm not sure the *good girl* was strictly necessary though, Granddad.'

Her phone rings.

'Hi, Steve. You okay?'

'I might be if Mum wasn't in today's *Mail*.'

'Yes, we've just seen it.'

'*LifeTime predicts teacher's death!* They're saying her projection was only months out, they're hailing LifeTime as the modern Nostradamus.' He's clearly angry.

'I know. I'm surprised they didn't put it on the front. I'm relieved it's buried on page eight.'

'You reckon this is Dad's doing?'

Paula straightens up. 'I don't think so. You wanna talk to him, he's here.'

'Not now,' Mick hisses, shaking his head and starting the engine. He struggles to put on his seat belt as the car slews in the gravel under his heavy right foot.

'*Granddad!* Get me there alive or there's hardly any point!'

'Sorry, love,' he says, slowing to exit the drive, snarling at the gaggle of reporters and cameras, then accelerating away.

'You're on speaker, Steve. We're in the car. Ask him.'

'What do you want, son?' Mick shouts as he hauls the steering wheel straight.

'Have you put Mum's projection in the papers?'

'What are you talking about?'

'The *Mail* has Mum on page eight, *LifeTime predicts teacher's death*, exclamation mark. Did you do this?'

'Course I didn't bloody do it. I only got her projection this morning in the post. How could I get it in the *Mail* before I've seen it myself?'

'Where did they get this from? Is it right? You say you've got her projection.'

'Yes, it is right. And it means you should look at yours *now*! Make sure you don't have a dicky heart same as her and your grandmother. And open Will's too. Any of you got less than a lifetime ahead of you, I want you getting every test done money can buy, and my money's going to buy it. No discussion. We're on the way to Paula's now to see what hers says.'

Jaz is waiting for him as Adam's Segway curves down the slope and stops next to a mixture of hoverboards and bicycles at the start of the path that circles the lake. They shake hands on the step and Jaz leads him through the lounge.

'Glad you could make it,' Jaz says as they enter. 'You are hot property at the moment.'

Adam mumbles a reply. There's a gathering underway on the back deck, which he hasn't been expecting, that's taking the lion's share of his concentration. He can see dark suits and cocktail dresses, waiting staff doing the rounds with trays of drinks and nibbles.

'I wish you'd warned me,' he says, sheepishly. 'I would've worn a tie.'

'No sweat, it's informal,' Jaz says. 'You're fine.'

Fine for some line dancing, Adam thinks, but doesn't say, while attempting to squash a couple of the creases out of his shirt.

'What's the occasion?'

'Nothing special, some people from the top table. Hannah Lennox wants to show you around, I think. She was mighty impressed with your performance yesterday; she told me to get you over here. You're still obviously her golden boy and all that. I reckon you might be in for a bonus, or something.' He shows him a bottle of Bushmills and raises an eyebrow.

What the fuck? Adam thinks to himself, nodding. He might as well enjoy the free booze if he's going to be grilled by Popeye. Might as well act the maverick if he's going to be touted as one.

'On the rocks.'

'It was great work, Adam.' Jaz pours the drink and hands it over. 'We were in a hole before you sorted it out. If Michaela's long projection had got out, Mick would've been humiliated.

We wouldn't have looked too clever either. You've heard about the negotiations that are underway with the Brits?'

Adam doesn't know whether he knows, or he doesn't know. Ron had said he shouldn't be telling him.

'I've heard a whisper.' He shrugs, noncommittal, then switches to amazed, completely disbelieving. 'Are you saying it's *true?*' If it'd been a movie, the Oscar would've been wrapped already. Jaz nods, moves in closer.

'It's enormous. They say, and don't tell anyone I told you this—' He nods towards the suits and evening dresses, switches to a whisper. '—they say they're way over a hundred billion dollars and still haggling. Can you imagine that? Over a hundred billion dollars?'

Adam whistles his inability to imagine it, and wonders how he's going to keep track of who he can admit what to.

Yolanda appears in a dress that's almost non-existent, barring a couple of scraps of turquoise material that seem to hang in just the right places. She drapes a long, bare arm across Adam's shoulders, leans in and lets a kiss linger underneath his ear. He can feel her soft breath caressing his face, smell her scent invading his sinuses like a powerful decongestant, working its way all the way up and into his brain, triggering instant responses, like a burglar alarm has been set off inside his head. His heart kicks from the overwhelming nature of her contact. He feels like his senses have been mugged.

'So lovely to see you again, Adam,' she breathes into his ear, her closeness breaking all social norms of decency and decorum. Adam's never visited a high-class brothel, but he has a feeling that this is an extremely close approximation. To his relief, she glides away, letting her hand stroke the full length across his shoulders as she blows him a kiss and releases a soft giggle.

Adam tenses, in case Jaz is already unloading a left hook, but he simply nods towards the deck, there's soft music audible over the chatter. 'Come on. Let's mingle. Jazelle's about. Dying to see you again...' He puts his baseball mitt of a hand on the back of Adam's neck and gives it a firm squeeze – the way you might maul the Christmas turkey, as you wait for the oven to warm up.

Chapter Thirty-Three

'Britons' earlier deaths linked to NHS underinvestment – study.
Major King's Fund report finds Britons more likely to die of
biggest killer diseases than in many other richer countries.
NHS's mounting failures and political neglect laid bare in
sobering study.'
—*The Guardian*, 26 June 2023

Mick pulls the Jag up outside Paula's and waits at her
front door as she waddles around the car. She feels like
a duck and doesn't appreciate being watched or hurried – and
especially not *both*.

'I'm coming, I'm coming, don't rush me,' she gasps, holding
her bump in position with her hands. She opens the door and
Mick squeezes past her, almost knocking her over in his haste.

'Where is it?' he demands as she shuts the front door.

'It's upstairs,' she says, slipping off her coat.

'I'll get it,' he snaps, grabbing the banister. 'Whereabouts?'

'It's either in my sexy knickers drawer, or it's in my sexy bras drawer. Can't remember which, you might have to have a rummage around in both.'

Mick stops on the third step, turns and gives her the most censorious glare he's able to muster for her. At least that makes her smile.

'Alternatively, you could put the kettle on, and I promise to be down within the hour. I need a quick tinkle. Being preggers and all that, my bladder seems to have shrunk to the size of an egg cup.' She hauls herself up the stairs.

'I'll put the kettle on,' he grumbles, heading slowly towards the kitchen.

'Adam, so good to see you again.' Hannah Lennox kisses him on both cheeks and introduces him to a couple of faceless suits, one from data resourcing or recycling or regurgitating, and the other from some humane influencing unit or something equally baffling and well paid. He nods acknowledgement. The suits nod back.

'And congratulations on your work. You're doing great things,' she continues.

'Thank you, it seems to be going quite well.'

'Adam's heading up our programme in the United Kingdom. It's going *phenomenally* well. I've warned you about underselling yourself, haven't I?'

'Oh, you're our guy in Blighty, right?' says a suit. 'So, you're the key to the mega contract with the British government, are you?'

Adam shrugs, drains his glass. 'I'm more in sales–'

'Yes, but we hear you were working the back channels to make sure that lady who died had an accurate projection. Great job. It's work like that could tip the scales our way.'

Adam's unsure how to respond without losing his job. He lifts a glass off a passing tray, no idea what's in it, and downs half of it in one swallow. *Champagne*, he thinks. *Maybe fizzy wine.* He'd prefer a beer but none of the trays are bringing beer, just tall glasses full of bright colours.

'How is Dr Strong?' Hannah Lennox asks, a concerned expression switching on around her heavily made-up eyes, like a button has been pressed in a darkened control room in some hidden SphereCity bunker.

'He's doing okay. Michaela's death was a shock. But he's stoical, he's that generation. Emotions in a locked box.'

'He still using his LifeBuddy?'

'Oh yes, still trying to get himself fit enough to outrun his projection.'

They all laugh, politely. Suit touches Adam's arm with his forefinger.

'Let's hope he doesn't outrun it too successfully, eh?'

'No, that wouldn't do at all, would it?' the other suit responds, nodding at Adam, hunting for agreement.

Hannah Lennox catches Adam's eye and gives him a look: it's the one doctors use when they say *hmmmm* while removing their glasses.

There's a tap on his shoulder. 'Hi, Adam. Great to see you again.'

Adam turns, his heart already starting to canter at the sound of her voice.

They haven't done badly, Mick thinks, looking around the kitchen as he waits. His might be four times bigger but this is fine, better than the rabbit hutch they'd been renting. Yes, Adam's come good for Paula, although the money he's making as

LifeTime's main man in the UK is a relief. He might not leave the amount people would've guessed the Manor was worth, but he won't leave them penniless now.

He wanders into the through-lounge and looks out of the French windows into the garden. Again, his is four or five times the size but what would they want with a garden that big? His is taken up by brambles most of the year so what does *he* want with it? They've done the room out nice, what he thinks they call 'minimalist', not that he's a fan of programmes that show you the inside of other people's houses. Nor cookery programmes, especially not *children's* cookery programmes. Christ, they don't know how to make TV shows anymore. Still, he's got his *Sweeney* DVDs.

Where the hell is she?

'Paula? Everything okay?' he shouts up the stairs.

She appears at the top, golden envelope open in her hand, worry lines creasing her face.

'Jazelle! Hi, likewise. How are you?' Adam swaps his glass on another passing tray, touches the waiter's arm to slow him down and gestures to Jazelle.

'Oh, no, thank you. You're not trying to get me *drunk*, are you?'

'Christ! No, I simply didn't want to... No.' He drains two thirds of the glass. The same shit as before. Why don't they have any beer?

There's a pause. He looks across the lake; she stares straight at him. He can feel her eyes, taunting him. *Look at me, look at me.* He turns to face her, her lacy yellow dress marking her out from the overwhelming sea of grey and charcoal, like a small rubber duck about to be engulfed in a tsunami of driftwood. She plays with a strand of her freshly washed hair. Her perfume wafts across with a breeze, firing his memory like a match to a fuse on a bundle of dynamite.

'I hear things are going well in the UK. Dr Strong won some reality show?'

'Yeah, that's right. All very tame over there. I hear you've got them wrestling snakes and eating live caterpillars here.'

'No, don't be silly, course they aren't.' She touches his arm with, what seems to him to be, practised casualness, continues to look up at him, smiles at his joke, flutters her eyelashes, gnaws gently at her lower lip. Is there a book she's read to learn all this stuff? Or some YouTube Flirt-Wiki channel?

Adam's eye catches a movement behind her. There's a group of about six over by the edge of the deck. One has turned his head and is staring at them. Jaz.

'Look, would you excuse me?' Adam says, draining his glass and deciding not to elaborate.

In the bathroom he splashes his face with water, studies his reflection in the mirror, can't recognise the stranger he sees, wallows in shame. *Stop drinking!* He orders himself. *Enough!* He wonders if he'll be missed if he cuts for his hotel now? Probably. Jaz said Hannah wants to spend the evening pressing his flesh into the hands of admirers. He dries his face, the towels reminding him of the best hotels he's ever stayed in. *Stop drinking!*

He slides out of the bathroom and crosses the lounge, scans the deck for yellow, spots her standing with Jaz, heads back indoors and sees Ron over by the bookshelves, talking to someone and waving frantically.

'Adam! Long time no see; look, I really have to have a word with you. Would you excuse us...' He grabs Adam by the elbow and steers him outside. Adam makes sure they avoid Jazelle by nudging Ron leftwards as they step onto the deck. If you were watching them, you'd conclude they were drunk. They end up half-hidden behind a palm in a pot.

'I saw you yesterday,' Adam says, mystified.

'Yes, I know, got caught by Larry. Makes it a sort of bus driver's vacation. Is that the phrase?'

'Yes, I think so.'

'Drink?' Ron gasps, stopping a waiter with a full, kaleidoscopic tray. He lifts two, hands a pink one to Adam, keeps the yellow. 'Cheers.'

'Cheers,' says Adam, emptying it in two gulps. Different colour, same taste.

Adam spends the late afternoon having the strength of his metacarpals tested almost to destruction by whoever is in Jaz or Hannah's range. He meets people from departments he's never heard of, doing jobs he doesn't understand even when they explain them to him.

It's dark and the place has practically emptied by the time Jaz beckons Adam to follow him into his office. Adam wonders if Jazelle has been telling tales out of class and he's about to be fired. He's managed to avoid her for the rest of the evening and was more than relieved to see her leave with a young suit wearing a tie that looked like a weight-watching badger cadging a ride.

Jaz takes a new bottle of Bushmills from a glass cabinet along with two crystal glasses. He breaks the seal, pours two merciless measures, and offers Adam a toast.

'Success.'

'Success.' Adam sighs.

'You've surprised me,' Jaz begins, sitting heavily in his chair across the desk from Adam. 'Shocked me, even.'

Adam tries to clear his head. He's drunk too much, needs a clear head if Jaz is about to make accusations. Why has he drunk so much?

'Oh, yeah?'

'Yeah. I didn't think you could do this. I told you as much at the start, but you've surprised me. You've done well.'

Adam shrugs.

'And you and Ron checked out the good doctor's numbers, yeah? You don't think his projection's gonna be too far outta kilter?'

'No. It seemed reasonable. He's obviously not affected by his wife's heart issues, they're not blood relatives. So, no, it appears okay.' He decides he'll keep Mick's cancer confession to himself, trusting Ron to do the same.

Jaz nods. 'We hope so, don't we. There's a lot riding on Dr Strong – as far as the fortunes of LifeTime is concerned, that's for sure.' Their eyes meet, there's something in Jaz's that disturbs Adam. 'Everything well at home?' Jaz continues, change of subject – or is it?

'Yeah, it's good. Busy, but good.'

'And the family? Pregnancy progressing well?'

'Great, thanks.' Adam isn't sure how Jaz knows about Paula's pregnancy, maybe he's in contact with Mick. He doesn't remember telling him, but then he can barely remember where he's left his jacket.

'I hear you also have a new house.'

'Yeah, all good there.' Again, he's puzzled that Jaz knows this, cares even. The conversation's odd, but he can't work out if it's odd because he's drunk, or because Jaz is drunk, or because it's simply odd. Why would Jaz bring him into his office for a man-chat?

'That's good. You've got responsibilities now. Big mortgage

to pay, baby on the way. You need to keep riding that wave of success you're on. Long way down if you fall...'

Adam says nothing. Jaz sips his drink. Behind him, Adam hears the outer door opening and closing. There's a tap on the office door.

'Yeah?'

Adam hears the door open, smells the perfume before he hears her voice.

'Night, Daddy... oh, hello, Adam, I didn't know you were still here.'

Adam turns in his chair. Smiles and nods.

'Yeah, just chatting with your dad...' Your *dad*? Why didn't he say Jaz? *Just chatting with Jaz. Just chatting with my boss, who's a foot taller than me and used to play college football. Muscles like coconuts. And he has a beautiful daughter who keeps smiling at me...*

'Well, bedtime,' she says, staring straight into Adam's eyes. 'Come up and see me before you go, if you like, I'm a light sleeper...'

The door closes with the softness of a kiss.

Adam feels like he's been punched.

Chapter Thirty-Four

'A Stressful Workplace Could Take 33 Years off Your Life
Expectancy, Study Finds.'
—*The Independent*, 29 October 2015

'What does it say?' Mick gasps, starting up the stairs, regretting ever having bought a LifeTime projection for her.

'It's okay,' Paula replies, signalling for him to go back down. 'It's fine. I just took a while to take it in.'

He leads her into the lounge, tea is off. She sits on the sofa, he sits beside her, desperate to snatch the golden envelope out of her hands, knows he can't.

'It's fine, Granddad, really...'

'What is it?' he pleads.

She hands him the envelope, he flips the folds open, studies it, his face changing from concerned to concerned and confused in microseconds.

'How old are you? Twenty-five?'

'Yes.'

'So, twenty-five and forty-seven is seventy-two.'

'It's fine,' she says, as brightly as she can. 'A ripe old age.'

They stare at each other. He can see that she's trying not to upset him, trying not to let him down by showing her disappointment; he knows women in the UK average nearly eighty years, although it used to be higher before the austerity years, and the cost-of-living crisis, and the Universal Credit meltdown, and the crisis after that, whatever it was called. He looks down at the numbers, has he added them wrong? Is it *eighty*-seven? She can't live a shorter life than him. He puts his arm around her shoulders.

'You can't take this as gospel, you know. You've heard what Adam says about projections and predictions; it's one of them, not the other. Remember that.'

She smiles at his concern, and his complete naivety: how is he still practising as a doctor?

'You understand that, don't you? A few more sessions of your aerobics, fewer takeaways, you're young enough to add years to that. Not that you can trust those numbers anyway.'

'Yes, no problem, Granddad. Come on. Let's have that tea.'

Adam stares at the door, wonders what's happening behind him. Knife? Gun? Baseball bat? He imagines sitting, staring at the door until the end of time, too afraid to turn around and discover what's waiting for him.

'Don't sweat,' Jaz says finally, taking a pull from his glass, running his finger round the rim. 'She's a big girl, enjoys life. I don't hold her on a chain...'

Adam turns and reaches for his glass for the want of anything better to do. His heart is pounding, he can feel a sheen of sweat on his neck, his shirt is sticking to his back.

'...and the video's under strict lock and key.'

Adam tries to control his facial muscles, but he doesn't know what he wants them to do. He can feel the slack-jawed expressions of confusion, realisation, then finally disbelief working their way across his features with no effort on his part.

'It's a fetish she's got. I don't see the harm. She uses one of our grace and favour apartments as her... *entertaining* suite. The video is a thing she does, for *personal* amusement. The quality is very good, apparently. Sound as well. But, as I say, lock and key. Never gonna get out. As long as you keep doing well...'

'I think, it's late,' Adam says, standing, his mouth like desert sandstone, tongue a small, dead desert animal. 'I should be going.'

'I can help,' Jaz says, reaching into one of the desk drawers and pulling out a dull, silver-coloured tin, the size and type a Bond villain would have handy, to store a deadly syringe of poison or three venom-tipped darts. He places it on the desk between them. 'I can help you do well. Very well.'

Adam eases himself back down into his chair: better judgement closes the door behind itself and disappears into the night.

'You know the deal with the UK government is worth at least a hundred billion? I know you do. They want our services to help them plan their pensions, health service, insurance companies want a slice, whole load of things. They're on the verge of signing. And you've moved it much closer to fruition with your recent work on Michaela Strong's projection. That was good work, thoughtful, proactive. And we're all very appreciative of the work you've done to check out Dr Strong's projection, make sure that's as accurate as possible, because the more accurate it is, the more likely they are to sign.'

'What's in the tin?' Adam asks. His voice cracking on the final word. He clears his throat, sips more whiskey. He doesn't need the alcohol, only the moisture: his mouth now has the physical characteristics of a thirsty camel's arse, and it continues to worsen.

'In the tin is a million dollars, Adam. A million dollars for you.'

Adam wants to make a crack about a million dollars not fitting in the tin but thinks better of it. Well, he doesn't make the crack. Whether he's capable of much thinking, or even speaking, is now debatable.

'We need one more piece of your thoughtful, proactive work. One final special moment to push the deal over the line. Something that will capture the imagination of the British press, the British public and – finally – the British government. Something to make them open their sterling pocketbook with confidence. Something big, something that really shows how valuable our services are, how *accurate*, something everybody is waiting for.'

Adam shakes his head. 'I don't know what you're talking about.'

'I'm talking about a good friend of ours. Taken recently to a bit of power walking, I hear. Maybe even running by now, who knows? Maybe not the best thing for him to be starting at his age, could be dangerous. Old ticker, you know? Might give up on him. Would surprise nobody. Wouldn't raise an eyebrow. If it were to happen in the next few weeks it would be, how shall we put this? *Advantageous?* What with time pressing on as it is...'

He opens the lid; it falls back on a hinge, clinking lightly on the shiny tabletop. Inside, it looks like two slightly oversized condom packets, silver again, no branding or lettering. Jaz lifts them out, holding them one in each hand, like two playing cards that he might be about to make disappear.

'In each of these packets is a wet wipe towelette, a very special wet wipe. Don't use it yourself by mistake. One wipe of one of these on bare skin, will give us the result you need within minutes.'

'What are you talking about?'

'Give it to him when he's hot, sweaty, fresh from a long, exhausting power walk, and he needs to cool down. Solve all your problems.'

'You're crazy!' Adam stands, his chair topples backwards. 'You're absolutely crazy!'

'Post-mortem will conclude a heart attack because that's what will have happened. There'll be no traces of anything internally. All you have to do is tidy everything away *extremely* carefully. I'd suggest high-quality surgical gloves.' He turns the packets over in his fingers, puts them back in the box, closes the lid. Pushes it across the table to Adam.

'You must be joking!'

'A million dollars. A million dollars *and* the recording are yours. Otherwise, I can't be responsible for the lock and key.'

'That's blackmail.'

'I call it *incentive*.'

'You're mad.'

'You'd be mad not to. Imagine if the tape got into the hands of your wife. Or maybe the general sludge of social media, Jazelle can be a little *unpredictable*, I'm sure you're aware of what girls like her can be like...'

'You're out of your mind.'

'And if you find yourself out of a job, what will you pay your enormous mortgage with? This is foolproof. Everyone must be expecting the inevitable – the amount of exercise he's doing, the amount of booze and cigars he's packed away, no one will suspect a thing. The most natural event in the world.'

'I'll suspect!' he shouts. 'I'll know. I can't do this. Christ alive, Jaz, what are you thinking?'

'I'm thinking more money than you ever dreamed possible,

or you take your chances that your lovely wife will be understanding when she sees your debut on screen, full colour sound and vision, and learns that you're out of a job, and your home is in the hands of the bank, and her new little motor needs to be sold. It's your choice, but if that box is on my table when I get up in the morning I'll take it as your resignation and put the rest in motion. Think on that. Have a safe flight.'

Jaz drains his glass, stands up and walks around the desk. Adam hears him stop at the door. 'And don't disturb Jazelle on your way out, she needs her beauty sleep.'

Adam barely hears the door close.

Adam checks-in his bag and heads for the security lines, passport in his hand.

'You got a minute?' Hand on his shoulder. He spins, heart pounding.

'*Fuck!* Ron! Don't do that.'

'Just one?'

'Okay. One!'

'You gonna tell me what's going on?'

'Meaning?'

'I'm getting whispers you're on the way out.'

Adam glances left and right, then cuts out of the line. 'Let's go outside for that minute.'

Outside, they find a quiet corner, away from the herd of smokers, and lean on a barrier.

'This just got a whole lot more serious, Ron. Listen to me carefully; I'll only say this once.'

'What?'

'Remember what you were saying the other day? About LifeTime wanting Mick's death to follow Michaela's pretty quickly? So that he dominates the news, not her? Well, Jaz asked me to *kill* Mick. Sometime near his date, before is best as we're pressed for time on a hundred-billion-buck deal. Offered me a million dollars to do it. Tried to give me some wet wipe that he said would induce a heart attack. If I didn't do it, I'd be sacked, and he says he has a video of me and his daughter from that hotel. I'm freaked out here. No idea what's happening.'

Ron lights a cigarette, bugger the smoking zone.

'What'cha gonna do?'

Adam breathes in, breathes out, offers Ron his hand.

'I'm gonna catch my flight home, buddy. Catch my flight home.'

Chapter Thirty-Five

'UK life expectancy falls to lowest level in a decade.'
—*The Guardian*, 11 January 2024

P aula opens the writing desk in Michaela's living room and sighs. *Only a teacher would have these*, she thinks, surveying the bundles of worksheets and *Kipper and Biff* books that slide down onto the writing surface. She picks one up, *The Whatsit*, and is sure she remembers reading it when she was in primary school. She flips through the pages.

'Did you read these when you were young?' she asks, sliding it across the floor.

Cathy picks it up. 'Yeah, loved these. I wanted to be Biff when I grew up.' She sits on the sofa and pores over the pages.

'Thanks for helping me with this, I knew Steve wouldn't want to, and I couldn't ask Adam or Granddad,' Paula says, collecting six more *Magic Key* books and dropping them into a box marked SCHOOL.

'It's no problem; I understand you wouldn't want to do it on your own. Being an only child, when my parents died, I had to.'

'That's tough. Did they die long ago?'

'The year before I met Steve. Otherwise, I would've roped him in, no question.' She pauses, stares into the air. 'I loved Michaela, she was a bit like a mum to me. I think she took it upon herself, knowing that I had no parents alive. You've been a bit of a sister too. I'm glad you asked me to help.'

When Paula doesn't respond for a couple of seconds, Cathy turns, stands and crosses the room. Paula's sitting with her back to her, something in her hands.

'Found something?'

'This.' She holds up a LifeTime package, torn open as if Michaela had opened it in a rage. The golden envelope has been folded in half and stuffed back into the Jiffy bag along with the data disc.

'Oh, I'm sorry. I wish I'd found that,' Cathy says, putting her hand on Paula's shoulder.

'It's okay, just a bit of a surprise. I thought she'd thrown it away.' She pulls the golden envelope out absent-mindedly, fiddles with the flaps. 'I can't believe she's gone; she was so full of life.'

'I know. Christ, she'll be missed at the school.'

'Yeah.' Paula opens the golden envelope out flat, spreads her hands over the writing. Neither of them speaks for fifteen seconds. Twenty.

'I don't understand,' Paula finally says, like it's a gas bill for ten times the usual amount.

Cathy takes the envelope, stares at the numbers. 'This doesn't make sense. The paper said she had a couple of hundred days.'

'I know. I saw it. Granddad had it when I visited him last week.'

She takes the envelope back from Cathy, flattens it some more on her lap, stroking it softly.

'Twenty-four years? She should've lived until she was seventy-three,' she says quietly, one tear rolling unnoticed. 'I don't understand.'

Mick pounds up the hill from town. He has one eye on his watch: if he puts on a spurt, he might break a hundred minutes. He feels good: heart is racing but that's the blood flowing; legs are strong; he sucks air like a brand-new Dyson, feels the rain plastering his hair flat.

Ahead, at the gate to his drive, he can see half-a-dozen hacks, cameras and phones at the ready, huddled under a canopy of umbrellas, like a wake of black vultures feeding on a corpse that mourners have left unburied. He's warned them. He puts on another burst of what a child with a lively imagination might call *speed*.

'How do you feel?' a voice from the crowd shouts.

'Fucked!' he gasps. 'You can quote me.'

'Any plans for the day?'

'Nope,' he hisses petulantly at the Curry's trolley full of Dictaphones and cameras that seek his every (hopefully last) word. Behind him, Lucky Boy yaps and prances past the clicking cameras like a newborn celebrity on his first red-carpet appearance.

Paula, inveterate Airport Reunions Anonymous member, long before *Love Actually* made it a certifiable addiction, breaks the invisible cordon and rushes into Adam's arms.

'Missed you,' she whispers into his chest.

'You too,' he replies.

They run to the car through a curtain of rain that has been incessant for more than twenty-four hours. Paula shivers as she runs: ten per cent cold, ninety per cent cinematic romanticism. She negotiates the car park hunched forward in her seat and doesn't sit back until she's safely on the M11 heading north. It's a couple of hours to home where they're due at the Sunday share, the first for a few weeks after the disruption of the funeral. She asks about his trip, listens to his bland replies, then takes a breath.

'I found Mum's LifeTime envelope when I was clearing out her house.'

'I thought she threw that out,' he mutters, after the briefest of pauses.

'Apparently not. She'd clearly opened it and slung it in a drawer.'

'Did you look at it?'

'Of course, it gave her another twenty-four years. That's what I don't understand. Granddad had one that gave her a couple of hundred *days*...'

Adam breathes in heavily, stares out through the rain-drenched window.

'I told you Mick asked me to get it reissued, he was searching for it.' He continues to stare at or through the glass. She wonders if he's going to say more without prompting. 'So, I talked to Ron, and we discovered that Mick hadn't included details of Celia's heart attack when he made the application. So, your mum's projection was way out, her medical history should have included Celia's heart attack. We decided it would be more honest if we included a fuller family medical history before we issued the projection again. Make it more accurate. We also didn't want to embarrass Mick. It would probably have got out to the press; we didn't think Mick would want to be humiliated. Doctor doesn't keep his records up to date, that sort of thing.'

'Shit!'

'We thought it was the best thing to do.'

'No, it's not that. He's now beating himself up for stopping her from opening it. He thinks they might have saved her life had she known what the projection said.'

'Well, if she'd opened her projection as soon as he gave it to her, it would've said twenty-four years. So, he's no need to beat himself up.'

'But it's not that simple. Even if we tell him her figure would've said twenty-four years, then he's going to regret leaving out her family history. What was he thinking? He's still going to see it as his fault.'

'True. Christ, what a mess. You haven't told him about the original projection?'

'No.'

'Do you want to?'

'I don't know. It doesn't seem to make much difference either way. As it is, he's blaming himself for stopping her from opening it. If we tell him, he'll still blame himself for not including the details about Granny. Either way he'll blame himself for something. And there's something else...'

'What?'

'The *Mail* have splashed on Mum, saying LifeTime predicted her death pretty accurately.'

'You're joking!' He turns in his seat; she can tell he's truly shocked.

'Everybody thinks you gave them the story.'

'What? Why would they think that?'

'Because you sent the projection to Mick and the next morning it was in the *Mail*. We've got journalists around the house fishing for quotes. It's horrible.'

Adam shakes his head; he's still staring at her.

'Do *you* think I gave your mum's projection to the press?'

'No,' she says, 'but I do think it came from LifeTime.'

'Of course it did,' he says. 'There's no other explanation. But I promise you, I didn't leak it.'

Adam quickly freshens up before they head across to the Sunday share. He closes the bathroom door, turns on the shower, then, under cover of the noise, he places a seecall to Ron.

'Hey, buddy, how ya doin'? Good flight?'

'Yeah, great thanks. Look, a quick question. When we reissued Michaela's projection the other day, did you send it to the British press?'

'You're not seriously asking me that. No, of course I didn't, but we can both narrow down the field of suspects to one or two names if that's where it's ended up.'

'My guess is Jaz Forrester?'

'There's your boy. Him or maybe Popeye, possibly the pair of them in tandem. I imagine they might not have wanted to approach you with the idea, so probably went freelance before you got wind.'

'Bastards.'

'You're too kind to them. I don't *know*, but I'm not at all surprised. Why?'

'Oh, we've got press hammering on every door, and the family here thinks it was me who leaked it. Well, not Paula, but everyone else. I can deal with that, don't worry. Catch up soon.'

'Yeah, take care.'

Adam quits the call and starts to undress. His phone rings again. It's Jaz. Adam hesitates. What could he want? He accepts the seecall, deciding to pretend last night never happened. He's got a job to do; he's going to keep doing it.

'Hey, Adam. Good to see you. How are things?'

'If you're going to go over my head sending stories to the British press, it leaves me looking kinda dumb when I don't know they're coming. Could you, or whoever on your team did it, at least give me a heads-up next time.'

Jaz nods slowly. 'Well, that's fine, Adam, but the biggest heads-up I can give you is that things are going to be moving quickly over your way quite soon. While you may have your boots on the ground, so to speak, we're planning on sending a few tomahawks over the horizon to add to the sense of occasion. Take it from me, you can expect the visibility of the media to increase markedly going forwards, we want to build the feeling of expectation over there. Not exactly a countdown, but you know, get people talking. So, it might be a good idea for you to get on with your most *pressing* matters before there are telephoto lenses following the good doctor every place he goes.'

Adam says nothing.

'Another thing,' says Jaz. 'We're getting disturbing reports that Dr Strong isn't treating our very good and extremely valuable friends in the media as well as we would hope and expect. You'll have a word with him, no doubt, and remind him of his contractual obligations?'

'What are you talking about?'

'We heard he no commented a TV crew the other day, that's my polite way of telling you he told them to go fuck themselves, or words to. Not exactly the sort of engagement our most high-profile member in the UK is contractually obliged to provide, and has been handsomely paid for. I appreciate you were over here at the time, but you really need to have him better trained and more on-message than that.'

'Anything else?' Adam says, biting his tongue on an acerbic response.

'I notice you forgot to collect your *gift* when you left mine yesterday, so I took the liberty of couriering it over to you, maybe encourage you to change your mind. Otherwise, the sell-by date is exactly a week, Adam. After that, you don't work here. Don't let it all slip through your fingers, buddy, you got a lot to lose...'

Jaz disconnects, leaving Adam to stare at the small package that he picked up off the mat as they arrived back from the airport. It's as plain as they come: brown padded envelope, couple of Express Delivery stickers, typed address. No logos, no holograms. But, somehow he knew what it was, knew Paula couldn't see it. He rams it into his jacket pocket for want of a better place to hide it.

The broadcast vans with the satellite dishes on their roofs are almost blocking the drive as Steve and Cathy arrive for the Sunday share.

'What the hell is this?' Steve shouts through the rain as he winds down the window.

The van's passenger window opens halfway, a woman's face peeks out.

'Hello, sir, are you a member of the family?'

'Bugger off and get your bloody van out of the way.' He squeezes past it, scattering gravel as he accelerates up the drive. Will waves excitedly through the back window at the camera eyes.

Mick is at the door as they run through the rain from the car; Lucky Boy stands sentry beside him. 'Are those ruddy great vans still down the bottom there?'

'Yeah, I told them to bugger off. What do they want?'

'Oh, what do they ever want? Some news where there isn't any. Come in anyway, drinks?'

'Beer for me,' says Steve.

'Yeah, me too,' says Cathy. 'What about you, Will?'

'What are you drinking, GG?' Will asks.

'Water for me, son. Water of life.'

'I'll have that too.'

'Where do you want these?' Cathy says, holding two large pizza boxes out to Mick, while looking askance at Will.

'Bring them out and we'll put them in the oven to keep warm, shall we? Adam's landed safely; Paula called. They're "freshening up", or whatever Americans do. They'll be over in half an hour.'

He takes some beers from the fridge, fills a couple of glasses from the tap, leads them through to the lounge and takes command of his favourite armchair, Lucky Boy silently following every step like an electronic tag.

'You still on the water kick?' Steve starts, nodding towards Mick's glass.

'And feeling a lot better for it,' he says, raising his drink in toast. 'To absent friends.'

They respond in kind, although Cathy wonders if Mick means Celia and Michaela, or Adam and Paula. She says nothing; Steve continues.

'I hear you're power walking as well. Wonders never cease.'

'Don't mock. I do five miles a day, that's nearly four microlives added to my LifeTime. You should come.'

'How long does five miles take you?'

'My best time is a hundred and four minutes, thirty-eight seconds, but that includes the hill up to the clifftop. I'm aiming to break the hundred minute barrier.'

Steve shoots Cathy a *He's lost it* look. Cathy, meanwhile, is more concerned by the fact that Mick has two glasses of water on the table next to his chair, and there's another over by his music collection. A car pulls up in the drive.

'I'll let them in,' Cathy says, heading for the front door. Lucky Boy springs up and starts to follow her but stops, like he's tethered to the chair, when Mick doesn't move.

'Hi, all,' Paula shouts from the doorway, shaking her coat out in the porch. 'Anybody mind if we eat straight away? Adam's starved.'

'No, no, bring it in,' Mick says, getting up and leading Lucky Boy into the kitchen. 'Drinks, you two?'

'Two beers?' Paula says, glancing at Adam, who nods.

'You take that in. Adam, come and get the pizzas.'

While Paula takes salads and dips into the lounge, Adam collects the pizzas and Mick picks up two more beers and fills a glass with water.

'So, Adam, how was your trip?' Mick opens, as Adam lifts a slice of pizza and settles back onto the sofa next to Paula.

'Oh, the usual,' he says, shrugging. 'Meetings, meetings and more meetings.'

'You'll be able to get that truck off my drive?'

Adam chews pizza and shrugs again. 'Would if I could. I imagine they're a gang of freelancers; I didn't see Sky or the BBC or ITN out there. The mainstream media seem to have stuck to the deal to leave you alone. You might find that breaking down a bit as we get closer to *the day* as the bottom feeders hunt for something exclusive.'

Everybody concentrates on eating, nobody keen to continue that thread – except Will.

'It's thirty-three days now, isn't it, GG?' he says, as Steve winces.

'Might have added another couple of hours after my walk this morning,' Mick says, rolling up his sleeve.

319

Will shakes his head. 'Yeah, it did, but it's still thirty-three days.'

There's a moment, as everybody wonders why Will's comment strikes them as odd.

'How do you know that?' Adam says, ahead of the rest with his thinking, and his fear.

'It's on the LifeTime website live feed,' Will says, tapping buttons on his webwatch and showing it to the room.

Adam closes his eyes; he knows what's coming.

'Are you saying Mick's projection is live on the internet?' says Steve.

'Yeah. Look, I've got it here.'

'Don't they need my permission for that?' Mick asks, glaring at Adam.

Adam sighs, shakes his head. 'When you had the Buddy fitted, did they ask you to sign anything?'

Mick shrugs. 'Yeah, I think so. There was something on a tablet Jaz asked me to sign when we came off stage.'

'Did you read it?'

'What? Are you joking? It was all small print, pages long. I just signed it.'

'I can check at head office if you like, but I think your permission will be in the small print.'

'Bloody hell! That's totally out of order. I got journos camped out on my drive and now the world is watching my life ticking down on my arm. If I'd known I was signing away my right to privacy, I'd never have signed the bloody thing.'

'Breakfast TV have a countdown clock running,' Will adds to a stunned silence.

'I'll make a call,' Adam says, without much conviction. 'But I imagine that's the deal; you get a ten-thousand-dollar piece of kit for free, and they get permission to publicise the data. I'm guessing, but that's what I imagine they're thinking.'

'You went walking in *this* rain?' Paula gasps, breaking the awkward silence, hoping to protect Adam from further incoming fire.

'I skipped out when it eased off. The rain's quite exhilarating.'

'Do you really think the press are going to take more of an interest as, you know, it gets nearer?' Steve asks Adam.

'I would imagine so,' Adam says, taking a pull at his beer. 'Big story.'

'Well, they'd better back off,' Mick says angrily. 'I'm not having them parked on my drive and poking microphones in everyone's faces. That girl the other day was quite rude, wasn't she, love?' He looks at Paula, who smiles.

'I'm not sure she knew quite what she'd taken on, Granddad.'

They all laugh, except Adam.

'What happened?' he asks.

'We were doorstepped by some teenager with a tape recorder and her girlfriend with a camera. I sent them packing, politely but firmly.'

'You want me to try to re-establish the guidelines we agreed at the start,' Adam asks, sipping his beer and lifting another slice of pizza.

'No. I want them to bugger off. I think they've had their pound of flesh. Now it's time they left us in peace. If I am nearing my end, which I don't honestly think I am, not in thirty-three days anyway, not if I have anything to do with it, then it's only seemly that they leave us in peace, don't you think? Bit of dignity.'

'Exactly,' says Steve. 'Well said.'

'I'm not sure the great British media will be looking at *this* news story in quite the way you might be hoping,' Adam says, fearing he's tossing a lit match into a firework factory. 'I imagine there'll be a bit of extra interest as the date of your projection comes and goes. It'll probably settle down after that.'

'They're not getting another word out of me, I'm afraid. I've had my fifteen minutes of fame and now I've had enough of it, thank you very much.'

'Good for you, Mick,' Cathy says, lifting her beer bottle.

'We should be ready for Mick to get a bit of a surprise if he's really decided not to speak to the media anymore,' Adam says as he turns the car in the drive and heads for home.

'What do you mean?' Paula asks.

'Well, he's spent his time so far courting them; he's going to find it hard to push them away now he's generated so much interest. They don't work like that. He must realise; they won't all lose interest and go home if he goes all Mona Lisa. That'll simply make the next exclusive more exclusive.'

Paula leans back in the seat, watches the wipers losing their battle, the rain obliterating the view faster than they can clear it. Adam peers forwards, negotiates the gap between the van and the gatepost carefully, rolls the car out into the road.

'I know what you mean,' she says at last, almost to herself. 'I think he might simply be a bit tired of it all. He's not really an extrovert. I know what he's like with the family, but aside from that, what does he do? A few rounds of golf, a pint in the Fish, Sunday share? He's hardly celebrity material, is he?'

'No, not really, until he decided to die on live TV.'

'Hardly.'

'Yeah, I know. But you don't need a deck of tarot cards to guess what the media will be like as the appointed hour approaches. They'll want a countdown and quotes from everyone involved: from the family to his butcher. It could turn into a bit of a bear pit around the Manor for a while.'

'Can't you do anything about it?'

'Up till now, he's agreed to give a regular flow of interviews and comment to the mainstream media, our admin department have kept his Facebook and Twitter feeds lively, but as it gets closer to D-Day, the vloggers and the also-rans will want their piece of the action for free. There's no way we're going to be able to stop them setting up shop in the village and pestering anyone who wants their face made public. If he stops feeding tidbits to the mainstream, they'll be forced to join the stakeout, he's only gonna make it worse. Plus, if he's aggressive, it plays into their hands. He seems to think they'll have no copy if he swears at them, but social media ain't so squeamish. They love that stuff; he's feeding the meme machines and they're flooding the internet. Here, check out my latest WhatsApps from work.'

He hands her his mobile and she clicks to his messages. A rain-splattered Mick fills the screen. *Fucked!* He shouts. Paula gasps, hand to her gaping mouth.

'My God!' she whispers, shutting the phone down.

'That's gold dust to the meme factories, he's simply encouraging them. There's probably not much we can do about it no matter how he responds, but he's right about one thing – a bit of dignity would go a long way.'

'Could you speak to him?'

'I could try, I'm not sure what I can do except explain how it's going to be and try to stop him making an exhibition of himself. As you can see, that simply feeds the gutter elements.'

'Talk to him.'

'Okay.'

'Did you notice his water?'

'He's drinking gallons.'

'No, he's forgetting he's got a glass on the go. I also found the

Cornflakes in the fridge this evening. He's doing stuff like this more and more. I can't say anything to him; he gets so grumpy and what does that serve? Cathy's noticed too; she thinks he's going downhill fast. She says she phoned him the other day and he thought it was Mum. Had this whole conversation with her about school and the shopping. It spooked Cathy.'

'I can imagine. I'm not sure I can do a man-to-man chat on his health, or otherwise, but I can talk to him about the media. The other stuff? We'll simply have to hope he's on a slow decline. Something manageable. I'm not sure the extra stress will help.'

'I can't see him humiliated, you know. I can't take that.' She puts her hand on his on the gearstick, another of her unconscious tics that makes her feel connected, on the same trajectory, safe.

'I'll go see him tomorrow evening, maybe go for a power walk with him,' he jokes.

Paula smiles. 'Reckon you can do five miles in a little under a couple of hours? I'm worried enough about *him* having a cardiac, I don't want *you* in the next bed. Talk to him.'

'Don't worry about me,' he says softly, struggling to peer through the enveloping darkness. 'I'll keep up with him.'

Mick's a light sleeper. Especially since he's given up the booze. So, a tinkle of broken glass on the kitchen tiles is easily enough to rouse him. He sits up. Listens. There's a scrabbling sound, like someone's reaching through a broken pane, trying to locate the key on the inside of the lock. But Mick isn't stupid. He never leaves the key in the lock. He gets up, puts on his dressing gown, opens his bedroom door and switches on the landing lights.

'I've called the police!' he bellows. 'And I've got a shotgun. And I'm on my way down to blow your fucking head off!'

Lucky Boy wakes and starts barking wildly.

Mick stamps down the stairs, noisy under the lightest of treads, his arrival is well and truly announced.

'You'd better be fucking bulletproof!' he yells as he reaches the hall and turns towards the kitchen. His heart is thumping. Faster than it ever does on his walks, but he's damned if some smackhead is going to intimidate him in his own house. An Englishman's home and all that.

He opens the kitchen door.

Part Four

<u>The End</u>

'When the world is destroyed, it will be destroyed not by its madmen but by the sanity of its experts and the superior ignorance of its bureaucrats...'
—John le Carré, *The Russia House*

Chapter Thirty-Six

'NHS is suffering its "worst heart care crisis in living memory",
experts warn as early deaths from heart disease among under-
75s hit highest level in more than a decade.'
—*Mail Online,* 22 January 2024

A dam parks the car parallel to the steps that lead up to
Mick's front door. The rain finds the cracks and empty
knotholes in them and disappears into what must be a dank,
unhealthy space underneath. Dark thunderclouds, dusted by
the light of a nearly full moon, punch the stars out of sight one
by one. The rain, which has been heavy, starts to intensify
rapidly until the downpour is suddenly biblical. Even the
moonlight is quickly overwhelmed by the demonic gloom. *Good
place for a horror film,* crosses Adam's mind.

'Isn't it wonderful?' Mick shouts, stepping out into the
elements from under the porch, and tipping his face upwards to
feel the full force battering on his closed eyelids. Adam remains
in the car, wondering if Mick is back on the booze. Lucky Boy

watches from the shelter of the porch, looking as though he's thinking much the same thing.

Then, like a bathroom shower has been switched off, the deluge stops, leaving only a few heavy droplets slapping loudly on the roof of the car.

'One minute,' Mick gasps, wiping his dripping brow and heading indoors. He returns, towelling his hair with a large SpongeBob beach towel. 'Brilliant,' he gasps, throwing his drenched training top onto the floor, and rubbing his upper body like he's trying to force life into his pale skin. Then he drops the towel next to his top, slips on another sweatshirt, and steps out again.

'C'mon, let's get this done,' he beckons, and starts marching purposefully down the drive, the scrunching of the gravel unusually loud in the sudden stillness after the downpour.

'We still going?' Adam shouts as he steps out of the car.

'Course,' Mick yells back. 'We said we'd do it. It's stopped now.'

'Well, only for a minute, maybe?' Adam looks up as the moon reappears and sheds a silvery brightness. They are right on the edge of an enormous bank of towering storm clouds that are shuddering inland. Below the clouds, away to his left, he can make out areas of dark, smoke-like rain down towards the village. The other way, up towards the cliff, the sky is a star-studded cobalt, the sea below it whitened by the moonlight, until a kink at the edge of the cloud covers the moon again and the whiteness recedes to the distance, like a spotlight following a performer offstage.

He catches Mick at the bottom of the drive. There's only one hack on duty, asleep at the wheel, the rest probably in the pub waiting for dispatches. Mick points, sends his eyes to heaven, turns down the hill on tiptoe.

'Storm's that way,' Adam warns.

Mick stops and looks up. The world is suddenly black and white, storm or calm, dark or light. He nods to himself and smiles.

'You wanna go up? Okay,' he says, as he starts walking purposefully up towards the cliff. 'Can you feel the energy? The power?'

Adam feels the wet seeping into his trainers as he follows dutifully, zipping his lightweight jacket tighter to his neck; he has no official sports clothes. He stares ahead to gauge the likelihood of another cloudburst: his jacket's as waterproof as newspaper, his shoes evidently less so.

'Come on, keep up!' Mick barks as he pounds up the hill. 'Trick is to get your rhythm going. One-two! One-two! Come on, you're a fit lad. Steve won't dare come with me.'

Adam jogs up beside him and drops into his rhythm. He should be able to keep up with the old bastard. He hears scampering paws behind him and is overtaken by Lucky Boy who bounds along beside them.

'Feel good? I love this. Should've started years ago. It's best at night too, nobody about. Even the hacks are all in the pub, except that dozy bastard back in the car. Nice and peaceful up here. Come on.'

It's a good mile or so to the top of the cliff. Mick swings his arms like he's punching balloons, Adam marches alongside feeling his breathing start to increase. The pace is faster than he'd expected; Mick's certainly not out for a stroll.

They reach the top, Adam's lungs complaining; he slumps down onto a wooden bench facing the sea. Mick supports himself on the back of it, breathing heavily, stretching his calves out, arching his back, his breathing slowing. 'Wonderful!' he gasps. 'That's the warm-up, long way to go. You ready?'

'Two seconds, catch my breath.'

The view along the top is lit by the moonlight. The cliff

resembles a cake that has had bites taken out of it by a hungry, not very well-mannered giant. Mick takes a dozen paces and stops at the cliff edge. Lucky Boy takes one step but pauses, afraid to go further. He whimpers slightly, sits in front of Adam and watches Mick.

'Some fucker tried to burgle me last night, you know?' Mick says.

'Really?'

'Yeah. Broke a window in the back door. Thought the key was on the inside. Thought I was stupid.'

'Did you call the police?'

'No. I scared the shit out of them instead. Turned all the lights on, shouted I'd called the police and that I was going to shoot them with my shotgun.'

'You've got a shotgun?'

'Course I haven't. But they knew that as much as you did.' He laughs.

'Kids?'

'I thought it might be. But I saw him running off across the garden. Big guy. On his own. He won't be back.'

The storm splits the sky in two. Back down the hill, pockets of heavy rain are visible over the sea and the land, like the giant is now sneezing through the clouds; in the other direction, along the cliff path, the moon paints the sea white and makes moon shadows behind the nearest trees. Mick watches the inky clouds, still moving inland like a slow invading army, no end to them in sight on the horizon.

Adam sits on the bench and listens to Mick's breathing, hears him sigh with contentment. He notices his own breathing has steadied, but his heartbeat is thundering. It's an odd feeling, breathing slowing, heart getting faster and more insistent. It was quick when he sat down, the walk up the hill took it out of him, and it's now accelerating almost uncontrollably.

He fingers the package that's still in his pocket, strokes it nervously, wonders if he's really got it in him to go through with this. Wonders if it serves any purpose except his own. Wonders if he has any choice.

You need a wet wipe?

It's all he has to say. The rest will do itself, apparently. Just tidy up the bits and pieces afterwards, very carefully, all done, nice and tidy, nice and tidy life secured.

You need a wet wipe?

'Isn't life wonderful?' Mick shouts into the sky. 'You've got to live it to the full, eh?' He points down the hill towards the village. 'We were married there, you know? She's buried there as well, near Michaela. Can see them both from the Manor, can see them whenever I want. That's where I'll be buried too.' He puts his hands on his hips, stares down the hill towards the small town, lights in a few of the houses, darkness in the majority.

Adam stares down the hill too, it's clear all the way to the bottom: no cars, no one walking, no mad bastards running, no hacks with cameras or notebooks. The other way, along the clifftop is the same, deserted of life. No one mad enough to be out on a night like this. Nobody.

You need a wet wipe?

Mick spreads his arms, Christ-the-Redeemer style. 'You know, I don't fear death, not anymore. I'd like to see another grandchild, I'm certain I will. A month or two either way is well within the margin of error, yeah? But whenever it happens, it happens. I'm ready for it.'

Adam stands.

Paula sits on the sofa and opens the tray of microwaved korma on her plate. It's her favourite – the one with the chopped almonds. She always tosses in a few sultanas to add a bit of whatever *je ne sais quoi* is in Hindi or Urdu, or whatever language it is the wonderful korma makers in M&S speak. The steam and the bubbles say it's ready, but she doesn't sniff it. Four minutes ago, it was the only thing in the world that would satisfy her hunger; now, her stomach turns gently, it's the last thing on the planet she could eat. She leaves the plate on the coffee table and returns to the kitchen, fills a glass from the tap and sips it.

She feels heavy, her legs don't seem able to support her weight. She waddles to a kitchen chair and sits. Not comfortable enough, she gets up again. The pain is like someone is squeezing her stomach softly, but with iron gloves. She's feeling queasy too: pint and a half of lager and a curry queasy, although her korma deluxe remains untouched and she's yet to pop her first alco-free can. She sits back on the chair and groans softly.

'No, no. Not now, don't be silly. You stay exactly where you are.' She combs her brain. She's weeks away. It *can't* be now. The pain intensifies, doubles her over, tears drop onto her dress but don't show on the material – the front of her dress is already soaked.

Mick turns. As he does, there's a sound like a million glass marbles pouring onto the beach a couple of hundred feet behind and below him. He's about to turn back to see what it is when he's shaken almost off his feet; he staggers to retain his balance; the ground shudders again and he falls to his knees. Ahead of him Adam suddenly seems to rise above him, then disappear behind a wall of brown mud that's appeared straight in front of him.

Adam sees Mick drop from view. Where there were a dozen

paces in front of him, there's now only two or three: a new cliff edge has appeared. Lucky Boy is barking frantically, taking half-steps forward, retreating instantly. Adam takes a couple of steps, peers over: a massive slice of the cliff edge, close to the size of a tennis court, has slid down from its previous position, like a drunk leaning back on a pub wall sliding to the floor. It's now two, maybe three metres below its previous position, Mick kneeling in the centre of it, surrounded by loose mud and almost-liquid soil.

Mick looks up as Adam appears at the newborn cliff edge. The slither of another million marbles fills the air.

'Get back!' Mick shouts. 'Fucking cliff's going!'

'Climb up here, give me your hand!' Adam screams, flattening himself on the wet grass, stretching his hand down towards Mick.

'No!' Mick yells. 'You get away! Bloody thing could go any time!'

'Get up here; give me your bloody hand!'

A waterfall of mud and gravel starts to dislodge and pour away from under Adam.

'Get back!' Mick screams, pointing uselessly as yet more heavy sludge starts to cover his thighs and spread up to his waist. 'Save yourself, get back to Paula, leave me here.'

Without warning, the land that Adam is lying on shunts down half a metre, then another. More mud and gravel slews onto Mick's legs. Lucky Boy barks and whimpers, walks in tight circles. Adam hesitates.

They say your life flashes before your eyes when you're dying. The reel of your time on the planet: if it were Mick, he'd see a pram in the sun, feeding a joey; a long boat journey; boys taunting his accent in a damp schoolyard; a 'Bridge Over Troubled Water'; a first patient; a wedding ring; a firstborn; the promise of a second...

But it's not Mick who's watching his life flash from Super 8 to GoPro – it's Adam. And Adam's brain hasn't adopted the traditional review format, Adam's brain has hit fast-forward. It takes a split second for him to see two versions of his life-to-be flash before his eyes. In the first, Mick dies here. It's a heaven-sent gift. The cliff takes Mick, and Adam's deal with Jaz is over. Jaz won't get the timely 'natural' death he so desires, but he wouldn't be able to blame Adam for that. Adam would be off the hook, free to live his life, if Mick dies here.

The second version is much more complicated.

'Your hand!' Adam yells, now clearly within reach. 'Give me your *fucking* hand!'

Mick heaves himself up out of the sludge, then wades, knee-deep, through the slurry-like goo in front of him, but his feet sink, and he gains little height. He scrambles at the wall of saturated mud, his shoes slipping like he's trying to scale plate glass. He grabs a stray root, Adam's fingers are touchable, but neither can get a grip. Adam inches further downward, their fingers brush, then the block of cliff under Adam shudders and rocks again, drops another few centimetres, and they grasp hands.

'Up!' Adam yells, heaving with his arm, his eyes bulging, his face reddening. Mick kicks with his feet, grabs whatever he can with his free hand, pulling, pushing. 'C'mon!' Adam shouts, digging his toes into the wet grass, pushing backwards with his free hand, pulling with all his might. Lucky Boy barks incessantly. Mick reaches up, finds a tuft of grass and grabs at it, the wetness making it impossible to hold. So, he drives his fingers into the mud at the top of the cliff, burrows into the soft soil, feels purchase, and heaves.

'Yeah!' Adam bellows, pulling again. 'Get a grip here!'

They heave and pull and swear, all the time unearthly noises and sensations of the land groaning and slipping provide a horror film backdrop. Mick scrambles up to Adam's level and they sit, exhausted, spit and snot dribbling down their mud-splattered faces, the dog circling them and barking furiously like he doesn't want to play this game.

The edge of the storm blankets the moon, heavy drops of rain start to splat all around them.

'Let's go!' Adam commands. 'Need to get outta here.'

This slice of clifftop is now nearly two metres below the height it was a few moments earlier. The grass under their feet is half covered by a sheen of muddy debris. Adam scrabbles for finger and footholds in the wall, notices he's alone. He turns – Mick hasn't moved.

'Come on!' he shouts, angrily. 'We can do this!'

Mick, his back to Adam, shakes his head.

'Nothing left,' he gasps. 'Go on! You go.'

'The fuck, I will!' Adam slips and slithers back towards Mick, hauls him up by the armpits. Mick offers little resistance but does nothing to help either. Adam turns him round. His phone starts to ring in his jacket pocket.

'Please answer!' Paula prays. 'Please answer.'

She had crawled to her bag in the hall and turned it upside down to find her phone, realised she'd put it on the coffee table ready for *Pride and Prejudice* and the korma. So, she crawled back, leaving a slug's trail of wet on the hall tiles, hardly believing she had the brain width to worry about the mess she'd make of the new carpet. She reached for the phone, collapsed backwards onto the floor, the only position that gave her any relief from the pain, and punched Adam's number.

'Please answer!' she prays. '*Please* answer!'

'Hi, Adam here, leave a message and I'll get back to you.'

'Jesus, no. *Please!*'

'Come on, Mick! We can do this! Between us we can do it!'

'You go,' Mick breathes in reply, 'don't feel so good.'

'Come on! I'm not leaving you here.' He half pulls, half carries him towards the brown wall that's shedding material like a springtime waterfall, his phone no longer bleating its muffled call. The rain is now steady. He offers Mick his two hands, linked together for Mick's foot.

'No,' Mick gasps, shaking his head wearily. 'I won't have the strength to pull you up. You go, then pull me.' He links his own hands and offers them to Adam. Adam places his muddy shoe in them and, with one heave and a lot of desperate pulling, gets his chest onto the clifftop and hauls himself up. He turns and reaches out to Mick. Mick steps backwards.

'You go,' he says, shaking his head.

'Do I have to come back down and fucking push you?'

'Fuck off, will you? Leave me.' Mick sighs. 'I've had enough! And I don't want Paula to be a widow. Go!'

Adam stares, arm outstretched.

'We go together, or we stay together,' he finally says. 'Give me your hand.'

Mick looks up, then raises his hand. Adam grips him as far down as he can.

'Now pull!' Adam shouts. Mick's a heavy man; he seems to make no progress as the steady rain pours down his arm. Mick's phone starts to ring.

Paula prays again. She hasn't prayed this much since she was in primary school and wanted a Barbie for her birthday. Barbie, Ken and the open-top car, the whole boxed set. The pain scorches through her middle, causing her to double over into a foetal curl again.

'Please answer, Granddad.' She weeps.

Adam grabs at Mick's sweatshirt with his other arm, trying to get a different leverage, but the shirt rides up, stretches uselessly around Mick's neck. The rain intensifies, lightning flickers behind him, brightening Mick's face.

'Leave it.' Mick sighs. 'It's okay. You go to Paula, before the whole place goes and you go with it.'

Adam shakes his head. 'Let go a second. Take your sweatshirt off.'

Adam's already got his flimsy jacket off. Mick shrugs, hasn't the will to ask or argue.

'Sling it up here,' Adam shouts. He knots the ends of two arms together, then repeats the process with the other two, creating a makeshift loop. 'Put your head and arms through,' he yells, dropping one side of the loop down to Mick, as a clap of thunder threatens to drown him out.

'The dog first,' Mick yells, lifting Lucky Boy and passing him up. Adam then wraps the other side of the loop around his wrist and pulls again. Mick, now with two free hands, scratches for holds in the muddy wall. Adam is able to stand, kick his heels into the soft grass, brace himself backwards, and use his bodyweight, although it feels like he might break his back from the effort. Slowly, half a kicked step by half a kicked step, Adam inches his way backwards until he reaches the bench, bolted into a concrete base. He leans back on it and heaves.

First Mick's hands, then his arms, then his face, appear up over the edge of the cliff. With one last desperate pull, Mick manages to get his legs up beside himself. He crawls up to Adam as the rain intensifies and slumps on the ground next to the bench, the dog joining them, lying across Mick's legs.

'Saved my life!' Mick gasps.

They feel the torrent of rain, savouring the relief, listening to Mick's phone until it stops ringing. Adam forces himself to move.

'It's not safe here, Mick. We gotta go. Come on.' He stands, untangles the sodden clothing from his wrist. His jacket is soaked with rain and mud but he hauls it on, zips it up. 'Come on, Mick!' he says again, bent double, his stomach muscles aching like he's been hit with a plank. He pushes Mick's shoulder. There's no response. 'Mick!'

Ignoring the pain, Adam stands astride Mick, grasping his face in his hands and shaking it. Mick's eyes open and he shakes his head wearily.

'Heart,' he says quietly, closing his eyes again in a grimace of pain.

'The baby's coming! The baby's coming!' Paula screams into the mouthpiece.

'Are you sure?' Cathy snaps back, trying to stay calm.

'Yes! My waters have gone and I'm in agony.'

'Where's Adam?'

'He's at Mick's, not answering his phone.'

'Have you called an ambulance?'

'No, I called Adam and Mick.'

'Are you at home?'

'Yeah.'

'One second. Steve! *Steve!*'

'What?'

'Get the car out, Paula's having the baby! And tell Jenny next door to take Will. Listen, Paula, I'm calling an ambulance then we're coming straight over. Lie down, try to get comfortable, I'll be with you in five minutes. Okay?'

'Hurry, Cathy. I'm afraid.'

'We're on our way.'

———

'You sure?'

'I'm a fucking doctor,' Mick puffs, pain crumpling his face.

'What do I do?' Adam shouts, afraid Mick's lapsing into unconsciousness. 'Tell me what to do.' He has no idea how to do CPR, afraid he'll do more harm than good if he tries.

'Ambulance.'

'Ambulance,' Adam repeats. 'Phone,' he says aloud. There's something in his mind telling him to keep talking to Mick. They do that on the TV, when paramedics arrive. Keep the patient talking. He pulls his phone out of his pocket. One missed call. Paula. He wipes the screen to clear the raindrops that are still falling, but less heavily now, dials 999, it rings once.

'Hello, emergency services operator, which service do you require?'

'Ambulance.'

'Connecting you now.'

———

'Ambulance service. What is the address of the emergency?'

'Um, 21 Wellbrook... No, sorry, they've moved. Steve!

Steve! What's Paula's new address? Sorry, my husband's getting the car. Steve!'

'What?' Steve replies.

'What's Paula's new address?'

'Umm, The Meadows, isn't it?'

'It's The Meadows, the new estate outside Overstrand. They've just moved.'

'Do you know the number?' the operator asks.

'Number, Steve?'

No reply, just the sound of the car starting.

'It's on the other side of the lake there, it's a small estate, there's only a dozen houses, so maybe five or six, their house is in the middle. We'll be there in five minutes; we're driving a white Berlingo people carrier. We'll be parked outside.'

'Tell me exactly what's happened.'

'He says he's having a heart attack,' Adam says. 'He's a doctor; he says he's having a heart attack.'

'How old is he?

'Seventy-five.'

'Is he conscious?'

'Yes, but I don't know for how much longer, he's sorta drifting in and out...'

Steve slews the car around the small lake at the heart of The Meadows estate. He parks it side on and hits the hazards to help the ambulance driver find them. Cathy pushes the door that Paula has obviously managed to open. She finds her on the floor in the living room, lying against the sofa, head back, sweating and grimacing.

'It's all right, love. Ambulance is coming. Steve, get some towels.'

'They're coming, Mick. They're coming,' Adam babbles, searching the horizon in both directions. He knows there's an ambulance station in Cromer, probably one in Hunstanton, maybe Fakenham. Twenty minutes if they leave immediately, he estimates. *Fuck!*

'Keep talking to me, Mick; I don't want you passing out. Talk to me. How are you feeling?'

Mick shakes his head. 'Sit me up,' he gasps.

'What?'

'Help me sit up.'

'No, stay where you are, don't try to move.'

Mick shakes his head again. 'Sit me up, best position, trust me.'

'Okay.' He sighs, not daring to contradict the doctor. He rolls Mick around and helps to sit him up against the side of the bench. Lucky Boy positions himself next to him. The new cliff edge is only a metre away and they can hear a steady spew of saturated gravel and mud tinkling away from it. The rain patters steadily. 'Can you move further away?' Adam asks.

Mick shakes his head again. 'Just sit here.'

'If the cliff starts to go again, I'm dragging you like a sack of spuds, Mick. You hear?'

'You're a good lad, Adam.'

Adam scans the horizon again. East towards Cromer he can't see much, the cliff rises and falls cutting the view. He can see more to the west where the land falls to the village and beyond towards Hunstanton. In the far distance, God knows how far, he sees blue lights flashing.

'They're coming, Mick, I can see them. Here they come. You okay?'

Mick nods, his breathing is shallow, laboured. Adam stands and watches the lights as they cut through the village but instead of climbing, the ambulance turns inland.

***

Blue lights start to flash on the ceiling.

'Thank Christ,' gasps Paula.

'They're here!' Steve yells from the front door, waving furiously. Two paramedics bustle through to the lounge, padded like astronauts with radios chirping and puffy bags swinging.

Steve and Cathy move back as the paramedics set to work calming Paula. While one talks quietly to her, the other unzips a bag and begins to take out pieces of kit.

'I'm sorry, I didn't know what to do,' Cathy butts in. 'I wasn't here, and I just phoned you when Paula called me.'

'No worries,' says the medic who's making the closest examination. 'Were you planning a home delivery?'

'No,' says Paula, hesitantly.

'Well, you're having one,' she replies. 'All hands on deck, please. Warm water, towels, chop chop!'

***

Adam paces. Scouring the horizon for more blue lights. Mick has lapsed into unconsciousness, slumped forward. Nothing Adam tried could keep him awake. But he's breathing steadily. Adam can only hope, and wait, and watch.

Seeing a face you know in a strange place, an unusual

setting, can be a particularly disconcerting experience. Your mind freezes as you recognise someone, then you doubt yourself because they're in a location you've never seen them before, one where you'd never expect to see them.

Adam would never expect to see Jaz's face here.

He's running up the hill from Mick's house. It's a hunched-up sort of run, like he's trying not to be seen against the dark background, dressed as he is, in dark clothes, a dark beanie hat, and dark gloves. Everything dark, except his left hand, which has a patch of white in the palm, a neat square held up and away from his body as he runs.

Adam stands, takes two or three steps away from Mick. Jaz slows, halts a couple of metres away.

'You've done it?' Jaz asks, breathing heavily, nodding towards Mick, who's slouched against the bench, head on his chest.

Adam stares. Can't believe what's happening. Has Jaz seriously come here to make sure...?

'Can I check?' Jaz takes a step. Adam stiffens, holds a hand up.

'Stay where you are.'

'Is he dead?'

'He's had a heart attack.'

'He's not dead?'

'Ambulance is coming.'

Jaz looks down at the ground, back up at Adam, steel in his eyes.

'Let me finish him. Nobody will know. It's worth billions if he dies here. I can make you rich. Ten million? Name your price. Nobody will know. He won't feel a thing, he's already unconscious. Let me make sure—'

'Stay where you are. You're not touching him.'

'Don't be stupid, Adam. It's worth more money than you've

ever dreamed of if this deal goes through. Mick's death would push it over the line, the publicity–'

'Shut up. It's over, Jaz. You're not getting near him. The ambulance is com–'

From nowhere, Jaz throws a punch. A straight right. Adam sees it coming and sways backwards, but it clips him above the left eye. He feels the warmth of blood rolling down from his eyebrow. Jaz tries to edge closer to Mick, but he's having to keep his left hand out of range, clearly not wanting two, or even three, LifeTime employees dead on a Norfolk clifftop. Adam feints a punch to force Jaz back a step or two, all the time keeping his eyes on Jaz's left hand, the deadly white square clutched in it.

Without warning, Jaz ducks, charges, pummels his right shoulder into Adam's chest, but Adam still has his eyes on the white square. As Jaz hits him, Adam grabs his left wrist in both hands, they spin together, the force of Jaz's charge taking them both down onto the grass where they slither and wrestle, Adam concentrating on keeping Jaz's gloved hand away from Mick, and himself. Jaz throws punches with his free fist, but he's on his back, under Adam, can get no purchase, no power. Lucky Boy snaps and snarls as he pounds a circle around them. A siren sounds in the distance, Adam can see blue flashes lighting the trees.

'It's over,' he shouts into Jaz's contorted face. The rain intensifies, the wind gusts, Jaz's eyes suddenly lock in a stare of pure fear, he turns his face away, and Adam sees, almost in slow motion, the white square flutter in front of his face, before landing on Jaz's cheek.

'Jesus!' Jaz gasps, shaking his head furiously, attempting to dislodge the towelette.

Adam lets go of Jaz's wrist. Scrambles to his feet. Jaz flaps at his face, knocking the small sheet off onto the grass where it spins in the wind, takes off, whisks past Adam's face, and disappears out over the cliff edge.

They stare at each other: Adam standing, Jaz on the ground, the rain falling in another deluge, the wind blowing, the siren louder, blue lights lighting their faces. Adam wonders if the rain will wash the poison before it can take effect. Then Jaz chokes, his eyes bulge, his hands reach for his chest but never make it. They flop to his sides, and his eyes close.

Adam's mind spins. He pats Jaz's jacket until he feels the metal tin in the breast pocket. He slips it out and zips it into his own pocket, next to the one already there.

An ambulance crests the hill and pulls to a halt. The rain pounds heavily. Two paramedics climb out, collecting bags and equipment.

'Where's the patient?' shouts the first paramedic.

'There are two,' Adam replies. 'Careful, the cliff's given way. This is Mick Strong. I called you out for him. That's Jaz, a colleague from work. He was helping me with Mick when he collapsed.'

The paramedics take a patient each, Adam stays with Mick who's coming round again.

Mick's paramedic makes a quick assessment, peers over the cliff edge, a metre or so away, then looks up at Adam. 'We need to move him. That cliff is very unstable.'

'I can walk if you get me up,' Mick says, groggily.

'Let's go,' the paramedic replies, gesturing for Adam to get on the other side of him. 'After three – one, two...'

'...three! That's it. Well done. It's a girl!'

The baby's bawling splits the tension as the paramedic

busies herself with the cord. She wraps the baby up in a towel and gently lowers her down into Paula's arms.

'There you are. That was the easiest job of the night, Paula. And Cathy, you timed that phone call just right. Now, I hope someone's got the kettle on...'

Chapter Thirty-Seven

'NHS privatisation drive linked to rise in avoidable deaths,
study suggests.'
—*The Guardian*, 29 June 2022

A dam knocks gently on the door, pushes it open.
'Nurse says it's okay to surprise you?'

Mick waves him in, then double takes as Paula follows
Adam – carrying a baby.

'Mother of God! When did this happen?' Mick exclaims.

'Last night, when you were out playing on the cliff with
Adam. I'm not sure you'll be allowed to hold her.'

Mick sighs, readjusts his position in the bed, looks down his
chest at all the stickers and cables, then left and right at the
bleeping and flashing monitors.

'Bring her over here, they can't stop me taking a peek.'

Paula squeezes past a monitor and holds the baby so that
Mick can peer in.

'You've got the full set of great-grandchildren now,' she says.

'She's gorgeous, but how are you?'

'I'm great. Apart from a brand-new carpet that needs deep cleaning, I'm fine. But more to the point, how are *you*? The nurses said you are doing really well.'

'I'm still here, still kicking, thanks to your husband. I'd given up on it all last night. He saved my life, two or three times.'

Adam smiles modestly. 'You can be a bit of a contrary bastard at times, but I managed to talk you round.'

'You did. And I'll never be able to thank you.'

'Were you aware that Jaz showed up last night?' Adam asks, tentatively.

Mick looks shocked. 'Jaz? From Utah? Turned up where?'

'On the cliff. I didn't have time to ask him what he was doing, some kind of surprise visit I imagine. I was too busy dealing with you. Anyway, he was helping me to lift you when he collapsed. Heart attack they've told me. He died.'

'Dead?'

'I'm afraid so. They tried to resuscitate him but couldn't.'

'I can't believe it.'

'Neither can I.'

They stare at each other for a few moments, each having their own, rather distinct, memories of Jaz running through their minds.

The door opens again; a doctor enters.

'Hello, how are we all?' she says, standing at the foot of the bed and checking a tablet. There is a mumble of assent until the doctor spots Paula and the baby. 'And who's this?' she says. 'My goodness, this one looks very young.'

'Yesterday,' Paula says. 'We thought we had to get her in to see Great-Granddad as soon as possible...' Paula's tone and pleading eyes warn the doctor of her fears.

'Oh, I wouldn't be worrying about him,' the doctor says, smiling. 'I'm Dr Jill Barnes, by the way. How are you feeling this morning, Dr Strong?'

'Do you want us to leave?' Paula asks quietly. The doctor shakes her head sternly and motions for them to stay with a steely glare that says she has an agenda that she wants them in on. Mick studies all his gadgetry again.

'Maybe you should tell me,' Mick says dryly.

'You look a lot better than you did last night, that's for certain.'

Mick smiles, nods. 'What's all the hi-tech stuff telling us?'

'It's telling us you're in good shape; I'm not even going to say *for your age*. How do you feel?'

'I feel better than I did yesterday, pretty sore around here though.' He rubs across his chest a couple of times. 'I feel I might survive after all?'

'Oh, you're going to survive, Dr Strong. I've never known anyone die from costochondritis before.'

'*Costochondritis?*'

'We're sure that's what you've got. You certainly haven't had a heart attack, which I know was worrying you last night.'

'What's costochondritis?' Paula asks, not quite sure whether it's a better or worse diagnosis than a heart attack.

'Bruised bloody ribs,' Mick mutters in astonishment.

'It's a bit more than that,' the doctor says. 'It's inflammation of the costochondral joint, that's the cartilage that joins the ribs to the sternum.' She turns to Adam. 'I think all the pulling and tugging you were telling me about last night are the cause. There's also a couple of cracked ribs, but they're not going to kill him either.'

'You're joking. I was sure I was having a heart attack.'

'Of course you were, as you'll know, costochondritis is often mistaken for heart attack symptoms. But you certainly haven't had one.'

'Well, that's wonderful,' Paula says, 'isn't it? He'll get better?'

'Oh yes, a few painkillers, anti-inflammatories, rest. I'm not worried about that. But I am worried about these...' The doctor leans forward and points at the mole-like spots scattered across Mick's chest. '...especially as I can't find any records for you in our wonderful oncology department here.'

Paula gasps. 'Oncology's *cancer*, isn't it?'

'Yes, it is,' the doctor replies. 'I'm sorry, I assumed...' The doctor stares at Paula, and Paula knows that she's confirmed her suspicions. All eyes turn to Mick, who's decided now is the right time to tidy up a thumbnail.

Chapter Thirty-Eight

'How to die: five positive steps to deal with death.'
—*The Guardian*, 5 May 2014

D-Day. As some of the red tops are calling it. The curtains are drawn on all the Manor House windows. The group of journos and snappers at the bottom of the drive is the largest it's ever been. They take turns to send one up to knock on the door, post notes through the letter box. There are reports that Mick's been offered a million pounds for a camera in the room. His phone is going to voicemail. The pack all have their phones set to Breakfast TV or the LifeTime website, which are following the countdown like it's Apollo 11 all over again. It is time.

T-minus thirty minutes and counting...

———

Mick lounges on the sofa at Paula and Adam's, enjoying a late breakfast. The TV is showing the scene at the Manor House, a countdown clock in the bottom corner of the screen. Paula fusses gently.

'More OJ, Granddad?'

'No, I'm fine thanks, love. Come and watch. They've just had a report that I'm in the Fish and Anchor. Couple of cars of journos are on their way now, live camera feed. It's like the Keystone Cops, hilarious.'

Paula sits next to him, takes his hand. He smiles at her. As the crowd at the Manor had grown over the last couple of days, Paula suggested to Adam that they spirit Mick over to theirs for what she's calling 'the day'. Feeling precious little loyalty to LifeTime, Adam had agreed and protested ignorance when calls from Utah began to arrive enquiring about Mick's whereabouts.

When Will started to angle for a day off school 'to be with Great-Granddad' Adam had taken Steve, Cathy and Paula aside to tell them that in his opinion, the chances of Mick dying on cue were slim to non-existent. He revealed a little about the variable quality of Mick's responses to the LifeTime application questionnaire, and also apprised them of the fact that none of Mick's medical records from his childhood in Australia had been available, and not much either from his early years in the UK. Paula had taken all this in with a rising sense of hope – but she still holds his hand as the countdown on screen passes ten minutes.

Mick notices her staring, squeezes her hand. 'Wanna see something?'

'What?'

'Watch.' He takes a strip of tablets out of his pocket, pops one out of its blister and swills it down with a mouthful of orange juice. Paula stares, bemused. Mick shows his LifeBuddy with nine and a half minutes displayed, until suddenly it flips to thirty-nine and a half. Paula gasps, stares at the TV, which seconds later also flips to thirty-nine and a half.

'What happened?' she asks, elation, fear and confusion playing havoc with her expression. Mick hugs her.

'My daily statin,' he says, shrugging and smiling. 'Worth a microlife, thirty minutes a day.'

Paula smiles, cautiously. Then her face breaks into a huge grin as a tear rolls down her cheek.

'Oh, Granddad. Tell me you're not going to die today. Tell me.'

Mick beams. 'What? Because this piece of crap says I'm going to? No, Paula. I'm not going to die today.'

Cathy and Steve bowl up unannounced with Adam in tow. Mick gives them an enormous sigh and rolls his eyes.

'Come to watch me die? Ghouls,' he teases as he takes their drink orders.

They turn the TV off for the final minute, Paula wanting it to be just family, no nosey nobodies intruding on the moment. She squeezes Mick's hand, tears rolling down her cheeks as his LifeBuddy finally flips to three, two, one, zero.

And then...

Nothing.

Nothing happens.

The counter stays on zero. Mick gives his arm a little shake, like his watch has stopped. But the zero shines brightly.

'Bugger!' He sighs.

'What?' Paula begs, still not sure that she can breathe out, that she'll ever be able to.

'Well, I was expecting it to start counting *up* after reaching zero. You know? I've beaten my prediction by a minute. By an hour. By a week. Bloody thing's just sitting on zero.'

Paula smiles, slowly starts to laugh.

'What?' Mick says, almost annoyed that she doesn't share his grievance.

'Well, Gramps. I suppose we should have listened to Adam, shouldn't we? He did tell us, from day one, it's not a prediction...'

They all turn and stare at Adam, who looks the most relieved person in the room.

Chapter Thirty-Nine

'We're one step closer to a blood test that predicts when a
person will die.'
—*TIME* (Time.com), 21 August 2019

Celia wore the christening gown in 1951; Michaela
followed her in 1975; Paula was next in 2000; and now
it's the turn of baby Celia Michaela Strong-Collingworth. From
the church, the family stroll up to the clifftop, Mick leading the
way at a briskish pace. He's booked a large table outside the
Watch Café and orders hot chocolates and eclairs for everyone.
They follow this with a walk further along the cliff, now
cordoned off with red and white hazard tape where the latest
collapse occurred, Mick continually fussing and warning Paula
not to walk too close to the edge with the pram, Lucky Boy
keeping further from the edge than anybody, whimpering
plaintively to himself.

The party follows in the garden at 6 The Meadows. It's an
informal affair: no set speeches, no long table, no silver service,
no waiting staff in uniform – no Bushmills. Mick had offered

Sacklow Hall, tried to insist, but Paula stood firm. It would be at home, smart casual, everyone could bring something, and she would do the pudding. Close family and a few, a very few, selected friends only. Plus two pairs of paramedics, not on standby, but guests of honour in significantly less colourful garb than they usually wear.

Mick is doing the rounds, showing off his LifeBuddy to anyone who's never seen one, still showing zero days, as it has for the past few weeks. He's still grumbling that it doesn't display the increasing number of days that he's beaten his projection by – but no, it sits on zero, as if waiting to be proved correct... one day. The paramedics are willing victims to his unending spiel.

As the afternoon wears on, and he allows himself a glass or two of champagne (*for the baby*), he even starts opening his shirt to show Paula's co-workers at the chemist his scars where they've successfully removed his benign growths. He also boasts that he's beaten his hundred-minute target for power walking the cliffs.

Steve and Cathy are swapping golf tips with one of Paula's new neighbours. They play eighteen holes, once a week with Mick – no buggies, everybody walks. Steve turns out to be a bit of a natural, out-driving Mick, although not always ending up on the fairway. Cathy's short game puts the pair of them to shame. They lunch at the Nineteenth Hole, where they do a rather good quinoa salad. Over lunch, Steve often discusses what the cardiologist he shares with Paula has said about their progress. The doctor's happy with their loyalty to the suggested dietary and fitness regimes; Mick's delighted with the BOGOF deal he negotiated for the pair of them. Steve is particularly religious about his cycling and squash; he does twenty K at least once a week with his running club; and is mid-table in the squash league, playing twice – sometimes three times a week.

They've paved the garden, and have an active loyalty card at the wholefood shop.

Cathy and Steve have never spoken about her decision to buy herself a LifeTime projection. She secretly squirrelled her money away and took delivery without fanfare. She hasn't told him what it says. Steve, for his part, has never asked whether she went ahead; it's a secret they don't share.

Adam watches Paula with the baby. He's painted his resignation from LifeTime as a mutual agreement thing, suggesting that he really wasn't coping with being a media mogul, and he didn't particularly want his old job back, which wouldn't have paid the mortgage anyway. So the house will have to go. He's got a couple of interviews lined up which, if he lands one, would allow them to buy something. Mick has hinted that his LifeTime war chest (as he calls it) will help them on their way, if they need it.

The only thing Paula and Adam can't agree on concerns the issue of a LifeBuddy for baby Celia Michaela. With the deal between LifeTime and the UK government inching towards completion, the prime minister has been leaking morsels suggesting that anyone fitted with a LifeBuddy before the age of five will have free access to all NHS services for life, as opposed to the insurance-based system introduced after the post-Brexit agreement with the United States. This deal will apparently apply as long as the LifeBuddy confirms that the person never smokes, takes illegal drugs or drinks more than one unit of alcohol in any twenty-four-hour period. There are other restrictions on sugar, salt and fat intakes, plus minimum requirements for daily exercise. Paula wants Celia Michaela fitted up as soon as the deal is finalised, and she's working diligently on Adam, who's yet to be convinced, especially since he's lost his staff discount and the price of membership has already more than doubled with further price hikes threatened.

Adam also keeps a regular eye on his social media and the newspaper headlines, which, for now, remain gratifyingly dull.

The doorbell rings; Adam heads inside. They're not expecting anyone else, unless it's the press again, but they finally seem to have got the message with Mick refusing to say anything except polite requests for respect for a grieving family. No journalist dares to challenge him that Michaela has been dead for months.

A couple of other LifeTime members have now joined Mick in passing their projected dates without suffering a sudden demise. One paper is celebrating their victories and is running Cheating the Grave day counters for each of them. Making bigger headlines in the tabloids is the steady stream of LifeTime members who are closing in on their own finish lines in the Race to Death, as one red-top has started calling it.

With the British market still only warming up, the *Mail* and the *Express* are running regular stories of LifeTime members in the US who 'sadly passed' on, or close to, their projected death dates. The LifeTime Corporation provides a steady flow of names and photos and headline quotes from its vast database of members' achievements. Social media conspiracy theories that suggest some of these timely deaths might have been assisted suicides with secret compensation payouts made by LifeTime to the family are vigorously challenged by the company's legal vultures if the tabloids go anywhere near those stories. The vast bulk of LifeTime members, those who died before their projected dates, or have survived them by months or years, are rarely mentioned in the tabloids' search for their *Isn't That Amazing?* columns. A close, almost symbiotic, relationship is rapidly developing between LifeTime, the tabloids and the opinion TV channels, with LifeTime benefitting from the free publicity, and the mouthpieces enjoying regular stories to feed the appetites of those among their readers who are keen to cheat the grave.

LifeTime announces regular upgrades to their software (at a price) promising greater accuracy, increased functionality, and a lot of other technological doodah going forwards.

One conspiracy theory, floating in the toxic ether online, but rarely making it into the mainstream, suggests that Mick Strong, erstwhile LifeTime poster boy in the UK, somehow cocked-up the application process for his, and by extension, his family's projections, thereby explaining why he's still alive. The mainstream UK media won't go near it, partly because they're still occasionally running pieces on how Mick's doing, explaining his continuing survival as an inexplicable outlier, or the result of his superhuman fitness regime, or maybe a lack of available data from his early years in Oz. Mick only broaches the subject from the angle of his exercise programme. Adam doesn't contradict him, what would be the point?

Adam, of course, knows that Mick's handling of the application process was flawed, and the truth about LifeTime's whole modus operandi, but again says nothing, knowing what Cathy thinks, knowing what Will thinks, now that he's opened his projection, still unaware of the fact that it's a substitute – or why.

LifeTime is also busy, constantly rewriting its terms and conditions, threatening legal action against anyone who *maliciously or carelessly provides LifeTime with inaccurate or incomplete data during the application process, and then goes on to publicise stories that are damaging to the reputation of LifeTime.*

Adam opens the door.

'Ron!'

'Happy christening! Congratulations, mate.'

'What are you doing here?'

'Brought you a christening present. Two actually...'

Adam gets him a beer and they tour the garden, shaking hands, kissing the baby, patting the dog, inspecting Mick's LifeBuddy, before retreating into a quiet corner of the lounge. Ron shuts the door.

'So, you out?' Adam asks.

'I'm out. Tidied up my finances and I'm a freelance consultant. Getting no help from anyone at LifeTime but it's probably best that way. I can breathe easy now, sleep better at night.'

'Good for you.'

'And you?'

'Well, you know.' Adam casts a hand around the living room, shrugs.

'Nice place.'

'*Expensive* place.'

'What are your plans?'

'We've put it up for sale, it should move quite quickly.'

'Paula okay with that?'

'Yeah, she's got an easy come, easy go attitude to it.' He shrugs again. 'She says it isn't really us, and she's right. I feel we should be having famous actors and actresses over for drinks, film stars for dinner parties. Maybe have a few footballers and their WAGs around for beers. But the only people we have are Mick, Steve and Cathy.'

'And now me...'

'Yeah, well...'

They chuckle briefly. Ron turns semi-serious again.

'Any luck with a new job?'

'I should be okay. There's a full-time post at the university I've put in for. My old head of department is still there so she knows me. Couple of other things in the technology park next to the university, I'm not worried.'

Ron smiles, lifts his small knapsack onto his knee. 'I need to give you your christening present.'

'Oh, you shouldn't have, let me get Paula—'

'No, this is for your eyes only,' he replies, pointedly. Out of his bag he pulls a sleek tablet, hands it to Adam.

'What's this? It's not even wrapped.'

They smile.

'Play it,' Ron says.

Adam shakes his head in mystification, as Ron finds the play button for him. The screen brightens.

The scene is a large bedroom, probably a hotel, shot from a high corner, black-and-white but high quality. The bed is made; the room is tidy and empty, awaiting guests. Action begins at the bottom of the screen; the camera is clearly above the entrance door. A man enters carrying a body, fireman-style. He moves towards the bed and dumps the body onto it. It's lifeless. He's followed by a girl: short dress, long dark hair, high shoes, carrying a small knapsack. Adam's mouth slowly opens.

'I can't watch this...'

'Trust me,' Ron says gravely, his hand on Adam's wrist, stopping him from reaching to kill the screen. 'You'll want to see this.'

The girl disappears into what Adam knows is the bathroom. The man, recognisably Jaz, starts to undress the body, Adam's body, on the bed. He searches the jacket for a moment, slips something into the wallet before replacing it, then he tosses jacket, shirt, shoes and socks to the four corners of the room. He rolls Adam's naked body to the far side of the bed, rips the bedclothes down, rolls Adam back into the middle and half covers him. He then messes up the bed, throwing a couple of pillows onto the floor.

The girl, Jazelle, appears from the bathroom dressed in jeans, sweatshirt and trainers, her hair now up in a businesslike ponytail. She scatters her dress and other clothes across the floor, carefully hangs a dark bra on the back of a chair. Adam notices how she *hangs* it there, *places* it. Everything else is scattered, but she's careful with the bra, stages it. Then she takes a champagne bottle out of the minibar, opens it carefully, half fills two glasses, takes a long swig from the bottle, offers it to Jaz. He takes it, toasts her, and drinks. She retrieves the bottle and disappears into the bathroom for a few seconds before returning to put it on the table, next to the glasses and a white powder that Jaz has been busy pouring from what appears to be an envelope.

They survey the scene together, nod with evident satisfaction, then leave. Neither seems to have spoken although Adam has heard scrapes and clonks as they've arranged the room. The video ends.

They sit in silence for twenty seconds or so before Adam speaks. 'They set it up!' he says, almost to himself. 'Bastards.'

'Jaz doesn't have a daughter,' Ron says quietly. 'Nor a wife.'

'So, who...?'

'Far as I can discover, Jaz used an escort agency in town.'

'How did you find *that* out?'

'He charged it to his LifeTime expense card. How brazen could you get?'

'So, it was a way to, what, *blackmail* me? I didn't actually–'

'No, you didn't actually anything. My guess is they drugged you, probably one of the benzodiazepines. I mean, see the way he landed you on the bed? You can't have drunk *that* much. You look like you were in a coma. The whole thing was staged.'

'I had a few drinks, but not enough to do that. I don't know how to thank you, that's such a relief. I've been feeling so guilty, wondering if I should tell Paula.'

'You didn't?'

'No.'

'Good.'

'How did you get hold of this?'

'Oh, knowing I was leaving, I could take a few risks. I went snooping, asked a few people a lot of awkward questions. I have a good friend in SecDiv who showed me the security system as a kind of leaving present. Every grace and favour property has automatic filming; I imagine the real reason is straight security. Seems to me like Jaz had no idea that the room was *really* being filmed. They didn't even hide their faces. It's clear he was bluffing, there *was* a video, but he didn't know that, and it wasn't the one he led you to believe. There's another reason why I think he didn't really know how much was being monitored.'

'What's that?'

'His house, the one on the lake?'

'What about it?'

'It's not his.'

'What do you mean?'

'It belongs to the LifeTime Corporation, another grace and favour residence. For him, it was just his office.'

'So... it's *monitored?*'

'So, it's monitored. Roll 'em. Your second christening present.' Ron points at the tablet. Adam presses the play button.

The scene is a small office. Adam recognises it instantly as Jaz walks in and pours drinks and they toast. The sound quality is surprisingly good. They watch it through to the end, where Adam departs, leaving the silver tin on the desk.

'He's clever,' Ron says when it's over. 'He didn't use the magic words *kill him*. So, although it's embarrassing for LifeTime, I don't think it's a go-to-jail card, not that it matters now anyway. And even if the towelettes are covered in Jaz's fingerprints, he could feasibly have argued that he had them to put down his sick dog or something. But I have learned something else interesting.'

'What's that?'

'Remember I said I'd heard rumours that they'd included some AI in their strategic planning?'

'Yes.'

'Well, I've had that confirmed. And it was MarktDiv that made the changes to our algorithms. It probably explains why our original data has been downgraded under a much more commercial drive for profit.'

'So, this was all Jaz's doing?'

'That's what that old Friar of Occam would conclude, and I'm with him. And something else I picked up on my valedictory tour...'

'Go on...'

'Jaz had been loading up on LifeTime stock, borrowing heavily to acquire it, millions of dollars' worth. My guess is he was keen for Mick to die in a timely fashion as the stock would no doubt have gone through the roof if he had, and the UK deal got confirmed in the subsequent publicity. Not that I'd think you'd need that much intelligence, artificial or any other kind, to work that out, but maybe Jaz wasn't the brightest button on the coat. Whatever, he stood to make millions.'

'He offered me ten.'

'Ten million? That would have been a small price to pay given what he could have collected. The stock is riding high as it is, even without Mick's death, the progress of the negotiations seems to be driving the price up, there's a feeding frenzy on LifeTime stock in anticipation.'

Adam nods, deep in thought; it looks like he might sit there for the rest of the afternoon without speaking. Ron breaks the silence.

'The British police interested in Jaz's death at all?'

'No. Post-mortem said massive heart attack. No case to open.'

They stare at each other in silence, each harbouring their own thoughts and memories.

'A chance to move on?' Adam says quietly.

———————

Ron takes his leave and Adam returns to the garden, which has emptied somewhat as the sun has started to set. Mick has collected a putter from the boot of his car and is giving lessons to Will, Lucky Boy acting as retriever. Cathy, Steve and Paula are sitting around the table on the patio, deep in conversation. Adam surveys the scene, feels relief wash his conscience clear and congratulates himself on never sharing what was, but is no longer, his guilty secret with Paula.

Baby Celia starts to cry. Paula picks her out of the pram, walks down the garden; Adam follows. She sits under the shade of a willow tree. He joins her, gingerly, his stomach muscles still giving him twinges, reminders of his night on the cliff with Mick.

Paula gives Celia her pinky, while Adam relishes the feeling of freedom that his resignation from LifeTime has given him. A clean break is what he wants now, especially as he knows for certain that there isn't, never was, an incriminating video stored somewhere in the LifeTime labyrinth. He wants an ordinary life back; no jet-setting to Utah, no high-pressure sales role, and no high-stakes meeting with people he doesn't fully trust. He sits quietly, watching Paula fussing gently with Celia. All is right in his world. He wants to keep it that way.

'Can I ask you a question?' Paula suddenly says.

Adam smiles, knowing that if Ron hadn't recently shown

him the two videos from Utah, he'd be panicking that Paula had been sent something terrible.

'Shoot,' he says.

'Do you ever wonder how much the world is going to change between today and the time when Celia will be Mick's age? Seventy-five years?' Paula asks, looking straight into the baby's staring eyes.

Chapter Forty

'How long will YOU live? Check life expectancy with new calculator.'
—*Daily Express*, 3 September 2020

The sun is high; the temperature is perfect. Adam's wearing jeans and a *Born to Run* T-shirt – it's the great-grandson of the original he bought at The Garden when he was nineteen. He's got no window to roll down, but he's got his buds in, and the wind's blowing his hair back as his Segway takes him from his hotel towards MarktDiv. Life's good.

He checks his watch. His appointment's at eleven. It's ten minutes past. He's fashionably late. Not a problem. The invitation to a meeting had landed in north Norfolk out of a miserably cloudy sky. No reason given. No agenda. Just the invitation and a first-class ticket. He's had little contact with LifeTime since his resignation. He'd helped with the repatriation of Jaz's body, but that was dealt with through the lower echelons of the LT hierarchy, so an invitation from Ms

Hannah D. Lennox, Director MarktDiv (LT Global), to a meeting, expenses paid, was unexpected.

Paula had wondered if Hannah wanted to thank Adam formally for his work at LifeTime, maybe award him some kind of a leaving bonus, so she was keen for him to go. Adam has darker thoughts. Has Hannah found out – or has she known all along – about Jaz's plan to expedite Mick's death? Is there some kind of a payoff for Adam in the offing? But not to thank him, more to shut him up, ensure there are no scandalous rumours heading for the darker parts of the web from a disgruntled ex-employee?

He parks, stows his buds and rides the elevator. Hannah rises from the white leather sofa, checks her watch, and crosses half the room to greet him. Adam checks his own watch before shaking her hand.

He notices she's been mixing her paints again, blue this time, the sort of blue you used to get on the covers of travel brochures, before they joined twin tubs and phone books in the dustbin of technological advance.

'Adam. Come and sit down, so good to see you again. Good flight?'

Adam settles himself in an armchair. 'Yes, fine, thank you. Are you well?'

'Why yes, thank you, I'm fine. How about you? Family all okay?'

'Yes, very good, Celia's giving us fewer sleepless nights now, so fingers crossed.'

'Indeed. Drink? Coffee? Or maybe tea, have you taken to English tea?'

'I'll have a beer,' he says.

She makes no move to arrange this, so he assumes the waiter, who he mistook for her on his first visit, is listening in. She already has a pot of coffee on the go. They chew the transatlantic fat for a few more minutes until, sure enough, his drink is served by the smart young exec in traditional penguin colours. Adam waves the iced glass away and offers Hannah a toast with his bottle.

'Long life,' he says, before taking a slug.

Hannah smiles, sips her coffee, settles back in her chair and nods slowly.

'So, how is life treating you? You have a new job, I assume. I can't see you being out of work for long. Sad though I was to see you go, there is a wonderful reference on file, please make sure you name me as a referee.'

'Thank you. That's kind. I have a couple of applications in at the moment, both for academia; I'm optimistic.'

Hannah nods again. Sips her coffee. 'It was a blow to us, to lose both you and Jaz in such quick succession. I wonder if I could ask you something?'

Adam shrugs. 'Sure. Fire away.'

'It's a little something that's puzzled me, mainly because Jaz never mentioned a plan to fly to England. Exactly what was he doing there?'

Adam picks up his bottle. Wonders if this is some kind of a trap. Can't see the angle she might be coming from if it is. So, he repeats the story he concocted for the police when they were asking questions.

'He came out to check up on Mick. Jaz thought he was getting a little fed up with all the press attention, wanted them to back off. I'd noticed it myself. I think Jaz simply wanted to put a hand on Mick's shoulder, remind him that we were all behind him, in the same corner, you know?'

Hannah nods again, a little sadly, Adam thinks.

'We miss him. He was so good at his job. The team he'd assembled under him were, well, *are* wonderful. I don't know how we're going to replace him. And then your resignation was another huge blow to us. Nobody saw that coming. Least of all, me.'

'No. It was a bit of a sudden decision.'

'Would I be wasting my time completely if I tried to tempt you back?'

This floors him. The last thing he, or Paula, had contemplated was that LifeTime would try to coax him back.

'Are you serious?'

'Have you ever known me not to be?'

'No. I suppose not. I have to admit, this is a bit of a surprise.'

'Really? You never did rate yourself as highly as we rated you, did you, Adam?'

He smiles, isn't sure how to continue. He and Paula haven't considered this as an option. The housing market in the UK is difficult. Nobody seems to be looking for four-bedroomed detached properties at the moment, and the prices of all the two-beds are rocketing. He's also slightly sugar-coated his response to Hannah's question about his job prospects. While he still, technically, has two applications in the pipeline, the pipeline is turning out to be a lot longer, and somewhat more blocked, than he had been anticipating. Paula is certainly getting worried.

'Look, Adam. How about I cut to the chase? There's a job here for you if you want it.'

'Seriously? What job?'

Hannah smiles. Adam wonders if it's a first.

'Well, it's not really a question of what job,' she says, sitting forward and staring into his eyes. 'It's *whose...*'

THE END

Also by Tom Alan

Hitting the Jackpot

Author's Notes

I started writing *The Last App* in 2018. The original idea came to me after seeing the types of newspaper headlines that I have used to head up each chapter. The book was in the genre of speculative fiction. Well, it was, until September of 2020, when the University of East Anglia announced news of their *MyLongevity* app which would '... use big data from anonymised electronic health records to calculate life expectancy...' So, no longer quite as speculative as I'd first imagined.

The concept of a 'microlife' was outlined by Michael Blastland (creator of the BBC Radio Four programme *More or Less*) and David Spiegelhalter (Professor of the Public Understanding of Risk at Cambridge University) in their book, *The Norm Chronicles; Stories and Numbers about Danger* (Profile Books 2013).

Note also that the UK National Institute for Health and Clinical Excellence (NICE) uses a measure called a QALY (quality-adjusted life year) to help determine whether a medical intervention is accepted as cost-effective. The guidelines consider costs between £20,000 and £30,000 'may be deemed cost-effective' if the treatment is expected to prolong life by one healthy year (1 QALY). Taking the upper figure, and a year equating to 17,520 microlives, that indicates that the cost of one microlife (one extra half-hour of life) is priced (by British health authorities) at £1.71, about the same as a small bar of chocolate...

Acknowledgements

A lot of people have helped to bring *The Last App* to publication. I'd especially like to thank Betsy Reavley at Bloodhound Books for her advice and encouragement to make some important changes when I first submitted the book for consideration. Her suggestions helped turn a 'maybe' manuscript into a 'yes'. She was also instrumental in the choice of *The Last App* as the title.

My editor, Abbie Rutherford, also deserves thanks and praise. She was always willing to explain the changes she was suggesting, and answer my many questions. I pride myself on being a quick learner: I hope if we work together again in the future she will have less to do next time.

Also at Bloodhound, I'm grateful to Tara Lyons, Hannah Deuce, Katia Allen and Fred Freeman for all that they do to put our ideas in front of potential readers. Thanks also to Better Book Design for another inspired cover.

Away from Bloodhound, I'd like to thank my team of beta readers: Laura, Beth, Jude, Gail, Peter, Shaz, John, Grace and Pete. It's a few years since I first asked them to give me some feedback on (what was then called) *The Chance of a LifeTime*; I hope they enjoy its metamorphosis into *The Last App*.

Finally, thanks to my wife Jill for her constant encouragement. This one was always your favourite, so here it is. *Por fin!*

A note from the publisher

Thank you for reading this book. If you enjoyed it please do consider leaving a review on Amazon to help others find it too.

We hate typos. All of our books have been rigorously edited and proofread, but sometimes mistakes do slip through. If you have spotted a typo, please do let us know and we can get it amended within hours.

info@bloodhoundbooks.com

Printed in Great Britain
by Amazon

41435304R00219